Bestselling author **Jules Bennett** has penned nearly forty romance novels. She lives in the Midwest with her high-school-sweetheart husband and their two daughters. Sign up for her newsletter to stay up-to-date on releases and monthly contests for subscribers only. Find Jules on Facebook, Twitter or her website, www.julesbennett.com.

To all the readers who've asked about Ryker...
you're welcome.

# One

With one hand clutching the forgotten cuff links and one hand firmly over her still-flat stomach, Laney pulled in a deep breath and willed courage to make an appearance.

She was an O'Shea, damn it. She didn't back down in the face of fear. Fear was nothing but a lie. A bold-faced lie capable of defeating most people. Laney wasn't most people.

She'd come this far, all she had to do was knock…and make a life-changing confession to a man she'd been in love with since she was old enough to notice boys. Forget the fact he'd been ten years older. Age meant about as much to her as fear did.

Tears clogged her throat as emotions threatened to overwhelm her. Whatever his reaction, she owed him the truth. But if he rejected her, the pain would slice deep.

Laney pushed aside the hurt, the fear and the nausea, and pounded on Ryker Barrett's front door.

No turning back now.

Ryker had been part of her life since she was a child. He'd worked for her father, was best friends with her brothers. Her family had taken him in when his own had turned him away. He was mysterious, intriguing and frustrating.

And for the past five weeks he'd been pretending nothing had happened. He gave no hint that he even recalled tearing her Chanel dress from her body before holding her against her hotel room wall and bringing her every desire to life.

Nope. It was business as usual. When she'd had to feed him information via email or text for O'Shea's auctions, he'd never given any indication that their one heated night had made an impact on his life whatsoever. Was he that emotionally detached?

Well, he was about to sustain one hell of an impact. He may try to ignore her, but there was no way he could ignore the consequences of their night.

The door swung open and the entire speech she'd rehearsed all morning vanished from her mind. Ryker stood before her wearing only a pair of running shorts, a tatted chest and glorious muscle tone.

She'd never seen him this way. The man who traveled the globe in designer suits, the man who donned a leather jacket and worn jeans to blend in when necessary, had never presented himself in such a beautiful, natural manner. He should do this more often.

Casual as you please, Ryker rested a forearm on the edge of the door and quirked a brow as if she'd disturbed him. Yeah, well, he deserved to be put out. She'd been fighting her feelings for him for years.

Rage bubbled from within as she slapped his cuff links against his bare chest and pushed past him. In all the years she'd known him, Laney had never come to his house in Boston. When they met, it was always on neutral ground, usually at the O'Shea family home her brother Braden now lived in.

As infuriating as Ryker could be, Laney was the first to admit that her family would crumble without him. He may be the "enforcer," the guy who kept them protected and took the brunt of any backlash they ever faced, but he could easily cut ties and leave. This billionaire never threw his money around like most men she knew. Loyalty meant much more to Ryker than finances ever would… one of the many reasons she was drawn to him.

The door closed at her back. Laney shut her eyes and tried to forget the intensity of their complicated relationship, tried to ignore the way her body instantly responded to this man. She was here for one reason. And the fact that he worked for her family, was practically *part* of her family, wasn't making this confession any easier.

"If you're here regarding the painting in L.A. that you emailed me about last week, I've already—"

Laney whirled. "I'm not here about work."

Crossing his arms over his broad chest, Ryker widened his stance and gave a brief nod. "I can't believe it took you this long to come to me."

Laney's heart kicked up. So he knew she would bring up that night, and he'd what? Been waiting on her? Jerk. Uncaring, unfeeling, stupid, sexy jerk. Why couldn't he put a shirt on? She was trying to keep her anger going, but lust was creeping into the mix.

"You could've come to me," she threw back. "Or, I don't know, actually talked to me when we were exchanging work information."

The O'Sheas were a force all their own, known around the globe for their prestigious auction houses. Laney had ignored the whispered "mafia" or "mob" rumors her entire life. She knew full well what her family was, and she was a proud member. They remained on the right side of the law thanks to the connections her late father had made and the ones her brother Braden, who was now in charge, and her other brother Mac continued to work at.

And Ryker Barrett, other than starring in her every fantasy for years, was the family's right-hand man, security detail and any other job they needed him for. He did the dirty work and lay low, staying out of the limelight and behind the scenes.

Laney waited for him to say something, anything, but he stood there staring at her, which only made her nerves worse. How could he have so much power over her? She was an O'Shea, for crying out loud, and he was just standing there.

Standing there looking all half-naked, sexy and perfect.

*Focus, Laney.*

Ryker held up the cuff links. "Was this all?"

Laney narrowed her eyes. "Am I interrupting something?"

*Or someone?* It hadn't even occurred to her that he may be entertaining. A sick feeling in the pit of her stomach grew, and she hated the spear of jealousy that ripped through her.

"Yeah, my morning session with the punching bag."

Which explained those perfectly sculpted arms, shoulders and pecs, though Laney figured he used a punching bag as a means of releasing his emotions rather than to stay in shape. Ryker was the epitome of keeping to himself and never letting anyone get too close. So what did that say about that night they shared? Clearly he'd thrown all of his rules out the window because they'd been as close as two people could get.

Nausea pushed its way to the front of the line, bypassing her worry, her fear. Laney closed her eyes, waiting to see if she needed to find the bathroom or take a seat and let the wave pass. *Please, please, just pass.* Of all times to appear vulnerable, this was not the one.

"Listen, I get you want to discuss what happened," he began, oblivious to her current state. "I take the blame. I shouldn't have followed you into your room and—"

"Ripped my clothes off?" she finished, holding a hand to her stomach and glaring across the room at him. "I'm not sorry it happened. I've been waiting on you to notice I'm not just Mac and Braden's little sister. I've fantasized about you ripping my clothes off, and I don't even mind that you ruined my favorite dress. So, I'm not sorry a bit. I'm only sorry about how you treated me after."

Other than the muscles ticking in his stubbled jaw, Ryker showed no emotion.

"This wasn't just some one-night stand," she argued.

"It was."

Okay. That hurt—the truth often did—but still. They were more, so much more, than a quick, albeit amazing, romp.

"How dare you act like I was just some random stranger?" she yelled, throwing her arms out wide. "I've known you almost my whole life. You think it's okay to have sex with me and—"

He moved in a flash, gripped her shoulders and hauled her against his bare chest. "No, I didn't think it was okay, but I couldn't stop. Damn it, Laney."

Ryker released her and took a step back, letting her go as if she'd burned him. "I couldn't stop," he whispered.

She had to get out of here. The last time they'd been alone his control had snapped, and he was barely hanging on by a thread now that she was in his living room, on his turf.

He'd purposely been avoiding her since their one-night stand, only communicating through texts for stuff related to O'Shea's. They'd been working together for the past several years. He could admit that when she came on board, his job had become so much easier. With her being able to dig deeper, to infiltrate systems he never could've…she was invaluable. Laney's computer hacking skills were eerily good. If she ever worked with the wrong crowd, she could be dangerous. Granted, some considered the O'Sheas the wrong crowd, but whatever. He couldn't do his job without her, so avoiding her altogether wasn't an option

The torture of working so close together was worth it, though. Even the slightest communication with Laney kept him going. He shouldn't enjoy the pain of being so near, unable to fulfill his every desire, but he chalked up his masochistic tendencies to his less than stellar childhood.

When he wasn't on assignment, he typically would hide out at his home in London or take a trip to some random destination just because he could and had no ties. When he was in Boston, he was too tempted to give in to his desires for his best friends' and bosses' little sister.

When Laney started to reach for him, Ryker held up a hand. "No." If she touched him, this whole distance thing would crumble. He'd been playing with fire when he'd grabbed her a second ago…but damn if she didn't feel good against him.

This had to stop. He owed it to the family who saved him from a living hell. For years he'd ached for her, watched from afar as she grew into a breathtaking woman who managed to slip beneath his defenses. When she'd dated other men, it had nearly gutted him, but what right did he have to say anything?

She was the mafia princess, and he was the family… problem solver. He'd been involved with a lot of dark deeds before her father passed away and left the family business to Braden. Now they were all on the path to being legitimate. But legitimacy didn't change what he'd done in the past. And no matter that his bank account had more zeroes than any one person would need, that didn't change the fact he wasn't worthy of Laney. Not only was she the daughter of one of Boston's most powerful men, but she'd never made it a secret she wanted a large family, complete with babies and pets. He opted for lovers in other states and countries, to keep things physical and void of all emotions.

To put things simply, they were on opposite ends of this warped world. Since Patrick's death months ago, Braden and Mac protected her, and rightfully so, from the harsh realities their family faced each day. Actually, Laney's protection had also been part of Ryker's job.

Not that he needed the money or the job. But he owed the O'Sheas. Anything they asked for, he would provide or die trying. And it was all of that watching over Laney that had damn near done him in.

Blowing out a breath, he shook his head and faced her, but froze. Laney had stepped back and was leaning against the wall. Her closed eyes, her long, slow breaths had him narrowing the distance between them.

"Laney?" He was near enough to touch her, but kept his hands to himself. See? He could do it. He'd just be right here in case she needed something…like his hands on her.

With shaky fingers, he shoved her hair away from her face. Her lids fluttered open, but a sheen of sweat had popped up over her forehead. Was she that nervous about being here?

"I know you don't want me here, but I have to tell you something."

She pushed from the wall, swaying slightly.

Now he didn't resist contact. Ryker grabbed her around the waist and held her against him. "Are you all right?"

"Let me go."

Those vibrant green eyes came up to meet his. The punch to his gut instantly forced him back to that night, to her pinned between his body and the wall. She'd panted his name as she'd clung to his back. Never had he experienced anything so…perfect. And he didn't deserve one second of her affection. Mac and Braden would kick his ass if they knew… Well, they'd try, anyway. He could handle himself in a fight, but he deserved at least a punch to the face over the way he'd seduced Laney like she was just another woman he'd met on one of his trips. Laney was nothing like those other women, and he needed to remember that.

Ryker dropped his hands but didn't step back. He couldn't, not when she still seemed so unsteady and his body was wound so tightly. She was a drug, his drug. They were bad for each other for too many reasons, yet he wanted more.

"I'm pregnant."

Ryker stilled. Had she just...

What the hell? He hadn't heard her right. No way. When they'd been in Miami, he hadn't planned on having sex with her after the party at the new O'Shea's location, but she'd assured him she was on birth control. So, no. He hadn't heard right.

But Laney continued to stare up at him, and Ryker waited for her to say something else, anything else, because there was no way in hell...

"I'm sorry." Laney leaned her head back against the wall and shut her eyes once more. "I didn't know how else to say it. I mean, there's really no good lead-in to something like this."

Pregnant. As in, a baby. Their baby.

Ryker turned away as dread consumed him. How the hell had he allowed something like this to even be a possibility? A child was definitely not something he ever wanted in his life. No damn way would he purposely bring an innocent baby into this world. Into his darkness.

"You said you were on birth control."

He didn't mean for the words to come out as an accusation, but he was confused, damn it. And angry. Angry at himself, because had he kept that control of his in line, Laney wouldn't be dropping this bomb.

"I was." She pulled in a breath and squared her shoulders. "I had to switch the one I was on and started a new one the week before Miami. I don't know if that's why it happened. I just don't know..."

He remembered so clearly her tugging his shirt over

his head and telling him she was on birth control, that she had just had a physical and was clean. He knew full well he hadn't been with anyone for a while, and he'd never gone without protection. So in their frantic state of shedding clothes and getting to the good stuff, they'd had a two-second conversation about contraception.

So here they were. Laney was expecting his child and he was…screwed. Literally.

Bracing his hands on the antique table behind the sofa, Ryker dropped his head. He'd kept his hands, and all his other parts, to himself this whole time. Out of respect for the family who took him in and saved his life, Ryker hadn't given in to the one desire he'd had for years. Until Miami, damn it. How would he ever make things right with the O'Sheas?

Patrick had taken Ryker in at the age of twelve when Ryker had stood up for Braden and Mac on the playground, and the boys had become best friends. Ryker had instantly become like family, but he'd never thought of Laney as a sister. At the time, he'd ignored her because she was so much younger. But by the time she graduated high school, Ryker was deep in the family business, and more than aware that his dirty hands should never touch the sophisticated Laney O'Shea.

When her computer hacking skills were made apparent, Ryker knew she'd be an asset. He'd just had no idea how difficult it would be to work with her. He could afford to hire anyone to do the behind-the-screen work, but he trusted only her.

Braden and Mac were going to kill him. They would kill him and bury his body, and no one would ever know…and he deserved nothing less.

Damn it. Ryker blew out a breath. This was how he

repaid the family who trusted him, who was loyal to him when no one else cared?

"This isn't your fault."

Her soft voice washed over him, and he let out a curt laugh. "No? Am I the one who pushed his way into your room, tore that dress off and demanded you wrap your legs around me? Or was that another man?"

He threw her a glance just in time to see her flinch. Great. Now he was being an ass. All of this was on him. Laney didn't deserve his anger—she was just as innocent as the child.

His gaze dropped to her flat stomach, and fear engulfed him. Images of his biological father flooded his mind, and Ryker vowed that second to never be that man. Never would he lay a hand on his child, never would he choose the next fix over putting food on the table.

Ryker's childhood may be a sad cliché, but that was life and all too often kids were mistreated while other adults turned a blind eye to the abuse.

Ryker looked down. Random scars covered his knuckles, his forearms. His life was made up of more ugly than anything else, yet this beautiful, vibrant woman stood here giving him something so precious and all he wanted to do was…

Hell. What did he want to do? He never wanted Braden or Mac to find out about the night he'd spent with their baby sister. Not that he was afraid of them. He could handle anything thrown his way—almost anything.

They trusted Ryker to keep the family safe, to keep all threats away. Wasn't that why he'd been ordered to follow her back to her hotel that night? Because there had been a threat against her?

For years he'd kept asshats away from her. A few

months ago he'd had to use physical force and pull some major strings to get her ex out of her life. The man had made a menace of himself and had started harassing Laney. He hadn't told Laney what happened, and he never would, but he knew she wondered. Wondered if Ryker had done something sinister. And maybe that was for the best. Maybe she wouldn't get those stars in her eyes like she'd had when they were intimate in Miami.

Pushing off the table, Ryker ran a hand down his face. Stubble rustled beneath his palm, and he honestly had no idea what to do next. He'd never faced something this life-altering, this damn scary.

"I don't expect anything from you." Laney stood straight, apparently feeling better. Her coloring was back. "But I wasn't going to keep this a secret, either. I know you don't want anything to do with me—"

"Stop saying that," he growled. "You have no idea what I want."

She tipped up her head, quirked a brow, as if issuing a silent challenge. "Enlighten me."

If only things were that easy. If only their relationship was about sex and nothing else. *If only* was the story of his entire messed-up life.

"I will be here for this child," he told her, turning to face her fully. "I'll keep you protected."

"You've been looking out for me for years."

He took a step forward. "Not like this. If you think I was protective before, you haven't seen anything."

Laney rolled her eyes. "Don't do this. Don't be over-bearing. If I hadn't gotten pregnant, I know you would've gone on to ignore me on a personal level. That night we spent together wasn't supposed to happen, but we were on that path for so long, it was inevitable."

He hated when she was right. Hated even more that every night since then, he'd had to replay it over and over in his mind because he would never be that close to her again. And she'd ruined him for any other woman.

"I can take care of the baby and myself just fine." She glared back. "But I don't want my brothers to know just yet. I'm not ready."

As much as he hated hiding from anything that threatened him, he was in total agreement. Braden and Mac would find out soon enough, but for now, just no. First, he and Laney had to grasp this news themselves.

Ryker took another step until the gap between them was closed. "Let's get something straight now. I will take care of you and our baby. You need anything, I'm providing it. You won't shut me out. If I have to haul you off to my home in London and watch you personally, I will."

Laney snorted. "Really? Now you choose to let me in?"

"I don't have a choice," he muttered.

And maybe he never had…not where Laney was concerned.

So how the hell did he even attempt to keep his loyalty to this family when he'd betrayed them? And how was he going to be closer to Laney than ever before and keep his hands off her?

Ryker Barrett had lived through some rough times, but he had a feeling he was entering a whole new level of hell.

# Two

How cute was he, thinking he could be all protective and overbearing? Poor Ryker. He clearly forgot he was dealing with an O'Shea. She may be the baby sister, she may be the one everyone loved to keep safely tucked away behind the computer, but she knew more than they'd ever realize. She wasn't naïve, and she wasn't blind.

And going to London? Not an option. She was working on something right here in Boston that was so near to her heart, she refused to walk away. Pregnant or not, she'd see this project come to fruition.

Once she'd left Ryker's house earlier, she headed home, changed her clothes and went for a run. Her doctor had informed her that keeping up with her regular exercise routine was perfectly fine. She needed to release some pent-up energy and blow off steam anyway. Perhaps she should've joined Ryker in his punching bag workout. Although she feared he'd have pissed her off and she'd have ended up socking him in the face to knock some sense into that thick head of his.

Why did she have to be attracted to such a stubborn, frustrating man? Why did she still have to feel how amazing he was weeks after their encounter? The imprint of his powerful touch would be with her forever. Laney had always wondered if the reality of being with Ryker would measure up to the fantasy…and it was better. So much better than anything she could have dreamed up.

But now that she was pregnant, she wasn't going to use the child as an excuse to get closer to him. She wasn't a pathetic, desperate woman. She may have loved Ryker for as long as she could remember, but she would never use an innocent child to get a man.

She'd worried about telling him, though. Worried because she knew enough of his childhood to figure out he probably had no dreams of becoming a father. Ryker never spoke of his birth family—his family had become the O'Sheas the instant Mac and Braden brought him home after school one day. All she knew was that his first twelve years had been hell, and nothing any child should have to go through.

Ryker may be ten years older than her, but that didn't make him out of her reach. By the time she'd been old enough to notice boys, she'd had eyes for only one man. Oh, she'd dated, but nobody had captured her attention like Ryker. And for years he'd ignored her.

Then one night, as if the dam had broken, he'd quite literally torn off her clothes. Never had Laney been so thrilled, so relieved to finally have a dream become reality. But no dream could've ever prepared her for the experience Ryker gave her.

Laney pulled her damp hair into a loose topknot. Now that she'd exercised and showered, she was ready to get some work done. Her brothers were so close to finding their family's missing heirlooms, and she so wanted to be the one to crack the mystery.

For years, decades actually, their family had been searching for nine missing scrolls. The precious documents dated back to the sixteenth century, when one of their ancestors, an Irish monk, transcribed some of William Shakespeare's work. The scrolls had been handed down from generation to generation.

But when the Great Depression robbed so many people of their normal lives, the O'Shea family lost their home and everything inside. The home actually ended up falling into the possession of Zara Perkins's family, which was how Zara and Braden met. Braden had thought that cozying up to the pretty event coordinator and getting inside her house would help in their search. Little did Braden know he'd fall in love.

The scrolls weren't found, so now the search continued. And Laney would love nothing more than to be the one to find the missing treasure. Her entire life she'd been sheltered, kept at an arm's length from the dangers of the family business. If her father and brothers hadn't needed her mad computer skills, she had no doubt they wouldn't have told her a single thing.

Well, if she found these scrolls, they'd have to acknowledge just how much she brought to the table and how she wasn't afraid to get her hands dirty. Family meant everything, and, now more than ever, she was determined to take a stronger role in the business. Proving to her brothers, to Ryker, that she could keep up with them wasn't going to be a problem. She was an

O'Shea. Determination was ingrained in every fiber of her being.

Laney pulled up her email and slid a hand over her flat stomach. This baby would be so hardheaded and strong. There was no other option, considering the genes.

Scrolling through messages, Laney tried to forget Ryker and his demanding ways. But it was those demanding ways that had rocked her entire world at a hotel in Miami.

Maybe she could distract herself with some online Christmas shopping. Maybe that would take her mind off Ryker and the fact she now carried his child. Laney couldn't help but wonder how her overbearing brothers would react to this news.

Dread filled her stomach. How would Zara take the pregnancy? She and Braden had miscarried a child several months ago. Were they trying for another one? Laney hated to pry, but she also didn't want to seem insensitive. Especially if they tried and were unsuccessful.

Oh, they'd be happy about the baby, but privately would they be hurt? Laney loved Zara like a sister and didn't want to cause her any more grief.

With Mac and Jenna planning a wedding, Laney seriously hesitated to say anything to anybody. There wouldn't be a perfect time, but at least she could wait for a better time.

Laney clicked on an email she'd been waiting on. Her offer had been accepted. Finally. She'd been wanting this news for over a week, and the timing was perfect. One more step closer to her goal of revamping an old, run-down building in Boston's south side... Ryker's old neighborhood.

She'd set these plans in motion before Miami. Over

the years, she'd heard Ryker talk about unfortunate kids, never of his own childhood, but she knew his worry stemmed from where he'd come from. So Laney wanted to help. She hated the idea of kids feeling like there was no hope, no one there who really cared about their future.

Her father had instilled in her that commitment. To help the unfortunate. When he'd taken in Ryker, he'd done so without another thought. If more people reached out like her father had, maybe this world would be a bit brighter.

She was keeping the project a secret because she wasn't in it for the praise or the recognition. And she definitely wasn't out to make the O'Shea name look better in the community, which was what many would think if they knew she was involved.

Laney starred the email and laid her phone on the desk in her office before taking a seat. It had gotten so dark since she'd finished her run. She longed for summer and sunshine, where she didn't have to worry about getting back in time before sunset. She also wondered if running alone was the smartest choice. She always had done it by herself to clear her head and think, but now that she was pregnant, she felt more vulnerable.

From the time she was little, her father had taught her to always be aware of her surroundings. But now she should take a few more precautions. Even though she lived in Boston and the streets were bustling with people, she might want to consider using her treadmill or finding a jogging partner.

A laugh escaped her as she thought of Ryker. She couldn't quite imagine the brooding man throwing on a pair of sneakers and running. No, he was more of a boxer type, a guy who lifted heavy weights, or did pull-ups with one arm. He was all strength, all power.

And the thought of all of that excellent muscle tone had Laney attempting to focus on something else. Anything.

Christmas shopping. Right. That's what she'd been planning to do. Why go to the stores and fight all the crazies when she could go braless at home and have everything delivered right to her door...wrapped even.

Online shopping was glorious.

She also had a few final touches to put on the O'Shea's holiday party they were having for the staff at Braden's house in two weeks. The annual event had grown even more since Mac had opened satellite offices in Miami and Atlanta.

Still, Laney loved working on the party and Zara was a professional coordinator, so her sister-in-law had done the majority of the work this year. Laney just needed to order the centerpieces she and Zara had agreed on.

She'd just opened a new browser to search for a dress to wear to the party when her doorbell rang. Glancing quickly at the monitors, she saw Ryker's hulking frame. He kept his head down, shoulders hunched against the brisk December air. He never came to her house...just like she had never gone to his. He'd followed her home before to make sure she was safe, but he'd never popped in of his own accord.

Who knew it would take a pregnancy to get him to come for a visit?

Pushing away from her desk, Laney headed toward the front door. Darkness had set in and snow swirled around, bright flakes catching in the streetlights.

Laney flicked the lock on her door and opened it, immediately stepping back so Ryker could come in out of the cold.

Without a word he strode inside. Those heavy black boots were quite the contrast to her bare feet with polished pink toes. And that was barely the beginning of all the ways they differed.

Laney closed out the cold and set the dead bolt. Crossing her arms over her chest, she faced the man she'd been half in love with since she was a teen.

"This is a surprise," she told him. "Did you come to talk or is something wrong?"

"I need to head out of town."

Laney nodded. His rushing out of town was nothing new. He did so many things for the family. The O'Sheas had gone global with their famous auction houses. Ryker sometimes traveled to obtain relics or random pieces for a specific auction. He'd been known to procure heirlooms that had been stolen. Some may look at him as a modern-day Robin Hood since he returned items to their right owner.

He also was known to go to his home in London for a quick escape, but he was always a text or call away. He put her family first above all else.

"I'm leaving in the morning, and I'll be gone a few days."

Laney tipped up her head. "You never tell me when you're going out of town unless you need my computer skills to pull up the blueprint of a building. If that's what you—"

"I'm not here for the blueprint."

The way those black-as-night eyes held her in place had her shivering. Why did she let him have such power over her? He had more power in one stare than most guys did in a kiss. And she'd dated some great kissers.

"Then why are you here?" She was proud of her strong tone but worried about what his answer would be.

"Are you feeling okay?" he asked, his eyes dropping to her stomach, then back up. "I didn't ask earlier. Or, hell, maybe I did. It's all still kind of a blur."

So he was here about the pregnancy. She should've known he wouldn't stay too far from her. He'd always been protective in that overbearing, bouncer kind of way.

"If you're going to hover, don't waste your time."

She didn't want to sound ungrateful, but she didn't want a babysitter. She wanted him, damn it. She wanted him to see her as a woman. As the woman he'd let down his guard with several weeks ago.

Up until then, she'd always thought he saw her as Mac and Braden's little sister. Someone he helped when necessary, but who was more family than anything.

"If I want to hover, I damn well will," he growled. "You're having my child. You're part of a very well-known family, and it's my job to protect you."

That was the crux of the entire problem. The slice to her heart shouldn't surprise her. Did she honestly think that after they'd had sex he'd come around? That when he knew about the baby he'd profess his undying love to her? No, but she'd at least hoped for him to treat her like…hell. Was it too much to ask for him to act like he cared about her as more than his friends' baby sister?

"I don't want to be your job."

Laney turned before he could see the hurt on her face. Heading back toward her office, she couldn't care less if he let himself out or if he followed. Trying to capture

Ryker's attention for so long was exhausting. She sure as hell didn't want it now due to a job or a baby. She wanted him to look at her for her. Nothing else.

Apparently that was too much to ask. With his traveling schedule, he probably did hookups and one-night stands. She'd never seen him in any type of a relationship or even heard him mention seeing someone. Laney thought she may take way too much delight in that, but whatever.

Just as she reached the threshold of her office, a hand clamped around her arm and spun her.

"Don't walk away from me."

Laney raised her brows. "You're not in charge of me, no matter what my brothers tell you to do. I can get along just fine without being coddled."

"Would you quit acting like you're so put out? Your brothers care about you and only want you safe."

Laney jerked free of his hold but kept her eyes on his. "And what about you, Ryker? Do you care about me?"

"Of course I do."

Laney swallowed. "As a brother?"

The muscles along the stubbled jaw ticked. "I'm not doing this, Laney. I'm not hashing out my feelings or letting you get inside my head."

Of course he wouldn't. Ryker would never let anyone in because he was made of steel. She'd never seen him show emotion, other than frustration and anger. But he never talked about what drove him to those feelings. The clenching of the muscles in his perfectly squared jaw indicated he was angry. Other than that, he played his cards seriously close to his chest.

"Whatever." She waved a hand in the air. "I'm feeling fine. There. Now you've checked up on me, and you can go on your way, guilt-free. This all could've been done in a text."

"Maybe," he agreed. "But if you were feeling bad you'd lie, and I wanted to see for myself."

Laney went for broke. "I think we both know between the two of us who would lie about how they feel."

When he remained still, silent, Laney was done. They were getting nowhere, and she wasn't in the mood to play games or whatever the hell else he wanted.

"I won't keep you out of the baby's life, but I don't want your attention just because I'm pregnant. I've waited for years for you to notice me. I thought Miami was something, but I was clearly mistaken, since you ignored me until you knew I was having your child."

All of that was so hard to admit, but at this point what did she have to lose? She wasn't one to hide her feelings, which only made Ryker squirm. Good. He deserved it.

The second she jerked the door open, a burst of cold air rushed in. "If you're done here…"

Laney turned and stared out at the blowing flakes. She didn't want to look at him, not when she still craved him. Putting up some type of emotional barrier was the only way she'd survive this.

Heavy boots moved across her hardwood floor. Ryker stopped right in front of her but kept his gaze out the open door. Laney stared at his black, leather-clad shoulder. The smell of his jacket, the familiar woodsy cologne and the unmistakable scent that she only associated with Ryker assaulted her senses. Why did he have to be the one to hold her emotionally captive?

"I've noticed you," he whispered as he remained rooted inches from her. "I've noticed too much for too long."

Laney's breath caught in her throat.

"But Miami won't happen again." Turning, he locked those dark eyes on her. "I'll check on you while I'm away."

And then he was gone. Shoulders hunched against the blowing snow, head down, Ryker walked off her porch and down the walk toward his car. Despite shivering, Laney waited until he was in the SUV with the engine running before she closed the door…but not before she caught him looking back at her.

Just that glance from a distance was enough to have her stomach doing flops, her heart pounding.

Ryker may be checking on her because of the baby, something she couldn't be upset about, but his telling words gave her hope. He'd noticed her. And from the way he seemed to be angry about it, he'd clearly been fighting with himself over the fact for a while now.

Laney leaned back against her door and wrapped her arms around her abdomen. She had no idea what was going to happen now that she and Ryker were on this journey, but one thing was perfectly clear. They were in this together, whether he liked it or not.

# Three

"I don't like this."

Ryker's cell phone lay on the console as he watched the house across the street. With Braden on speaker, Ryker could focus on who was coming and going.

"I'm not a fan myself, but I think there's something here," Ryker replied.

This was his first interaction with Braden since Ryker discovered Laney was expecting. The guilt of his betrayal weighed heavily on his chest. The O'Sheas had been everything to him over the years, and he'd purposely kept his distance from Laney because he knew what would happen if he touched her. Just one touch, that's all it would've taken at any given time for him to snap.

But she'd mouthed off at the party and between her sass and that body-hugging dress, his self-control had finally expired.

Damn, the woman could tempt a saint...not that he

was anywhere near that holy. But he'd completely lost it in Miami. Years of pent-up frustration, the fact she'd been receiving threats and not sharing that information, and the way she'd looked in that short black dress had been the combination for his undoing.

"How long are you going to wait?" Braden's low tone cut through the memories.

Ryker rubbed the penny between his thumb and index finger, hating the way he carried the damn thing around like some good-luck charm. He was pathetic for even still having it, but the reminder of where he came from always needed to be front and center.

"I've seen a member of the DeLuca family go in, but nothing else."

The DeLuca family was known for organized crime. Thugs, actually. They didn't even compare to the O'Sheas, though Ryker thought some members of law enforcement would lump the two families in the same category...or prison cell.

"What activity has Laney uncovered?" Braden asked.

Ryker raked a hand down his face. "She's seen some email chatter with several family members discussing moving a package. When she dug a little deeper, she found they have an old trunk in the basement that contains some documents. But we have no clue what they are."

Ryker didn't know how the coveted scrolls would've ended up hours away from where they were last seen or how they were in a basement belonging to an organized crime family, but this was the strongest lead they'd had in a while. Ryker had followed every tip that had popped up. He'd been to London twice, Mexico, Paris and several US states.

When Patrick passed several months ago, he had one dying request. He wanted the scrolls found and returned to the O'Shea family. He'd tried for years to recover them but to no avail. Ryker fully intended to finish the job… it was the least he could do for the people to whom he owed his life.

"Damn, Laney is calling me," Braden stated. "Keep me posted no matter what happens or what time it is."

Laney was calling? Was she okay? Did something happen?

Every time he'd thought of her since Miami, all he could think about was the way she came apart in his arms. She'd been so responsive, so passionate. Now when he thought of her, all he could think was that she was carrying his child. His. Child.

The words didn't seem real even in his own mind. How the hell was he going to take care of a baby? What did he know? His father had only taught him how to get high, get laid and steal. The essentials of every childhood according to dear ole Dad.

Ryker kept his eyes on the house, but his mind wasn't on the job. Damn. This was why he never got involved with anyone. His loyalties were with Braden and Mac now. And by default, as their baby sister, Laney. If he was worrying about anyone, especially a woman, he wouldn't be able to concentrate on the task at hand. And the task sure as hell wasn't Laney.

She'd called Braden, not Ryker. That shouldn't bother him, but it did. There was no denying that he wanted to be the one she called on when she needed anything. But he couldn't be that deep in her life and keep his distance at the same time.

His mind went into overdrive. If something was going

on with the baby, she wouldn't have called Braden, that much Ryker was sure of.

Ryker disconnected the call. The penny was heavy in his hand. Over the years, he'd tried to tell himself that the souvenir from the best day of his life was ridiculous and childish to keep. Yet each day he left his house, he grabbed his keys and the penny and shoved them in his pocket. He couldn't seem to let go of his past.

Story of his life.

After another hour of waiting, which brought the grand total up to six, Ryker decided to call it a night. Laney would let him know if more activity came through her. She'd managed to tap into several areas: emails, private messages on social media, a cell phone.

Ryker always marveled at how crazy brilliant she was. She was seriously the brains behind the operation when it came to research and hunting down people. For years, she'd managed to find anything online, while Ryker did the grunt work. They were a team in a sense, but he never wanted to look at things that way. If he did, then he'd have to admit there was a relationship. And even when their dealings had been platonic, he couldn't analyze things too deeply when it came to Laney.

The woman could make a man forget everything else in this ugly world. She had beauty, grace and a stubborn streak he couldn't help but admire.

And now she was having his baby.

Pulling himself up straighter in his seat, Ryker brought the engine of his SUV to life. Snow covered the streets and showed no sign of stopping soon. December in New York was just as brutal and unpredictable as in Boston.

Cranking up the heat, he maneuvered through the

streets toward the hotel. Another cold hotel. He always booked a suite. Mostly because growing up he'd lived in a one-room dump of an apartment. Now that he could afford to stay anywhere or buy anything he wanted, he fully intended to take advantage.

But he'd never look at another hotel the same after Miami. Laney changed everything.

He couldn't even wrap his mind around the fact he was going to be a father. What the hell did he know? His own father had used him as a punching bag when he was awake and only half drunk. Ryker never wanted marriage, kids, the minivan experience. He was just fine with the job he had. Though Braden and Mac would never tell him this was a job, to them he was simply a brother, a best friend.

Which made this pregnancy so much harder to comprehend. He couldn't come to grips with how he should deal with it, so how the hell could he figure out how to tell them?

Laney was such an innocent. They'd worked for years to keep her safe, to keep her behind the scenes. Ryker had made enemies all over the globe. Now that Laney was pregnant, he would have to be twice as diligent about keeping those he cared about safe.

Yeah, he cared about her. Too much. Being ten years older than her, he'd not paid much attention when he first came to the O'Sheas as a teen. Then he'd been out of the house mostly doing grunt work and earning his way in the family, so he didn't have to go back to his former hellhole.

By the time he'd started coming around the house more often, Laney was a teen herself and he was a bastard for looking at her twice. If Patrick O'Shea had ever thought Ryker was eyeing his daughter, Ryker doubted he'd still be here.

But Ryker had respected the man more than anyone. Patrick had shown him what a true father figure was. Patrick had cared for his children, put them first and kept them protected at all costs. He had demanded loyalty, and there was nothing Ryker had wanted to give him more.

Which was one of the main reasons he wanted to be the one to uncover the scrolls. Patrick was gone, but Ryker still wanted to do this one final job for the only real father he'd ever known.

And all the more reason Ryker needed to keep his hands to himself where Laney was concerned. Patrick had been extremely protective and cautious when Laney wanted to date certain men. There were guys who wanted to date her simply for her last name or because they thought they could get into the family and wanted to use her as a warped version of a job interview.

Ryker had done neither of those things. He'd just gone straight to taking her against a wall and getting her pregnant like a loser.

One thing was for sure. He may not be father material, but he wasn't about to ignore his responsibilities. If he had his way, he'd whisk Laney and their baby away and tuck them safely in his home in London…or he'd buy a damn private island. Anything to keep them safe.

He had the funds, that wasn't the problem. No, the problem came in the form of a beautiful, stubborn, Irish goddess who would rather argue with him than listen to reason.

Ryker pulled into a parking spot right outside the window to his room. Always on the ground floor, always near an exit.

Fear overwhelmed him for the first time in years. Not for himself but for Laney and their unborn child.

When he got back to Boston, they were going to have to talk. He couldn't outrun her any longer. He may not want a relationship with her, or anyone else for that matter, but he'd make damn sure she was taken care of… regardless of the cost to his own heart.

Most would say he didn't have a heart. Ryker would have to agree. But Laney made him feel, and he could see the train wreck coming. Someone was going to get hurt.

When Laney had called her brother because her Christmas decorations were too heavy for her to lift, she hadn't even realized the time of night. But here he was hauling box after box into her living room.

"Why do you have so much stuff to put up for only one month?" he growled as he sat the last box beside her sofa.

"So you can enjoy it when you come to visit." Laney smiled and patted his cheek. "Just think, in about four weeks you can come back and take this all back up to my attic."

"I'll hire someone. Hell, just leave it up all year long. I won't judge."

Laney pulled the lid off one box and stared down at the contents. Christmas decorations were her crack. She loved everything about them. The lights, the glass ornaments that belonged to her mother, the garland she strung over her mantel and down her staircase. Everything was so magical, so perfect, and it made her remember how amazing her childhood had been. A house full of family and laughter, the parties they'd thrown in the O'Shea ballroom.

Tears pricked her eyes. She wanted that for her baby.

She wanted her child to know the meaning of family gatherings. There was nothing more valuable to Laney than her family. She needed them now more than ever, but she had no idea how to tell them a little O'Shea was about to join their ranks.

She wasn't afraid of how they'd react to the baby; her brothers would welcome another O'Shea. But how would they treat Ryker? He was such a staple in their family, and he was so much more to Braden and Mac than just an employee. He was…everything.

Laney sighed and blinked back tears.

"Hey, you okay?" Braden stood beside her, bending to look her in the eye. "Oh, damn. Please don't cry. I'll help take them down later, I swear."

Why was it that the strongest of men couldn't handle a little water?

"I'm fine," she assured him, waving a hand. "It's late and I'm tired. That's all."

His dark brows raised in disbelief. "And you opted to start decorating now?"

"I've got a lot on my mind." Wasn't that an understatement. "I'll work on this until I think I can fall asleep."

Crossing his arms over his chest, Braden straightened and pinned her with his eyes. "Is there a problem I need to know about?"

Laney picked up an ornament and began to peel away its bubble wrap. "Just worrying about my brothers. Nothing new."

That wasn't a total lie. She always worried about them. Their business kept them busy, traveling, sneaking around. Thankfully they had enough law enforcement in their back pocket to keep them out of the hot seat, but still. Laney always worried something would happen. There were worse fates than being arrested.

"We're all fine." Braden took the ornament from her and waited until she turned her attention toward him. "I'm asking about you. Are you still receiving threats? I'd hoped after Shane—"

"Stop worrying about me."

She didn't want to talk about her emails or Shane. Ryker had taken it upon himself to…handle the problem of Shane when he'd attempted to abduct Laney from in front of her home in Beacon Hill. Shane had been the bane of her family's existence for years, but he'd crossed the line when he'd harassed Braden's wife, Zara. When he'd tried to grab Laney, Ryker had had enough.

And Laney knew the way Ryker had managed the situation had been an issue between him and Braden. Since Braden had taken over the family business after their father passed, he'd been adamant about going legitimate, and that included how they took care of their enemies. Ryker insisted that ending their old practices so suddenly would make them look weak and invite retribution.

Laney was still unsure what happened to her ex, but she was fine about being kept in the dark regarding that.

"Why don't you get back home to your bride?" Laney suggested. "It's late. I'm just going to sit here and tear up a little over Mom's things."

Braden looked as if he wanted to say more. That intense stare could make even the most seasoned criminal break, but Laney wasn't caving. She'd grown up around strong-willed alphas her entire life. Not much fazed her.

"If you have any issues, you call me or Ryker immediately."

Laney nodded, though if she had an issue she'd deal with it herself. She wasn't a helpless female.

Once she hugged her loving, overprotective brother good-night, she reset her alarm and glanced around at the mess. The tree sat completely naked in the corner near the fireplace where she always put it. She wasn't even sure at this point if she had any working lights. She tried to buy new ones each year, but, well, this year had been a bit exceptional and her mind had been elsewhere.

Laney found the box with her garland and decided to work on the staircase. That would be simple enough and keep her mind occupied for a few minutes.

She'd barely started when her thoughts drifted to Ryker. There was always a level of fear anytime she knew he was working. But the not knowing was frustrating. She knew the lead he was working on, she'd supplied him with the intel, but she didn't like how he insisted on going out alone. He always stayed just detached enough to be in the know but keep to himself. Damn frustrating man.

Laney carefully wrapped the banister, fluffing the greenery as she went. This time next year she'd be playing Santa and buying the baby's first Christmas things— tacky bibs and ridiculous ornaments would be welcome here.

What would her world be like with a child? Laney smiled. As scared as she was to tell her brothers, as worried as she was about what this meant for her and Ryker, there was no way Laney would change one single thing about Miami. This baby would never question how much he or she was loved, and the first person to call this pregnancy a mistake would be throat punched.

The thought of Ryker holding a baby was nearly

laughable. She'd never seen his softer side, though she knew he had one. He cared for her, even if he opted to show it in Neanderthal-type ways.

Those whispered words before he left kept playing through her mind. She wished he'd stayed so they could talk, but he was prone to run rather than discuss his feelings. Well, he couldn't hide from her forever. Eventually they had to talk about the future and their baby.

Laney's cell chimed from the living room. She hurried down the stairs and carefully maneuvered the minefield of boxes. She found her phone on the coffee table next to a wreath that was in desperate need of fluffing. Because of the time of night, she figured the text would be important.

And she was right.

Ryker's name lit up her screen, and she swiped her phone to read the message.

Nothing new tonight. Anything come through on your end?

Work. It was always work with him. A sliver of disappointment speared through her as she replied.

Nothing. I'll keep you posted.

Her thumb hovered over the Send button. She wanted to make this more personal. She wanted to say…something. But Ryker was all work. What would he say if she asked personal questions or called him out on what he'd confessed to her earlier? Could he talk about his feelings when he wasn't looking her in the face? She understood that. She totally got how people were more apt to open up when they could hide behind an electronic device.

She hit Send but immediately started typing another message.

Earlier when you said you think about me, why were you angry about it?

Laney sent the message before she could change her mind. She wanted to know. She deserved to know, but the screen seemed to mock her as no reply came. She waited several minutes, but still nothing.

Fine. She wasn't going to beg. Yes, she would give anything to get inside that head of his, but she didn't want to have to beat the information out of him.

The second she laid her phone down, it chimed once again. Laney stared at the screen. She almost didn't want to read the message, but she hadn't been raised to give into any fear.

Because it isn't right.

Laney resisted the urge to roll her eyes as she contemplated her reply. There was so much to be said, it was too much to text and should be said face-to-face.

But he wasn't completely closing her out, so she went for it.

Whatever you feel can't be helped. Why fight it?

Laney jumped when her phone rang. The cell bounced from her hand and onto the sofa, hit a box and landed on the floor. She snatched it up, thankful the screen wasn't cracked, and she was a bit surprised to see Ryker's name.

"I didn't think you'd actually talk to me," she answered.

"You wouldn't leave me alone until I did."

Laney smiled. Just that gruff tone had her nerves calming. Ryker could always make her feel safe, at ease. Even though they argued and got on each other's nerves, he was her comfort zone. Banter was their normal. Normal was so vanilla. What she and Ryker had, well…that was more Rocky Road.

"Where are you now?" she asked, scooting a box over and taking a seat on her couch.

"Hotel."

"Plenty of time to talk, then."

Ryker's heavy sigh resounded through the line. "I'm not in a chatty mood."

"Have you ever been?"

"What do you think?"

Laney toed the disorderly wreath aside and propped her socked feet on the coffee table. "Maybe it's time you stop fighting whatever you're feeling and just go with it."

The laugh that escaped him was void of any humor. "Life isn't that easy."

"It's your life, isn't it? Make it that easy."

"You think I enjoy pushing my level of self-control?" he asked, his voice gravelly, as if fighting back anger. "I have a responsibility to your brothers. I have a responsibility to you." He let out a deep sigh. "To our baby."

Laney's heart clenched. Closing her eyes, she dropped her head back on the cushion and focused on not botching this. Ryker was so much more to her than she could even put into words, but he may never comprehend that.

"You have a responsibility to yourself," she said softly. "You owe my family nothing. I know you think you—"

"I owe your family everything. And I've betrayed them."

His last words came out on a strangled breath. Laney stilled. Did he honestly believe that? Was he that torn up over the baby that he truly felt he'd gone against her brothers? Why did everything have to come back to his sense of loyalty to her family? They trusted him, they knew him better than anyone else and they might be angry, but they would still love him.

Tears pricked her eyes, and she cursed her stupid pregnancy hormones. Tears had no place here. She was fighting for what she wanted, what Ryker wanted. Hell, what they deserved.

"If that's how you feel, then there's nothing I can say. If you don't want anyone to know this baby is yours, we don't have to say anything. I can just say I'm not involved with the father and not tell my brothers any name at all." Though it would kill her. Pain like nothing before speared through her at the thought of Ryker not being involved. "I can't make you want—"

"That's the whole problem," he yelled. "I want, damn it. Too much. But I'll never turn my back on you or this baby."

Laney picked at the hem of her T-shirt and swallowed a lump of remorse. "Right. Responsibilities."

"Laney—"

"It's late. I'll let you go."

She ended the call, dropping the phone into her lap as she battled back tears. Why did he have to be so noble, yet so ignorant at the same time? Why did he feel that he had to sacrifice his own happiness in order to fulfill some past debt? Ryker had more than proved himself to this family.

At least he hadn't agreed to being left out of the baby's life. That would've gutted her. But he still only saw her as a responsibility, and Laney feared she'd never be more in his life.

# Four

"We need to get inside that house."

Braden nodded in agreement. "How soon can you get back? I don't want them moving that trunk."

Ryker leaned back on the leather sofa in Braden's study. He'd left New York after staying an extra day longer than planned, and had driven straight to Braden's house. He hadn't called or texted Laney after their talk on the phone. He'd revealed too much, she'd gotten too close to the raw emotions…emotions he feared he couldn't hide forever.

Damn it. He hadn't even been aware of suppressing them, so how the hell did he continue to hide them?

"I can go as soon as I get the blueprint."

Braden came to his feet. "Great. Laney is due here anytime."

The blueprint was a pathetic excuse to see her again.

He could've gotten it the other day when she offered, she could've also emailed it. But, he wanted to see her, touch her, consume her. But reality was cold and harsh. He'd had her once, and that would have to stay with him forever because he couldn't let his guard down again.

He'd not only betrayed Braden and Mac by slashing right through their trust, but he'd let Laney down, as well. He should've had more control in Miami, should've walked her to her room and kept going once he knew she was safe. How could he have let his all-consuming need for her change their entire lives?

"Ryker?"

Jerking his attention back to Braden, Ryker stood. "Lost in thought. What were you saying?"

"Laney just pulled in."

Ryker glanced to the monitors and saw Laney stepping from her car. While it had stopped snowing, the ground was blanketed in several inches. Braden's drive and walk had been cleared though.

He tried not to watch as she pulled her coat tighter around her waist or how her long, dark hair blew in the breeze. He didn't have to concentrate too hard to still feel that hair over his body. Ryker clenched his fists and ordered himself to get control before she stepped inside. This would be the first time the three of them would be together since he'd found out about the pregnancy. He couldn't give anything away. He couldn't—

On the screen, Laney slipped and went down. Ryker tore out of the study, down the hall and through the foyer. He whipped open the door, oblivious to the wind and the bitter air. Laney had a gloved hand on the bumper of her car and was pushing herself up.

"Stop." Ryker slid his arms around her waist. "Lean into me."

Laney pushed her hair away from her face and looked up at him. "I'm fine. Embarrassed, but fine."

Ryker didn't let her go as she came fully to her feet. "Is she okay?"

Ryker glanced over his shoulder to Braden who was coming toward them. "I think so."

Laney tried to push off Ryker, but winced. "Okay. Just give me a second."

His hands flattened over her stomach as his heart sank. "Laney?"

Her eyes held his. "It's my ankle. Just sore. I'm okay."

How did she know? Could she be sure the baby was okay? Ryker didn't know how hard she fell. Hell, he didn't know anything about pregnancies or babies, but seeing her go down had nearly stopped his heart.

Scooping her up in his arms, and careful to avoid random ice patches, he stalked past Braden and into the house. Zara rushed in from the kitchen, her dark hair flying around her shoulders.

"What happened? Laney?"

"I'm okay." Laney waved a hand. "Just slipped outside and my ankle is sore. Ryker is being overbearing as usual."

Considering he'd been that way with her for years, this wasn't out of the ordinary. He didn't give a damn if it was. Seeing Laney go down like that had ripped something open inside him. In the brief seconds it took him to get outside, all he could think of was their baby. How the hell was he going to handle parenting?

"I'll get some ice," Zara told them.

Ryker gently laid Laney on the chaise in the formal

living room. Her hand slid against the side of his neck as she let go. Even though she had gloves on, just that simple touch took him back to Miami when she'd—

No. That was then. A mistake. He couldn't live in the past. He'd vowed to move on and that's exactly what he had to do if he wanted to get their intimacy out of his life.

Unfortunately, Laney had imbedded herself into his soul…and he thought he'd sold that to the devil a long time ago.

But he felt her. When she looked at him, he swore he felt her. That delicate touch, the tender gaze. She was hurting now, and he needed to focus.

"I'll call our doctor," Ryker stated.

Laney immediately started to shake her head. "I just went down wrong. I'm fine. I didn't fall hard."

"Let's get your boot off and look at your ankle." Braden went to unzip her boot. "Can you move it at all?"

She wiggled her foot, and Ryker watched her face for any sign of discomfort. When her bright eyes flashed up to his, he had to tell himself not to look away. She could draw him in so easily…and she knew the power she possessed.

"It's a little swollen," Braden commented. "I'd say you're fine. Just stay off it for a while."

Laney smirked. Freakin' smirked at him like a child who'd been playing parents against each other. Ryker narrowed his eyes. "I'm calling the doctor anyway just to be safe."

Before he could slide his cell from his pocket, Laney laid a hand on his wrist. "I'm fine." Her eyes bore into his, completely serious now. "I promise. I'd know if I needed to be seen."

She didn't look away, her grip tightened. Ryker blew

out a breath he wasn't aware he'd been holding. Of course she would get a doctor here if she thought she needed one. Laney loved this baby and wouldn't make poor choices. Still, for his peace of mind, he'd feel better if she was seen.

"Relax," she whispered, her eyes darting toward her brother.

Yeah. Relax.

Ryker took a step back and glanced down at her ankle. He needed to get a grip. Being cautious and protective was one thing, but acting like a hovering boyfriend was—

Seriously? How had that word even popped into his head? He wasn't her damn boyfriend. This wasn't junior high. But she was right. If he didn't get a grip, Braden would wonder what was going on, and that wasn't a topic he wanted to dive headfirst into right now.

"Here you go." Zara came back in and placed an ice pack wrapped in a towel over Laney's ankle. "Let's put a pillow under you to keep it propped up."

Ryker stayed back as Braden and Zara got Laney situated. He wanted to scoop her up and take her back to his house where he could take care of her. He wanted her tucked away behind his state-of-the-art security system where she'd be safe at all times. But none of that was possible. She'd never be at his house on personal terms. He'd never see her in his bed.

Ryker reached into his pocket, his fingertips brushing over the penny. The reminder he wasn't cut out for family life.

"Do you feel like working?" Braden asked. "I hate to ask, but time is of the essence."

Laney shifted on the sofa. "I can work. My laptop is

out in the car, though. I was walking to the passenger side to get it when I fell."

"I'll get it."

Ryker needed more cool air. He needed to get his heart rate back to normal and to chill out. Laney had had to talk him down, and that had never happened. Damn it.

She may not want a doctor, but one thing was certain. When they left here, he'd be driving her. Whether they went to her house or his, that was her choice, but they'd be leaving together.

Laney concentrated on digging up the layout of the house Ryker needed to get into. Her ankle throbbed more than she wanted to admit, but she was absolutely certain nothing else was hurt. The baby was fine. If she even thought for a second that something could be wrong, she'd have a doctor here. But she honestly hadn't fallen that hard, just turned her ankle on the sliver of ice she hadn't seen.

Zara and Braden were in the study. Her brother had told her to yell when she found something because he was helping his wife work on finalizing the company party.

Laney's sister-in-law was a top-notch events coordinator and in high demand. The way Braden supported her business was adorable. He was proud of his wife, and their love was evident whenever they were around each other.

The miscarriage they'd suffered a few months ago had only forged their bond even deeper. But Laney still couldn't bring herself to tell them about her own condition.

"Will you stop brooding?" Laney's fingers flew over the keys, but Ryker's presence was wearing on her nerves.

"I'm waiting."

She glanced over to him and raised her brows. "You're leaning in the corner with your arms crossed, and you've been staring for twenty minutes. That's brooding. I can actually hear your frustration."

When he pushed from the wall and strode over to her, Laney realized she'd poked the bear. Fine. At least he was showing emotion.

Ryker loomed over her, hands on his narrow hips. "How much longer until you have something?"

"I'm downloading the blueprints now."

"Good. Then we're leaving."

Laney jerked back. "Excuse me?"

He leaned down, pinning her with those coal-black eyes. "You heard me. I'm driving. The destination is up to you."

O-kay. The clenched jaw and the no-nonsense tone told her he wasn't giving her an option.

"Fine. We're going to my house. I have things I need to get done."

Ryker shoved his hands in his pockets. "Not with that ankle. You're relaxing, and if I even think you're trying to put weight on it, I'll have the doctor at your house so fast you won't know what hit you."

Laney believed him. He didn't take chances with her on a good day, but add in a pregnancy and a fall, and Ryker was dead serious.

"Oh, don't worry." She offered him her sweetest smile. "I plan on letting you do all the work."

Poor guy. He had no idea he was about to be covered head to toe in glittery garland, lights and delicate glass ornaments. She'd most certainly have her phone at the ready to snap some pictures of Ryker decorating her house.

"Oh, here we go." She glanced back at her screen, surveyed the pages that had downloaded and quickly emailed them to Braden and Ryker. "All done."

Ryker stalked from the room. There was no other word to describe his movements. He was angry, most likely with himself, or maybe with her. Whatever. He was about to be doused in Christmas happiness. He wanted to order her around and demand he leave with her? Fine.

Laney hesitated for a second but quickly pulled up her emails. Nothing new on the property in Southie. She'd had some contractors survey the building so she could get some quotes. After she signed the paperwork next week, the place would officially be hers and she could get to work. She seriously wanted the place open by spring so kids could come and play when the weather got nicer.

Opening the community center in Ryker's old neighborhood was perfect. She couldn't wait to have children filling the place. Children who may not have an exemplary home life and just needed a break.

Laney wondered where Ryker would be today if someone had intervened and helped him earlier than her father had. Would he still be part of their lives? Would he still be as hard, as jaded as he was now? He'd made it a point to be her personal security detail from the time she was a teenager. Was that because no one had protected him?

Laney's heart clenched. Had his worry for her led to whatever happened to her ex?

No. She wouldn't believe that Ryker would do anything to him beyond a few harassing calls and texts. Ryker could be over the top at times when it came to people he cared about, but she truly hoped he hadn't done anything rash.

Laney swallowed as she closed her laptop. Ryker cared about her. Beyond their intense night together, he'd admitted as much…and he didn't mean the sibling type of caring, either.

Ryker may think he'd been keeping her safe, but she always had his back, too. She held the reins with the intel coming in, and she chose what to feed him and what to keep to herself.

Laney would be even more diligent now that he was going to be a father. There might be times she made sure he didn't get a case because of the danger it posed to him, and she'd deal with the backlash from her brothers. Ryker needed someone to look after him; he was long overdue for it, actually. And Laney was just the woman for the job.

# Five

The second Ryker stepped into Laney's house, he froze. He'd been duped. He glanced at her, only to see a smirk on her beautiful face. Now she mocked him.

Why did he find himself so attracted to her again? Oh, yeah. She was sexy as hell, and she took charge. A perfectly lethal combination to his senses. If he were ever considering a relationship, those were the qualities he'd look for. But a relationship with Laney was not only risky, it was suicide.

"Don't even tell me I'm decorating."

Laney leaned on him because she wouldn't let him carry her, yet she was limping slightly. Stubborn woman.

"I can do it, but you'll just get all grouchy and make me sit down."

Ryker reset her alarm system, still wishing he'd ignored her request and gone to his own house. After escorting her over to her sofa with an attached chaise, he got her settled and pulled off her boots. He grabbed one of her fluffy yellow throw pillows and set it beneath her ankle.

"Still sore?" he asked, glancing down at her, trying to ignore how perfect she looked all laid out.

"It's fine."

Ryker crossed his arms over his chest and sighed. "You've said that at least five times since it happened, which means it's anything but fine."

Laney tipped her head back on the cushion, her hair falling around her shoulders. Try as he might, he couldn't help but recall how all those strands felt on his bare skin. A memory he prayed never diminished. He needed that to keep him going, especially since he'd never have her again.

"Stop hovering. My ankle is fine, the baby is fine." She laced her fingers over her abdomen. "Do you want to put the lights on the tree or would you prefer to decorate the mantel?"

Ryker narrowed his eyes. Testing his patience was a surefire way to get him to take her back to his house. Did he look like a damn interior designer?

"Maybe you didn't notice, but I don't do Christmas."

"I always buy you a gift. In fact, you're the first person I buy for."

Yeah, and he'd kept every single one of them. He always felt like a fool for not buying her something, but what would he get her? What was an appropriate gift for a woman he wanted but couldn't have? So he never did gifts…for anyone.

"You don't have to buy me gifts," he growled. He'd rather put up lights than get into this uncomfortable topic.

Laney shifted on the chaise and patted the spot beside her. "You're staring down at me like I'm a bug on your shoe. So, either sit down, get to work or leave."

Ryker loved how she always spoke her mind. Except when she kept revealing her feelings for him. Nothing good could come from her making an impossible situation even more difficult.

And if he sat next to her, he'd want to touch her. Touching would lead to what they both truly wanted, and he refused to betray this family again by giving into his selfish desires.

Ryker turned and grabbed a box. "What's in here?"

From the corner of his eye, he saw Laney's shoulders fall, her eyes close. He'd hurt her. He couldn't sit close to her. Didn't she get that? She had to understand this wasn't about them. There was so much more to it than just a man and a woman who were attracted to each other. So he'd have to keep his distance…as much as possible, no matter how much he wanted her.

"That's the ornaments," she told him. "I have a bag of lights I just purchased. It's on the steps. There's also a bag from All Seasons there, but be careful because I just bought the cutest Nutcracker there."

Fine. He'd put the damn lights on the tree. He'd decorate her house to put a smile on her face. He knew full well how much Laney loved Christmas. She used to go to her parents' house, which was now Braden and Zara's, and cook an elaborate dinner on Christmas Eve. She'd pass out gifts she'd bought and wrapped in thick, sparkly paper. Most likely she'd hand tied her own bows, too. Laney's face would light up as she sat and watched her family open their gifts. Ryker was always so mesmerized, so humbled he got to experience Christmas with them.

Damn it. They were his family. The only family he'd truly considered his own—the only one that mattered.

He'd just reached the steps and spotted the bag when Laney's soft voice stopped him.

"I know you don't want to be here."

Ryker glanced over his shoulder. Those bright green eyes locked him in place from across the room.

"I never said that."

Smiling, she said, "You didn't have to. You regret sleeping with me. Probably feel trapped because I'm pregnant. And I'm positive you think you betrayed my brothers. But please, don't patronize me or pity me. I'm fine on my own, Ryker."

When she held her ground and didn't glance away, he ignored the bag and started back toward Laney. She was a strong woman, what man wouldn't find that a complete turn on? She was everything he'd want in a woman, but she was the little sister of his employers, his best friends. She was off limits. And he'd ignored that unwritten rule.

Taking a seat on the edge of the chaise, he faced her. "I don't regret sleeping with you. I've tried, but I can't even lie to myself."

She reached out, tracing his scarred knuckles with her fingertip. "That's something, at least."

"I don't feel trapped," he went on. "I feel sorry for you, for this baby. I know nothing, Laney. The most impressionable years of my childhood were spent in hell. I couldn't begin to tell you what a baby needs. I don't even know how to help you adjust to this. I'm not made to be in a relationship or to be a parent. But that doesn't mean I'm turning my back on you guys. It just means…"

Ryker shook his head and turned away so he didn't have to look her in the eye. Apparently she was the stronger of the two. "It means you deserve better, and this is what you've got."

He barely heard her shift before her fingers threaded through his hair. "There's nobody better than you, Ryker. You're a fighter, you're noble and you're loyal. I know you'd do anything to keep me and this baby safe. What makes you think I'm so unlucky?"

Reaching up, he gripped her wrist, but didn't pull her hand away as he turned to meet her questioning gaze. "Because you deserve a man you can share your life with. You're the type who wants a family, who wants that big Christmas morning celebration with chaos and Santa stories. I can't give you that."

Laney smoothed his hair from his forehead. He should stop her. He should remove her hand, but he was such a selfish bastard. One more touch. He just needed one more and then he'd get up.

"Have I asked you for anything? You're already family. Just because we're having a baby doesn't mean you have to marry me."

Just the thought of marriage had him trembling. He traveled too much, took too many risks to bring a wife into the mix.

Laney's hand fell to her lap. "I didn't realize you were so put off by the thought of marriage. Glad I didn't propose."

She'd tried to make light of the situation, but the hurt in her tone gave her away.

"Laney—"

"So, if you want to bring me that sack of lights, I can

get them out of the boxes, and you can put them on the tree."

He stared at her another minute, to which her response was to stare right back, as if daring him to turn the topic back around. Ryker didn't necessarily want to get into a verbal sparring match with her, so he nodded and went to get the bag.

He'd thought Christmas decorating was torture, but seeing Laney hurt, knowing he'd caused her feelings to be crushed, was even worse. He was going to have to learn how to make her smile again or...what? It wasn't as if he could remove himself from her life. He worked for her family, and she was having his baby.

For once in his life, Ryker had no idea what the hell to do. He'd lived on the streets, he'd fought for his next meal and he'd taken risks that not even Mac or Braden knew about. But the shaky ground he stood on with Laney was the scariest thing he'd ever had to face.

Laney wasn't sure what was more amusing, Ryker cursing at the tangle of lights that had somehow wrapped itself around his shoulders, or Spike and Rapture continually getting into the tree and swatting at Ryker's hand.

Poor cats. They thought Ryker wanted to play each time he reached for another branch. Most of the time her cats kept to themselves, ignored her completely. But the excitement of the tree and the boxes had brought them out of hiding.

Laney realized she had completely forgotten about the pain in her ankle. The entertainment in her living room was more than enough to keep her distracted.

But part of her couldn't help but drift to the "what-if" state. The scenario right now with Ryker decorating,

Laney pregnant, resting on the chaise, the fire roaring and the cats playing, it was like a scene from a Christmas card.

Laney couldn't lie to herself. She wanted that Christmas card. She wanted to have a family like the one she'd grown up in. The O'Sheas were Irish—they knew how to do family gatherings. She had always dreamed of having her own home, having a husband and children. She'd never seen her future any differently.

Perhaps she was going about her plan in the wrong order, but she still had every hope of having children and a husband.

So, how would Ryker fit into this mix? He wasn't exactly the type of man she'd envisioned when she'd been doing her daydreaming. She'd never thought of being with a man who had scarred knuckles, tattoos, constant scruff along his jawline and an attitude that matched that of her cocky brothers.

Still, Ryker was absolutely everything that got her excited. He turned her on and made her want more—and not just physically. Ryker always made her feel safe, even if he drove her out of her mind.

Perhaps that's why she was so drawn to him. He didn't back down, he didn't care what her last name was and he matched her wits.

Laney stared across the room as Ryker reached toward the top of the tree for the last section of lights. So what if she was admiring the way his T-shirt rode up when he reached or the way his worn jeans covered his backside.

"Why are you staring?"

Laney blinked, realizing Ryker had glanced over his shoulder. Oops. Oh, well, it wouldn't be the last time she'd be caught ogling.

"I've never had a hotter decorator," she told him with a smile. "Next you can start on the ornaments."

Ryker turned. Hands propped on his hips, he shook his head. "This isn't going to work. Whatever is in your mind, get it out."

Laney shifted on the chaise to prop her elbow on the arm. Resting her chin in her hand, she raised her brows. "I don't know what you're talking about."

"The innocent act also doesn't work on me."

Laney laughed. "No? Offering to strip my clothes seemed to work."

Ryker's stony expression told her he didn't find her nearly as amusing as she found herself.

"Listen, we're going to have to learn to get along," she told him. "We can't always be griping at each other. You need to relax."

"Relax? You think I'll ever relax, especially now that you're having my child?"

Laney shrugged. "Shouldn't I be the one freaking out? I mean, I'm carrying the baby."

Ryker raked a hand over his jaw, the bristling of his stubble against his palm doing nothing to douse the desire she had for him. She recalled exactly what the coarse hair felt like on her heated skin. She'd give anything to feel it all over again.

"Are you that worried about my brothers?" she asked. "I mean, once they find out about the baby, they'll get used to the idea of us being together."

"We aren't together."

Laney met his dark gaze. "We could be."

Laying it all out there was ridiculous. Her hint about as subtle as a two-by-four to the head, but she wanted him to see that they could at least try to be more.

"No, we can't." Glancing around the room, he located a box marked Ornaments and pulled off the lid. "You know why and I'm not going to discuss this every time we're together. I already told you I'd support you and our baby."

"I don't want your money." Laney swung her legs over the side of the chaise and pushed off, using the arm of the sofa for support. "I want you to stop dancing around this attraction. We already know we're compatible between the sheets."

"Sit down before you hurt yourself." In three strides he'd reached her and was ushering her back down. "I hope you don't care how the ornaments are put up because I've never done this before."

Laney didn't budge, but it was difficult to hold her ground when he was pushing her and she was putting her weight on one foot.

"Why are you so stubborn?" she demanded, then waited until he looked her in the eyes. "Seriously. Can't you just tell me why you won't even consider giving this a chance?"

His fingers curled around her shoulders. "Because you see something in me, in us, that isn't there."

"I see potential. I see a man who wants something and never goes after it. He's too busy working his ass off for everyone around him."

The muscles in his jaw clenched. "That's enough, Laney."

"Is it?" she threw back. "Because I don't think it's near enough. I think you need someone to tell you just what the—"

His mouth slammed onto hers. For a split second she was stunned, then she was thrilled. Finally. He was finally taking what he wanted.

Those hands moved from her shoulders at once. One went to the small of her back, pulling her closer to his body. The other crept up beneath her hair, fisting it and jerking her head just where he wanted it.

Laney held on to his biceps to steady herself. A full-on attack like this required a bit of warning. She supposed her warning had been his intense gaze, the way he stalked across the room toward her. The way he'd torn her dress weeks ago.

Ryker broke the kiss, his forehead resting against hers. "You have to stop."

*Excuse me?* "You kissed me."

"To shut you up," he growled. "I can't keep fighting this with you. You push and push until I snap."

"Maybe I push so you can see what it is you're missing."

Ryker pulled in a deep breath and took a step back. His arms dropped to his sides. "Believe me, I know what I'm missing."

If she'd ever met a more frustrating man, she couldn't recall. "What would you do if I quit pushing?" she countered. "Maybe one day I'll give up, move on. What would you do then?"

# Six

Ryker shoved his hand in his pockets, a futile attempt at reaching for her. There was nothing he wanted more than to take her and rip those clothes off and make use of that sofa.

The penny in his pocket mocked him, reminding him of where he came from, of who he actually was. If he were a better man, a man who could offer Laney and their baby something of worth, he wouldn't think twice about taking her up on her offer.

"I won't wait on you forever," she whispered. "I feel like I've already waited most of my life. We had one night and you flipped out. And that was before you found out about the baby."

Ryker didn't know what to say. He didn't do feelings, and he sure as hell didn't discuss them. Laney was right, though. He'd flipped out after their night together.

Never in his life had he ever felt something so perfect—he didn't deserve perfect. In the midst of betraying the only family he'd ever loved, he'd found a dose of happiness he never knew he was longing for.

"I think we're done here." Laney eased herself back onto the chaise. Clearly she'd taken his silence as rejection. "I'm tired. Set the alarm on your way out."

"You think I'd leave when you're this upset?"

Laney's bright green eyes misted. "I'm not upset. I'm exhausted. I've beat my head against the proverbial wall for too long, and now I have a child who needs my attention. I have to look out for myself now, and if you can't see what we could be, then we have nothing left to discuss."

Getting shut out was not what he wanted, damn it, but he couldn't let himself in, either. There was no right answer, but there was an answer that would keep Laney and their baby safe.

"We need to tell Mac and Braden soon." Ryker ignored the pain in his chest. Pain was just a by-product of doing the right thing for those he cared about. "I'll do anything for you and our baby, Laney, but I can't be that perfect man in your life. You know why."

She kept her focus on her lap where her hands were folded. "I know you're a coward, so maybe you're not the man I want."

Her harsh words gutted him. The idea of her being with anyone else made him want to hit the faceless bastard. How could Ryker let her go so easily?

Because she was an O'Shea. Her father had taken Ryker in when he'd been on the verge of going down a path of complete destruction. Respecting Patrick, keeping his relationships with Mac and Braden, that's what

Ryker needed to do. He'd built his entire life around working for them, taking risks to keep them safe and going through hell in keeping his distance from Laney.

He'd failed. His penance would be to let her go.

"Let me at least help you to—"

"I don't need your help." Laney held up a hand, her lips thinned in anger, though her eyes still held unshed tears. "Since you won't take a chance, then I have nothing left to say to you right now. I'll let you know when my doctor's appointment is, and I'll fill you in on work. Other than that, we're done."

Swallowing, Ryker nodded. "I'm going back to New York since you got me the blueprints of the DeLuca property. I don't know when I'll be back, but shouldn't be more than a couple of days."

When she said nothing, Ryker moved around the coffee table and the storage boxes. He grabbed his coat off the hook by the front door and had just jerked the leather over his shoulders when her soft voice stopped him.

"Be careful."

With his back to her, Ryker closed his eyes.

"I may be angry with you, but I still care and I want you safe," she went on. "Your baby is counting on you to be here."

His baby. Words he never thought would come to mean so much to him.

"I can take care of myself." He opened the door and typed in the alarm code.

He thought he heard her mutter, "That's what scares me," before he closed the door, but he didn't stop to ask. The bitter cold whipped around him. Ryker pulled his jacket tighter around his shoulders and made his way off her porch and toward his SUV. Walking away from

Laney was the hardest thing he'd ever done. Before Miami, he'd always thought not knowing what being intimate with her felt like was the worst thing, but he'd been wrong. Because now he knew. Now he was fully aware of how perfect they were, how compatible they were. Now he had to live with the knowledge that he'd never have something that amazing in his life.

As Ryker slid behind the wheel of his car, he cursed himself. In the long run, this was the right answer. He'd been teetering on the wrong side of the law for so long, and he should finally feel good about a decision he was making.

So why did he feel like hell?

"It's a trap." Laney gripped her phone and tried not to panic as she left Ryker a voicemail. The third in as many hours. "Don't go inside. It's all been a setup."

She stood in Braden's office, staring out the massive wall of windows that overlooked a snow-blanketed backyard. She'd come here after her first call and several texts had gone unanswered. It was late, too late to be worrying about Ryker and this damn job. She should be at home asleep. Ryker should be safe in his hotel room. But she'd been given intel that the DeLuca home was going to be empty around eight in the evening, and Ryker had been given the green light to go in, check the trunk in the basement and get out before they arrived back sometime around midnight.

It was now one in the morning, and nobody had heard a word.

"Find out something, damn it." Braden's frustration level was just as high as hers as he shouted into his cell. "Call me back."

Laney turned to face her brother. "Anything?"

"I called one of our FBI guys in that area, and he's looking into where Ryker is."

Which meant they still knew nothing. Laney tamped down her fear because Ryker had been in sticky situations before. For years she worried each time he went out, but he'd always come back. On occasion he'd dodge the topic of why he had new scrapes or bruises, or a run-in with the law, but he always returned.

All Laney could think of was how they'd left things last night. Why had she told him that she was done? If he came back right now and told her he wanted to give things a shot, she'd be right there with him. He was it for her.

Laney smoothed her hand down the front of her tunic and over her flat stomach. She needed to remain calm for the baby. Ryker was okay…he had to be.

"He'll be fine," Braden assured her. "It's Ryker. You know he's probably somewhere laying low. Most likely he's hiding in that house with his phone on silent and dodging the DeLucas. You know he loves a challenge."

Laney jerked the leather chair from behind the desk and sank into it. "You're not helping. It's all my fault for giving him that information."

"Laney, you were going on a lead. That's all."

Exhaustion had long since set in. She hadn't slept well after Ryker had left last night. Then today she'd been searching for the root of her troublesome emails that had been sent a couple months ago when she'd gotten another bit of information on the DeLuca property. She'd instantly noticed something was wrong when the chatter turned to humorous banter about a setup. She'd almost gotten sick. After her texts to Ryker went unanswered, she called. And called.

She hadn't suffered much morning sickness yet, but the constant state of I-need-a-nap was ever-present. This situation with the DeLucas wasn't helping. All the worrying, all the fear. She wanted to believe the best because she wasn't sure she could handle it if Ryker got hurt...or worse.

Laney crossed her arms on the desk, making them a pillow for her head. Strong hands came to rub her shoulders.

"Relax," Braden told her. "Any minute he'll walk through the door and get angry because you're worrying."

Yeah, that was so like Ryker. She wished for that scenario more than anything.

"I swear, when you two aren't at each other's throats, you're both worrywarts."

Laney couldn't respond. She was too busy enjoying the massage and trying to wrap her mind around how she'd survive if something happened to Ryker.

Oh, she'd live and get along, but she'd be empty. Her child would be fatherless. She couldn't imagine anything scarier. Ryker had been in her life for so long, she truly didn't know how to exist without him.

When Braden's cell chimed, Laney jerked her head up and turned to stare as he answered.

"Yeah?"

Her brother's hard jaw, set mouth and grip on the phone weren't helping her nerves, but that was just typical Braden. As head of the family now, he was all business, all the time. Mac, their more carefree brother, was still down in Miami with his fiancée, Jenna. Those two had danced around their attraction for years…which reminded Laney of another stubborn couple she knew.

"Where is he now?"

Laney jerked to her feet, hanging on each and every word, watching to see if Braden's expression changed. Was Ryker okay? She wanted answers. Right. Now.

"I'll be waiting."

Braden pocketed his phone. "He's fine," he assured her. "But he was arrested. After some strings were pulled in the right direction, my contact with the Bureau managed to get him released. Ryker is being escorted by my acquaintance. I'm going to meet them just outside the city in a few hours."

Laney gripped the desk for support. "I'm going with you."

Braden put a hand on her arm. "You're going home. He's fine and it's late."

When she started to protest, Braden shook his head. "No, Laney. I don't know what's gotten into you. This is Ryker. You know he's fine. He'll be annoying you by morning, I'm sure."

What had gotten into her? Well, the father of her baby had been arrested, though the charges wouldn't stick because of their connections. He'd been set up in a trap that could've gone so much worse than what it had been.

How could she do this? How could she keep letting herself get all worked up over a man who kept pushing her away?

Finally Laney nodded. "Will you text me once you see him? Just to let me know he's really okay?"

After she grabbed her purse and keys, Braden kissed her cheek. "I will. Now go home and get some sleep."

Laney wouldn't sleep until she knew for sure. And

a text from Braden wasn't good enough. She wanted to see with her own eyes.

As she let herself out of her childhood home in Beacon Hill, Laney knew just where to go.

# Seven

The last thirty-six hours had been a bitch. Ryker wanted nothing more than to get into his home and crawl between the sheets of his king-size bed. So much could've gone wrong in New York, but he refused to dwell on that. All he could concentrate on was the fact that he'd failed. One more dead end.

No scrolls. He hadn't even gotten to the mysterious damn trunk in the basement before he'd been caught off guard and cuffed.

Punching in his security code, Ryker let himself in. The sun was bright and promising a new day…and he was thankful for thick blinds. He hadn't slept since he left Boston. He sure as hell hadn't been able to relax when he'd been taken into custody. Not that he'd been worried. This wasn't his first run-in with the law, but he didn't have time for all this nonsense.

As soon as he stepped through his door and closed it behind his back, Ryker took in the sight before him. Without turning, he reached over his shoulder and reset the alarm. He wasn't about to take his eyes off the sleeping beauty perfectly placed on his leather sofa.

Laney wasn't quite lying down. She had her feet curled up to the side, her hands were tucked under her face, which rested on the arm of the couch. She looked so fragile, so small. But he knew she was neither. There was a vibrancy, a strength in her that terrified him. She feared nothing. He'd never found a woman who was willing to verbally spar with him like Laney. She wasn't afraid to throw back anything he dished out. She was absolutely perfect.

And she was the most beautiful sight he'd seen in days.

Ryker released the grip on his bag until it thunked onto the hardwood floor. He shed his coat and hung it up. She still didn't stir. Pregnancy was taking its toll on her. It wasn't like his Laney to be tired all the time.

Ryker froze. *His Laney?* Not in this lifetime. She'd never be completely his. But he was on a slippery slope and wasn't going to be able to hold on much longer. He'd told her before he was selfish, he'd proved that in Miami. But there was going to come a point when he wouldn't be able to turn her away.

Laney stirred, blinked until she focused on him, then jerked awake. The tousled hair, the slight crease on her cheek from where she'd lain, the flawless face void of any makeup staring back at him…maybe that time had come.

He started forward as Laney swung her legs off the side of the couch and stood. "I'm sorry. I didn't mean to fall asleep," she stated, tugging her long shirt in place over her leggings. "I just wanted to wait until you got home so I could see you were safe."

Something stirred inside him. Something primal. No one had ever waited to see if he was okay. Nobody had ever gone to the trouble of checking up on him. Oh, Mac and Braden checked in, but they were friends, brothers.

Laney was...special.

"I didn't think you'd mind if I used your code."

She'd only been to his house once, but every O'Shea had his code for emergency purposes and he had theirs. This was clearly an emergency for her. That primal feeling turned into a warmth he didn't want to recognize.

"But now that I can see for myself you're okay, I'll just go." She was adorable when she was nervous. "I'm sure you're tired and need to rest."

Ryker moved closer as she rambled, his eyes never coming off that lip she was biting. She'd been scared—for him. More scared than he'd ever seen her—for him. She was the most beautiful sight, and after the hellish past day and a half, he needed something beautiful in his life. He needed Laney.

"After we left things, and then we couldn't get in touch with you—"

His mouth slid over hers, cutting off her words. His arms wrapped around her waist, jerking her flush against his body.

*Finally.*

He felt like he'd waited forever to have her in his home, in his arms again. There were countless reasons why he shouldn't have been doing this, why he should've let her walk out that door.

But he needed this. He needed her, and he hadn't realized how much until he'd walked in and seen her curled up on his couch.

Laney melted against him, her fingers threading through the hair at his nape. Her mouth opened to his instantly, and Ryker didn't hesitate to take everything he wanted from her.

He wanted to devour her, wanted to take her into his bedroom and lay her flat out on his bed, taking his time the way he should've in Miami.

Laney was in his home, and this was one fantasy he'd had for way too long. No way in hell was he turning her away. He needed this. They needed this.

Before common sense or those red flags could wave too high, Ryker secured his hold around her waist, never breaking away from her lush mouth. He lifted her up, arousal bursting through him when she wrapped her legs around his waist.

"I didn't think you wanted me," she murmured against his lips.

Ryker spun and headed toward his bedroom. The sleep he'd needed moments ago was no longer on his radar

"I never said that. Ever."

Laney nipped at his lips. "You push me away."

Ryker stopped, pulled away and looked into those engaging eyes. "Do you feel me pushing you away now?"

Her hips tipped against his as her ankles locked behind his back. "I wouldn't let you at this point. But what about tomorrow? Next week? What then, Ryker?"

On a sigh, he closed his eyes and rested his forehead against hers. "Right now, Laney. Let's concentrate on right now."

She hesitated a second longer than he was comfortable

with, but finally nodded. "I'm going to want answers, Ryker. I'm going to want to talk, not fight, about us."

*About us.* Those words terrified him and thrilled him at the same time. He'd worry about that conversation later. Right now he had the only woman he'd ever wanted in his bed actually here. He sure as hell wasn't going to talk, not when his emotions were raw. He had Laney and that was enough.

The second he crossed the threshold to his master suite, he hit the panel on the wall to close the blinds, encasing his room in darkness—much like the way he lived his life. Laney was the brightest spot he'd ever had, and he didn't need anyone to tell him he didn't deserve her, or their baby.

But heaven help him, he wanted both.

Laney tucked her face into the crook of his neck, her warm breath tickling him as he led her to his bed in the middle of the room. Easing down, he laid her on his rumpled sheets. He hadn't made a bed in...well, ever.

As much as he wanted to follow her down, he pulled back because he had a driving need to see her splayed out. He'd never brought another woman into his house, into his bed. If he thought too hard about this moment, he may let fear consume him, but he latched on to his need for Laney and shoved all else aside.

Her long shirt pulled against her breasts, her hair fanned out on his navy sheets and her eyes held so much desire, he didn't know if he was going to be able to take his time.

"If you are reconsidering, I'm going to kill you myself."

Ryker couldn't help but laugh. He reached behind his back and jerked his T-shirt over his head, flinging it across the room. Her eyes raked over his chest, his abs, lower. Pure male pride surged through him. He kept in shape and had never cared what anyone thought of him, not even his lovers, but he wanted Laney to care. He wanted her to…hell, he didn't know. There was nothing of worth in him, yet she wanted him. He was humbled and proud at the same time.

Laney sat up on the bed, pulling her shirt over her head as she went. Ryker was rendered speechless at the sight of her in a pale pink bra that did little to contain her full breasts. And when she reached behind her to unfasten it, staring up at him with those wide eyes, Ryker's control snapped.

With a need he couldn't identify, Ryker reached down and gripped the top of her leggings and panties. In one jerk he had them off and flung over his shoulder.

Laney lay back on his bed, a smug grin on her face. Ryker couldn't get his jeans unfastened fast enough.

"You think you've got me where you want me?" he asked, remembering he still needed to get his damn boots off.

She lifted one bare shoulder. "I've got you where you want to be."

No truer words were ever spoken.

After freeing himself from everything, he placed a knee on the bed beside her hip. Laney trailed her fingertips up his bare leg, sending shivers through him. Damn shivers. He was trying to keep some semblance of control here, but one touch from her and he was powerless.

Ryker glanced to her flat belly, worry lacing through him. He glanced up to see her smiling.

"It's fine," she assured him. "I promise."

He was clueless when it came to pregnancies or babies. Hell, he couldn't even deal with his own emotions, let alone care for another person. What was he thinking? Why was he letting his desire for Laney cloud his judgment?

"Hey." She reached for him, her fingers wrapping around his biceps. "Don't. Wherever you just went, come back. We'll deal with it later."

The war he'd battled with himself for years had no place right now. He couldn't deny her, couldn't deny himself. She was right. Whatever they needed to deal with could wait.

Laney eased her legs apart, tugging on him until he settled right where he needed to be. With his hands on either side of her head, he lowered onto his forearms so his hands could be free. He smoothed her hair away from her face, letting his fingers linger on her smooth skin.

"My scarred hands don't belong on you," he whispered, the words spilling from him before he could stop himself.

"I don't want anybody else's hands on my body," she purred, arching into him. "You're perfect."

*Perfect*. A word never associated with him before, let alone said aloud. Laney closed her eyes, blowing out a slow, shuddering breath. Ryker slid his body against hers, finally taking the time to appreciate how incredibly they fit together.

Laney flattened her palms against his back, urging him even closer. Her knees came up on either side of his hips as she let out a soft sigh. He couldn't take his eyes off her as he watched her arousal consume her. She could easily become a drug that kept him addicted forever.

But forever wasn't in his vocabulary. Forever wasn't a word for a man with his lifestyle.

"Tell me if I hurt you," he muttered. "I mean, with the baby…damn. I just don't—"

She leaned up, capturing his lips. "We're both fine."

Ryker captured her hips once more and rolled them over so she was straddling him and he was on his back. She sat straight up, her hands resting on his abdomen.

"I like this view better." He could look at it forever.

Damn that word for creeping into the bedroom again and making him want things he had no business wanting.

"You're letting me have control?" she asked, quirking her brow.

Ryker reached between them, rubbing his fingertip against her most sensitive part. Laney gasped, throwing her head back.

"I'm still in control, baby. Always."

Laney shifted, and in seconds settled over him, joining them, and Ryker's eyes nearly rolled back in his head. She was a vixen and she damn well knew it.

Her hips shifted, slowly. Too slow. Agonizingly slow. Enough.

Ryker gripped her hips between his hands and held her in place as he slammed into her at a feverish pace.

Laney's fingers curled into his bare skin, her nails biting into him. Perfect. This was what he'd missed. Her passion, her need for him that stirred something so deep within his chest, he refused to analyze it.

Laney tossed her head, her hair flying to cover part of her face. She clenched her eyes shut as her knees tightened against his sides. Ryker held his palm over her stomach a second before curling his fingers back around her side.

*Mine.*

The word slammed into him as Laney cried out her

release, and there was no stopping his now. Ryker's entire body trembled as he let go, Laney's pants only urging him on. He locked his eyes on her, shocked to find something in hers. Something much more than desire, much more than passion.

Damn it. Laney had love in her eyes. Love for a bastard who didn't deserve her, who'd betrayed her brothers. Love for a man who'd been told he was unlovable for the first twelve years of his life.

Ryker shut his eyes. He couldn't face this now. Not when he'd told her they'd talk later, not when he was feeling too damn exposed, and not when he knew there was no forever for them.

# Eight

Monday morning had Laney heading to O'Shea's, the actual office in downtown Boston. Apparently there were some computer issues Braden needed fixed ASAP, per an employee's plea. Braden had told her this was top priority in an early-morning text.

Laney had only met the newest employee a handful of times, but based on what she'd seen of her and how she'd corresponded with her via emails and texts, Viviana was exactly the type of professional, poised person the business needed. The woman had been with them for nearly a year now and was proving to be an extremely loyal, trustworthy team member. She fit right in with the O'Shea family.

Laney let herself into the old building, which had been renovated into something of grand beauty back in the fifties. A few modern touches had been added to keep the ambiance up-to-date, and for security purposes, but overall, the building had been restored to its original grandeur. The old etched windows were kept, as well as the intricate trim and crown moldings. Scarred hardwood floors had been buffed and refinished to a dark, sparkling shine.

They wanted potential clients to feel at home. Because that's what O'Shea's was all about. Family.

Shaking off the cold, Laney turned and smiled at Viviana. The striking beauty was around the same age as Laney's brothers, but she could easily still be carded. She had glossy black hair, almost as if she had some Native American heritage. Her dark eyes and skin only showcased how gorgeous she was naturally.

"I nearly froze just walking in from my car," Laney stated, tugging off her gloves.

"Maybe I'll ask for a transfer to Mac's store in Miami," Viviana joked, her painted red lips parting in a stunning smile. "Just during the winter months. Boston can be brutal."

Laney nodded in agreement, recalling the snowstorm nearly a year ago when Braden and Zara ended up trapped together. Of course, if not for that storm, Zara may not be in the family now.

Laney couldn't imagine being trapped with Ryker. Actually, if their encounter two days ago was any indicator, their private time would be absolutely glorious. Maybe being trapped together would do them some good. Then he couldn't run away from what they shared and he'd have to listen to reason.

But Laney knew if they were alone, their clothes would be off and that would be the end of talking.

"We love you too much here to let you go," Laney replied, heading toward the back office. "Braden said the new program was giving you fits?"

Laney glanced at the framed images lining the walls. Ancestors in front of the store, some of her grandfather and father at the auction podium, another of her great-grandfather at his desk in the backroom…the same desk she was heading toward.

Viviana fell into step beside her. "I tried to go back through some records to find a piece we auctioned last spring in London, but the program shows a blank, like nothing was entered until two months ago."

Two months ago Laney had installed a simpler program; she'd put all the history of their auctions on there for easy access. Something was definitely wrong.

"Let me take a look." Laney moved into the spacious office and circled the antique desk her great-grandfather had found at an estate sale in Spain. This piece was part of O'Shea's history, passed down through generations. "Do you have any clients coming in this morning?"

Viviana crossed her arms over her plum suit jacket and shook her head. "Not today. I was hoping to get some pieces logged in to the system. We've already received quite a few framed pieces of artwork and several items from a recent estate sale Mac handled in Naples."

Laney settled into her comfort zone behind the screen. She pulled up the system she'd created and saw everything was up-to-date from the time she'd installed it. Then when she tried to retrieve backdated records, the files were completely empty. That was impossible. Everything should have been in chronological order just like she'd programmed.

"If you want to work, you can still get into the system

to add new items. You just can't go back." Laney didn't look up as she continued going from screen to screen to see what happened. All of her codes were still as they should be. "I'll let you know if I need you."

Laney's cell chimed from her purse, which was on the leather club chair beside the door. "Would you care to grab that for me?" she asked without looking up.

Scrolling down the screen, Laney dissected each and every entry she'd made. Nothing was off, but—

Wait. She scrolled back up. That couldn't be possible. She stared at the screen again.

"Something wrong?" Viviana asked.

Laney leaned closer to the computer, sure she was mistaken. But she didn't want to say anything to anyone until she could research things further. Braden would explode when he found out about the security breach. Still, she wanted to double-and triple-check everything before she went to him with this. There was no need to alarm anyone if she was misreading everything...but the odds of her being wrong were pretty much nil.

Her stomach turned. Who would hack into her system? Who had the balls big enough to go up against the O'Shea clan? How the hell had anyone gotten through all the security she'd installed?

The answer was simple. They weren't hacked. This was an inside job.

"Laney?"

Fury raged through her as she turned to look at Viviana, who held out Laney's phone. "You sure everything is okay?" she asked.

Laney nodded. "I think I've found the problem, but it's going to take some time to fix. I'm going to take this laptop with me. Can you use one of the others?"

Viviana's eyes widened for a second before she glanced around the office. "Of course. Is there anything I can do?"

*Be on the lookout for the enemy?*

"No. I've got it handled." Laney looked at her phone, still in Viviana's hand. "Oh, thanks."

She saw Ryker's name on the screen and opened the text. She'd left him sleeping the other night because she knew if she'd actually stayed, she'd want to spend every night there.

She had to make Ryker realize he wanted this. Perhaps if she wasn't so available, he'd ache for her the way she did for him. She wanted him so needy for her, so desperate to have her in his life, he'd ignore his demons and take a chance. She wasn't playing a game, she was simply opening his eyes to what they had.

Pulling up his message, she read:

We need to talk. Meet at Braden's now.

Laney closed the program and shut the laptop. "I need to go. Call me if you have any more issues, no matter how minor."

Viviana nodded and scooted back, and Laney headed toward the office door. "Of course."

Laney tossed her phone back into her bag. Pulling on her wrap coat, she knotted the ties before grabbing the laptop and sliding it into the side of her bag, as well.

"There haven't been any strange calls or emails, even from regular clients?" Laney asked as she slid the bag onto her forearm.

Viviana shifted, her head tipped as she glanced at the floor. "I can't recall any. It's pretty black and white here," she told Laney, looking back up. "You think someone has been messing with the system?"

"I think it's a possibility, and I want you to keep your eyes and ears open. Call me, not Braden or Mac, if you notice anything odd."

She'd figure out what was going on in the meantime.

"Of course," Viviana stated.

Laney headed through the main part of their office area and back out into the swirling snow. The streetlights lining each side of the street were decorated with simple, elegant evergreen wreaths with bright, cheery red bows. The garlands twisting around the poles ran from the wreath to the base. The city was battling the snowfall by keeping the sidewalks salted, the streets cleared. Laney absolutely loved her hometown of Beacon Hill and never wanted to be anywhere else.

As she climbed behind the wheel of her car, she wondered what Ryker wanted. Did he actually love Boston like she did, or did he love the lifestyle he led of traveling, going from one adventure to the next? Would he slow down, take fewer risks now that he was going to be a father?

Knowing Ryker…no. He would think he could do it all, as if he were invincible.

She headed toward her childhood home and pulled in behind Ryker's SUV. Large, menacing, just like the man himself. That whole dark, mysterious persona he oozed was so damn sexy, but there was infinitely more to Ryker. The layers that made up that man were tightly woven together, but she wasn't giving up on removing each one until she uncovered the very heart of him.

Grabbing her bag from the passenger seat, she got out of the car, careful where she stepped this time. Watching the ground before her gray boots, she started when a pair of black boots came into view.

"Easy." Ryker gripped her arms to steady her. "I came to make sure you didn't fall again."

Laney's heart flipped. She didn't want to keep sliding further in love with him, but there was no way to stop. Regardless of the baby, Laney loved Ryker. She'd love him even if they'd never kissed or slept together. Nothing could ever diminish her feelings for him.

"Well, startling me is not the way to go about helping."

Ryker took the bag from her arm and slid his other arm around her waist. "I wouldn't let you fall. Ever."

"If you keep tossing gallant gestures my way, I'm going to think you're trying to get all romantic."

Those dark eyes locked onto hers. "I don't do romance, Laney. I do reality."

Laney rolled her eyes. The reality was that she loved him, and he could ignore it all he wanted, but he had feelings for her, too. She wasn't offended by his words, not when his actions were booming louder than ever. Laney was optimistic that Ryker would come around… the question was how long would she give him before she finally told him how she truly felt? If she pulled out the cringe-worthy *L* word at this point, he'd sprint back into his steel shell and never come out again.

Ryker was vulnerable, not something she'd ever say to him or he'd ever admit, but the truth was glaring them both in the face. The don't-give-a-damn attitude, the rough exterior he offered to the world, wasn't who she saw. She looked beneath all of that and found the man he truly was…a kind, gentle and generous man with so much to give, one capable of so much love. It was a man he probably wasn't even aware existed. Or one he was battling to keep inside.

Regardless, Laney was about to rip his mask off and shove him in front of a mirror.

"Ankle okay today?" he asked.

"Just tender, but nothing I can't put weight on."

His arm didn't leave her waist, which was fine with her. She wanted his hands on her, and clearly he wanted them to be there.

"We have a problem."

Laney froze on the sidewalk, jerking her gaze up to his. "What?"

After the security breach, she didn't need more bad news. Dread curled in her stomach.

"We had a call from one of our contacts with the Bureau." Ryker ushered her toward the steps. "Let's get you inside. It's too cold out here."

"No." Laney placed a gloved hand on his chest. "First tell me what he wanted."

Ryker clenched his jaw. "Apparently someone is feeding them information. Intel only someone in our organization would know. They've discovered some pieces of art that are in our computer system, that only we have the log for. And I know you put those in like any other items we obtain legally, but they have a list of our back auctions."

Laney pulled in a breath, the air so cold her lungs burned. "This isn't a coincidence," she murmured.

Ryker's grip on her tightened. "What?"

"I have something on my laptop to show you guys. Let's get inside."

She could pull up any company document on a family computer, but she was most comfortable working with her own. She knew what documents and files to access right from the start. Time was of the essence.

As she turned, everything seemed to shift all at once. She tilted, thankfully against a firm, hard chest.

"Easy," Ryker told her, his arm around her waist tightening. "What happened?"

Laney held a hand to her head, shutting her eyes. "Just got a bit dizzy, that's all."

Before Laney could say another word, her world tilted again as she was swept up into Ryker's arms. "Put me down. I can walk."

"And I can carry you and your bag, so be quiet."

There it was. That emotion he held so hidden within him, one he didn't seem to recognize. If she thought for a second he didn't want her, she'd let it go. But when she saw a need in him, a need that matched her own, she couldn't ignore the facts…or let the best thing in her life slip right by because she was afraid to take a chance.

Laney wrapped her arms around his neck, nestling her face against the heat of his. She closed her eyes, relishing this pivotal moment. The baby would not be a tool in this path she was on to show Ryker how much she loved him, and that's not what this moment was about. Right now, he cared about her.He wasn't about to let her fall or get hurt. Laney only prayed by the time this was all said and done, that would still be the case.

She also refused to let him fall. She'd do anything to keep the man she loved safe. She was an O'Shea. The fact she was a female made no difference because she was brought up to be strong, fierce and resilient. Nothing could stop her from staking her claim.

"What happened?" Braden's worried tone brought her out of her thoughts. "Did she fall again?"

Ryker brushed by Braden and into the warmth of the house. "No. She started getting dizzy."

Ryker eased her down because it wasn't as if he could hold her forever. Shame that. Plus, if she clung to him too long, Braden would get the idea something was going on. Which reminded her that they were going to have to tell her brothers soon. Their unknown reactions terrified her.

"I'm fine," she assured them both, offering a smile. "See? Standing on my own two feet."

"Did you eat breakfast?" Braden asked, his brows still drawn together in worry. "Go sit in the living room, and I'll bring you something."

"No, no." She waved a hand, then opened the ties on her coat. "I ate. I must've just moved too fast, and with all that's going on with work, I'm just stressed."

Oops. Wrong choice of words. Ryker's eyes darkened, narrowed. His lips thinned.

"You'll be taking it easy. I'll make sure of it."

He delivered the threat in that low, sexy tone of his that left no room for argument. Laney merely nodded because now she was facing down two of the most alpha men she knew.

"Have a seat anyway," Braden told her, gesturing toward the living room.

Laney headed into the room that screamed Christmas: from the sparkly garland draped over the mantel, to the twelve-foot-tall noble fir standing proudly in front of the old windows, to the various candle stands, berries and other festive decor.

Quite the opposite of Ryker's house. Not one sprig of evergreen was to be seen there. A testament to what he came from. The child who didn't do Christmas had turned into a man who didn't, and it was one of the saddest things Laney had ever seen.

She took a seat on the high wing-back chair her mother had fallen in love with at an estate sale when she and Laney's father had first gotten married. Patrick O'Shea had never been able to say no to his wife. Their love, though cut too short in Laney's opinion, was something Laney wanted. That love, the family, the bond was what Laney dreamed of. And they weren't little girl dreams. She was going into this situation with Ryker knowing full well she could get hurt, but the chance of a love and family of her own was worth the risk.

Weren't O'Sheas built on all the risks they'd taken? A challenge was never avoided, but met head-on. And conquered.

"Ryker told me you had a call from the Bureau," she started, not wanting to waste any time. "I don't know what all you found out, but Viviana's problem at the office was the system's backlog. I was looking into that when I got Ryker's text."

Ryker leaned one broad shoulder against the mantel, crossing his arms over his chest. "Tell me what you found."

Braden remained standing as well, right by the leather sofa across from her. The tension in the room was palpable.

"When I go into the records, there is nothing showing from before I changed systems," she explained. "Everything should be in the files I added by year and then broke down into months. Before October, there is nothing."

"Define nothing," Braden said between gritted teeth.

Laney faced him, staring into eyes exactly like her

own, exactly like their father's. "Not one document is on there. Don't worry, I have backups of everything at home. I'm not sloppy, Braden."

"I never said you were, but what the hell is going on and what does this have to do with my call from the Feds?"

"When I first started digging to see what happened, it appeared someone hacked into our system. But that would be virtually impossible."

There was no easy way to deliver such a statement, so she went for it.

"The only way someone could access the system is if they work for us. My security is so tight—"

"Not tight enough," Braden growled.

Laney straightened her back, squared her shoulders.

"Chill, Braden." Ryker's warning couldn't be ignored. "Respect."

Braden turned his attention across the room. "She's my sister, I can damn well say what I want."

"No, you can't." Ryker's sneer even made Laney shiver. "She's the best programmer I've ever met, and I know some shady bastards."

Even though she could've handled herself, and her brother was justifiably angry, Ryker's quick defense warmed her. He'd always protected her, but he'd never spoken back to Braden in such a manner.

"Who the hell are you to tell me?" Braden countered. "We may be facing a real issue here, not to mention the scrolls are who knows where. But the Feds are on our back and our system was hacked? Doesn't take a genius to figure out we have a mole."

The idea horrified Laney. They were so careful about who they hired. The background checks were extensive, their training and "babysitting" period was just as meticulous. Now the question was how did they narrow their search down to one office? They had branches all over the globe. Their main one, of course, was in Boston, and a year ago one opened in Miami and in Atlanta.

Could the traitor be one of the employees down South?

"We need to warn Mac," she stated, thinking aloud. "He needs to start scouring his crew while we look at ours. We clearly should start with our US locations. I doubt the threat is coming from overseas. That wouldn't make any sense."

Braden nodded. "I agree. What I want to know is how someone fractured your system."

Laney rubbed her forehead, wondering the same thing. Closing her eyes, she willed the slight dizziness to pass. Maybe she should get some orange juice or something in her stomach.

"I'm going to figure that out." Laney eased back in the chair, rested her elbow on the arm and opened her eyes. "I took one of the laptops from the office, and I plan on looking through its history. I'll do the same for the rest of them."

Braden's hardened gaze held hers. "I love you, Laney. I'm not doubting you. I'm shocked, actually. We've never had this kind of breach before, and the last thing I need is the Feds sniffing around."

Since Braden had taken over after their father's passing, the O'Sheas had been moving into more legitimate territory—which meant staying off the radar of the law. To her full knowledge, they'd been so careful. Minus Ryker and Shane's incident, there wasn't anything that she knew of that would cause this level of scrutiny...well, she still didn't know what happened to her ex.

What a mess. Having the Feds involved did not bode well for the O'Sheas.

"I promise you, there won't be a problem. I'll get this fixed, and we'll find out who the snitch is."

She risked a glance at Ryker, who looked even more menacing than usual. Those dark lashes fanned out over coal-like eyes, his hard-set jaw was clenched, his arms were crossed over that impossibly broad chest. Ryker was pissed, and she only prayed she could get to the bottom of this betrayal before he took matters into his own hands.

# Nine

Laney had just grabbed a bottle of water when her front door slammed. Because she lived in an old brownstone, she didn't have that whole open-concept thing going on. She liked her rooms cozy and blocked off into designated areas.

"Hello?" she called as she made her way to the front of her house.

She wasn't too concerned about an intruder, considering she had alarms, cameras and an insane security system she knew her brother and Ryker had paid quite a bit for. They'd insisted on making sure she was safe the second she moved out of the O'Shea mansion.

The bottle crinkled in her hand as she stopped in the entryway to her living room.

"What are you doing here?"

Without taking his eyes off her, Ryker jerked out of

his leather jacket and tossed it onto the couch. "I'm making sure you're okay, and then I'm helping you get to the bottom of this damn mess."

Nerves stirred in her stomach. He was here because he cared, and he was here for work. Their worlds collided on so many levels, there was no way she could find separation.

"I'm fine."

"You were dizzy earlier, then you weren't feeling well when you were talking with Braden."

Laney twisted the cap on her bottle of water and took a drink. He hadn't made a move to come in any farther, but clearly he was staying since he'd taken off his coat. This was becoming a habit...one she would gladly build on.

"I was feeling a little light-headed while we were talking. It passed."

"You're not driving anymore."

Laney screwed the lid back on and cocked her head, sure she'd heard wrong. "Excuse me?"

Now he moved, like a panther to its prey. He crossed to her until they stood toe to toe, causing her to tip her head back to meet his intense, heavy-lidded gaze.

"You heard me."

"I did," she agreed. "I'm giving you the chance to choose different words."

A hint of a smile danced around those kissable lips. "I'm not backing down on this, Laney. Until your dizzy spells pass, I'll be your chauffeur."

Even though she knew he wouldn't back down, Laney waited a minute to see if he wanted to add anything...or retract such a ridiculous statement.

Finally, when he said nothing, Laney stepped around him and headed toward the corner of the sectional she'd been cozied up in. Well, as cozy as one could be while working on discovering who hacked into her family's computer system. Clearly the O'Sheas were smarter than to have all of their skeletons exposed for anyone to see. But there were items, especially in the past when her father was at the helm, that could be looked at twice. Some may find their "mysterious" auction pieces to be a red flag, considering the majority of them had been reported stolen.

Laney eased back into the curve of the couch and picked up the laptop she'd laid to the side.

"Glaring at me and using this whole silent predator vibe definitely will not change my mind," she told him without looking at him. She typed in the password for the laptop. "So, did you want anything else? Or are you ready to move on to work?"

Laney had just pulled up the system, but before she could go any further, a delicate pewter ornament appeared between her and the screen. Jerking her eyes up to his, she gasped.

"What is that?" She looked back to the ornament. "I mean, I know what it is, but—"

Well, damn. There she went, tearing up. She hated all these pregnancy-induced crying jags.

She reached out to take the likeness of a woman wrapping her arms around her swollen belly. The simple pewter ornament would look absolutely perfect on her white-and-silver tree. She clutched it against her chest.

But when she looked back up, Ryker glanced away, shoving his hands in his pockets. "I wasn't sure what to get. I mean, I didn't set out to get anything, but I was passing by that Christmas shop near the office."

"All Seasons."

He nodded. "Yeah. I knew you liked that place since you mention it every year."

Her favorite little shop because they literally transformed their store into a completely different place depending on the season. She could spend a fortune in there…and she had. A fact he well knew because he'd taken her there a few times when he felt she was in danger of being in public alone. Of course he'd kept his brooding self out front or waiting in the car at the curb.

"They have a tree in the window that reminded me of yours, and it caught my eye," he went on. He looked at his feet, the wall, the tree…anywhere but at her. "Then I saw this and…"

How adorable was he, being all nervous? This was definitely a side of Ryker Barrett she'd never seen before. Laney set the laptop aside and came to her feet. Tears flooded her eyes as she held tight to this precious gift.

She slid her arms around his neck, tucking her face against his. "This might be the sweetest thing anyone has ever got me."

Slowly he returned her embrace, and Laney wanted to sink into him. "You deserve more," he whispered into her ear.

She knew he wasn't talking monetary items. Ryker could buy her an island and a private jet to get there if he wanted. There was a fear in Ryker that allowed him to touch her, yet not get too emotionally involved. He felt he didn't deserve her, but she was just getting started in proving him wrong. He was everything she deserved.

"This doesn't mean you're driving me," she muttered.

Ryker laughed. The vibrating sensation bounced off her chest. "We'll talk about that later."

There wasn't going to be a later for that particular

topic, but he'd find out soon enough. They didn't have time to argue.

Laney pulled back, kissed him briefly, then shifted from his hold. Crossing the room to the tree, she hung her ornament right in the center, then stepped back to look at how perfectly it fit.

"I love it," she said, turning. "You didn't have to get me a gift, but it's my new favorite decoration."

Ryker nodded, which was about as much of a reaction as she was going to get from him.

"Now, we need to get to work because whoever is fighting us has chosen the wrong family to mess with."

Before she could settle back onto the couch, Ryker's arm snaked out and wrapped around her waist, pulling her against his hard chest. He closed the space between them, covering her mouth with his. Heat, instant and all-consuming, swept over her as she wrapped her arms around his neck.

All too willingly, she opened to him. He eased her back slightly, keeping his hold on her tight, protective. Laney threaded her fingers through his hair, wishing they didn't have to work, wishing they could go to her bedroom and use this kiss as a stepping-stone to something much more erotic and satisfying.

When he pulled back, nipping at her lips, Laney waited for him to say something…anything.

"I'm not complaining," she started when he remained silent. "But what's going on between us? You keep me in your bed the other day, you buy me the sweetest gift ever and now you kiss me like your next breath depended on it."

Ryker's hands slid to her hips where he held her still. "I have no idea," he stated on a sigh. "I can't put a label on this. I only know I did want you in my bed all day, I knew you had to have that ornament and just now my next breath did depend on kissing you."

Laney stared into his dark eyes, eyes that had terrified many enemies. Eyes she'd fallen in love with when she'd been only a teen. She'd seen him come and go many times while she'd been in high school. While her friends were out at the malls or movies with other boys, Laney was home waiting on Ryker to show for a meeting with her father. She'd get a glimpse of him as he'd come into the house. When she was lucky, he'd turn his gaze toward her, meet her with that intense stare for a half second before moving on to the study.

That split second had been worth skipping a night out with her friends.

"Don't fight whatever is happening," she told him. "And don't be afraid of it."

Ryker grunted. "I'm not afraid of anything, Laney. I think you know that."

Again, she wasn't going to argue. They didn't have the time. But he was so terrified of his feelings, he refused to even acknowledge them. Or perhaps he didn't even know they existed.

She eased back into her seat, set her water bottle on the cushion next to her and pulled the laptop back into her lap. Ryker grabbed the large ottoman from the accent chair and pushed it in front of her.

"Put your feet up."

Laney waited a second, but he merely raised a brow and continued to glare. Okay, no point in arguing. Propping her feet up, she started pecking at the keys. Ryker stood.

"It's going to be a while, maybe even days. Might as well have a seat."

"We don't have days."

Laney prayed she would find something that would lead them in the right direction. "You think I don't know that, Ryker?" She didn't even bother to spare him a glance as she worked. Time was of the essence—the only reason she didn't pursue that kiss. "I'm an O'Shea, a glaring fact my brothers and you often forget. I know what's at stake."

Laney ignored the silence as she scrolled through code after code. Let Ryker process her words because it was rather ridiculous how they attempted to keep her sheltered at all times, but expected her to twinkle her nose at the first sign of a computer problem. She wasn't naive; she knew exactly what her family did, what they stood for. She also knew Braden was doing his best to make sure they kept their reputation impeccable within the auction world while cleaning up their act on the legal side. Well, as much as it could be cleaned up. She knew Ryker had done things at her father's request…

She shut her eyes, forcing away any mental images. A shudder rippled through her.

"Laney?"

Instantly he was at her side. Sure. Now he chose to take a seat.

"I'm fine," she assured him. "Just a chill."

More like a clench to her heart. That was the part of her family's past she preferred to keep under wraps. She knew there were justifiable reasons for their actions, she even knew there were times it was self-defense. She'd been fifteen years old when she'd overheard a twenty-five-year-old Ryker describing a trip to Sydney to her father. Ryker had been telling Patrick about a guard who'd attacked him with a knife. Laney recalled standing on the landing of the house, curled up on the floor and holding on to the banisters in the dark. At that moment, she'd realized how dangerous Ryker's job truly was and what he put on the line for her family.

"I don't know how the hell you comprehend all that," Ryker muttered.

Laney kept scrolling, slowly, looking for any hint as to how their security had been breached. She knew the threat was on the inside. Which meant if she had to access every employee's computer, she damn well would.

Her mind kept returning to the timing. The newest stores had been opened a year ago in Miami and Atlanta. The Boston office had been around since the beginning. Where was the mole more likely to be?

Laney didn't know how long she searched. Losing track of time was an occupational hazard. Her stomach growled, and she waited for Ryker to make some snarky comment, but when he remained silent, she glanced over. The man was out. Head tipped back on the cushion, face totally relaxed. Laney wasn't sure she'd ever seen him this peaceful, this calm.

When Ryker was in work mode, which was nearly every time she saw him, he was hard, intense, focused. When they were intimate, well…he was exactly the same way.

Laney's hands went lax on the keyboard as she studied his facial features. His brows weren't drawn in, his mouth was parted just slightly, as if waiting for a lover's kiss, black lashes fanned over his cheeks. She could study him forever.

Forever. If she even said that word to him he'd build yet another wall to protect himself.

Without tearing her eyes away from him, Laney slid the computer off her lap and onto the cushion beside her. She tipped her head back on the cushion as well, needing just another minute of this. One more minute of nothing but Laney and Ryker. There was no outside world, there was no issue with work and there was no fear of telling her brothers that she was expecting Ryker's baby.

Given how fiercely he protected her, Laney knew he would be an amazing father. He doubted himself, but she'd be right there showing him how perfect he was. She wasn't experienced at being a mother, but she knew love. Between her love and his protection, their child would have everything.

Laney bit her lip to keep from tumbling into that emotional roller coaster that seemed to accompany pregnancy. She shifted her thoughts to what their baby would look like. Dark hair for sure since they both had black hair. But would the eyes be green or coal-like? Would Ryker's strong jawline get passed down?

Suddenly those coal-black eyes were fixed on hers. "How long are you going to stare at me?"

# Ten

"You scared me to death," she scolded him, swatting his arm. He lifted his lids and couldn't help but smile.

Ryker had known the second Laney had stopped working. He'd heard her stomach growl and was about to say something, when he'd felt her shift. The sudden awareness of her eyes on him had him holding still. He'd felt the slightest dip in the cushion next to his head, and he wondered what she'd been thinking.

Then he'd worried where her thoughts were. He knew Laney had dreams of a big family. She had that innocence about her that would cling to romance and love. She had hope. He'd lost that when he'd been in diapers.

"Find anything?"

Laney kept resting her head on the cushion next to his. "Nothing new. We've already established that it was an inside job. Braden doesn't like hearing that one of his employees is a mole, but we have to find out who it is before they cause more damage."

Rage burned in his gut. There wouldn't be a hole deep enough for this bastard to hide.

"Don't." Laney's hand slid up his forearm. "I'm furious, too, but don't let it ruin this moment. I just want a minute more of no threats, just us."

*Us.*

"We're always threatened." Unable to resist, Ryker flipped his hand over and shifted to lace their fingers together. "The authorities who aren't on our side are always looking for things to pin on us. On me."

Laney closed her eyes. Ryker hated this. Hated wanting her with an ache that was indescribable. Hated that he couldn't have her fully because of who he was. Hated most of all that he was the one who put worry into that beautiful life of hers.

"I can't stand the thought of you being hurt, being a target." She met his gaze once again. The fear in those eyes gutted him. "I've known for years how much you put at stake, but now it's different."

"The baby—"

"And me." She leaned forward, resting her forehead against his. "Before the baby, before Miami. I started falling for you."

He'd known. Hell, he'd known for years, but hearing her say the words seemed so official and real. He couldn't have her committing herself to him. There was no future for them as a couple, only as parents to this innocent child. That's all they could share.

But, damn it, he couldn't hurt her. He couldn't reject this gift she'd just presented. Laney was everything perfect and pure in his life. She was that place in his mind he went to when he was on assignment and the world around him turned ugly. She'd been his salvation for so long…but telling her that would only give her false hope.

"I know you don't want to hear those words." She eased back, leaving Ryker feeling cold. "But I can't lie to you."

He didn't know what to say, so like a complete moron, he said nothing. Laney shoved her hair away from her face and turned to get her laptop, instantly diving back into her work. The moment was gone.

Ryker reached over, gripping her hand beneath his. Her fingers stilled on the keys. She kept her eyes on the screen, her throat bobbed as she swallowed. Nerves were getting to her, he needed to at least reassure her…what? What the hell could he say? Ryker had no idea, all he knew was he wanted that helpless look gone.

"I'm out of my element here, Laney." He decided to go with honesty. "You've been part of my life for so long, but—"

"I know," she whispered.

How could she know when he didn't know himself?

"No, you don't." Damn it, he needed to make her understand. "You can't possibly know what I feel. You have no clue what those words mean to me."

Her head dropped as she pulled in a deep breath. "I know you better than you think," she said quietly.

Silence settled heavily around them. Ryker had never been this close to a woman. He'd had lovers, mostly when he traveled and needed a stress reliever. The possibility of a serious relationship had never entered his mind. It had no place in his life.

"I know who you are," she went on, still not looking his way. "I've known all along."

Now she did turn, those vibrant green eyes piercing him right to his soul. Until now he hadn't even been aware he had one.

"I know full well why you're trying to keep me at a distance. I'm not backing down, Ryker. You need to know that I intend to fight for what I want, and I want you."

Laney's words should have terrified him. But damn if her fire wasn't the sexiest thing he'd ever seen.

"I'll consider myself warned."

Her eyes narrowed. "If we weren't in so deep with this traitor mess, I'd show you right now how much I love you. That will have to wait."

Ryker's body stirred. He'd never put his work second to anything or anyone before…but right at this moment he was seriously considering doing just that.

"Get that look out of your eyes." She laughed. "How about I keep working and you go see what you can find in the kitchen?"

Ryker came to his feet. "Because I'm all for equal rights, I'll cook for you. But I expect you to open doors for me and buy me flowers."

Laney laughed, the exact response he was hoping for. He couldn't handle tension…not with her.

"That wasn't sexist at all," she said, grabbing a throw pillow and smacking him.

That smile lighting up her face never failed to warm him in spots only she could touch. Guilt slammed through him. There was no way in hell Braden and Mac were going to allow their baby sister to have a relationship with Ryker, even if he thought he could risk it. No, Laney's brothers were looking out for her, and they would be justified by telling her *hell no* when it came to Ryker.

Baby or not, the O'Shea brothers wouldn't budge in

this area. They'd had him follow Laney's boyfriends over the years. Ryker had investigated worthless jerks, and he'd scared off the ones who posed any threat to Laney or the O'Sheas in general. Each time he'd had to intervene, Ryker had selfishly felt relieved that Laney wasn't going to be with some jerk any longer.

Now here he was taking that role...and Mac and Braden were going to have to be the ones to talk some sense into Laney because he sure as hell had no willpower where she was concerned.

And she was wrong. This baby did change everything. Ryker knew he'd never be the same again.

Dinner consisted of chips, salsa and, surprisingly, a taco salad. Apparently Ryker's favorite food was Mexican, and he'd made it happen. She hadn't known those ingredients were in her kitchen, but Ryker had worked a miracle and produced something amazing.

Hours later, Laney's eyes were crossing. She closed the laptop and glanced across to Ryker, who was on his phone, leaning against her newly decorated mantel.

"I'm waving the white flag," she told him around a yawn.

He straightened, shoving his cell in his pocket. "It's nearly one in the morning. You need to sleep."

"What about you? You need sleep, too."

Looking at him in her living room, all dark and menacing, he actually seemed to fit. Amid the sparkling tree, the garland, the Nutcrackers and especially the new ornament, Ryker worked perfectly in her living room, in her life. He'd been a sport and had hung the rest of her ornaments and even added the newly fluffed wreath to her front door. He did draw the line sprinkling the iridescent glitter across the silver and white decor on her mantel..

But he'd stayed. He'd brought her living room to life with Christmas, made dinner and put the empty storage boxes back in her attic. There was something to be said about a man who put his woman's needs first. And she was his woman. He'd figure that out on his own soon enough.

Ready to make good on that promise to fight for what she wanted, Laney set the laptop to the side and came to her feet.

"You need sleep, too," she repeated, slowly closing the space between them. "It would be ridiculous to go out in this weather."

His half-lidded perusal of her body from head to toe and back up sent shivers racing over her, through her. The man's stare was nearly as potent as his touch. She practically felt him when he licked his lips as if she were a buffet. And he could devour her anytime he wanted.

"I'm not afraid of snow," he told her.

Taking a risk that the hunger in his eyes was his weakness, Laney gripped the hem of her shirt and pulled it over her head, tossing the garment to the side. His eyes remained fixed on her, exactly where she wanted them.

"But why take the chance?" she asked, reaching around to unhook her bra.

In a flash, Ryker reached out, wrapping those strong hands around her upper arms. For a second she feared he was going to stop her. Then she focused on his face. Clenched jaw, thin lips, desire staring back at her.

"You want me to stay?" he growled. "Then I'll be the one doing this."

He tore away her bra, jerked down her pants and panties. She had to hold on to those broad shoulders as he yanked the material over her feet. Standing bare before him sent another thrill through her. He stood back up, his hands roaming up the sides of her body, over the dip in her waist, cupping her breasts. His thumbs brushed against their peaks.

Laney couldn't help but lean into his touch. But then his hands moved back down. His hands covered her stomach.

"No matter what happens with us, this is all that matters. I'll do everything to protect our baby."

Laney nodded. There was so much uncertainty between them, but the baby's security was top priority. Until the arrival of their child, Laney would show him just how much she loved him, how much he deserved to be loved.

"If that means you have to move to my house in London, then you'll do it." She started to say something, but his hard eyes stopped her. "I'm serious, Laney. We don't know what we're dealing with, and I'll be damned if I take a chance with our baby."

Fear fueled his words. She knew this unknown threat had him as worried as the rest of them. Now was not the time to bang her chest and be all independent. They were a team.

"I promise," she whispered as she went up onto her toes to slide her lips over his. "Anything you want."

Ryker's hands shifted to her backside. Pulling her flush against his fully clothed body, he growled. "I want to take you up those stairs and keep you locked in your bedroom naked for the next week."

Oh, if only…

"But all I can promise is right now."

He kept saying that. All of these "right now" moments were adding up. Did he notice? He would. One day he'd wake up to the fact they were it for each other. Laney dared her brothers to even try to stop her happiness.

"Then show me," she muttered a split second before his mouth came crashing down onto hers.

He lifted her with ease, carrying her toward the staircase as his lips demanded everything from her…and promised so much more. As if she weighed nothing at all, he took the four steps onto the landing. Just when she expected to feel him turn and head the rest of the way up, he stopped. Laney tore her mouth away, ready to ask him what he was doing, but she found herself being eased onto the built-in, cushioned bench.

She tipped her head back to peer up at him, the soft light from the lamp in the living room casting a perfect yellow rim around his frame. She had no idea what he intended to do, but he reached behind his neck and jerked his T-shirt over his head. After he tossed it behind him, he quickly rid himself of his black boots, sending them back down the steps with a heavy thunk.

Laney couldn't take her eyes off that impressive chest. Spattered with dark hair, a scar over his left pec and a tattoo of a menacing dragon over his right, Ryker was all man…and he was still stripping.

"This is the best show I've ever been to."

The snap to his jeans popped open, he drew the zipper down, all without taking his eyes from hers. "I don't want to hear about the time you and your friends went to Poppycocks."

Laney gasped. "You know about that?"

"Baby, I know everything about you, and I sure as hell am not getting into this now, nor are we discussing the fact I had to do damage control with your father and tell him you were at the mall."

Laney bit her lip to keep from laughing because Ryker clearly didn't find the humor in her sneaking into a male strip club when she was only seventeen. Those fake IDs she'd made for herself and her friends as a joke had come in handy.

Laney opted to keep her mouth shut and enjoy the view as Ryker ridded himself of the rest of his clothes. Unable to keep her hands still, she reached out. She needed to touch him, explore him. Every time they were together her ache for him grew.

Ryker took her hands before she could touch him. Jerking her to her feet, he tugged her until she fell against him.

"I'm calling the shots here. No touching."

Laney quirked a brow. "Then this night is a total bust if I can't put my hands on you."

Strong arms banded around her waist, and instantly she was lifted once again. Laney wrapped her legs around him as he continued up to the second story.

"I'll tell you when you can touch me," he ordered. "I'm going to lay you down and do this right. We're always in a hurry."

Laney rested her head against his shoulder. "Does this mean you're staying all night?"

He reached the double doors to her bedroom and shouldered them open. Looking down into her eyes, Ryker nodded. "I'm staying. Saying no to you is becoming impossible. I don't know what the hell that means, but for now, I'm staying."

Laney knew exactly what that meant. It meant Ryker was hers, and he was finally, *finally* coming around

# Eleven

Ryker rolled over in bed. The canopy with white sheers draped all around the posts was definitely not his bed. This was Laney's world, a world she'd graciously let him into.

No. Scratch that. A world she'd woven him into, and he was getting to the point where he wasn't sure if he ever wanted to leave. It would be the smart thing to do, but he had needs, damn it…and he wasn't just talking physical.

He had no clue what time it was, but the sun wasn't up yet. The soft glow from Laney's phone had him squinting to see what she was looking at.

Baby furniture. Something twisted in his gut. All this time he'd been worried about their safety, about how he'd handle Mac and Braden. The reality was this child would need things. Probably lots of things he had no damn clue about. But he'd learn. He refused to be a deadbeat dad like his had been. Ryker would go out of his way to make sure his child, and the mother of his child, was comfortable and wanted for nothing.

Ryker slid an arm around Laney's waist, flattening his palm on her stomach. "I'll buy whatever you want," he murmured, nuzzling the side of her neck.

The warmth of her body penetrated him, never failing to warm areas that had been iced over for years.

"I can get the things for the nursery." She scrolled through a variety of white cribs. "I really want yellow and white, no matter the sex. I can always add accent pieces once we find out what we're having."

Ryker swallowed. This was a conversation he never, ever thought he'd be having…especially with his best friends', his *employers'*, little sister.

"Do you care what we have?" Laney turned her head slightly to look at him.

Ryker eased back. "I hadn't thought about it, actually."

Blowing out a soft breath, she turned back toward her phone. "No, I'd say you haven't. This isn't something that excites most men, and when you weren't wanting a baby at all—"

Ryker lifted enough to roll her beneath him until she was on her back and staring up at him. He rested his hands on either side of her head.

"A baby may not have been on my radar before now, but that doesn't mean even for a second that I'm not excited about this life, Laney."

Her face lit up. Her brows rose, a smile spread on her lips. "You're excited?"

Hell. He hadn't realized he was excited until he'd said the words aloud.

"I am. I'm scared as hell, though. I haven't thought

about the sex because it doesn't matter to me." Ryker kissed her softly. "All that matters is you two are safe, healthy, happy. That's my goal here, Laney."

Cupping the side of his face, she stared back at him. Her brows were drawn in, the happiness in her face vanished.

"I'm scared for you," she murmured. "When Braden and Mac—"

He silenced her with his lips. "I'm not worried about them."

"They won't like this." She blinked as moisture gathered in her eyes. "They'll blame you, and I've been half in love with you my whole life, and Miami was—"

"Amazing." He nipped at her lips, her chin, along her jawline. "Miami had been coming for a long time. There was no way I could've avoided you forever."

The screen on her phone went dim, plunging the room into darkness. He settled perfectly between her spread thighs.

"I can resist many things in this world, but you're not one of them." He ran his lips along the side of her neck as she arched her body against his. "I'm only human, Laney. And I can only ignore my body for so long. I've told you before, I'm a selfish bastard."

"No, you're not. You're one of the most giving people I know." Her arms and legs encircled him as he slid into her. "You know this is more than just the baby and chemistry between us, right?" she asked.

Ryker stilled for a second before moving his hips slowly. "I can admit that, yes. But beyond that, let's just—"

"I know. Concentrate on now." She returned his thrust

with a quicker pace. "I'm all for what's happening right now."

But they would get back to this topic later, he knew.

Ryker framed her face between his hands again and covered her mouth with his. He'd never wanted to take his time like this, never wanted to enjoy the process of getting to the climax. Fast and frantic had been just fine with him. Slow, passionate...that meant getting more emotionally involved.

And God help him, he had plunged headfirst into this...whatever this was...with Laney.

Her nails bit into his back. She opened her mouth fully for him, completely taking him in every way she could. There was a fire, a burning for her that hadn't been there before. The all-consuming need he'd had in the past was nothing compared to right here, right now. She was taking him and wrapping him into her perfect world where she believed such things as love actually existed.

Ryker tore his mouth from hers, ran his lips down her neck, to one perfect breast. Her hands came up to his head, as if to hold him in place. Her soft gasps only fueled him further to make sure she had everything she wanted.

"Ryker..."

He eased back, then pushed forward hard. Once, twice. Her entire body shuddered beneath his. It was almost too much to bear as Laney cried out his name, arched beneath him and came undone all around him.

And it was all Ryker needed to follow her over the edge.

The papers for the new property had been signed a few days ago, the contractor had been hired and Laney couldn't wait to get her hands dirty and dig into the process of renovating the old, neglected building in Southie.

Right now, though, she was having a difficult time breathing in the damn dress she'd purchased for O'Shea's annual Christmas party. She'd thought it was fine in the store, but, the overflowing cleavage and the slight pull of the emerald green satin at her waist gave her pause. She hadn't noticed her midsection getting any larger, she was only eight weeks pregnant now, but something had happened overnight because she was seriously worried about popping that side zipper.

"Being so gorgeous and built like that should make me hate you."

Laney spun to see Jenna, her arm looped through Mac's. Crossing the ballroom, Laney threw her arms out wide.

"I'm so glad you guys made it in." She hugged her brother before turning to Jenna, taking in the gorgeous red dress that highlighted her curves. "Like you're one to talk. You look stunning."

Jenna had a voluptuous figure, not model-thin like some women felt they needed to be. Jenna was a beautiful woman and looked even more striking now that she was in love. Mac, Laney's globe-trotting playboy brother, had finally been tamed by his best friend when he had to pose as her fiancé. Laney would've given anything to see the moment her brother realized Jenna was the one. She had seen this coming for years and couldn't be happier for the two of them.

"I was worried the snow would delay you all getting here."

Mac shrugged. "I checked the area before I took off."

Her brother doubled as a pilot. "I was confident we'd be safe. If not, we could've gone into DC and rented a car."

"He'll fly in almost anything," Jenna joked. "He's had me white-knuckling it more than once, but he assures me he has everything under control."

Mac's pilot's license came in handy since he hated Boston winters and was now living it up in Miami.

"Next year I vote we move this party to my house," he suggested. "Too damn cold up here."

"Are you complaining already?" Braden stepped into the room, Zara by his side. He slapped Mac's shoulder. "You haven't been in town an hour and already a hater."

Laney noticed Zara scanning the room and tuned out her brothers' banter. "I came a little early and made sure all the centerpieces were set up like we'd discussed. I hope you like them."

Her sister-in-law smiled. "They're beautiful."

"You're beautiful," Laney countered. "That gold dress is perfect on you."

"I think we all look amazing." Zara continued to look around, her brows drawn in a frown. "Is Ryker here? I thought he told Braden he'd be here early."

Laney's heart quickened. It had been several days since he spent the night in her bed. He'd gone out of town on business to acquire some authentic pieces for the spring auction. He'd only gone to Toronto, then to Chicago, but she hated not knowing he was in town. Not that she ever felt at risk, but she definitely felt safer knowing he was around.

"He's in the study," Braden stated. "He...had to take a call."

A call? Why had Braden hesitated? Laney knew Ryker's personal life was technically none of her business, but she still wanted to know what was going on. And if Braden had been in the study with Ryker, then the call was most likely business…in which case she still wanted to know.

"The room looks amazing," Jenna said as she pulled away from Mac's side and started walking around. "The lights, the tables, all of it looks magical. You all really know how to treat your employees."

"Loyalty deserves to be rewarded," Mac stated simply. "And O'Shea's wouldn't throw a cheap party."

"Neither would I," Zara chimed in. "I totally use you all to boost my own company."

Braden smiled, leaned down to kiss his wife on the head. "You do an incredible job. You don't need us."

Her brothers had found two amazing women to share their lives with. Laney wanted to tell them all about the pregnancy, but she wasn't ready. Beyond the fact that she worried how they'd treat Ryker, Laney wanted to tell Zara privately so she didn't have to absorb the news around others. Zara would most likely be elated, but Laney didn't want to take any chances. The miscarriage was still fresh, but did that loss and ache ever really go away?

Laney prayed she never had to find out.

She pulled in a breath, as much as her dress would allow. "I'll be right back."

She wasn't going to make up an excuse to leave the room. The guests weren't due to arrive for another hour, so her presence wasn't needed at the moment.

The foursome continued talking as the caterers entered through the side doors to set up the food tables in the back of the room. Laney saw her chance to slip out. She headed toward the wide, curved staircase and made her way up to the study. Nobody would think twice about her and Ryker talking.

Once she reached the landing, she glanced over her shoulder to see that she was still alone. She didn't hear Ryker on the phone as she approached the study, then she realized the door was closed. Laney turned the knob slowly as she pushed the door open a crack. When she peeked inside, she didn't see Ryker on the phone at all. His hands were on the desk, his back to the door, his head bowed.

Opening the door wider, Laney let herself in. Her heels were quiet on the carpet, but the shift in the full skirt of her dress pulled Ryker straight up. He spun and froze. Laney stilled, as well.

She'd seen him in a tux before, but something about seeing him now that she knew him so intimately…damn, he was one sexy man. His all-black tux played up the menacing male he was on a daily basis, but the expensive cut screamed money and class. Ryker was every type of fantasy man wrapped into one delicious package.

And something was troubling him. His tight face, clenched jaw and worried eyes stared back at her.

"What's wrong?"

Shaking his head, he pushed off the desk and walked toward her. "Nothing now that you showed up wearing this killer dress."

As much as her ego appreciated his approval, she wasn't letting his compliments distract her from digging deeper.

"Tell me." She stepped back when he stood right before her. Touching him now would get them nowhere… except naked, which was a bad idea, considering her family was downstairs. "Something happened."

Raking a hand over the back of his neck, Ryker blew out a sigh. "Nothing for you to worry about."

When he reached for her, Laney held up her hands. "No. You're not blowing me off. I do worry, Ryker. It's what happens when you care about someone."

"It's just work, nothing I can't handle." He moved lightning-fast and wrapped his arms around her, pulling her body flush with his. "You didn't tell me you'd look so damn sexy tonight. I'm going to have a hard time keeping my hands to myself."

Laney wanted his hands all over her, but she also wanted to know what he was hiding from her.

"You better keep your hands off. If we expose ourselves here, you and my brothers will have a fight and that's not the atmosphere we want for this party."

"I'll just have mental foreplay until I can get you back to my bed tonight."

Laney lifted a brow. "Your bed?"

He slid one fingertip up her arm, across her collarbone and down to the V of her plunging neckline. "My bed. Where you belong."

Laney could barely process the meaning of those words for all the delicious tingles shooting through her. Finally, he was coming around and admitting he wanted her. They were making progress and she was going to continue to build on this, to show him exactly what they could be together.

Ryker's eyes held hers, so much desire and passion staring back at her. She couldn't get to his house soon enough.

The click of the door had Ryker easing his hand away and crossing his arms over his chest. Laney took a step back.

"Everything okay?"

Laney kept her back to Mac, who'd just come in. Her eyes stayed on Ryker, who was looking over her head.

"Yeah. Laney was just following up on an email she sent me earlier."

When Ryker moved around her, Laney turned in time to see the one-armed man hug between the two.

"I hear we got the Feds on us now." Mac shoved his hands in his pockets and rocked back on his heels. "If you all need me here, let me know. I doubt the source is coming from down South."

Laney shook her head. "I disagree. I think the timing is too coincidental, since you opened two new stores and now we have a mole."

"We can't rule out anything yet," Ryker, the voice of calm and reason, interjected. "I'll pursue every angle, and Laney will dig deeper to get to the bottom of this. She's been losing sleep over it."

Mac's eyes darted to her. "You can't take on all of this by yourself."

Guilt hit her hard. "I set up the system, I did background checks on every employee. By default, the blame comes back to me."

"We don't work that way," Ryker told her, his gaze hard. "We're a team. Remember?"

The burn in her throat, the prickling sensation in her eyes came out of nowhere. Now was not the time to cry. But damn him for reminding her of that fact.

"He's right," Mac agreed, oblivious. "We're all in this together, and we'll get out of it together. We just have to pool our efforts like we always do."

Laney pulled in a shaky breath and nodded. "You're right. I still feel responsible, but I will get to the bottom of this. I just need more time with the computers to eliminate our main office as the source of the snitch."

"Not tonight," Ryker told her. "Tonight we're all taking a few hours off and not worrying about work. We have enough Feds in our pocket to hold them off for a bit."

Between the Feds and worrying about the baby and when to drop that bombshell, and trying to analyze Ryker's sudden change of heart about sleeping with her, Laney had a headache. No surprise there.

She rubbed her forehead and closed her eyes for a moment. The guys continued to talk, and she willed the oncoming migraine to cease. Maybe it would help if she ate something. The caterer they'd hired was the best in the area. Laney's mouth watered at the thought of the filet mignon on the menu, and the chocolate fountain and fresh fruit sounded amazing, too.

"Laney?"

Ryker's worried tone had her opening her eyes, offering a smile. But the smile was moot when she started to sway.

Instantly Ryker took one of her arms and Mac had the other.

"You all right?" Mac asked.

Laney nodded. "Just getting a headache. No big deal."

She glanced between her brother's worried expression and Ryker's questioning gaze. She knew where Ryker's mind was, but she couldn't reveal too much here.

"I'm fine, I swear. I just need to eat, that's all."

Ryker's grip on her elbow tightened. "Then let's go downstairs and get you something."

Nodding, Laney pulled from both strong holds. "I can take care of myself. I'll just go into the kitchen and grab some crackers to hold me over."

"No, you'll eat more because when guests arrive, you'll be talking, and you'll forget to get a plate for yourself."

Laney stared at Ryker and he glared right back. While the whole protective thing was cute and sexy, she couldn't stay around him during this party. Their guests—her family—would be on to them in a second. Laney saw how Zara and Jenna stared at their men, and Laney knew for a fact she had that same love-swept gleam in her eye.

"I'll grab some fruit or something, too," she assured him. "I'm fine."

Without waiting for another argument, she turned from the guys and headed out of the room. Once in the hallway, Laney leaned against the wall, held a hand to her stomach and took a moment to relax. She needed to stay focused on finding who was betraying her family, but she couldn't neglect her body. This baby was everything to her. She'd wanted a family of her own since she could remember, and she'd been given this gift. It might not be how she had pictured things would fall in line, but did life ever really work that way?

Laney pushed off the wall and headed downstairs. She needed to get a hold of herself and put on her game face. This night had to be about the company and her family. And discovering the traitor in their midst.

# Twelve

Ryker moved about the room, never straying too far from Laney. That damn dress was going to be the death of him. He wasn't sure if he wanted her to leave it on later when they were alone or if he wanted to peel it off of her. Those curves, the breasts that threatened to spill out and the fact she was carrying his baby were a lethal combination.

"You think our betrayer is here?"

Ryker gripped his glass of bourbon and nodded to Braden. "Yeah, I do. I think the bastard wants to keep close, thinking if they didn't show up, we'd see it as a red flag. They'll act like the doting, perfect employee."

"Damn it." Braden took a sip of whatever he was drinking, *Scotch by the smell of it*, Ryker thought, and let out a sigh. "I knew they'd be here. When I find out who I opened up my home to, my family to, they will be sorry they ever crossed us."

Ryker scanned the room. Laughter, chatter, hugs, everything seemed like a regular O'Shea's Christmas party. Women wore glamorous gowns and the men wore their finest suits. The tradition had been started decades ago. Before the O'Shea clan had taken him in, he never would've dreamed this was where he'd end up. A boy from a broken home with a deadbeat, druggie father had turned into a billionaire by simply being loyal and valuing what family was all about.

And Ryker would do it again even without all the money.

Zara joined them, swirling her glass of wine. "I'd say this party is another success."

Braden nodded. "Of course it is. I married the best event coordinator in the world."

Ryker listened, but his eyes were on Laney. She was chatting with Viviana and whoever her date was. Some guy with a beard and an expensive suit. Ryker had never seen the man before, but he'd met Viviana and knew the family trusted her. Laney hugged the woman and turned, her gaze catching Ryker's. His heart kicked up as she made her way across the floor. The way her body shifted, the way that dress hugged her until mid-thigh then flared out, those creamy shoulders exposed...he was going to have to think of something else because Laney was seriously killing him. And from the smirk on her face, she damn well knew it.

"Feeling better?" Braden asked when Laney stood before them. "Mac said you'd gotten dizzy or something earlier."

"I'm fine."

"You're not taking care of yourself," Braden added.

"This is the second time this has happened recently. Have you been to the doctor?"

Laney nodded. "I have, and I promise I'm perfectly healthy."

Ryker hated this. Hated lying to the only people he truly cared about.

"Have you tried this white wine?" Zara asked Laney. "It's the best I've ever had. I already asked the caterer the name, and I'm going to order it for my next event."

Laney shook her head. "Wow, it must be good."

"Let me get you a glass," Zara stated.

Ryker froze at the same time Laney's eyes widened. "Um, no. I'm just going to have some water for now."

Zara's brows drew in. "Are you sure?"

"Positive."

Ryker needed to move this conversation in a different direction. Laney was uncomfortable, and that was the last thing she needed.

"Braden, are you—"

"Oh, Laney." Zara's words cut him off. "Are you… are you pregnant?"

The last word was whispered, and Ryker gritted his teeth. He scrambled for a defense, but he couldn't out-right lie. It wasn't as if they could keep the baby a secret forever. Damn it, he wanted, needed to come to Laney's aid here, he just had no idea how.

"Laney?" Braden jerked his attention to his sister. "Are you?"

The party went on around them, but the silence surrounded their little group, blocking everything else out. Ryker opened his mouth, not sure what he was about to say, but Laney's one word response cut him off.

"Yes."

"Oh, honey." Zara stepped forward and hugged Laney. "I'm sorry. I just blurted that out because I recognized the symptoms. I shouldn't have said anything."

Laney returned the embrace. "It's okay. I was waiting to tell you all. I wasn't sure how you'd take the news."

Zara leaned back. "I'm happy for you if you're happy. Braden and I are confident we'll have children, so don't worry about me."

Laney's smile widened as she turned her attention to Braden. "Well, do you have something you want to say?"

"Who's the father?"

His low, anger-filled tone cut right through Ryker. To Laney's credit, she didn't even flick a glance his way as she continued to smile.

"Right now we're just keeping things low-key. I'm not ready to say who the father is just yet."

Part of Ryker was proud of her response, honest but still keeping their secret. The other part of him, the bigger part of him, hated the fact he was kept out of the equation. He wanted to be part of this child's life from the start. Not hidden in the background.

And he sure as hell didn't want Laney defending him. That wasn't how this was going to work. He may not know where the hell they were headed, but he wasn't going to hide behind a pregnant woman.

"I'm the father."

He ignored Laney's gasp and concentrated on Braden...who slowly turned his eyes to Ryker.

"You're lying," he stated in a low, threatening tone. "You'd never do that to me."

Laney reached forward, putting her hand on Braden's arm. "Don't. Not here."

Braden shrugged her off. "I will kill you myself."

Ryker clenched his fists. "You can try."

"No bloodshed." Laney stepped between them, her back to Ryker. "Now is not the time to discuss this."

Zara tugged on Braden's arm. "She's right. You need to step back, and we can all talk after the party."

Braden's hard eyes never wavered from Ryker's. This was his brother and he'd betrayed him. Ryker didn't blame Braden for wanting to kill him. Whatever Braden, and Mac, threw his way, Ryker knew he deserved every bit of it. But the worst part, the scariest part, was the possibility that he'd no longer be part of the family.

Braden shifted his attention to Laney. "What the hell were you thinking?"

"My personal life is none of your business," she spat.

"What is going on?" Mac moved to the group, Jenna right on his heels. "You all are causing a scene."

"Laney's pregnant and Ryker is the father." Braden delivered the blow to Mac in a disgusted tone, but never took his eyes from his sister. "She was just about to explain what the hell she was thinking."

"I wasn't about to explain anything to anyone," Laney said, lowering her voice. "I don't owe any of you a defense. And I sure as hell am not getting into this here."

When she turned away, Braden reached out and snagged her arm. Ryker saw red.

"Get your hand off her," he gritted out. "Or I won't care what type of scene we cause."

Braden's anger was palpable. Ryker would gladly take the brunt of his rage, but he refused to have Laney shoulder the blame.

"This isn't the place," Mac stated. Ryker glanced to him, but was met with equally angry eyes. "But we are going to talk when this party is over."

Ryker nodded in agreement. Laney jerked free of Braden's grip and gracefully walked away. She wasn't going to cause any more of a scene than necessary, and he applauded her for her poise and determination. Ryker, on the other hand, was ready to throw his fist through a wall.

"Come on, Braden. You have a party to host." Zara wrapped her arm through his. "Getting angry isn't going to change a thing."

Braden remained still for several moments before being led away. Ryker turned to Mac and Jenna.

"You want to say something now?"

Mac's jaw clenched. "Later. I'll have plenty to say later."

"What your sister and I do is none of your concern."

Mac's sneer indicated otherwise. "You got my sister pregnant. I'd say every bit of this is our business, *brother.*"

The parting shot did the damage Mac had intended. He walked away, leaving Ryker feeling even more like a bastard than he already did. He'd never thought he was good enough for Laney—and her brothers had just hit that point home.

There was no certainty how things were going to go down, but Ryker vowed to keep Laney safe. He'd told her he wouldn't let her get hurt, and he damn well meant it.

Oh, he wasn't concerned her brothers would physically harm her. No way in hell would they do that. But words could cause more damage than any actions, and tensions were running high.

Ryker felt for the souvenir penny inside his pocket, the reminder he needed right now. Family was everything to him, and he'd slashed right through that shroud of trust.

Now he had to pick up the pieces and make some vain attempt to put them all back together.

Laney's nerves were shot. She didn't have the energy to argue with her brothers, and she was furious at Ryker for dropping their bombshell the way he had. She'd had things covered, she was trying to keep him out of the hot seat until her brothers had a chance to process the pregnancy.

And she could think of so many other times that would've been more appropriate.

The caterers were gone, the room now a skeleton of a beautiful Christmas party. The employees had all mingled, chatting about the upcoming spring auction, the biggest one of the year. Laney had tried to zero in on who she thought could be capable of betrayal, but after the intense scene with her brothers and Ryker, she had lost focus.

"I'm so, so sorry, Laney."

Laney turned toward the doorway to the ballroom leading off the foyer. Zara had her hands clasped in front of her as she worried her bottom lip.

"None of this is your fault." Laney moved toward her sister-in-law and let out a sigh. "I have no idea where the guys went, but I hope Ryker is still alive."

Zara nodded. "Braden and Mac are outside, and I saw Ryker go up to the study. Jenna is finishing up in the kitchen, but I wanted to slip out and see you without the others."

Tears pricked Laney's eyes. "I was so worried how you'd take the news. I didn't want to bring back all of those memories."

Zara reached out, taking Laney's hands in hers. "The

memories are always there. The hurt will never go away, I imagine. We are trying to have another, and my doctor says he sees no reason why we can't get pregnant again. Don't worry about me, Laney. This is a special time for you and Ryker."

Laney blinked back the burn and moisture. "I don't know what Braden and Mac are going to do. I mean, they're all like brothers, they're best friends. Ryker needs them in his life. He had no one before coming here. He—"

"You love him," Zara said softly.

There was no denying the truth. "Yes."

"Then fight for this. Your brothers are in a state of shock, and most of their anger stems from getting caught off guard. Make them see how much you care for Ryker. Does he feel the same way?"

And wasn't that the question? How did Ryker feel? The man was so closed off. She knew full well how he felt about their physical relationship, and she was almost positive he had feelings for her, but she wanted him to say it. To admit how he felt and stop hiding from everything.

"It's okay." Zara squeezed Laney's hands. "Go on upstairs. Your brothers will be up shortly, I'm sure."

Laney wrapped her arms around Zara. "I'm so glad you're in our lives."

Returning the embrace, Zara whispered, "Me, too."

Pulling herself together, Laney made her way upstairs. She wasn't ready for this talk, didn't think she'd ever be. She knew going in that harsh words were going to be exchanged, some things that could never be taken back. But she wouldn't let her brothers blame Ryker. That was an issue she refused to back down on.

When she eased open the study door, she saw Ryker

across the room, facing the floor-to-ceiling windows behind the desk. With his hands in his pockets, he looked as if he didn't have a care in the world. Laney knew different. He carried everything on his shoulders.

She closed the door at her back, and the click had Ryker glancing over his shoulder.

"You need to leave," he told her, turning back to look out the window. "I've got this."

Yeah, carrying the entire weight, as if this pregnancy was one-sided.

"We're a team, remember?"

She moved across the floor, nerves swirling in her stomach. If he shut her out now, Laney didn't know how she'd handle his silence.

"Why didn't you let me manage things earlier?" she asked as she came to stand beside him. When he didn't look at her, Laney's heart sank just a bit more.

"I don't want you to think I was keeping your name from them for any reason other than it wasn't the time or place to get into this."

Ryker whirled, eyes blazing with fury. "I'm not hiding behind a woman. You think I was just going to stand there and let Braden speculate? How would that have worked out for either of us when he did find out the truth? If we'd let that go, his rage would've been worse."

Once again, Ryker was the voice of reason. Plus, it wasn't his style to let a woman take the fall, especially her. She should've known he wouldn't stand by while she made excuses and skirted around the truth.

"I just want to go home with you and be done here," she whispered.

"I'm not sure that's the best idea right now."

Laney froze. "What? Don't even tell me you're letting them come between us already."

He turned back to stare out at the dark night, illuminated only by the glow from the patio lights below. "I've told you before there is no 'us.' Their reaction should have told you that."

Laney crossed her arms over her chest. "And we're not going to fight them on this?"

The muscles in his jaw clenched. His silence might as well have been shouted through a bullhorn.

The door to the study opened, then slammed. Laney glanced up to see her brothers. Furious over Ryker's stance, Laney had had more than enough.

"If you're going to come in here and beat your chests over how you're supposed to protect me and Ryker knew better, save it." Laney glared across the room as her brothers started in her direction. "I'm expecting a baby. We didn't plan it, but your anger won't change a thing."

Mac stopped behind the leather couch and rested his hands over the back. "Maybe not, but we're still pissed. We're family, Laney. Ryker crossed the line."

Laney rolled her eyes. "I assure you, he didn't make the baby himself."

"So what now?" Braden asked, his eyes on Ryker. "What do you plan to do with my sister?"

Laney stilled, her back turned to Ryker as she waited on his response.

"I plan on helping her raise our baby and continuing to keep her safe. This changes nothing."

Laney's heart broke. Cracked right in two, then splintered into shards on the ground. She wasn't going to beg anymore. She'd tried to show him how perfect they'd be together, but clearly he wanted to keep that bit of distance in place so he could hold together the only family he'd ever known. She understood his fear, admired him for clinging to what he'd built, but to throw away her love was the last straw.

Laney turned to face Ryker. "You're right. This changes nothing. We're going to have a baby, but that's all."

Those dark eyes stared back at her. Lips thinned, jaw clenched, he was seething. Laney continued to stare, tipping up her chin in defiance. If he wanted to expand, then he needed to do so now. If he wanted to come to her "rescue" like he always had in the past, he needed to say what he felt. Why did have to be so set on doing the right thing? He was human, and they were attracted to each other. He'd showed her with his actions that he cared. Why was he choosing her brothers over her—again?

"We have too many problems going on right now for you two to be at odds," Mac cut into her thoughts. "Laney, are you feeling okay? Are you sure you can keep working?"

Throwing her arms in the air, she spun. "For heaven's sake, I'm pregnant, not terminal. I've had a few dizzy spells, but that's all normal."

Braden ran a hand over the back of his neck and glanced toward the ceiling. Laney waited for the back-lash.

"Don't take this out on Ryker—"

"Stop, Laney."

She glanced over her shoulder. Ryker had turned from the window. His dark eyes held her in place, and she wanted to say so much more. She wanted to beat some sense into him until he relaxed his moral compass. He was so damn worried about getting shut out, he was lit-erally letting her slip away.

"I'll handle my end," he told her.

His end? So they were on separate sides?

"Yeah, I guess you can." She swallowed the hurt, ignoring the threat of tears. She had no time for tears, she was too angry. "I'm going home. I'm tired, I've had a long day."

Gathering the skirt of her gown in one hand, she marched toward the door.

"Laney."

Ryker's voice stopped her.

"I'll drive you home."

Letting out a humorless laugh, Laney turned. "Like hell you will. I can handle this myself."

Throwing his words right back at him should've made her feel marginally better, but she only felt empty. She shot a glance to each of her brothers.

"If I come across any new leads on the mole, I'll let you know."

She couldn't be in this room another second, and at this point she didn't care what they did to one another. They were all morons. Laney wondered how the hell she'd been cursed to be surrounded by idiots. Not one of them was thinking beyond this moment. Her brothers weren't looking to the future, to a new generation of O'Sheas, and Ryker was being so damn stubborn, she was getting another headache thinking about it.

By the time she got home, all Laney wanted to do was soak in a bubble bath and think about her precious baby. Designing a nursery in her head was exactly what she needed to relax. No work, no men, just sweet little baby thoughts.

# Thirteen

Ryker's eye throbbed. He'd deserved the single punch to the face…hell, he had expected so much more. Braden had delivered the blow, and Ryker hadn't even attempted a block.

How could he fault them for being protective of Lanoy? Ryker had done several interventions on her behalf when she'd been with men who weren't appropriate. He expected nothing less from Braden and Mac.

But Ryker had hurt her. He'd lied when he said the baby changed nothing. This baby changed everything. He'd been void of emotion for so long, something uncomfortable kept shifting in his chest, and he was scared as hell. Not that he'd ever admit such a thing aloud. He'd meant what he said when he'd told her there was no "us." Even so, he couldn't seem to stay away.

Though it was late, Ryker found himself standing outside Laney's house. It was time for damage control. He didn't text her first, nor was he about to knock. He knew O'Sheas hurt deeply and wanted to be left alone.

Too damn bad.

Ryker let himself in, punched in her security code and locked the dead bolt behind him. The Christmas tree lit up in the corner drew his attention to the pewter ornament hanging front and center. She'd genuinely been surprised and happy when he'd given that to her. He'd never seen her smile like that, at least not directed his way. He wanted to see that again. He needed to know he hadn't damaged something inside her.

Damn it. He raked a hand through his hair. He knew more than most how deeply harsh words sliced, and once they were out, there was no way to take them back.

"What do you want?"

Ryker glanced up the staircase. Laney stood on the landing, belting her robe, her damp hair lying across one shoulder.

He remained where he was, though everything inside him demanded he rush up the stairs, grab her and beg for forgiveness. Pride wouldn't let him…the same damn pride that was making her hurt.

Why did he have to be such a bastard? Why didn't he have normal feelings like everyone else? He'd been fine with his callous ways…until Laney.

"I came to apologize, though I doubt you'll accept it."

Crossing her arms over her chest, she nodded. "You're right. Which brother hit you?"

"Braden."

"Neanderthals," she muttered before starting down the steps. "I should get you some ice."

Ryker paused. "You're going to play nurse after what happened?"

Laney reached the landing, her hand braced on the newel post. "Braden had no right to hit you because we slept together. That's none of his business. But don't mistake the bag of ice as my forgiveness."

Even when she was pissed, Laney wanted to help. She managed to do things to him, things he never thought possible. She made him feel as if he actually had a heart. Problem was, he had no idea what the hell to do with it.

When she reached the bottom step, Ryker pivoted just enough to block her. With her up just those few inches, she was at eye level and right where he wanted her to be.

"Don't make this more difficult," she whispered, biting her bottom lip. "I'm tired, Ryker. You said enough earlier."

Jasmine. She'd used some form of Jasmine soap or shampoo, or whatever other potion women used. And she smelled absolutely delicious.

"I didn't mean those words the way they came out," he told her, clenching his fists. He wanted to reach for her, was desperate to touch her, but he didn't want his other eye blackened. He may be desperate, but he wasn't stupid.

"Yet you waited until we were alone to tell me that." She quirked a brow. "Your apology is accepted, but the damage is done. Do you want ice or not?"

"No."

"Fine. Then let yourself out and reset the alarm. I'm going to bed."

Before she could turn, Ryker placed his hand over hers on the post. "I'm lost, Laney. I have no idea what the hell I'm doing."

Her hand relaxed beneath his, giving him a minor

hope she wasn't ready to shut him out. If there was ever a time to spill his thoughts, it was now.

"I can't lose any of you," he went on. "Do you understand that? You're all I have. Braden and Mac are my brothers. I have no idea where this is leading between you and me, but I have to have some stability. I know you think I'm some superhuman, unfeeling bastard right now, but I feel…too much."

Laney's eyes closed, and Ryker had no idea what she was thinking. Everything was new to him. He'd been infatuated with her for so long, but never thought anything would come of it. Yet, here they were, expecting a baby and trying to wade through this mess he'd made.

And she loved him. Words he could never, ever forget.

"I can't do this with you." Her misty eyes landed on his, touching him right to his soul. "You know how I feel and when you do this push-pull. I have no idea how to react. I get that this family is yours, I completely understand you can't lose us. But are you willing to ignore everything between you and me?"

The hurt in her tone destroyed him. Ryker couldn't stand another second, he had to offer some comfort, but he knew the comfort was mostly for himself.

Taking her face between his hands, he stared directly into those vibrant green eyes. How could she pierce him so deeply? Nobody had ever even come close to touching him the way Laney had. But if he risked everything, *everything*, and they fell apart, it would kill him.

He eased forward, resting his forehead against hers and pulling in a deep breath. "I need time."

"I've given you most of my life," she whispered. The direct punch hit its mark.

"I'm new here, Laney. I can't mess this up, for you, for our baby. Just...don't give up on me."

Silence settled heavily around them, and Ryker hated the vulnerability he was showing. But this was Laney, and he was starting to see exactly what it would take to keep her waiting until he figured out his jumbled emotions.

She didn't say anything, didn't touch him in return. Ryker knew he wasn't done baring his soul. Stepping away from her, because he couldn't slice himself wide open *and* touch her, he started pacing her living room.

"I had the sad, clichéd childhood," he began, ignoring that instant burn to his chest when he thought about those first twelve years. "My father was a user, a man-whore, a worthless piece of trash who never should've been allowed to keep a child. I witnessed more by the time I was five years old than most people see or hear in a lifetime."

Ryker stopped in front of the mantel, catching Laney's gaze in the large mirror hanging above the greenery. "He'd leave me alone for days. I stole food to eat, I got myself ready for school, I picked fights on the playground so I could go to the principal's office."

Bracing his hands on the mantel, Ryker lowered his head. "I just wanted any contact with a male adult. I didn't care if it was negative. They'd try to call my dad, but of course he never answered. Half the time our phone bill wasn't paid anyway. So I'd stay in the office and finish my schoolwork, which was what I wanted. I wanted to be left alone to do my thing."

Pushing off the mantel, he started pacing again. He'd never let his backstory spill out like that. But now that he'd started, he wasn't about to stop. Laney deserved this part of him, she deserved it all, but this is all he could give for now.

"When I saw your brothers in a fight, I was all too eager to jump in. My dad had been gone for nearly a week, and I was pissed. I needed to take my aggression out on someone."

"How did nobody notice this for twelve years?" Laney's quiet question broke through his thoughts.

"People are so wrapped up in their own lives." He shrugged and reached for the ornament he'd given her. He rubbed his thumb over the roundness of the silhouette's belly before letting it go to sway against the branches. "I was so skeptical about meeting Patrick, but the second I saw him, I knew he was one of the good guys."

Laney let out a soft laugh. "Only a select few would lump him into that category, but I agree. He was the best."

"From the second I came to stay with you guys, then started working with your brothers, I felt like I had a place, a real home. Braden and Mac treated me like family. You were so young at first, I ignored you. But once you got to be a teenager, I was looking at you in ways that I shouldn't. Had your dad had even the slightest idea of what my thoughts were, he would've killed me himself."

"You never looked at me twice," she stated.

Ryker threw a glance over his shoulder, just in time to see one of her cats dart up the steps and disappear. "I looked. I fantasized. My penance for lusting after you was to watch you grow into a beautiful woman, to see other bastards on your arm. Then when we saw how eerily good you were with computers, I realized my penance had just begun."

He moved to the wide window in the front of the

house. Staring out onto the darkened night, with only a street lamp lighting a portion of the view, Ryker was forced to look at his own reflection. Fitting, considering he barely recognized the man who was spouting off his life story.

Slipping his hand into a pocket, he pulled out the penny. "I have been just fine keeping my distance from you. I mean, I wanted you, but I knew you were on another level, and nothing between us could ever happen. I've never forgotten where I came from, no matter how much money I have in my account or how many houses I own."

When he turned, he found her exactly as she'd been moments ago. Standing on that bottom step, her hand on the post, her eyes never wavering from him.

Holding up the pathetic piece of metal, Ryker walked forward. "I keep this ridiculous reminder in my pocket of what I came from. I've had this with me every single day since I was ten years old."

He stood only a few feet away, but held the penny out for her. Laney took it, examined it.

"This is one of those flattened pennies with your name on it." She brought her eyes back to his. "What's this from?"

"My dad was actually sober for a few hours one time." How sad was it that Ryker could pinpoint the exact hours his dad had gone without a drink or a fix? "There was a carnival outside the city, and he took me. He got this with my name on it, maybe because he felt he owed me something. I have no clue why, but this was the only thing he'd ever bought for me. This was the only time in my childhood he'd actually taken me anywhere."

Laney's eyes filled as she clutched the penny in her hand. "Are you worried about being a father?"

"Hell, yes, I am." Ryker rubbed the back of his neck, glancing to the floor before going on. "What do I have to fall back on? What part of my past says I'm ready to help raise another human being? I won't leave either of you, but I'm scared as hell, Laney."

"You're not afraid," she countered, her voice softening. "You're refusing to accept what already is. You have all of these wonderful emotions inside you. I know you care for me, I know you care for this baby. If you'd let yourself relax, you'd see there's so much more than fear. Fear is a lie. If my father showed you nothing else, he showed you that."

"There can't be animosity between your brothers and me, or them and you. There can't be. This family needs to be unified, and I swore to your father we'd find those scrolls, we'd keep this family going. I promised, Laney."

Still clutching the penny, she crossed her arms and nodded. "And we'll continue to do just that. My brothers aren't part of what you and I have going on. You need to understand that because if you don't, then we have nothing."

"If I were Braden, I would've killed someone like me."

Laney's hard stare held him in place. Damn, when she got that look, she was every bit Patrick O'Shea's daughter. She meant business—and she was sexy as hell.

"Braden's not going to harm you. Well, other than the black eye."

"You're aware of the man I am, what I've done to keep your family safe."

Laney nodded. "I'm not naive."

"You never ask me, you never look at me as if you disapprove."

Laney shrugged. "I know my father had his reasons.

I know Braden wants no more violence and that you had to take care of Shane because he tried to hurt me." She swallowed, bit her lip and pushed on. "And I know when my ex disappeared—"

"I didn't kill him. I couldn't. I sent him away with a fat check and a promise that if he returned, he would be finished."

"I thought you…"

Ryker nodded. "I know what you thought. I let you think that because I was trying to keep some wall between us, but it didn't work."

Laney blinked, glanced around the room as if trying to process what he'd just said. "I'm glad you didn't hurt him, but why didn't you? You hated him."

Hate was such a mild term for the man who'd verbally abused Laney. The guy was lucky he was still drawing breath in his lungs.

"I didn't want you to look at me like I was a monster."

"I could never look at you that way."

Ryker took a step forward. "I couldn't take the chance."

Laney uncrossed her arms, handed the penny back to him and pulled in a breath. Ryker shoved the memento back into his pocket.

"How much did Braden give you to send Shane away?"

"He didn't give me the money."

Her perfectly arched brows drew in as she tipped her head. "You used your money?"

"I'd have paid him every last dime I had to leave. I didn't want to have his blood on my hands, and I wanted him out of your life."

Laney pushed her hair over her shoulder and clutched

the V of her robe. She'd looked so damn gorgeous earlier in that red ball gown. She'd nearly stopped his heart and was the envy of every woman there; she was also most likely most guys' fantasy tonight.

But right now, she stood before him, void of all makeup, wearing nothing but her silk robe and smelling like everything he didn't deserve.

"Don't shut me out," he murmured. "I need time, and I know it's not fair to ask, but…just don't push me away, even when I'm being a selfish bastard."

It seemed as if an eternity passed as he waited for her to say something. Instead, she reached out, took his hand and turned to go up the steps.

"Laney."

She stopped but didn't look back at him. Ryker moved up to where she stood, lifted her in his arms and carried her the rest of the way.

"This is more," he told her. "Just let me catch up."

When she laid her head on his shoulder, Ryker knew he was breaking ground on learning how to live with a heart that actually feels. Now if he could only figure out a way to make sure she didn't get hurt…and prove to Braden and Mac that he wasn't just messing around with their baby sister.

# Fourteen

Laney was no closer to finding the traitor than she had been three days ago. Her family was counting on her. Their reputation, their…everything hinged on her finding the person who dared go against them. Until they knew who was behind the leak to the Feds, they were each taking turns manning the main office. Laney still wasn't convinced this was where everything went down; the clues the internet was giving her could be deceiving.

Mac and Jenna had decided to stick around through the holidays and definitely until this mess was cleared up.

Working in the office of her ancestors, Laney started looking at keystrokes with a program she'd downloaded. Every laptop in the office had to be checked. They had eight. The Boston office had to be ruled out first. Even though the new offices seemed coincidental in timing, if someone were going to attack, they may do it from close range where they could keep an eye on most of the key players.

Laney reached for another cracker. Normally she'd scold anyone for eating around their computers, but time was of the essence and her little one demanded some food.

"Anything?"

Laney didn't spare Braden a glance as he stepped into the office. "Not yet."

"How are you feeling?"

She hadn't seen him in three days, since the night of the party. He'd texted her to talk work and ask if she was feeling okay, but that was it. Ryker's name wasn't mentioned, and Laney was perfectly fine with that. The more her brothers stayed out of her personal business, the better.

"Hungry. I'm either tired or hungry. It's a cycle."

"Zara is out running errands. I'll have her bring you something."

Laney shook her head. "No need. I practically packed my kitchen in my bag because I knew I'd be here all day and evening."

Braden took a seat across from her. "You can't work yourself to death. You're expecting. I know how tired Zara was."

Her fingertips stilled on the keyboard as she glanced over the screen. "I'm sorry if this hurts you."

Braden shook his head. "You being pregnant isn't what bothers me."

Laney tried to keep the anger at bay. If they were all going to move forward, they had to stay levelheaded and remain calm. And after Ryker had spent the night simply holding her, Laney had a newfound hope that things would work out. They had to.

"You don't want to hear this, but Ryker and I aren't just fooling around."

Braden crossed his ankle over his knee and curled his hands over the sides of the chair. "No, I don't want to hear that my best friend, a guy I call my brother, is taking advantage of my sister. It doesn't sit well with me."

"You think that's what this is? That he's some sex-crazed maniac and I'm his poor, unsuspecting victim?" Laney shook her head and reached for another buttery cracker. "You have no clue, then. I love him."

"Damn it, Laney." Braden jerked forward in his seat, his hard stare holding her. "You're going to get hurt. A guy like Ryker doesn't do relationships. Have you ever wondered why he hasn't had a woman around us? That's not his style."

"It wasn't your style, either, until you got trapped with Zara. Now look at you."

That narrowed gaze didn't intimidate her. She took a bite of her cracker. "If you're done throwing your unwanted opinions around, I have work to do."

Braden came to his feet and blew out a breath. "You're going to get hurt," he repeated, his tone softer now.

"I'm a big girl."

She refused to look at him, refused to give him the power over her, because he had no say in how she handled her emotions or what she did with Ryker.

When he stormed out, Laney let out a breath. *That went well.*

Her cell chimed, but she ignored it. Braden was here, so if there was anything pressing going on, he'd know. The more she looked over this laptop, the more she was convinced it was clean. She'd just shut it down when her cell chimed once again.

Leaning over, she dug into her purse and fished it out of the side pocket. Giddiness burst through her when her contractor's name appeared.

She swiped her finger over the screen to open the message.

Inspections all passed. Moving forward on reworking the electrical.

Finally. Some good news. With the initial building inspections passed, she could push forward and hopefully come in ahead of her original spring opening.

After Ryker had shared his story with her the other night, she was even more determined to raise awareness for children who didn't have a proper home life.

She may not be able to help them all, but if she even helped one, then that was one less child who would doubt his or her self-worth. These kids needed to know someone cared about them, genuinely cared, because that was the struggle with Ryker right now. He didn't know what to do with the love she offered.

Laney sent off a quick reply that she'd be by tomorrow to discuss lighting and a few other questions she had regarding the kitchen area and the rec room.

She was making headway with the project, and possibly with Braden since he didn't seem so full of rage. Now if she could only figure out this puzzle of who was betraying her family. She didn't feel a bit sorry for the person on the other end of this investigation. Whoever had gone against the O'Sheas deserved everything they had coming.

* * *

Ryker had a sinking feeling, and he never ignored his instincts.

As he pulled in front of O'Shea's, he killed the engine and let his mind process all the intel that had come in regarding the scrolls. There were obvious dead ends, so he dismissed those immediately. But there was something eating away at his mind. It only made sense for the works to be fairly close. They were last known to be in Zara's home, or the home that the O'Sheas had lost in the Great Depression. If they had gotten out, word would've traveled.

Braden had searched, Ryker had searched. There wasn't a square inch of that house that had gone uncovered. But Ryker couldn't help but wonder if he'd missed something.

Zara's house sat empty now, well, save for her grandmother's things, because Zara had moved in with Braden. But Ryker wanted to go back in. He refused to give up. He'd been all over the damn globe on hunches, on veiled hints, but nothing had turned up. Frustration and failure were bitter pills to swallow, so he was going back to the point of origin, starting at square one. Because he was fresh out of leads.

Now more than ever, he needed to find those heirlooms. He needed to prove his family loyalties.

He stepped from his SUV, pulling his leather coat tighter to ward off the bitter chill. As soon as he stepped into O'Shea's, Braden's glare greeted him.

"Your eye looks better," he commented before looking back down at a stack of folders on his antique desk.

Ryker didn't take the bait. His eye still hurt like a bitch, but he had no right to complain.

"I want to get back into Zara's house," he said instead.

He moved farther into the spacious lobby area, complete with a Christmas tree that Laney no doubt had a hand in putting up. It had the same damn glittery nonsense she'd wanted him to put in her house.

"That resource is exhausted if you're referring to the scrolls." Braden dropped his pen and eased back in his leather seat. "Why do you need back in?"

Ryker shoved his hands in his pockets. "There's something we're missing."

"You're wasting your time."

"It's my time to waste." He refused to back down on this. "You know I'll just go in regardless. I'm merely telling you for courtesy."

Braden slowly came to his feet. Ryker didn't move, didn't bother to get out of the way when Braden came around the desk and stood toe to toe with him.

"Oh for pity's sake. If this is another pissing contest, count me out."

Ryker caught a glimpse of Laney in the doorway to the back office. Her hair was tied up in a loose knot, and her outfit consisted of an oversize gray sweater, black leggings and brown boots. She looked so young. Granted, she was ten years younger, but the simple outfit had her appearing almost innocent. His heart slammed against his chest as he took in the sight.

He offered her a smile. "I'm just letting your brother know of my plans for the evening."

Rolling her eyes, she moved toward them. "Braden, I think I found something. If you can stop being a bully for two seconds and come look?"

She'd barely gotten the words out before Braden and Ryker were in motion. Once in the office, Laney settled back into the seat, and Braden took one side of her chair while Ryker took the other.

"I found an encrypted email. I had to dig, and the person tried to delete it, but here it is."

"Open it."

Laney shook her head. "I can't. That's the problem. But the subject is damning and it's from the general computer at the main office."

She pointed to the bold header: BACKLOG

"And look at the time and date." She pointed to the screen—it was as soon as the new system was in place. Hours after it had been implemented, in fact. Then they had clearly sent the email and quickly covered their tracks.

The mole was good, but Laney was better. This was the break they'd needed.

"Bastards." Braden slammed his hand on the desk, making Laney jump.

"It's a start," she said, attempting to console him, but there was no calming him. This meant war for whoever did this. "The email wasn't from our internal system, and the account is fake. I just have to dig to find who set it up."

"You can do it." Ryker placed a hand on her shoulder and squeezed. "We all know you can. We're just frustrated and need to get this sorted out before the Feds find something incriminating."

Braden threw up his arms. "They have our sales records. If they search through each and every item, they're going to find questionable pieces."

Feeling a surge of loyalty and protectiveness, Laney glanced up at her brother. "If they searched each piece, they would have speculation at best. I have nothing in the program that indicates where the pieces came from. All of that is stored at my house, in a safe that even you two couldn't crack."

"I'd shoot it." Ryker straightened. "So, you're going to work on this, and I'm going to go back to Zara's tonight. Are you staying with her, Braden?"

Laney leaned back in her seat, looking up at the two men who seemed to be having some sort of staring showdown. She crossed her arms and waited for the testosterone to come down a notch.

"I'm not leaving her alone in her state," Braden replied. "You go. I'll make sure she's fine."

"With all this going on, I think it's safest if she's with one of us at all times."

Braden nodded. "That we can agree on."

Laney jerked to her feet, sending her chair flying back and crashing into the wall. "*She* is right here. And *she* can take care of herself."

They both stared at her as if she'd lost her mind. "I'm serious," she went on. "I don't need a babysitter, and nobody has threatened us with physical harm."

"You're pregnant," Braden growled. "You're automatically vulnerable."

Laney turned to face her brother fully. "You know I'm capable of taking care of myself. Stay all you want, but when I leave, I won't be needing a shadow."

Braden glanced over her shoulder toward Ryker. "Will you tell her? Maybe she'll listen to you."

"She won't listen to me. I ignore her wishes when it comes to things like this anyway."

Yeah, which was how he'd ended up tearing her dress off in a Miami hotel room. He'd been worried for her safety…and then she'd been plastered against the wall, panting his name.

Ryker took her arm, urging her to look at him. Laney shifted her attention. "What?"

"Just listen. For once. I'll be back later. Go to my place. I'll meet you there."

Braden practically growled behind Laney. "Can you two not talk like this?"

"Leave the room," Laney spouted over her shoulder. "I'll go home. If you want to come there, you can. I have too much to do."

Ryker nodded. "I'll try not to be too late."

Once he was gone, Laney glanced back at her overbearing babysitter. "You know your hovering and childish attitude aren't going to make my feelings for him go away."

"I've thought about this. I don't like feeling betrayed, but there's so much more at stake. I want you both to realize what's at stake if you fall out. We need him, Laney."

"You think I'm not aware of that? I can't help who I fall in love with, Braden."

He blew out a breath and pulled her into his arms. "Damn it, Laney. I love you both and don't want either of you hurt—even if I'm still pissed at him."

Laney sank into his embrace. "I don't think it's me you have to worry about."

# Fifteen

Ryker searched the obvious hiding places at the former O'Shea home once more: closets, cabinets, old trunks. He made his way to the secret tunnel Zara had showed them. The space was rather small and had no shelves, just a chair in the corner. The tunnel could be accessed at one end from an opening at the kitchen and at the other end from the long hallway. Ryker knew if those scrolls were still here, they'd likely be someplace "hidden" like this where no one would think to look.

He ran his hands over the walls. He'd never thought to look for another secret passage. Who knew what surprises this house had concealed? He covered every square inch of the walls, then worked on the baseboards, the floorboards. The tunnel was clean.

He'd been there for five hours and had covered the basement and main floor. There wasn't a loose floorboard to be found. As he went up to the second floor, the steps creaked, groaning against his weight. He froze. Old steps were bound to crackle and settle, but he'd never explored the stairs. Hadn't even crossed his mind—until now.

Ryker went back down the steps and started there. He knocked on the boards, curious if any were loose or sounded different from the others. He tapped each post on the banister, as well. He'd nearly made it to the top when, two steps from the second-floor landing, he hit pay dirt.

He'd been excited before on other hunts only to be deflated when nothing happened. But he was damn well going to devote every bit of energy he had to fulfilling Patrick's dying wish. Ryker owed him at least that—especially because he hadn't been able to stay away from Laney. That was a debt he'd never be able to repay.

Wrapping his fingers around the outside edge of the wood, Ryker gave a slight tug. The wood creaked as it started to give way. The banister that rested in that particular step splintered. Ryker jerked it out, tossed it down the steps…he'd pay to have it repaired later.

His heart accelerated as he gave the board another pull. Finally it ripped free from the step. He eased down another stair and pulled out the minuscule flashlight he'd shoved into his pocket before coming here.

Bending to get a good view, his chest clenched as he spotted something inside. No way could this be the scrolls. The odds that they'd been right under their noses the entire time was pretty nonexistent. Yet something had brought him back to the old house.

Ryker slid the end of the flashlight between his teeth,

then, using both hands, he reached into the space and tugged out a metal box.

Sinking back onto the step, his back against the wall, he stared at the box as if it held every answer he'd ever wanted. Was this them? He wanted to rip into this box to see, but at the same time he wanted to wait, to hold on to the hope he felt right at this moment. If these were the missing scrolls, Ryker had just accomplished what no one else had been able to.

Zara couldn't have known about this hiding spot in the steps or she would've told them. Which made him wonder if her grandmother even knew.

He set the flashlight aside and pulled the lock-pick kit from his jacket pocket. The box was definitely an antique, turn of the twentieth century, if he was guessing right. He'd been working with and acquiring for the O'Sheas long enough to know antiques. This box may be the one the O'Sheas had used before the scrolls had gone missing.

Carefully he went to work on the old, rusted lock. The box was long but not very wide. Ryker wondered if the scrolls could even fit in something this size. Suddenly the lock clicked and the lid flopped open. Most old locks were harder to pick. Clearly this was meant to be.

"Damn," he muttered. There were tubes inside the box. Nine tubes to be exact. Nine tubes that possibly held the nine scrolls.

Ryker couldn't get into one of the tubes fast enough. He'd barely pried the lid off one when his cell went off.

He ignored it. Nothing was more important than this right here. He didn't want to pull anything out, because if these were the scrolls, they'd be beyond delicate. But once the lid sprang free, he grabbed the light again and angled it inside the cylinder.

This was it. He'd found them. Finally.

There were no words, there was nothing but a sense of accomplishment unlike anything he'd ever known. He'd done it. After years, decades of hunting, Ryker had been the one to find the heirlooms so important to the O'Shea family.

Quickly, but with care, he put everything back into the box.

Glancing at his watch, he realized he'd been at Zara's longer than he first thought. It was late, dark, but there was no way he could let this moment pass. He had to let everyone know.

He sent off a quick text to Mac, Braden and Laney, telling them all to meet at Braden's. Mac should already be there, since that's where he was staying, and Laney…well, who knew where she would be. He hoped at Braden's so she could be safe, but knowing her, she went home and was up to her chin in jasmine-scented bubbles.

Ryker had procured many pieces over the years. He'd traveled all over the world. He'd learned languages, used disguises, made enemies all in the name of loyalty and love for this family.

And he was finally coming home with the one true gift he'd always longed to deliver.

"How the hell had we missed this?" Braden asked.

Laney couldn't take her eyes off the tubes. Nine of them lay on Braden's desk. And they were all there to witness this important moment in the O'Shea family history: Mac, Jenna, Braden, Zara, Laney—and Ryker.

She'd never in her life seen him so excited. The pride on his face… Laney couldn't put into words the transformation.

She'd had news to share with them about some antiques at an old estate not far outside the city that they needed to acquire, but that could definitely wait. This moment had been a long time coming. Decades. And here they all were gathered around her father's old desk. Laney couldn't help but feel as if he were here in spirit.

Tears pricked her eyes, but she blinked them away.

"I never even knew that step was loose, let alone came apart," Zara stated. Shock laced her voice as she, too, continued to stare. "I'm sure my grandmother didn't either or she would've told me. She was only a baby when she went to live there."

"Dad was adamant that there were no hidden areas," Braden chimed in. "We knew of the small tunnel that led into the kitchen, but nothing like this."

Braden turned his attention to Ryker and slapped a hand onto his shoulder. "You did it."

Ryker nodded, not saying a word. He may have appeared to have it all together in that typical Ryker fashion, but Laney knew that inside, he was trying hard to keep his emotions in check.

"I had to," Ryker finally murmured, his eyes fixed on the layout. "I owe you all—"

"Nothing," Braden confirmed. "I know I was pissed at you for the whole Shane incident—and I won't even get into Laney—but I see why you took matters into your own hands this time. If you do it again, though, I'll kill you."

Ryker's mouth twitched, but he merely nodded.

"But this is something I honestly never thought would

happen in my lifetime." Braden's voice grew thick with emotions. "Dad would be so damn proud of you."

A tear trickled down Laney's cheek. Zara wrapped her arm around Laney's shoulders, giving silent support. They were all feeling years' worth of frustration, hope, determination, all rolled into this moment. So many leads, so many cities… Ryker had single-handedly trekked all over the globe in an attempt to bring these home where they belonged.

"We need to get these in the safe," Mac chimed in. "Nobody can know they're here, and the security should probably be bumped up."

"I'm already on it." Work mode, that's what Laney could concentrate on. She swiped her damp cheek. "I have an alarm you can put on just the safe. It's sensitive but necessary."

Braden nodded. "Great. How are you doing on the search for our mole?"

"It's got to be one of the employees at the main office." A sick feeling settled in her stomach at the thought of anyone doing this to her family. "That narrows it down to six. Viviana is the newest employee, but I almost feel she's too obvious. Maybe whoever is doing this is using the timing of her coming on board."

Braden carefully capped the narrow tubes and placed them all back into the shallow box. "Keep everyone working on a regular schedule."

"What?" Mac questioned.

"Keep the enemies close," Ryker added. "Now that we know it was one of them, Laney can keep an eye on everything they're doing on our system."

"And they won't have a clue," she added with a smile.

"This is my favorite part of work. Oh, also freezing assets. I do enjoy knowing our enemies are broke."

Jenna laughed. "I'm so glad I'm on your good side."

Laney couldn't help but widen her smile. "You're safe. The DeLucas on the other hand…"

"What did you do?" Braden asked, his hand resting on the now-locked box.

With a shrug and a surge of pride, Laney met the questioning gazes of her brothers and Ryker. "Merely closed some credit cards, possibly drained their off-shore bank account."

Ryker's eyes widened, his nod of approval giving her another burst of excitement. No way was she going to let them get away with the petty little game they played with Ryker. Braden said no more violence, fine. She didn't get involved with that part anyway. But she could sure as hell ruin someone's life. Hard to keep being a jerk when you were broke and powerless.

"I swear, you scare me sometimes," Braden added. He came around Ryker and gave her a brotherly hug. "Just be careful. I know you make sure things can't be traced back to you, but I still worry. Especially now that you're pregnant."

Laney patted his back, meeting Ryker's gaze over Braden's shoulder. "I'm fine. The only time I'd ever been in physical danger was with Shane."

And thanks to Ryker, Shane was a nonissue.

Laney stepped back, smoothing her sweater over her torso. "Since we're talking work, I have a house out in Bradenton that has several antiques that could be of interest. The owner actually called me today asking if we could come look and discuss adding them to the spring show. I'll give you a heads-up. The price they're wanting is a bit over what I would estimate. But I haven't seen them."

"I'll go." Ryker shoved his hands in his pockets. Laney wondered if that penny was still there after his emotional purging session the other night. "Now that the scrolls have been found, I won't be so tied up and consumed with them. I'll do something normal for a change."

Laney held her breath while Mac and Braden stared at Ryker. After all that had happened—her pregnancy, finding the scrolls—Laney prayed her brothers kept Ryker in their brotherhood.

"You do that," Braden finally said. "Good change of pace for you, and it's only thirty minutes away."

Laney let out the breath she'd been holding. "I'll let them know you'll be there the day after tomorrow."

"All this excitement has me exhausted." Zara circled the group until she came to stand next to Braden. The look she gave her husband implied that she was more than ready for their company to leave. "Ryker, thank you, and please don't think a thing about tearing up the staircase."

Shifting in his stance, Ryker rubbed a hand over the back of his neck. "I'll fix it, you have my word."

"I'm going to head on home," Laney told them all. "I'm pretty tired, and it's way past my bedtime."

She gave her brothers a hug, said her farewells to Jenna and Zara, and when she turned to Ryker, there was no mistaking that hard look he gave her.

"Fine. You'll drive me home, and I'll get my car tomorrow. You don't even have to say it."

"Just to make sure she's safe," Mac chimed in.

Laney whirled. "Not now. We've had a good night. Let's not get into another pissing contest. His eye still hasn't healed."

"I can speak for myself," Ryker added. "I'll take her home, and from that point it's nobody's business."

Braden opened his mouth, but Zara elbowed him in the side. "You love them both. Let them figure out their own relationship."

Braden kept his eyes on Ryker, but Ryker only let out a slight grunt. "I get it," he said, holding his hands up. "If I hurt her, you'll bury me, nobody will find me. You all are the only ones who would look anyway."

Laney placed her hand on Ryker's arm. "Braden and Mac will get over it. We're having a baby. Let's focus on that for now."

She couldn't help but borrow his earlier verbiage. Everything that was happening between her and Ryker was going minute by minute. That's the only way her brothers could take it, as well. Besides, how could she tell them what was going on, where she and Ryker were headed, when she didn't know the answers herself?

Silence surrounded them, and Laney was beyond done with all this veiled testosterone tossing.

"Get her home safely," Braden finally said before Laney could open her mouth.

"That's what he's done for years." She had to remind them of how loyal Ryker truly was. And wasn't that ridiculous? He'd been around for decades and had proven himself over and over. "Ryker isn't the one who betrayed you. Remember that."

Laney marched from the room. Still thrilled about the scrolls, she tried not to let her brothers' archaic attitude ruin her mood. She didn't care where Ryker took her, his house or hers. She intended to show him just how thankful she was about his discovery.

# Sixteen

Whether it was due to the euphoric state of finding the missing scrolls or the fact that he held Laney until she fell asleep, Ryker didn't know, but he'd been unable to relax in her bed. Last night, after they'd left Braden's house, Ryker had every intention of going to his place, but Laney had nearly crawled in his lap in the car, suggesting they go to her house because it was closer. Who was he to argue?

Now he wished he were anywhere else. As he sat in the middle of one of the spare bedrooms, Ryker glanced at all the pieces to this crib. How did all of these damn pieces go together? The picture on the large box in the corner showed what he should end up with, but he'd never built a crib before. Hell, he'd never built anything. His hands had always been used in other not-so-innocent ways.

Ryker glared at the directions, trying to make sense of the pathetic diagrams. Why the hell didn't the company just send someone to assemble the damn thing when you ordered it?

He'd known she'd been looking at furniture, but until he'd walked past the spare bedroom this morning on his way to get coffee, he'd had no idea she'd actually bought a crib. He couldn't sleep and didn't want to wake Laney, so he figured he'd give it his best shot.

He'd stood in the doorway so long just staring. It had never occurred to him where the nursery would be—her house or his. Both? This was where things started to get even murkier. He didn't want to concentrate on all the reasons this path he was on could go wrong.

Yet he couldn't help himself. The level of comfort he was settling into with Laney was hinting at something so much more. He'd spent nights in her bed, the selfish jerk that he was. Ryker just couldn't tear himself away. He'd mentally pushed Laney away for so long, for so many reasons—his childhood was crap and didn't know how to do a relationship, her father had trusted Ryker to always do the right thing, Laney was ten years younger. The list went on and on, pounding away at Ryker's mind.

Frustrated at his insecurities, he pulled over two of the long boards and a pack of screws. That took no time to put together. Perhaps this wouldn't be such a pain and he could have it done by the time Laney woke up.

The sun hadn't even come up yet, so hopefully she'd sleep a little longer. She needed it. Their baby needed it.

Maybe if this crib got assembled, and didn't fall apart, he'd take her out to pick out something else she wanted. He hadn't gotten her a Christmas present. Hell, what would he even get her? She was all sparkles and grace, and he was a wolf in an Italian suit when his leathers wouldn't suffice.

Their worlds may have collided and run parallel for the past several years, but that didn't mean they were on the same playing field.

By the time Ryker got to the sides of the antique, white sleigh-style crib, he was ready to chuck the entire thing out the window and buy her one already assembled.

"I was going to have someone come in and do that for me."

Ryker jerked around. Laney stood in the doorway, her silk robe knotted around her still-narrow waist, her dark hair tousled all around her shoulders. A lump settled heavily in Ryker's throat. How could he take the mob princess and attempt to fit into her world? Not physically, but mentally. He was a damn mess inside, and he didn't need to pay anyone to tell him that.

"Why aren't you asleep?" he asked before turning back to the mayhem that posed as a baby bed.

He wasn't sure how long he'd been in here, but he needed a break. Ryker came to his feet, brushing his hands on the boxer briefs he'd slept in.

"The bed was lonely," she told him, raking her bedroom eyes over his nearly bare body.

Her smoldering looks never failed to make his body stir. The need for her had never been in question. If all of this was physical, if she wasn't Patrick O'Shea's daughter, hell, if she were anybody else, none of this would be in question.

"What's that look about?" She tipped her head to the side and crossed to him. "You found the scrolls, but you still look as if the weight of the world is on your shoulders."

Maybe because it was. The baby, the need to want Laney in his life more... Ryker wasn't even getting into how Braden and Mac still didn't approve. That he could handle. It was the rest of it he wasn't sure of.

"Ryker?"

He closed his eyes and willed his demons to stand down, but they were rearing their ugly heads even harsher than usual.

"We need to take some time—"

"What? Are you seriously going to tell me you need time?" Laney crossed her arms over her chest. "Don't be clichéd, Ryker. I already told you I was waiting for you, that I'd be here for you."

At least one of them was strong right now.

He ran his hands through his hair, his eyes burning from lack of sleep. "I can't get this damn thing together."

"The crib?" Her brows drew in. "This isn't a big deal."

It was everything.

"Do you know my father threw a glass table at me when I was seven?" he asked, needing her to understand. He ran a fingertip along the scar on his chest. "A piece ricocheted off the wall and hit me here. That wasn't the only time he lost his temper, Laney."

"And you think this is going to change how I look at you? Because you're nothing like him."

With a snort, Ryker shook his head. "I'm exactly like him. You do know what I've done for your family for years, right? When you were learning to write cursive in school, I was already doing all the dirty work."

Her eyes narrowed. In a move he didn't predict, she reached up, planted her palms on his bare chest and gave him a shove.

"If you're going to be a coward and worry about losing

your temper with me or our baby, then get out. I won't wait around for you when you're acting like this. I know the man inside, but clearly you have yet to meet him."

Her rage shattered him. "Are you willing to take the chance? I've never done the traditional family thing, and I have one good memory of the first twelve years of my life. That's all."

"Then you should be more determined to make memories with your child."

Could he? Was that even in him? He had no clue what children wanted. All he knew was what Laney deserved.

*If you love it, set it free.*

He stared at her, willing his feet to move, to go into her bedroom and get his things so he could leave. But the pink in her cheeks, the hurt in her eyes and the grim line of her mouth were hard to ignore.

"You have to know I'm distancing myself for the sake of you and the baby." He wanted to reach out and touch her. To let her know he did care, too much, but he had to get inside his own head and sort things out. "I need to know you're safe. That's been my role for so many years, but now I need to know you're safe from me."

"Safe from you? Then stop hurting me," she cried, tears filling her eyes. "You can walk out that door anytime, but don't think it's revolving. You know I love you, damn it, you love me, too. I can see it. You wouldn't be so hell-bent on pushing me away otherwise."

Now he did reach for her, taking her hands in his, holding tight when she tried to jerk away. "There's so much inside me that I need to deal with. Everything hit me so hard all at once…"

Damn it. He shook his head, glancing down to their joined hands. "Your father, your brothers have been the only family I've ever loved. But there's still that demon inside me that is the twelve-year-old boy who wasn't given love and security. I need to get that under control before it controls me."

"It's already controlling you." Now when Laney pulled, he let her go. "You have shut yourself off from real feelings for so long you have no idea how to handle them. You found the scrolls, fulfilled your promise to my father, and now you have all this space in your mind that is filling back up with doubts."

She was so dead-on. There was nothing she hadn't hit directly.

Pulling the V of her robe tighter, she glanced away. "Just go, Ryker. You want to. You want to run and hide and be secluded from anything that threatens you to step outside of your comfort zone."

Damn it, she was his comfort zone. He just knew if he stayed in that space too long, he'd end up destroying it if he didn't get a handle on his past.

"For now, this is for the best." He leaned down to kiss her on the head, but she stepped away, her eyes blazing at him.

Swallowing back his emotions, he moved around her and went back to her bedroom to get dressed. He only prayed he was making the right decision because he wanted Laney, wanted their baby. But he couldn't pull them into his world when he couldn't even handle living in it himself.

So maybe going back to Southie wasn't the best of ideas. But Ryker figured if he wanted to rid himself of the past, he'd need to tackle it headfirst.

So here he stood outside his old apartment building.

The place looked even more run-down than he remembered, and he hadn't thought that was possible. The gutter hung off one side, the wooden steps were bowed, the railing half gone. There was no way this could be deemed livable because if this was the outside, he didn't want to know what the inside looked like.

Snow swirled around him. The house next to the apartments wasn't faring much better, but someone had attempted to brighten it up with a strand of multicolored lights draped around the doorway.

Shoving his hands into the pockets of his jeans, Ryker stared back at the door that led to his dilapidated apartment. For the first twelve years of his life, he'd called this place home. He hadn't known anything different. Much like so many of the kids in this area. Granted, some kids had a happy home life because money wasn't the key to happiness. Having a home that was falling apart was definitely not the same as having an addict father who didn't give a damn.

The penny in his pocket brushed the tip of his fingers. Ryker honestly had no clue where his father was now; he didn't much care, either. Most likely the man had killed himself with all the chemicals he put into his system.

Ryker had actually shed tears after Patrick's death, but felt absolutely nothing when he thought of his biological father.

This place did nothing but bring back memories Ryker hated reliving.

He turned, heading down the street. He'd parked a block away, needing the brisk walk. Keeping his head low to ward off the chill, he headed back to his SUV, which stuck out like the proverbial sore thumb. When he was a kid, if this big, black vehicle had come through, Ryker would've thought it was the president himself.

He'd just stepped off the curb and crossed the street when he noticed movement out of the corner of his eye.

"Mr. Barrett?"

Ryker glanced toward the old building that had sat vacant for several years. It used to be a store of sorts, then a restaurant, and he'd just assumed it would be torn down.

"I thought that was you."

Ryker eyed the man who was unlocking the door to the building. After getting closer, Ryker could see it was Mr. Pauley, a popular contractor around the Boston area. The O'Sheas had used him a few times in the past. The truck behind Ryker's vehicle bore the familiar emblem from Mr. Pauley's company.

"How are you doing, Mr. Pauley?" Ryker called.

"Good. Good. Did you come by to check on the property?"

Confused, Ryker stopped by his car. "Excuse me?"

"Miss O'Shea said she'd be by today." He tugged the door open and held it with his foot as he shoved his keys back into his coat pocket. "I figured since you were here, she sent you."

Miss O'Shea? Laney? What the hell was going on?

Ryker was an O'Shea by default, so there was no questioning why the contractor would think such a thing. Everyone around the area knew full well who the infamous family was, and who Ryker associated with and now called family.

Deciding to play along and figure out what Laney was up to—though after this morning he had no right—Ryker headed toward the open door. Once the two were inside, Ryker glanced around. The place was empty, save for the cobwebs that could only have come from tarantulas, some old boxes and some loose flooring.

"As I told Miss O'Shea the other day, I'm reworking the electrical." Mr. Pauley walked through the space and kept talking as if Ryker knew exactly what was going on. "I'm not sure about the kitchen. I may need to rewire some things in there, especially for the appliances she's wanting to use. This building is definitely not up to par for the two ovens she's suggested."

What the hell was Laney going to do with a building in Southie? Ryker continued following the middle-aged man toward what he assumed was the kitchen.

"She's got in mind she needs to crank out several meals a day. I admire her gumption, but this is going to take a lot of money to keep going."

Glancing at the cracked countertops, a rusted refrigerator, a sink that used to be white, Ryker started spinning ideas in his head. And all of them revolved around the perfectly generous Laney.

"But if anyone can help these kids it's her. Patrick was determined to save people." Mr. Pauley glanced back to Ryker with a side grin. "Anyway, this outside wall would be the best location for the ovens, but the wiring is all off. It can be run here. It's just going to cost more than the initial estimate I gave her. Same with the ventilation. Not much more, but—"

"I'll cover it."

His head was spinning, his mind racing over what could have possibly gotten into Laney's big heart that made her want to do this.

Damn the emotions she forced out of him. She wasn't even here and he was facing things he didn't want to. He was feeling so much...and he wasn't as afraid as he used to be. She'd come into his old neighborhood, she was renovating this old building to help kids…just like he used to be.

But he'd told her about his sordid childhood only days ago. There was no way she could've set things in motion that fast—no matter what her last name was.

Something twisted in Ryker's chest, some foreign emotion he almost didn't want to put a name to. The weight of this newfound feeling seemed to awaken something so deep within him, Ryker wondered how long he'd suppressed everything that was bursting through him now.

His entire life.

Ryker tried to focus back on what Mr. Pauley was saying as he pointed and gestured toward various parts of the spacious area that would become Laney's ideal kitchen.

Whatever Laney wanted, he was completely on board.

# Seventeen

For the second time in as many weeks, Ryker had made a purchase at All Seasons. Now he stood outside Laney's house feeling like a fool. Perhaps this wasn't the way to go about things. Maybe he'd blown his chance when he flipped out over the crib and let all those doubts ruin what they had going on.

Since he left yesterday morning, she'd only texted him once, and that was to remind him of the home in Bradenton. He hadn't gone yet; there were more pressing matters to attend to.

For the first time in his life since becoming part of the O'Shea family, he was putting work on hold.

Because he didn't feel like he deserved to walk right in using his key, he rang the bell and gripped the shopping sack in his hand.

He didn't wait long before the door swung open. Laney

didn't say anything, and he waited for her to slam the door in his face. To his surprise, and relief, she stepped back and gestured for him to come in.

The warmth of her home instantly surrounded him. She had a fire in the fireplace, her tree sparkled with all the lights he'd put on it. This was home, a perfect home for their child to be raised in.

"Did you get to the estate?" she asked, brushing past him and heading back toward the kitchen.

"This is more important."

Laney stopped in her tracks, just as she hit the hallway off the living room. Her shoulders lifted as she drew in a breath and let out a deep sigh. When she turned, Ryker didn't waste any time moving toward her. He was done running, done hurting her, hurting them.

"I brought something for you." He extended the sack, smiling when her eyes caught the name on the side. "You can open it now."

She quirked a brow, kept her eyes on his and reached for the bag. Laney fisted the handles and stepped aside, sinking into the oversize chair. With the bag in her lap, she pulled out the tissue paper. Ryker shoved his hands in his pockets, waiting for her reaction, hoping he'd gone the right route in winning her back.

When she gasped and pulled out a white-and-gold stocking, her eyes immediately filled. That was a good sign...wasn't it?

"There's more." He nodded toward the bag and rocked back on his heels.

She pulled out another stocking, then another. Tissue paper lay all around her, the stockings on her lap as she stared down. Ryker couldn't see her expression for her hair curtaining her face.

Unable to stand the silence, he squatted in front of her.

"I don't have a fireplace," he started, reaching for one of the stockings. "I was hoping we could hang these here."

When she tipped her head to look at him, one tear slid down her cheek. "You put my name on one and yours on the other."

Ryker lay the smaller stocking over the larger ones. "And this will be for our baby. We can have the name put on once we know it."

"How did you…this…I don't even know what to say."

Speechless and in tears. Ryker was taking all of this as a very good sign. But he also knew Laney wouldn't be so quick to let him fully in. He'd been so back and forth, he needed to lay it all on the line and explain to her just what he wanted. Holding back was no longer an option.

"I hope you don't mind. I made a few adjustments to your plans with Mr. Pauley."

Laney's eyes widened as she sat up straighter. Her mouth formed a perfect O, and she continued to stare.

"I went back to my neighborhood, thinking maybe I could settle those demons once and for all." Before he would've gotten up to pace or avoided looking at her face, but he reached for her hands instead. "Mr. Pauley thought I was there to meet with him since you mentioned going by today."

"I…I called him a little bit ago but got his voicemail."

Ryker squeezed her hands. "Why did you start this project, Laney?"

"I wanted to make a difference for some kids." She glanced down at their hands, a soft smile adorning her mouth. "I started this before you ever told me the full story of your childhood. I'd heard enough over the years and always wanted to do something of my own. When I thought about what you went through, I would get so upset. I thought opening a place for kids to come after school would be ideal. They can get help with homework, we can feed them. In the summer, they can play basketball, interact with other kids and hopefully stay out of trouble."

She kept talking until Ryker put his finger over her lips. "You humble me, Laney O'Shea. Those kids are going to love this, love you."

Reaching out, he tipped up her chin with his finger and thumb. "Not as much as I love you."

The catch in her breath had Ryker easing forward, closing the space between them as he covered her mouth with his. He stole only a minor taste, promising himself more later.

"I do love you, Laney. Maybe I always have, but I was damn scared of it." She laughed, her eyes sparkling with more unshed tears as he pushed on. "You knew it, and I'm sorry it took me so long to catch up. But I have this past that sometimes threatens to strangle me and I... I'm working on it, but I can't work on my own. I need you, Laney."

She threw her arms around his neck, crushing the stockings and tissue between them. "I don't want you leaning on anyone else. Because I need you, too."

"I want to be here, with you." He eased back but didn't let go. "Your house is warm, it's perfect for our baby, for us. Our family."

"You want to move in here?" she asked, her eyes widening. "My brothers—"

"Aren't welcome. This is about you, me and our baby. Your brothers have an issue, they can take it up with me. I love you, Laney. I've never loved another woman. I want to be a team with you. All of the things I worried exposing you to, you've understood all along."

Laney's hands framed his face as her eyes searched his. "All of this came from you discovering my project?"

"The project just opened my eyes," he told her. "But why didn't you tell me?"

Laney shrugged, nibbling on her lip. "I didn't tell anyone. I told you I wanted something just for me. I'll tell the guys later, but I didn't do this so you all would be proud. I'm doing it for the kids."

Ryker settled his hands on her belly. "You're going to be the best mother. I can't wait to be a family with you."

Laney rested her forehead against his. "We're already a family."

# Epilogue

"And who are you again?"

Ryker wasn't about to let just anyone into Braden's home. They were in the middle of a celebration. After a month of tiptoeing around the fact he and Laney were living together, the brothers had finally come to realize that Ryker and Laney were a done deal.

But it wasn't so much their relationship they were celebrating. Zara was pregnant again, and Mac and Jenna were closing in on their wedding date. There was plenty to be happy about…except this visitor at their door.

"I'm an investigator. Jack Carson."

Investigator. More like a nosey jerk with too much time on his hands.

"And what do you want?" Ryker asked, curling his fingers around the edge of the door and blocking the narrow opening with his body. "We have attorneys, so if you have an issue—"

"There's been a fire at the home of Mr. and Mrs. Parker in Bradenton."

Ryker froze. "A fire?" He'd just talked to them two days ago. They were still haggling over prices for their antiques. The young couple with a new baby had inherited the estate and all its contents, and they were hoping to earn some money by selling the larger pieces.

"You seem stunned by the news," Carson stated. "You wouldn't know anything about the fire, would you?"

Shocked, Ryker bristled. "How the hell would I know about it since you just told me? Are they all right?"

The investigator's eyes narrowed. "They were killed. Only the baby survived because the nursery was in the back of the house."

Ryker's gut clenched. The thought of an innocent baby without a mother and father was crippling.

"I hate to hear that," he said honestly. "Why are you here telling me this?"

Braden came up behind Ryker and eased the door wider. "Something wrong?"

Ryker nodded to the unwanted guest. "This is Jack something-or-other. Claims he's a PI."

"What's he want?"

Jack went on to explain the fire while Ryker studied the man. There was something about him that was familiar. Despite the expensive suit, the flashy SUV, the man smelled like a cop. But cops didn't make this kind of money, neither did the Feds. This guy was definitely suspicious…and ballsy for showing up here.

"That's terrible," Braden replied once Jack was done with the story. "I'm not sure where we fit in."

"We're just trying to find who set this fire because it appears to be a cover-up." Jack's assessing eyes kept

shifting between Ryker and Braden. "There was a rob-
bery, and most of the antiques were wiped out. The couple actually died from gunshot wounds."

Ryker remained still. "Why don't you quit dancing
around the reason you're here and just spit it out."

"The O'Sheas had been talking with this couple, cor-
rect? About taking some of these antiques to auction?"

Ryker narrowed his eyes. "Our business is none of
your concern."

"It is when there are two dead bodies."

Braden took a step onto the porch. Jack instantly
backed up, but merely crossed his arms as if he was
bored.

"Get the hell off my property," Braden growled. "If
you have a problem, take it up with our attorneys. We
don't talk to random strangers accusing us of something
we know nothing about."

Braden took a step closer, and Ryker wondered if he'd
have to step between these two.

Nah. It was nice seeing Braden get so fired up.

"What cop sent you?" Braden asked

Jack remained silent and tipped his head. The cocky
bastard was seriously getting on Ryker's nerves. Having had enough of this nuisance, Ryker stepped onto the
porch and wedged a shoulder between the two.

"While this is fun and all, we actually have lives to get
back to," Ryker told Jack. "So you're here of your own
accord? No Fed or cop sent you? Then get your nosey
ass off the property."

Clenching his fists at his side, Ryker tried to compose
himself. But if this guy didn't budge soon, he wasn't
going to be responsible for his actions.

Finally, Jack nodded and walked back to his car as if he'd been here for a flippin' Sunday brunch. Arrogance was a hideous trait to witness.

Once the guy was gone, Ryker turned to go back inside, but Braden hadn't budged. He was still staring at the spot where Jack's SUV had been parked.

"Don't let him get to you," Ryker stated. "It's a shame about that couple, but they can't pin any of that on us when we didn't do it."

Braden shook his head. "Did you see his eyes?"

"What?"

Braden looked to Ryker. "That guy. Did you look at his eyes? They seemed so familiar."

Ryker agreed. A shiver crept up his back. He didn't like when he got this feeling. Things never ended well.

"I don't think he was a PI." Braden ran a hand over the back of his neck and started heading toward the house. "We'll talk to Mac later, but for now keep this little visit between us."

Ryker fell into step beside him. "We need to watch our backs. Who knows who the hell this guy is."

It was hard for Ryker to put the mysterious man out of his mind, but when he walked into the house and Laney met him in the hallway, he found himself smiling. She had the slightest baby belly, only visible when she wore something tight. Today she had on a body-hugging dress with tights and boots. She was so damn sexy.

"I wondered where you went," she told him. "Who was at the door?"

Braden moved on into the living room, leaving Ryker and Laney in the foyer. "Nobody important," he replied.

They hadn't discovered the mole, yet, but it was only a

matter of time. Ryker wasn't giving up on bringing down the culprit who was hellbent on destroying the only family he'd ever known.

Laney's arms looped around his neck. "If you're done celebrating here, I'm ready to go home and celebrate privately."

Ryker whispered in her ear exactly what they would be doing in private, and Laney melted against him.

This was his woman, his forever family. They'd been his all along…all he'd had to do was reach out and claim them.

* * * * *

# The torment that blazed on his face solidified her belief.

"You don't know what you're risking."

"I have nothing more to risk, Ivan."

His head tilted back against her hand, a growl rumbling deep in his chest. He was resisting because he did fear he'd hurt her.

Anastasia had to make him believe her that he wouldn't, had to make him stop holding back. Her other hand slipped around his neck, coaxing his face down to hers, needing to snap his hesitation. "The only injury I could have sustained was letting you go without being with you one more time."

Moving closer, she lowered her arms to hug all she could of him, a breath she'd been holding for seven years flowing out in tortured relief. Until he stiffened in her embrace.

Before she could withdraw in mortification, his formidable body surrendered.

Then suddenly he was pushing away and she was off her feet and in his arms.

\* \* \*

**His Pregnant Christmas Bride**
is part of The Billionaires of Black Castle series—
Only their dark pasts could lead these men
to the light of true love.

# HIS PREGNANT CHRISTMAS BRIDE

BY
OLIVIA GATES

First Published in Great Britain 2016
By Mills & Boon, an imprint of HarperCollins*Publishers*
1 London Bridge Street, London, SE1 9GF

© 2016 Olivia Gates

ISBN: 978-0-263-91885-4

51-1116

Printed and bound in Spain
by CPI, Barcelona

*USA TODAY* bestselling author **Olivia Gates** has written over forty books in action/adventure, thriller, medical, paranormal and contemporary romance. Her signature is her über-alpha male heroes. Whether they're gods, black-ops agents, virtuoso surgeons or ruthless billionaires, they all fall in love once and for life with the only women who can match them and bring them to their knees. She loves to hear from readers, so don't hesitate to email her at oliviagates@gmail.com.

# One

The beeping of the instruments measuring Anastasia Shepherd's vitals quickened as she surfaced from her oppressive slumber.

But she didn't want to wake up. She preferred the horrors she faced in sleep over the nightmare her life had become after the attack that had ended her brother's life, and left her struggling for hers.

She squeezed her lids harder against the macabre images. The masked gunmen, the muted gunfire, the crimson blossoming over Alex's white shirt as he collapsed beside her, bullets tearing into her own body.

In her shock, she'd somehow known she wouldn't die, not immediately. She'd also known one other thing. That she'd needed to protect her brother from further injury with whatever was left of her life. She'd thrown herself over Alex's body as their attackers approached them like inescapable doom.

But she'd only seen them fall. Like disposable opponents in a vicious video game at the hands of an expert player. It had made no sense. Until she'd seen *him*.

Ivan.

The man who'd walked away from her without a word seven years ago.

He'd swooped down on her and Alex, and right before darkness had claimed her, she'd heard him say what she'd dreamed he'd come back one day and say.

*I'm here now.*

And he'd been with her ever since. Through the whole ordeal of the past three weeks. Always sitting beside her bed like a sentinel. Watching over her, catering to her every need. Answering none of her questions.

"It isn't a mercy anymore, Ivan."

The words she hadn't intended to voice just came out, laden with all her agony and frustration, before she even opened her eyes.

Ivan made no response, probably thinking she was talking in her sleep. But she felt him move closer, until he was standing over her.

She finally forced her eyes open and was once again overwhelmed by his sheer beauty and physical presence.

He'd always been the most incredible man she'd ever seen. The exact combination that had appealed to her every taste and enslaved her every sense. In the short time she'd known him, she hadn't been able to tear her eyes and thoughts off of him. Not to mention her hands, lips and every inch of her. No man had ever compared to him, before or since; she'd given up before she'd even tried.

But the thirty-three-year-old juggernaut she'd once known had been nothing compared to the forty-year-old god he'd become.

Everything about him had been…magnified, intensified, until it choked her up just looking at him, just feeling him near. Any softness she hadn't even realized he'd had had been chiseled away. What remained looked as if it had been carved from polished steel, perfect and impenetrable.

If she didn't feel like one raw, exposed nerve, she knew she would have found him even more attractive for it. But how could she possibly be more attracted to him now than she had been in the past? From that first glance, when her brother introduced him as a new friend and another expatriate from their motherland, Russia, she'd been helplessly drawn to him like iron filings were to a magnet.

"Anastasia, are you awake?"

It seemed he wasn't sure, even with her eyes open and locked on his. She must have sleep-talked too many times.

She answered him by pressing the bed's remote, bringing herself up to a reclining position. "Avoiding my questions, giving me no details or explanations, is only making it worse."

When she'd thought nothing could make the devastation of losing Alex so violently any worse.

Her brother, her mentor and champion and closest friend, was gone. *Murdered.* That she'd survived was irrelevant. Unfair. If one of them had to die, it should have been her. Alex was far more important, in so many ways, to so many more people.

But not knowing why or who had been responsible for this heinous crime ate away at her sanity.

Ivan had only told her that he'd snatched her and Alex from the scene before law enforcement or emergency services had arrived, had provided them with lightning-fast medical stabilization while transporting them to his partner, Antonio Balducci, the only doctor he could trust with their lives.

She'd known Ivan and his partners in Black Castle Enterprises were extremely rich and powerful, but this level of reach and resources was mind-boggling. Ivan had been able to intervene faster than the authorities, who clearly hadn't even been alerted, since nobody had come investigating the attack. While this state-of-the-art hospital that far surpassed any medical facility she'd ever heard about was off-the-map. That something of that caliber was unknown to the world spoke of unimaginable power.

But though Dr. Balducci's fame had reached even her in the nonmedical world, as a genius trauma surgeon whose work bordered on magic, he'd managed to save only her.

Dr. Balducci had told her Ivan's intervention had given them a shot at surviving when nothing else could have. But only she had been in any condition to do so, even with his unequaled skills. There had been no saving Alex.

And she still didn't understand *why*. Any of it. The attack, Ivan's reappearance, anything he'd done ever since. Each time she inquired, Ivan merely insisted she wasn't strong enough yet to worry about anything but recuperating. He wouldn't tell her a thing.

He'd been the only man she'd ever loved, and he'd streaked in and out of her life like a meteor, leaving only wreckage in his wake. For him to be back in her life in such an explosive, inexplicable way had at first paralyzed her ability to think. Now speculation and confusion were driving her insane.

"Just tell me everything. *Please*."

His solicitous gaze became a stormy sea-green in the warmly lit hospital suite, as he clearly struggled with his reluctance to do so. Then his massive chest finally expanded on a resigned inhalation.

"I only wanted you to recuperate without having to deal with distressing details. I also wanted to…resolve the situation before I told you everything." He lowered his head for a moment before he looked up at her again. "I'm sorry if I inadvertently added to your anguish. That was the last thing I wanted to do."

Had he also thought he'd been sparing her when he'd left her seven years ago? Had he been trying not to "add to her anguish" by leaving without a word or warning?

Now that she thought about it, probably. He'd always felt somewhat…detached from the rest of humanity. Now he seemed to be wholly so. He probably had no insight into how he made others feel, how his actions impacted them. It stood to reason he didn't realize that he'd almost destroyed her by his sudden and unexplained desertion in the past—and was as equally clueless how his actions affected her now.

Not that she could be bitter about his actions this time. He had saved her. Had been dedicated to her physical well-being. He was merely oblivious to the rest of her needs, emotional and psychological. Like he'd always been.

Raising the bed to a fully sitting position, she vaguely noted that the surgical wound across her abdomen where Dr. Balducci had put her back together barely pulled. It now caused her minimum discomfort, even with reduced pain medication.

"I'm sorry, too, Ivan. The last thing I want is to seem ungrateful after everything you've been doing for me. I'm more grateful than I can say. But I not only can handle the full truth now, I need it. Nothing could be worse than what already happened, and the only way I can deal with it is to make sense of it all."

That seemed to flabbergast him. She'd been right. He'd never even considered this could be how she'd be feeling.

When he finally nodded, his hands fisted at his sides. Hands that had once owned her body in total intimacy. But that had been in another life. In this new realm, he hadn't once touched her since he'd squeezed her hand as he'd told her of Alex's death.

"I'll tell you everything you want to know," he said, looking like he'd rather take a bullet himself than do so. "But I need you to promise something first." She nodded, wary at the flare in his eyes. "Never apologize for anything. Or feel grateful. Never to me."

It really seemed to offend him, even pain him, that she'd expressed her regret and gratitude.

Would she ever understand the enigma that was Ivan Konstantinov?

No. It didn't matter that she never would. This wasn't about him, or about them. This was about Alex. She had to know why he'd been murdered, how she could avenge him.

Once he had her conceding nod, he exhaled forcibly. "You were attacked because of Alex's discoveries and intentions."

Ivan waited a beat, no doubt to see her response. She had none.

He grimaced. "I know about the top-secret, alternative energy project Alex was helming for FuturEn in conjunction with the multinational International Energy Organization, and that you were taking part as one of his top physicists. No need to pretend you don't know what I'm talking about."

She shook her head dazedly. "I'm not pretending anything." He looked as if he'd cut her off, but she hurried to add, "It doesn't surprise me that you know this. Now that I have a better idea of the extent of your power, it would surprise me if you didn't know everything about everyone who's ever crossed your path. What I don't understand is why Alex would be targeted for assassination for his work. It isn't as if he's the first person to ever make a breakthrough in such a field."

"You really don't know, do you?" When she shook her head, his teeth made a terrible grinding sound. He clearly hated that he had to explain more than he'd bargained for. "I expected as his research partner and sister, he'd confided in you that he'd discovered tampering at the highest levels in both the private research facility and the IEA to falsify his results."

The revelation hit her like a punch to her tender gut.

She slumped back, the ever-hovering tears flowing down her cheeks again.

Ivan stabbed a hand in his raven mane, his frown one of realization. "He must have wanted to shield you from it all, must have wanted to expose the fraud without your involvement to protect you. Yet it's clear he didn't think they'd decide to silence him forever."

A sob tore through her even as she struggled to bring herself under control. "H-how did you find all that out when I didn't even suspect any of it?"

The reluctance to give her information about himself, what had always been his default, tightened his face further. "I have my ways, Anastasia."

Yeah. That he had. Being called the king of the cyber world must mean he had an ear and an eye, not to mention a hand, in just about everything that made the world go round.

"But if you found out the liquidation plan, why didn't you warn Alex? Or…did you warn him and he didn't believe it would come to that?"

"Alex was very careful in covering his tracks as he investigated the culprits and gathered evidence against them. So careful even I didn't trace it until he requested an emergency meeting with all key players in the project, no doubt to make his revelation. It was just a couple of hours before the meeting when I pieced together the whole thing."

She bit her trembling lip. "The meeting he told me he'd go to alone."

"He wanted you away from any possible fallout, which he probably thought would only involve professional setbacks or legal repercussions. It's clear he didn't realize how huge this was to those he was going to expose. He didn't imagine they'd kill to stop him." His jaw muscles bunched and those emerald eyes grew more turbid. "In the tight time I had, I had two options: alerting the police with an unsubstantiated claim, and only having them protect Alex temporarily if they even moved in time. Or I had to intervene myself, as the one equipped to effect comprehensive and permanent protection. I tried to call Alex to tell him to stay put until I came to extract him. I sent him messages, to no avail. And though I suspected you wouldn't be with him, I tried you, too. I had no response from you, either."

"He—he always forgot to take his phone off Mute. I keep mine on Vibrate, but I hadn't even looked at my phone that morning. I—I was too focused on getting to him before he left for that meeting."

"I almost went out of my mind being unable to reach either of you so I could warn you."

"But how did you get to us in time?" This she had to know.

His grimness deepened. "I didn't get to you in time."

"You almost did…"

"Almost doesn't count. I couldn't save Alex."

She swallowed another red-hot shard of agony at the reminder. "What I mean is, how were you so close that you reached us so quickly?"

"My Black Castle headquarters, with my apartment above it, is half an hour's drive from your labs. I came by helicopter."

He'd been that close? She'd spent the past years thinking he'd returned to Russia, or was flitting around the world, never settling in one place like he'd once said he never would. Had he been that close all along? So near she could have stumbled upon him on the streets?

Maybe she had. Maybe it was why she'd always felt him around her. Maybe he'd crossed her path many times but had remained out of sight.

He went on. "On the way, I saw the GPS signals of your phones next to each other. My blood froze when I realized you were together when you've been working in different labs during this phase of the research."

She nodded, stunned yet again at the extent of his knowledge of her and Alex's routines and the latest developments in their research, not to mention his ability to track them with such pinpoint accuracy. "I had a feeling Alex wasn't telling me something important about that emergency meeting so I went to him instead of going to my lab. To see if I could persuade him to let me join him."

His nod was terse, bleak. "The moment I realized you were together, I knew it would be the perfect time for them to strike. I knew they'd assume what I did, that he'd taken you into his confidence and you had to be eliminated with him. I have no doubt they would have leveled the whole building to destroy all evidence had I not arrived when I had."

The memories assaulted her, vivid and palpable. She choked as she felt as if she'd been thrown back into the horrifying moments all over again. "I'd just walked into his lab…and before I could say anything to him, they—they…"

Horror and agony filled her throat again, sealing it, cutting off her words, her breath. But she had to ask, had to know.

"I—I saw our attackers fall. Did you…?"

Ivan again looked as scary as he had during those moments when he'd swooped down on her and Alex. "I took care of them."

"You k-killed them?"

Her answer was a terrifying flare in his eyes. Not only affirming that he had, but also telling her he wanted nothing more than to resurrect them so he could have the pleasure of killing them over and over, this time slowly, agonizingly.

This was an Ivan she hadn't known, hadn't dreamed existed. Not the virtuoso cyber entrepreneur or the dream lover. This was a seasoned warrior, a remorseless exterminator. It made her wonder again if she'd ever truly known him.

Not that seeing this lethal side to him upset or scared her. It didn't even occur to her to be bothered about the illegality of his actions. He'd exacted immediate revenge that she considered just. Had she been able to, she would have done the same.

The need to know what else he'd done burned her. "What else did you do? Besides get us here?"

"I erased every sign of the attack."

"You removed the bodies?"

His nod was so matter-of-fact it made her wonder how many times he'd been involved in situations like this. It seemed this man she was discovering she knew very little about had dealt with lethal scenarios so many times before, he'd developed an unblinking ability to take ruthless action and had all the resources in place to resolve any problem. She'd only heard about such power and abilities in spy and black ops thrillers. So who exactly was Ivan Konstantinov?

She prodded him for more details. "What did you do with them?"

Ferociousness simmered again in his eyes. "No need to

concern yourself with them, ever again. No one will ever find them. Along with the evidence of what they did to you and Alex." At her confused expression he continued. "To your colleagues and employers, Alex had to cancel the meeting as both he and you had to leave on emergency family business. To your families, you're on sensitive, confidential work-related business that necessitated you leave immediately and remain out of contact until it's over. I send them messages from both your phones regularly to reassure them."

So he'd really covered every angle. Still, her breath came out in painful spurts as she imagined their families. Three weeks had passed since their abrupt disappearance. "They must still be going mad with worry."

His frown darkened. "I know. I try my best to placate them but I can only postpone their devastation, as this served many purposes."

Unable to contain her frustration anymore, she seethed. "What purposes? Why won't you let me contact them? Why don't you want the police involved even now? What—"

He cut off her agitated questions, his voice and gaze soothing, compelling. "Because I needed to keep the assassins' masters in the dark about what happened until I dealt with them all."

"That's why you didn't take us to a regular hospital and had Dr. Balducci take charge of us there?"

His eyes flooded with what looked like relief, that she'd reached that conclusion. "I couldn't even take you to one of his publicly known medical facilities where you could have been seen and recognized. I had to make sure those involved in the crime would never pose danger to you or anyone of yours, or anyone at all, ever again." At the fresh surge of tears in her eyes, he gritted his teeth again. "I know now I should have told you more of this sooner. But

I still wouldn't have let you contact your family. It would have placed them in danger if they'd learned any of it before I concluded everything."

"And did you? Conclude everything?"

"I'm putting the finishing touches on it all today."

This probably meant far worse than she, in her previously oblivious life, could imagine. Even now, she couldn't speculate on what he was doing. But after finding out the truth of the big picture, she no longer wanted to know the details.

But one thing she did know—Ivan was unstoppable. Whatever it took to end this with no more damage or danger to her or any of Alex's loved ones, he would do it. He'd already done it, was just wrapping up the loose ends now.

And no matter what he'd said, she was grateful, with all the ferocity of the agony and rage that were the only things fueling her will to live now.

He stood straighter, his eyes taking on a solemn cast. "Now you know. But there's one thing more I need you to understand. You have nothing to fear anymore, Anastasia. Never again. I pledge it."

His vow, along with the ramifications of his revelations, sank deep in her mind, drying her tears, stifling her agitation. She stared up at his hard, arresting face, and felt even more confusion and questions swamping her.

Years ago he'd been her lover, the embodiment of all her fantasies, the sum total of everything she could have never dreamed of. Then one day it was over. He'd said he was traveling on business. Then he'd never contacted her again.

The end had been so sudden she would have believed something terrible had happened to him if she hadn't read about him in media sources that covered the rich and famous. It had forced her to stop her efforts to contact him after one unanswered try. For only one thing could explain his ending it like that. In their incendiary, if short-lived affair, all the passion and emotion had only been on her side.

Yet everything he'd been doing since the attack contradicted that assumption. None of that was the actions of a man who cared nothing for her, or for Alex, whom he'd cut off as well. Everything he'd told her proved he'd kept close tabs on her. He'd come to their rescue without a moment's hesitation, and he continued to go to unimaginable lengths to eliminate any further danger to her and her family, and to avenge Alex. He'd been unwaveringly there for her through this ordeal, by her side from the moment he'd rescued her.

It was beyond confusing. But she was also beyond attempting to make sense of it all.

She could do nothing but let him steer the situation as he saw fit. He had all the knowledge, and all the power, while she was demolished, fragile in body and psyche.

She nodded weakly, accepting his vow and admitting her need for his protection, then lowered her aching, trembling body back to a supine position.

"I know you don't want thanks, Ivan, but you have mine. I'd do anything to repay you." His growl started to interrupt her but she closed her eyes, aborting his exasperation. Before she let exhaustion drag her into nothingness again, she whispered one last thing. "Let me know when you decide it's safe to contact our families."

Ivan watched Anastasia's breathing even out until it was the imperceptible movements that had at first sent him berserk, thinking it was a sign of deterioration.

But he'd been finding other things to compromise his sanity—her gemlike azure eyes, which had turned muddy, her peaches-and-cream complexion and even her long, thousand-hues golden hair that had become ashen, and her body, which had lost its lush curves and looked more fragile by the day.

But Antonio had kept assuring him she was getting better, and he'd been by her side day and night making sure she continued to do so, watching for every sliver of improvement.

Now the last words she'd said before she'd slipped back into oblivion reverberated in his head.

*Our families.*

She'd meant her and Alex's families: their parents, Alex's wife and children, and his in-laws, who were like a second family to both of them.

She couldn't know one of those families was his, too.

Keeping that fact a secret, keeping away from that family, had been one of the two reasons he'd forced himself to walk away from her and Alex years ago. Though he'd told her a lot today, that was one revelation he was keeping to himself. As it was, what he'd revealed of the tragedy had hit her hard enough.

But she'd made him tell her. And soon the need to keep their families in the dark would be over and her family's grief would only add to hers.

Dealing with the scum responsible for Alex's murder had been the easy part of this disaster. The hard part—and what kept getting harder—was dealing with everything that concerned Anastasia. His dread for her. His inability to give her her life back, with her body intact and her brother alive. And the expectation that he'd soon have to relinquish her again.

But the hardest thing of all was her very nearness.

When he'd deprived himself of it seven years ago, he'd thought he'd eventually become numb to the loss. It had taken one look into her eyes, in those nightmarish moments when he'd thought he'd been too late to save her, to prove how wrong he had been.

He hadn't been numb; he'd been shut down completely. It had been the only way to continue functioning. The injury of her loss, what he'd inflicted on himself, agonized and hardened him like none of the ordeals of his hellish past had. And that had been when she'd been alive and well. In the time he'd thought she might die, too, he'd known he wouldn't survive losing her for real.

But he hadn't lost her. Antonio had saved her.

At first he'd hidden Alex's fate from her, and the details of what he'd done, in order to hide his true nature. Anastasia and Alex had known him as Ivan Konstantinov, not Wildcard, The Organization's lethal mercenary with a body count that neither of them could have thought existed except in fictional tales or real-life stories of monsters.

But she'd insisted on seeing Alex until he had to tell her the truth. Watching her almost disintegrate with grief, he'd been grateful he hadn't told her she'd only survived because of the liver transplant she'd gotten from Alex.

As it had turned out, he should have told her, not about the transplant, but about the rest. Now that she was privy to everything, she was letting him deal with everything as he saw fit. He should have trusted her then to make the rational decision. After all, the Anastasia he knew never let emotions interfere with pragmatic priorities.

When he'd walked away, she'd only tried to contact him once. When he'd made no response, she'd gone on with her life as if those magical weeks they'd shared hadn't happened.

At first, instead of being relieved that his desertion hadn't hurt her, that she'd decided to just move on, he'd hated it, had felt such contrary bitterness that had made him even more ruthless and cynical.

But he'd still been unable to stop watching her and Alex obsessively. And as time had gone by and she'd been too busy with her scientific studies and research career to move on, he'd felt perverse pleasure that she hadn't replaced him. Even if she had, he still would have helped her. And he had, opening doors for her and Alex that would have remained closed otherwise. Their success had been deserved, but even in the world of science, it wasn't always merit that saw someone get their dues. He'd seen to it that they did.

It had remained a struggle to keep away even when he'd believed her better off without him. He lived in fear his past would catch up with him and he'd place her and Alex in danger. That had been the main reason he'd walked away.

It was such tragic irony that when fatal danger had targeted her and Alex, it had had nothing to do with him.

His phone buzzed in his pocket. Getting it out before the noise could wake her, he read the message he'd been waiting for. Fyodor, his right hand, affirming his latest move had been carried out.

Alex's murderers had been neutralized.

There was no reason to put off contacting Anastasia's and Alex's families anymore.

Not that his reluctance had anything to do with caring what *they* would suffer once they knew the truth. If not for them being Alex's family, if it wasn't for them continuing to impact Anastasia's life, he wouldn't have considered them at all.

After all, they were the people who'd sent him to hell.

# Two

"Don't discharge her."

Ivan blocked Antonio's path in the deserted corridor, intercepting him on the way to Anastasia's room.

His best friend's turbid eyes clashed with his unwaveringly, in their depths things Ivan had never seen before. Not even during their worst days as The Organization's captives and mercenaries.

Antonio had always been their brotherhood's most sangfroid member, at times seeming inhuman in his ability to deal with any level of hardship or abuse with a level head and a cool smile. Even as his closest friend from childhood, who'd seen deeper into him than anyone else ever had, he'd never thought Antonio could feel like this, let alone be unable to hide it. Despondent, desperate, even a little unhinged.

But then what had seemed impossible had happened. Antonio had fallen in love. Violently, irrevocably. And Liliana, the woman who'd created a heart inside him to worship her with—in his friend's own words—had discovered the truth. That he'd started their relationship as a plot to infiltrate their joint family, to destroy them from within. Liliana now believed he'd never loved her, had only proposed as means to an end. Devastated at the discovery, she'd run away from his efforts to explain... and she'd almost been fatally injured in doing so. After spiraling through ten different kinds of hell as he'd operated on her, too, he'd saved her life. But clearly, not her love. Liliana's rejection seemed final.

Now Antonio, the surgeon with nerves of steel, was a total mess. Which could actually work to Ivan's advantage right now.

The old Antonio, whose emotions never played a role in his actions and decisions, would have turned down his demand, since there was no medical merit to it. But Antonio the emotional volcano might sympathize with his plight and do what Ivan wanted.

And what he wanted was to postpone Anastasia rejoining the world, and her family.

Shaking his head, Antonio said, "I have already kept her longer than necessary, to be on the safest side possible. There's now no medical reason not to let her go back to her life."

A shiver ran down Ivan's spine. Antonio's voice now was the scariest thing he'd ever heard. Such barely contained instability from the most controlled being he'd ever known.

He only hoped dragging Antonio into his own concerns would distract him from dwelling on his regrets and the loss of the woman who'd become his only reason for living.

"Listen, Tonio, I'm eternally grateful for what you've done for...Anastasia." It was still hard to say her name, even to Antonio. He hadn't told him a thing about her until she'd realized her surgeon didn't even know her name and provided him with it. "I'm thankful that she has healed enough for you to think she should be discharged—" He grabbed Antonio's arm when he turned away. "But I'm still demanding you don't do it."

Irritation flickered in Antonio's eyes at Ivan's detainment. "And you're not going to give me a reason for your demand?"

Ivan's fingers dug harder into Antonio's steel arm in frustration. "My asking it should be reason enough for you."

Antonio finally took exception to Ivan's effort to coerce him, prying his hand off his arm with equal vehemence. "It was when you were asking me to help her. I didn't need to know anything then. I was willing to wait forever for you to tell me why she and her brother were shot or who they are to you. But now you're asking me to lie to her, to keep her here against her will."

"Who says it would be against her will?"

"She does. She wants to leave."

"She wants no such thing. And she certainly said nothing to you. I was there every second you were with her."

A ghost of the teasing they'd always engaged in from childhood came into Antonio's gaze. "Yeah, that you were. But I let you sit in during my checkups only as a courtesy to you as my best friend, against my professional and better judgment." Any hint of that indulgence vanished, and he started moving past him. "So don't push your luck, Ivan."

Ivan grabbed both his arms this time. He wasn't letting him walk away. "I'm pushing more than that, Tonio. You might think she's ready to leave based on her physical condition, but I know what's best for her."

Antonio gave the hands digging into his flesh a disdainful look. "It's clear your need to keep her here is blinding you to *her* needs. But *I* feel her need to leave."

"You might be an unequalled genius, Tonio, but not even

you are omniscient. Hell, you didn't even suspect what your own lover would feel if she knew the truth."

The moment the words were out, Ivan could have happily cut off his own tongue. The surge of self-loathing that came into Antonio's eyes would remain one of his stupidest, cruelest mistakes.

Ivan dropped his hands to his side, exhaled heavily. "I didn't mean it the way it sounded."

Antonio waved his qualification away. "I did know how she'd feel and that's why I hid the truth. *That* was my mistake."

"*I'm* not making one. She needs to stay here longer."

"If you think so, then you're having a serious judgment malfunction. She may not have asked to be discharged, but I sense she can't wait to bolt from here." Before Ivan could flay him with another contradiction, Antonio folded his arms over his white-coated chest. "Let me remind you that your specialty is ending lives, not saving them like me. Including yours, many times as I recall. So I'm the expert here."

"Not where Anastasia is concerned."

"Actually, in her case, your verdict is even more suspect, since you're clearly what I thought was impossible—emotionally involved. Even if it's in a way I can't fathom. It makes you even more ineligible to make decisions on her behalf."

Ivan felt his frustration rising to a suffocating level as his friend's eyes emptied of all agitation and became ice-cold blue.

Great. In his attempt at taking Antonio's mind off his estranged lover, he'd only brought out the immovable surgeon in him. To his own detriment.

He exhaled, pissed off at himself, at Antonio and all of existence. "Is this your roundabout way of forcing me to tell you about my involvement with her? You think you've found the best leverage to satisfy your curiosity?"

Antonio gave a disgusted shrug. "Right now I couldn't care less if the whole world, including you, disappeared, ended or even went to hell. But the one thing still functioning about me is my surgeon side." Yeah, like Ivan had just thought. "Professionally, I am obliged to tell her she's well enough to go. After that, she can choose to stay longer, or you convince her to stay. But I will tell her the truth. I won't let you hold her hostage to your own ends and convictions." Ivan started to protest, but Antonio raised a hand in a gesture of finality. "Either you give me a good enough reason not to discharge her, Ivan, or get out of my way."

So this was it. The only way Antonio would budge now was if Ivan played his last card. Much as he hated it, he had to tell him everything.

"Fine, I'll give you the reason." Feeling as if he was about to jump off a cliff, he inhaled a bolstering breath. "Got something stronger than coffee around here?"

Antonio turned away and started walking back toward his office. "I have medical-grade alcohol."

He fell into step with him. "Yeah, I forgot for a second there that you don't drink."

"Even if I did, I wouldn't keep my vices around my place of work."

"Yeah, well, for me to finally tell you what happened in my life before we met, we'll probably both need something."

"I have intravenous morphine." Antonio walked through his door, left Ivan to close it behind them. "Though I probably need sodium pentothal if I want anything approaching the truth. The maximum dose, for an elephant. You're the most drug-resistant ogre I've ever encountered."

Ivan threw himself on the black leather couch while

Antonio sat in his preferred armchair. "Still harping on when you wasted three times the dosage of anesthetic to put me under when you had to pull the shrapnel out of my thigh? I'd told you to do it with me awake. You're the one who wouldn't listen."

"I'll listen now." Antonio leaned forward and reached for the carafe on the table, poured one cup of black coffee. Ivan knew it was for him when Antonio added three spoons of sugar, as he knew he took it.

Grumbling that it was a poor substitute for Scotch, he took the cup from Antonio, at once taking a gulp, letting its contents scorch his throat.

Antonio sat back, leveled his gaze on him dispassionately. "So are you going to talk, or are you again going to be the elusive son of a bitch who never told even me anything about your past?"

Ivan snorted. "As if you were any better. You found out everything about your family and kept it to yourself, hatched this moronic vengeance plot that is now costing you the love of your life. If you'd told me, I would have probably saved you from making that catastrophic mistake."

"Yeah, sure. You would have saved me from myself."

"As I recall, I did, on a few notable, potentially fatal, incidents."

Antonio's frown took on a defensive edge. "I didn't want to share specifics until I felt I had something worthwhile to share. Besides, it's different. I didn't spend the last thirty years hiding the truth about my past from you. I didn't know anything about it until recently. But you came to The Organization old enough to know everything about yours."

"Touché." Ivan's grunt acknowledged the inequality of their positions. He'd always felt Antonio didn't like that he kept him, of all people, in the dark. But he'd never pushed.

He was pushing now. And maybe it was just as well.

Maybe he needed to purge the poison bottled up in his system. And who better to help him do it but his best friend and the world's leading healer?

When he didn't start talking at once, Antonio started to rise. "Seems you do need a shot of sodium pentothal to help loosen that calcified tongue of yours."

Ivan barked a mirthless laugh at his friend's threat and gestured for him to settle down. "I'll talk without a truth serum. But when I do, you'll end up doing what I demanded. So maybe you should just save yourself listening to the heap of crap that is my life story and just do as I say."

Antonio sat back, waving nonchalantly. "What's new? I've been taking your crap since I was eleven. Talk already. But whatever you say, there's no guarantee it'll change my mind."

"Oh, it will."

"*No* guarantee."

"All right, fine. Here goes, then." At Antonio's encouraging nod, he felt he got a glimpse of his oldest and closest friend again. It made it easier to start. "I was born Konstantin Ivanovich in Russia before the collapse of the Soviet Union." He paused as understanding flared in Antonio's eyes. Every member of their brotherhood had explained why he'd adopted his current name, except Ivan. "Yes, that's why I chose my name. Very predictable." He inhaled, went on. "During the upheaval leading to the collapse, my father found himself in a dangerous position. He'd inherited his job as a bookkeeper in Russia's organized crime and he needed out—out of the mob, and of the country. There was one great opportunity where he could take our family to the United States, and it all depended on me.

"I was only twelve, but I had long been recognized as a prodigy of computer programming. My abilities had meant a lot to my father's bosses. But he said there was this international organization offering children of exceptional abilities a unique opportunity to grow their skills to unprecedented levels, in return for developing the next level of technologies. If I joined them, they would use their influence to send my family to the United States.

"Everything was concluded quickly, and I was proud and eager to go in return for a safe and free life for all of us. My parents assured me I'd join them once I finished my two-year stint with The Organization and they'd established new identities. I soon realized that would never come to pass."

Like all the boys The Organization took, he'd realized after the first hellish weeks that he was a slave they had no intention of letting go, one they'd turn into a mercenary and lethal weapon.

At first he'd refused to be of any use to them no matter how much they tortured him, hoping they'd let him go. They'd only been too glad to escalate their abuse.

He exchanged a look with Antonio, filled with all the memories of their similar ordeals. "At one point I felt my mind and spirit breaking. I contemplated ending my life… and then you approached me."

Antonio had been a year younger, had introduced himself as Bones, as they'd been forbidden to use anything but the code names The Organization had given them. Antonio had already been selected for medicine because of his aptitudes—he'd been there since he was four. His friend had imparted on him the wisdom of his years with The Organization, convincing him to play along, so he'd become valued and be given privileges.

Then Antonio had offered him a lifeline. He'd asked him to join the brotherhood he belonged to. It was a group of boys selected and led by Numair, The Organization's top recruit, the older boy who'd been only known as Phantom then. Their secret brotherhood had become seven members when a year later their youngest member, Rafael, or Numbers, had joined them. The other three had been Raiden, or Lightning, Jakob, or Brainiac...and Cypher. None of them knew what he called himself now.

But when they'd been together, he'd taken their same vow: to become as skilled and knowledgeable as possible, so they'd one day escape, become powerful and wealthy enough to rule their own empires and bring down The Organization.

But meanwhile, they'd been The Organization's slaves and mercenaries, hired out to the highest bidder to execute any level of atrocities that no one else could: assassinations, sabotages, even starting revolutions, coups and wars.

It had taken over fifteen years to enact their escape plan. After they'd disappeared to build new personas, they'd surfaced to take the business world by storm and built Black Castle Enterprises, each presiding over his own segment of the global empire. Ivan ruled the cyber development world in ways that made his rivals call him Ivan the Terrible.

After they'd become established, and had begun untraceably dismantling The Organization, most of his Black Castle brothers had made finding their families or heritage a priority. Since most had come to The Organization too young to remember much, tracing their roots had been a lifelong endeavor. Ivan, though, knew his family and his brothers and had been certain that with his cyber reach, it would be the easiest thing in the world to find them once again.

But to his brothers' surprise he'd elected not to contact them. And he'd never told anyone, even Antonio, why.

He told him now. "I never told you this, but joining the

brotherhood, and having your friendship, was what saved my sanity. Saved my life. You gave me a reason to live after my family's desertion made me want to give up."

A sharp breath expanded Antonio's chest. "You think…?"

"I *know*. The people I would have gladly laid my life down for, traded my life for theirs."

Antonio's eyes filled with the empathy of the profound connection they'd shared from that first day. "That's even worse than what my family did to me."

Antonio's aristocratic Italian family had thrown him away at birth, discarding their daughter's illegitimate child from a nobody. The Organization had taken him from the orphanage he'd ended up in. It seemed he considered abandoning a newborn to an unknown fate a lesser crime than giving up a grown son to a definitely hellish one.

Ivan exhaled. "Not that I can't excuse my parents. We could have all been killed, or worse, and I was their only bargaining chip. They were forced to make a choice between two evils. Sacrificing me was the lesser one. But knowing that rationally and accepting it emotionally was— is—worlds apart."

"Of course it is. If anyone should exact vengeance, it's you." Antonio sat forward, his frown ominous. "I want in on it."

Ivan waved away Antonio's aggression. "I don't want vengeance. Never did. All I wanted was to come to terms. I placed them under surveillance, learned everything about them since they abandoned me. The Organization followed through and set them up in the States with new identities. They've since changed those twice more. They've managed to completely hide from the Russian mafia, the former soviets and their benefactors at The Organization."

"But no one can hide from you," Antonio said, an edge of vicious satisfaction and pride in his voice.

That was indeed Ivan's specialty. He'd always hunted down the most elusive of quarries.

He nodded. "Since then their lives have been running smoothly and uneventfully. My three younger sisters and brother, who came to America very young, integrated totally. They have successful careers and stable personal lives. My parents, now John and Glenda Evans, have lives that are as respectable, comfortable and secure. It's as if I never existed to any of them. I live trying to forget them, too."

"You shouldn't." Antonio shredded the words through gritted teeth. "For parents to toss their firstborn to the sharks, to live a prosperous life at the price of his life… No, Ivan, this shouldn't go unpunished."

He shook his head. "But it will, Tonio. I don't have the thirst for retribution like you did."

Antonio's fists bunched as he visibly struggled to bring his outrage under control. "Let me know if you change your mind."

Ivan nodded, his throat tightening at his best friend's solidarity.

Antonio sat back, the gears of his formidable mind clearly changing. "But what does all this have to do with Anastasia and her brother?"

Ivan sipped his cooling coffee before putting his cup down, buying himself time to rein in the memories of his family and the devastation of their betrayal.

"They come in seven years ago," he finally said. "After five years out of The Organization's prison, with only you and our brothers as my sole human connections, I'd resigned myself I'd never have anyone outside of you. Then one day, during the first conference I sponsored, I met a blast from my past. A man I recognized at once as my pre-Organization childhood best friend.

"Alexei Mikhailov left Russia with his parents just days

before I was sent to The Organization. It was one of the reasons I was so eager to leave. His parents, prominent scientists in soviet Russia, defected to the States and changed identities, too, becoming the Shepherds. The father, Sergei, became Michael, the mother Ludmila, Grace, and Alexei, who'd followed in his father's footsteps in the same branch of science in the States, became Alexander, or Alex. But because I'd changed too much..." They'd all made sure they did, so they'd be beyond recognition to their former captors even after they'd erased all evidence of their existence from their databases. "...Alex didn't recognize me. And I intended he never would. But I was still compelled to get closer. To my delight, even without knowing me, we hit it off all over again, resuming our former rapport as if the intervening years hadn't happened."

He paused, savoring the agony of the sweet memories. Then he went on. "Later that same night, I met Anastasia, Alex's younger sister, whom I remembered as a two-year-old child called Nastya, who used to be my youngest sister's playmate. She'd been twenty three years old then, and the most stunning creature I'd ever seen."

And the only woman he'd ever wanted, unstoppably, on sight.

From that first glance, the desire had been mutual and beyond either of them to resist...which they hadn't.

"For the next few weeks, as Alex and I became close friends again, I plunged into a passionate but secret affair with her." He leaned forward as echoes of this magical interlude that had never stopped haunting him deluged him again. Body hardening and heart thundering at the mere memories, he raked a hand through his hair, dragged himself back to the bleak reality. "I was overwhelmed by the ecstasy of being with her, not to mention by the delight of being with Alex again. Yet it haunted me that I might expose them to danger if one day the past caught up with me. And though that was my main fear, there was another problem.

"Through the escape and identity changes, not only had their family never lost contact with mine, they'd become like one family. My parents were like a second mother and father to them, with my sisters Anastasia's best friends and Alex in love with my youngest sister, Katerina, Cathy now. I knew being involved with Anastasia and Alex would bring my family crashing back into my life. My dread was validated when Alex kept trying to suck me into their extended family. It all came to a head when he asked me to be his best man."

He closed his eyes as memories of Alex, alive and in love and eager for his closeness, tore at him all over again.

His breath left him on a ragged hiss. "I considered putting the past behind me, for his sake, for Anastasia's. But I couldn't do it. I was unable to bear the thought of being around my family again. It was the shove I needed to leave them alone. So I told Anastasia and Alex that I had inescapable business on his wedding day and withdrew from both their lives."

Silence lengthened in the wake of his last words.

Then Antonio asked, "Without explanation?"

He'd driven himself crazy ever since thinking how he could have handled it better. He'd always come to the same conclusion. "Any excuse I invented to explain my withdrawal would have only hurt more than letting them think I was just an unfeeling jerk."

Antonio inclined his head. "So now you don't want her going back to her life because you can't walk away again and you're worried your family might somehow recognize you when they eventually see you with her? Or are you afraid you'd change your mind about punishing them once you see them again?"

"Neither. The years haven't lessened my aversion to being anywhere near them, but intensified it. If she goes back to her family, I won't be able to be there for her anymore. And she still needs my support, my protection. She isn't ready to face the world without them yet." He leaned his elbows on his knees. "So now you have the reason you asked for."

After another beat of silence, Antonio rose to his feet. "I will still discharge her, Ivan."

Ivan heaved up to his feet, blood shooting to his head. "What? After what I just told you?"

"I actually now believe it's even more imperative to let her go back to her life."

"You bastard, you make me spill my guts—"

"Which you should have done ages ago. But what you told me only reinforces what I already decided." An outstretched arm aborted Ivan's outraged step forward. "When you first told me you'd be there for her during the hard journey back to her old self, I assumed she had no one else. But she has a family who loves her. She needs to go back to them, to bury her brother, so she'll get closure and start the healing process. Keeping her isolated with only you hovering over her is keeping her in a limbo of unresolved tension and grief."

"That's only your opinion."

"It's the truth. And there's also another reason why I will discharge her against your wishes."

"Brilliant. You have more bloody reasons to screw me over?"

"You always turn into Richard when you're frustrated." Before Ivan could blast him for likening him to that pain-in-the-ass Brit partner and former jailor of theirs, Richard Graves, Antonio sighed. "But yes, I do have another reason. You."

"Me?"

"Believe it or not, I'm stopping you from making a catastrophic mistake with the woman you care about." Antonio waited a moment to let his words settle on Ivan before he went on. "No matter how justified you think you are, the day she discovers you kept her away from her loved ones when she most needed them for your own ends, you'll find yourself in my same position with Liliana, with her feeling manipulated and betrayed, and with you unable to reach her again. And you already have a huge strike against you with her for the way you deserted her in the past. I don't want you to meet my same fate."

Ivan almost staggered back under the barrage of truths he hated to hear. "Dammit, Tonio. You were supposed to be too messed up to offer any resistance, let alone come up with a reasoned argument this ironclad."

"Just your luck I have a separate compartment in my head for my inner Vulcan." Antonio took him by the shoulders this time. "Let her go, Ivan. And after she's done what she needs to do, find a way to be there for her, to help her become strong and whole again, while staying out of your family's range."

Ivan's gaze held Antonio's grim one, aversion and dread bubbling up to the surface. "Do I even have a choice here?"

Antonio's attempted smile came out as a grimace. "None."

Anastasia was sitting by the window overlooking the ocean—the Pacific, since Ivan had mentioned they were somewhere in Los Angeles—when he and Dr. Balducci walked in.

Apart from a couple of nurses and orderlies she'd barely

seen, those two had been her only company for the past five weeks. It sometimes felt as if she'd see no one else for the rest of her life except for the two men who'd saved her.

She watched them approaching her, and thought that if the gods came down from Mount Olympus, they wouldn't look that magnificent. She wondered again how they could look so much alike when one was one hundred percent Russian stock, like her, and the other was pure Italian. Their ethnicities were clear in their bone structure, but in their bodies, vibes and many other intangible things, they seemed to have been forged in the same higher-being manufacturing plant.

They stopped a couple of feet away, where the golden rays of a declining sun shining in through the window made them even more gorgeous. But though she mentally knew they were each other's equal, it was Ivan who embodied male beauty in her book. Or in her ledger. It felt as if everything that made her a female with these kinds of appreciations was frozen. Even gone.

Dr. Balducci spoke first. "Good news, Anastasia. I'm discharging you. I only ask that you resume your activities gradually and come to me when you can for a checkup. Of course, if you have any unusual symptoms, which I don't expect in the least, contact me at once. Ivan will provide you with every method to get hold of me day or night."

She blinked. "You mean…I—I can go?"

"Medically speaking, you're almost as good as new."

She hadn't even been considering her health. It wasn't what dictated whether she could go back.

Her gaze moved to the other juggernaut towering above her. Ivan's face was clamped in a disturbing expression.

"Is it okay for me to leave now?" She heard her voice wavering, imploring. "For my family to know…what happened?"

His eyes glittered a deeper green as a beat passed, and felt like an eternity, before he nodded. "Yes."

And the tears came again. As if they'd never stopped.

In her blurred gaze, she saw Dr. Balducci's image receding, and Ivan's hovering a breath away. But he didn't offer any comfort, just stood there, fists at his sides.

All she wanted was to throw herself at him, seek the shelter of his infinite strength, his encompassing protection. But she held back. She couldn't need him or lean on him any more than she already had. Ivan, from devastating experience, didn't stick around, and this time when he eventually left, it wouldn't be like before.

Seven years ago she'd been young and resilient. She'd suffered an indelible scar when he'd walked away, but she'd survived, even thrived. This time, in her bereft and damaged state, if her dependence deepened even more, she feared she'd be unable to recover.

Finally, feeling too wrecked to shed another tear, she slumped back in her seat limply, looking up at him. His gaze flayed her with its intensity. Yet he still said nothing.

She finally pushed to her feet. "Can I have my things back now, please?" she asked him. "I need them so I can arrange my return to New York. As for—for…"

He took an urgent step forward as she choked, and for a second, she thought he'd take her in his arms. He didn't.

Looking as if the words were being torn out of him, he said, "Don't worry about anything. I will deliver you—and Alex—to your family."

# Three

"What will we tell my family?"

Ivan looked up from his laptop at her subdued question. Anastasia had been trying to get herself to ask it ever since they'd left Dr. Balducci's secret medical installation and driven to a private airstrip to board Ivan's jet.

Until now, all she'd managed had been monosyllabic answers to his constant questions whether she needed anything.

Not that she possibly could. As he'd been doing for the past five weeks, he'd kept anticipating her needs, and far beyond. He'd barely let her feet touch the ground all the way to this luxurious seat in his state-of-the-art jet, barely let her lift a hand. The most she'd gotten away with had been going to the bathroom under her own power and feeding herself.

To escape his persistent focus and care, she'd had to pretend to fall asleep. Even then, she'd felt his gaze on her, no doubt counting her breaths, as usual.

She'd ended up falling asleep for real, and had just awoken a minute ago to find him finally doing something other than watch her. She'd been tempted to leave him engrossed in whatever he was doing. But she'd had to ask that question. They had to be on the same page during the coming ordeal.

It hadn't even occurred to her that he'd offer to take her home. But she'd still felt his aversion to the task and tried to convince him to let her go back alone. It had only made him more adamant that she was in no condition to deal with the upheaval ahead. Not to mention that only he could navigate the sensitive time until Alex was buried.

Now caught once more in his burning focus, she wished she'd kept silent. He closed the laptop, pushed aside the adjustable table and sat forward in the seat facing hers.

"Now that those responsible for Alex's murder have paid—"

She had to interrupt, her sluggish heart starting to hammer. "How exactly did they pay?"

His gaze stilled on her face. "You're sure you want details?"

She hadn't before. But now she burned for them. "Yes."

He didn't answer at once, as if trying to gauge if it was prudent to give her more information that might disturb her.

But he must have seen the steel hardening her nerves, the fire licking through her veins, her need to have vengeance for Alex fueling her, overriding any aversion she might have previously had to learn what he was capable off, what he'd done.

He finally gave a nod of acknowledgment. "Your immediate boss at FuturEn and insiders within the International Energy Organization had been exposed. Not for the crime Alex discovered—that they'd made sure his results would be publicly falsified, discredited and never see application, while bribing all energy competitors with the threat that those results were indeed a breakthrough that could deprive them of a big percentage of the market within years. And not for what they'd done to him—and you— since that will always remain a secret for your protection. I exposed every other crime they'd ever committed, which were many and equally as heinous. They'll never know who exposed them, but the evidence I made available to the authorities is copious and conclusive. They've been arrested and the dates of their expedited trials set. They've lost everything and won't see the outside of a maximum-security prison in this life."

"That's all?"

A chilling smile touched his lips as if he recognized and approved of her lust for a harsher punishment. "No. Those who gave the order to end your and Alex's lives will be locked up with their worst nightmares—those who owe them pain and suffering, and others who'll contribute imaginative punishments for one price or another. Those men will either meet their demise after protracted abuse or, worse, be deprived of its mercy."

She closed her eyes, struggling to suppress the vicious satisfaction that charred her blood. She was ferociously glad those monsters would pay, and that their punishment would be long and agonizing, and preferably unending.

It amazed her all over again that she was capable of such ruthlessness, that she would have exacted that punishment herself if she could have. She knew if Ivan hadn't taken action, she would have done anything to avenge Alex's death. But relying on the law wouldn't have done her any good. As a weak adversary with flimsy evidence, she would have gotten nowhere and ultimately would have been forced to resort to reckless measures. Which would have proven as ineffective and probably ended up in disaster for her and for her family, too.

So Ivan had saved her yet again, this time from the consequences of the vengeance she would have done anything to get, but wasn't equipped to enact. He'd given it to her, full and final, without a price for her or her loved ones.

Gratitude flooded her, along with so many other emotions that she felt she'd burst with it all. Needing an outlet, she reached a shaky hand to cover both of his as they interlaced loosely between his knees.

It was the first time she'd touched him in over seven years. And though it was nothing like that first touch that had changed her forever, that had told her this was the only man she'd ever crave, it was still as potent in its own way. The powerful hands that were capable of so much passion, skill and damage seemed to buzz beneath her trembling touch. His gaze crowded with so much she couldn't fathom.

She let out all her emotions on a quivering breath. "Thank you."

The stiffening of his body and face was an admonition, reminding her he'd demanded she never thank him.

"But I need to far more than thank you," she persisted. "For this. For everything you've done. And now for taking me—taking us—home." She shied away from thinking of Alex's body in the belly of the plane so she could go on. "Especially when I feel how much you'd rather not."

Sitting back, he moved his hands out of reach, a startled look coming into his eyes. No doubt he was surprised that she picked up on his reluctance.

He only said, "Alex was my friend, Anastasia."

The barely checked emotions that radiated from him whenever Alex was mentioned hit her full force again. Was that the reason for his reluctance? He hated that they were taking Alex home in a casket, to bury him? Did he feel, like her, that goodbye would feel real only then? Did it hurt him, too?

If it hurt him a fraction of how it hurt her, then it made sense. And it again rewrote everything she'd thought she'd known for the past seven years.

Ivan's friendship with Alex had lasted as long as their own relationship had. Exactly ten weeks. At the time, she'd believed the two men had shared a deep connection. Then his desertion had forced her to revise her opinion.

Though their liaisons had been brief, Ivan had left a gaping void in both their lives. Each had mourned his loss, had struggled with their own interpretation of its causes.

Alex had been resigned that someone of Ivan's caliber would surely not find him worthy of more than a passing acquaintance, that he'd been delusional to think they'd built the foundation of a lifelong friendship. As for herself, she thought she'd been nothing but another notch on his bedpost. Why else would he have simply walked away?

But after everything that had happened in the last weeks, after realizing he'd kept such close tabs on them, she was forced to reconsider everything. It was clear there was far more to this whole thing than she'd thought. Far, far more to Ivan. What, she couldn't even guess at. And if he never told her, she'd never know.

But for now, she had to tell him what Alex hadn't had the chance to.

"He was your friend, too, Ivan. He never got over your sudden disappearance from his life, yet always treasured the time he had with you."

It was agony to talk about Alex in the past tense, as she would from now on. And equally painful to reveal an intensely personal secret of his that only she'd known.

But Ivan had to know it. It was about him, and after all he'd done, she couldn't withhold it from him.

The next moment she wished she had. That look in his eyes as he met hers was filled with unbearable pain. The same look she'd seen before he'd declared he would deliver her and Alex to their family.

What did it all mean? How did his behavior, past and present, add up? Because it simply didn't.

Or maybe it did. Maybe he felt bad about the way he'd exited their lives, the remorse compounded by what had happened to them, by what he'd been unable to stop. Maybe he was appeasing his guilt by trying to put right as much as he could of this mess.

Not that it mattered what he felt or why he was doing this. For reasons he kept to himself, Ivan was hell-bent on seeing this tragedy to its resolution.

And though having him so near was like a dull scalpel opening old scars and new wounds, she was more grateful than she could ever express. She couldn't have survived without him. And once they broke the tragic news to their family, only his presence would get her through their grief.

After an oppressive silence, Ivan made no comment on her revelation and answered her original question. "I advise against taking anyone into your confidence about what happened, no matter how tempted you are. Not now, not ever. I've erased all evidence of the crime so I could deal with its perpetrators without repercussions. Any knowledge of it outside of us can someday cause untold trouble. I've constructed an airtight scenario to be told to the world, starting with your families, and I need you to always be consistent in telling it."

She nodded, hit again by how sinister this all was, how much larger than anything she'd ever thought she'd encounter in her life.

His eyes filled with approval of her unquestioning acceptance. Then he went on. "You'll say neither you nor

Alex knew which arm of the government recruited you for the top secret project, that all had gone smoothly, that you were supposed to go home when you were involved in a helicopter crash two weeks ago. The pilot died at once, Alex was gravely injured, while you had the least injuries."

She gave another nod as she absorbed the details that mixed reality with fiction. "How will I explain your role in all this?"

"You'll say I'm a previous acquaintance you contacted because I'm Dr. Balducci's partner, who transported you to his facility. But it was those in charge of your mission who didn't clear you to contact your family before now. You'll tell the truth, that Antonio operated on both of you, but could only save you, downplaying your injuries so you could be in this condition after two weeks. Part of the misdirection to the culprits is creating a different time line."

Her head spun at his scenario, what she'd now have to act out for the rest of her life. Not even their parents or Cathy would ever know the truth about how or why Alex died.

He went on. "That all said, I want you to say as little as possible from now on. To start, let me do the explaining."

Another surge of gratitude swept through her. "I'd prefer that, too. I doubt anyone will question anything you'll say."

"If anyone does, or if any authority investigates, I made sure all threads would lead to various government arms that no one would question. I made sure that each agency would have no way of making sure which one you were working for and would assume you were working for one of the others."

She shook her head in amazement. "How? How did you do all that?"

"I *am* in the business of monitoring, controlling and

even creating records and information. No one will ever know the truth, and you'll be forever safe from any fallout." She swallowed, flabbergasted yet again at another demonstration of his power. He sat forward, enveloping her in the heat of his body and aura. "Apart from all that, I assure you of another thing. Alex will be honored, his research and results will all be published. His legacy, which is substantial, will be applied, will get the recognition and rewards it deserves. His family will be given their full benefit, morally and financially."

The urge to launch herself at him, bury her face into his endless chest, cling and sob her heart out, almost overpowered her. Her every frailty reached out to absorb all she could of his strength. What he was so unreservedly offering.

Only her depletion and mounting dread of the impending reunion stopped her, made her unable to seek his refuge.

Which was just as well, since his offer of solace and protection didn't seem to extend to anything physical.

And she had to abide by his rules—this man she'd once loved, who'd injured her in the past and healed her in the present, both with no explanation.

But she didn't need to understand him to give him his due. It was what Alex would have wanted her to do. "Alex couldn't have hoped to leave his legacy in the hands of anyone better or more capable than you."

His eyes darkened again, whether at the mention of Alex's name or at the implied gratitude in her statement.

Before he could respond, she asked, "How long before we land?"

His turbulent gaze flitted to his phone. "Two hours."

She lowered her seat back to a flat position, pulled the blanket over her aching body. "I'll sleep again, then."

He surged forward, helping her adjust the seat and the covers. "Do that. Rest."

*You'll need it* went unspoken.

Ivan watched Anastasia sleeping, and knowing this would be the last time he did had bleakness expanding in his chest.

They'd landed an hour ago, but he couldn't bring himself to interrupt her sleep. As restless as it was, it was still better than what she'd go through when she woke up. This way, he had her beneath his eyes, where he could ward off the world, for as long as possible.

That had been one of the reasons he was escorting her home—to prolong his time with her. As Antonio had said, that was for himself as much as it was for her.

But the main reason he was doing this remained her, and Alex. Antonio had been right. He couldn't keep her any longer from the people she loved, those who were her lifelong support system. She needed her family, needed to bury her brother, give them all the chance to grieve, to say goodbye.

And he couldn't stomach letting her take the brunt of her family's shock alone. He couldn't bear that Alex would be buried without him being there. His abhorrence to being close to his family had been outweighed by his need to shield her, to honor Alex.

Now he had to rouse her. And they both had to plunge into their own version of a waking nightmare.

Two hours later, Ivan stood behind Anastasia on the threshold of the home Alex had shared with his wife, Ivan's sister, and their two children, his niece and nephew.

As they waited for the door to open, he felt Anastasia swaying, as if she was coming apart under the weight of the dread of confronting her best friend. And though it hurt to touch her, his hand clamped her trembling arm, offering her his strength, letting her know he'd step in anytime she needed.

In the next moment, he wondered if it was he who needed support.

The woman who opened the door had an eager smile that, in spite of all the changes twenty-eight years had wrought, was still the same as that of the baby sister he'd known. Her smile immediately froze when she saw Anastasia without Alex, looking desolate, and with him, a stranger, towering over her.

To say the next hour was harrowing would be to say that his time with The Organization hadn't been too bad.

At first, Anastasia had haltingly introduced him, so she wouldn't break down on the spot, needing to be strong for her best friend and sister-in-law. Then Katerina's— Cathy's—questions had come, the dread mounting until each answer fleshed out the scenario he'd created, validating her worst possible fears.

Then the agony had come. He'd felt every stab of it in his own gut as he watched yet another person he cared about in the throes of absolute anguish. For just seeing his sister in the flesh had brought back the memories of how much he'd loved her, from the moment his mother had told him she was pregnant again. In spite of her maturation from his Russian baby sister into a thoroughly American woman, she was still somehow his little Katerina.

He'd thought nothing could be worse than being ambushed by those kindred feelings he hadn't thought he could ever feel again, or than suffering shearing empathy for her loss. Until her—and his—parents arrived.

Seeing the man and woman he'd once loved completely,

whom he'd idolized, rush to their bereaved daughter's side, seemingly as overcome, rocked him to his core.

For almost three decades, since he'd discovered what they'd done to him, he'd imagined how he'd feel if he ever saw them again. He'd come up with a thousand scenarios. He'd known he'd hate it, had been determined never to expose himself to it. But he'd thought he'd braced for each possibility, that none could actually hit him too hard.

He'd been wrong.

After their desperate attempts to contain their daughter's agony, their focus had converged on him. He'd thought he was being too sensitive to their merest glance, but none of those who'd flooded the house, including his other sisters and brother, had looked at him like that.

As if they recognized him.

But of course they couldn't. Nothing remained of the twelve-year-old they'd bartered away for their freedom but his eye color. And then how would they even suspect a resemblance, when they must have believed him long dead?

A big percentage of the boys culled by The Organization couldn't endure their brutal training. Of those who did, more than half didn't last in the field. It was why they were always harvesting more, with their mortality rate so high. And the boy his parents knew, the slight nerd he'd been, wouldn't have been able to survive the inferno he'd been tossed in. If it hadn't been for his brothers, he wouldn't have.

He'd waited for anger to overtake him, but all he felt was desolation. Even now, he couldn't hate them. The only thing he felt when he looked at them—older, frailer and in their grief, even fragile—was pity.

There was no doubt in his mind they'd loved Alex as a son. Instead of that making him more bitter, it was like a knife of sympathy tearing through his guts.

The ordeal continued into the next day. Everyone, as if responding to his superior powers, let him steer everything. He'd fast-forwarded the process and arranged for the burial, laying Alex's body to rest, along with the true circumstances of his death.

Now they were back at Alex's house, and the true grieving had just begun. Alex's parents and Katerina seemed to be sinking deeper into despair. The only one who'd already gone through the stages of loss was Anastasia, and he felt her pour out her support to everyone who needed her. As he'd feared she would. But there was nothing he could do to stop that, to make her preserve herself, not give too much.

He now stood at the periphery of the jarringly sunny living room watching those who'd loved Alex flocking around his family in an effort to absorb a measure of their distress.

Then the agitation that had been rising and falling in jagged waves since they'd arrived crested again. The three people whose very presence tossed him from one level of turmoil to a higher one were approaching him.

Anastasia, and his parents.

The one who addressed him, puffy-eyed and broken, was his mother. "Mr. Konstantinov, Ana told us everything you've done for her and Alex. We—we wanted to thank you, even if there's nothing we could possibly say to express our gratitude."

"But we *are* grateful, beyond expression, on behalf of everyone." That was his father, looking nothing like the imposing figure he remembered, smaller, weaker, even helpless in his anguish. "Thank you, son."

He'd once had a bomb shower him with shrapnel, almost tearing his leg right off. The word *son* from the father who'd given him away tore through him with far more force and pain.

His reaction must have shown, for Anastasia came between them, no doubt mistaking it for his dislike of thankyous. "Ivan has a big problem with accepting thanks, so if you really want to express your gratitude, don't."

"But of course we have to express it," his mother exclaimed, her eyes, glittering with tears as they fixed on his face, with something that was feverish in its intensity in their depths. A…question? "And if there's ever anything at all we can do for you, we'd only be too happy and grateful to do it, my dear."

The sheer kindness and eagerness in her expression, what was reflected in his father's face as they awaited his response, felt like more stabs to his heart.

He could barely hold back from shouting, *All I ever wanted was for you not to abandon me to a life of servitude.*

As if feeling his critical condition, Anastasia intervened again. "I bet there's nothing we mere mortals can ever do for Ivan." His parents insisted that even the most powerful people had to need something, but she cut across their protests. "I'm sure if this is true, he won't hesitate to ask. You can count on him to make his wishes known, right, Ivan?"

He found himself nodding, his gaze riveted on her face, mesmerized by what he saw. A glimpse of his old Anastasia, the woman who'd glowed with life and candor, who'd captured him from the first glance.

"But as you know," she continued, "Ivan has already gone above and beyond and now he needs to go back to the life he's put on hold for so long to be there for us."

Clearly torn between disappointment that he'd leave and not wanting to impose on him, both his parents deluged him again with thanks and persistent hopes that he'd return whenever possible. It was all he could do to answer them coherently, then walk, not run, away from them.

His whole being in chaos, he felt Anastasia fall into step with him as he headed to the door. From her wary sidelong glances, it was clear she felt something was not right here, but was at a loss as to what it was and what had provoked it.

Not that he was about to explain. All he wanted now was to bolt as far away as possible from this place. Preferably to the ends of the earth, where he'd never lay eyes on his parents or the rest of his family ever again.

It would also serve Anastasia's purpose, too. It hadn't only been to save him from an uncomfortable situation that Anastasia had suggested he go. Clearly she, too, wanted him to leave. After all the time she'd been limited to only his company, she must have had way more than enough of it. Not to mention that he remained the odd man out here, and in this, of all times, she must be eager to be alone with her family.

But how could he just walk away this time, when he never wanted to leave her side again?

There was more to this than being unable to bear the thought of not seeing her again. Though she was out of danger, it was still a long road to complete recovery, physically and, more importantly, emotionally. She was outwardly holding together, being there for her parents, for Katerina, for the rest of the family, but he knew she was crumbling inside. And it wasn't only the brutal loss of Alex, but her own ordeal. Most probably she'd suffer one degree or another of post-traumatic stress.

But he couldn't help her himself now. If he stayed around to do so, he'd be too disturbed being in the vicinity of his family to offer her the stability she now needed. The best thing he could do was to make sure she had the best specialists to help her deal with the psychological repercussions. But he could not stay.

As she led him outside, he caught her arm in a gentle grip, stopping her.

The eyes that turned up to his were reddened, the lids swollen, her gaze hesitant and fragile. Yet those eyes were the most beautiful sight he'd ever seen, the most powerful weapon. They tore through his being with more force than bullets had torn through his flesh. For they made him want everything he couldn't have. They made him weak. They overpowered him when nothing else ever had.

Fighting the overpowering compulsion to crush her to him, feeling as if shards of glass filled his throat, he said, "I know you have your family now, and that you never ask for help, but…I am here for you. Don't let your independence or any other consideration stop you from letting me know what you need, now or at any time in the future. Promise me that if you need anything, anything at all, you'll ask me for it."

Her gaze clung to his, brightening with tears again, her still pale lips quivering in a semblance of a smile. "If I think it's something you can do, sure."

"I can and will do anything."

Her eyes darkened and a faint flush spread over her now sharper cheekbones, seeping into her dainty lips as they opened on a tiny, sharp inhalation. He had no idea how he stopped himself from snatching her into his arms and devouring her.

Then with a nod that encompassed reluctance and acquiescence at once, she accepted his carte blanche.

Though he doubted she'd ever use it. He'd just have to keep watching her, even closer this time, and do a far better job at anticipating her needs and protecting her from the dangers of the world.

Then it was the moment. His role had ended, and his one-time pass back into her life had expired. He had to let go. Until she needed him again. Knowing her, barring another catastrophe, that would be never.

Knowing her loss would be a worse injury than what he'd suffered in the past, knowing he'd never recover from it, he said what he hadn't the first time he'd walked away.

"Goodbye, Anastasia."

# Four

*But I can't say goodbye. Not again.*

The words kept reverberating in Anastasia's mind. Long after Ivan had brushed past her and walked to the limo that awaited him in the driveway. Long after it disappeared down the street.

And though the protest had exploded in her head when he'd said goodbye, out loud she'd said nothing. As if not saying goodbye herself wouldn't make his real.

Instead, she'd just watched him go, willing him to turn, to say something else that wouldn't make this final. Some promise he'd be back later, to at least check up on her. That this time he wouldn't disappear from her life completely. That he'd leave the door ajar. Leaving it up to her to approach him, and only with a need, slammed it shut, this time forever.

Because she'd never ask anything of him.

But he hadn't turned, not to qualify his goodbye, not

even to give her one last look. She'd watched his limo until it turned the corner, still feverishly hoping that the man who hadn't let her out of his sight for five weeks wouldn't go like that. She had no idea how long she'd stood there before her hammering heart had slowed to the rhythm of resignation, the knowledge of the centerpiece fact she'd now have to build her new shattered life around.

He was never coming back.

It felt like her world had ended, for a third time. Two out of the three times it had happened, it had been on Ivan's account.

But it wasn't her world that mattered now. Her family needed her. It was what had finally made her walk back into the house full of all who'd loved Alex, where she'd plunged again in the surreal realm of being in his house knowing he'd never be there again. Being among the people she'd been closest to since birth, contemplating all the ways their lives would be diminished and distorted in his absence had agonized her more with each passing second. But it had at least made it impossible to think of Ivan.

After a while, the presence of the mourners had turned from solace to suffocation for her parents and Cathy. As the one who'd dealt with the most brutal stages of Alex's loss, it was up to her to take charge. Using up her last traces of stamina and diplomacy, she'd made everyone leave, put the shattered Cathy and kids to bed and taken her broken parents home.

Once she'd settled them down as best she could, and sought the sanctuary of her own room, she'd finally taken off the mask of strength. Closing the door behind her, she'd collapsed where she'd stood, letting misery drown her again.

Gone. Alex was *gone*.

And Ivan, too.

She'd lost him all over again.

Not that she'd ever had him. He'd only reentered her life on a mission. Once it was accomplished, there was no more reason for him to stick around. Now she knew why this demolished her.

When he'd been by her side day and night, she hadn't been able to think ahead to the point in time when he'd leave again. She'd gotten so used to him being there it had felt as if the day would never come. That was why it had been such a shock when he'd not only walked away, but had also seemed as if he couldn't bear being around her anymore, couldn't wait to leave her behind.

*That* was what hurt until she couldn't breathe. What made her feel as if the ground had been swept out from under her, making her feel she was plummeting into an abyss. Not only had he removed his support, but also his fervor to be around her.

But no matter how vulnerable and lost she felt without him, she knew it would have been worse if he hadn't ended it now. Any longer with him, any more dependence on him, and his ultimate departure might have killed her. At least this way, she had a chance of survival.

Not that survival seemed like such a good thing now. For the few days since he'd left, she'd been going through the motions of living. Staying in both Alex's home and her parents', helping them with everyday chores, pretending things like food and homework and bath time and laundry mattered. Trying to ameliorate the unbearable. For herself and for them.

And it wasn't working. She only felt worse as every minute dragged by, Alex's absence solidifying into a gaping crater in her heart, a closed fist in her right side and a missing vital ingredient in her every breath.

Alex hadn't just been her older brother, he'd been her best friend, mentor, partner and confidant. Every single thing in her life was inextricably entwined with him. He'd been more to her than he'd been to their parents, to his wife and children. All of them had parts of them, interests and activities, that hadn't included him. She hadn't. He'd even been her squash and gym partner. And she didn't know how to plug the holes now that he'd been ripped from her. The feeling of being torn in half constantly gushed in, leaving her sinking.

But it was only in the last couple of days that others began noticing her condition. Though their anguish kept deepening, Cathy and her parents were slowly recovering their ability to think, at least enough to see beyond their own turmoil.

Though they didn't know the depth of her injuries— and never would—they now thought she was the one who had the most healing to do, and they said they would see to it. Just now they'd insisted she go home and rest. Making them promise to call her if anyone needed anything, she'd finally succumbed.

On her way home, she pulled into a shopping mall parking lot. She had no idea how long she sat staring ahead, trying to empty her mind, to not focus on Alex or her endless memories with him since the day she'd been born.

But not thinking about Alex only let her mind think of the other man who dominated her every waking and sleeping moment. Ivan.

It was like watching a movie of her life's transformative moments. For he'd been there in each and every one of them. Their cause or their conclusion.

Every moment replayed in her mind and impacted her senses. When he'd first walked up to her, looking like a supreme being right out of a fantasy. When he'd pulled her into that first kiss, an overwhelming seduction. When he'd loomed above her, invading her body with pleasure, branding her as his, a storm of passion in human form. When he'd snatched her from death's cold pull, like a lethal archangel. When he'd given her the only reason powerful enough to cling to life, imbuing her with his endless strength, like a guardian angel.

The images played in a loop, but always snagged on a specific one. His face filling with colliding emotions as he'd said goodbye. Watching it over and over as she sat there, she took it apart, looked at it from every angle, until she finally realized something.

How hard it had been for him to say it.

Jerking out of her stupor, she fumbled out her phone, her heart starting to thunder as she searched out the direct number he'd saved on it. She hit Dial as she restarted the car. He answered after only one ring.

"Anastasia?"

To everyone she was Ana. Only he called her by her full name. Every time he said it, he filled the simple utterance with so much, it filled volumes in her being. She'd once thought she'd heard how much he wanted her, and everything else he'd felt in the way he said it. She'd since come to believe she'd been only hearing what she'd wanted to hear.

But there was no mistaking how he'd said her name now. It was the very sound of agitation and solicitude combined. He was worried she needed something, and that it was big enough only he could deal with it, important enough to make her call him.

Before she could reassure him, his urgency silenced her. "I just hit Dial and the phone rang instead."

Did she get that right? "You were calling me?"

"I went to Alex's house and your mother told me you

went home, but I arrived here and didn't find you. I was calling you when your call connected first. What happened? Where are you?"

He'd been looking for her? Was at her home now? Why?

"*Anastasia.*"

His bark was pure anxiety now, clearly imagining another disaster had befallen her.

She rushed to allay his concern. "Nothing happened. I—I just stopped somewhere on the way." He didn't need to know that she had only sit there staring at a memory reel starring him. But *she* needed to know one thing. "Why were you looking for me?"

There was a long beat of silence on the other end, before his deep voice poured into her brain again, and his words snuffed out any light that remained in her world.

"I wanted to see you again before I went back to Russia."

Anastasia didn't even remember the drive back home.

Her brain registered nothing until she saw him sitting in his car outside her family home, like a predator lying in wait. He got out as soon as she neared, looking like a god descended to earth with the setting sun behind him. Even from a distance she felt the tension radiating from him. It swamped her as she drove past him into the garage, as he opened her door and helped her out.

Her throat tightening, her heart hammering, she invited him into the house. Every nerve fired with his nearness, with the intensity blasting from him.

Needing air, she led him all the way out back to her favorite part of her mother's garden—the gazebo. It was where she'd sat alone countless times with her laptop or a book, where her mind had always ended up dwelling on the man she'd loved and lost. She turned to him now.

He towered over her, his eyes that hypnotic green she'd

always drowned in, his expression singeing her blood with its heat. And she just couldn't do it.

She couldn't let him say goodbye. Not yet.

Not before she said what she'd called him to say.

"Anastasia—"

"I could have died, Ivan." Her quavering words cut off what he'd begun to say. "But I didn't. Because you saved me. Now I need one more thing from you."

He took a step closer, tight, barely leashed power in the move. Power she felt could move mountains, as he'd done for her and Alex. "Anything, Anastasia. Tell me what you need."

"I need you to show me that I didn't just survive, Ivan. I need you to prove to me that I'm still alive."

His eyes flared with such a blaze of emotions, she almost needed to shield her eyes. "Anastasia…"

This time he said her name as if it hurt, the inflection filled with seething hesitation. And she knew he wouldn't make a move. Either because he couldn't credit what she'd asked him for, or because he was taking it upon himself to protect her from any recklessness in her weakened, needy state.

But she couldn't take no for an answer. This was the one thing she needed. The last thing she'd have of him.

He'd nurtured her back to physical health, but she now needed a salve for her emotions, a reviving dose of passion from the only man she'd ever been intimate with.

Her move ate up the distance between them as a trembling hand rose to his face. The moment she cupped his rugged jaw and felt his strength fill her palm, overflow into her being it was like the years apart evaporated. Nothing remained inside her but longing, and it had taken only this contact to break the dam and have it all come pouring out.

"I need this, Ivan," she whispered. "I need you."

His flesh buzzed beneath her hand, electrifying her. "How could you? I left you—"

"It doesn't matter what you did or why you did it. The past is gone. Alex is gone." She stifled a sob that threatened to tear through her. "But I'm still here. And it's terrible, Ivan. Terrible to be alone, to know I'll always be alone because I'll never be able to share what happened, what changed me forever, with another person for the rest of my life."

"*Bozhe moi*, Anastasia."

He'd only ever spoken Russian when he'd lost his hold on his rigid control in the throes of passion and pleasure. But now different emotions compromised his control, eliciting his tormented "My God."

Her hand trembled around his neck, her fingers plunging into his luxurious mane. "But I share it with you, Ivan. It's only because you know everything, that you've lived it with me that I'm able to go on. And I want to share more with you, what might bring me back to life. The past is gone—"

"The past may be gone, but there's tomorrow—"

A finger on his lips stopped his protest, her tear-soaked voice breaking. "There's only now. And you said you'd do anything. That's the only thing I need. The one thing I'll ever ask of you."

His chest expanded, as if bracing under an insupportable burden. Not only wasn't he unfeeling, as she'd once thought, she now realized he probably felt too much, had to close himself off, to protect himself, and maybe the whole world from the power of his emotions. She'd seen him when a measure of these emotions—the violent, vengeful ones—had been let loose. He'd been lethal. She no longer doubted that he'd wreaked far more destruction in his life, that what she'd witnessed had only been the tip of the iceberg. And now she was chipping away at the barrier that restrained his devastating potential, and it was about to crack.

Not that it worried her. She wanted him to demolish her with all the ferocity of his fervor. He'd only ever hurt her when he'd deprived her of it.

"You need this, too, Ivan. You lost him, too." His flinch was proof that Alex's loss did hurt him. Her hand twisted in his hair in answering agony. "I need to share his loss with you, the one who knows, the one strong enough to live with it. And I'm the only one you can share it with, the one who understands, who's been part of it all."

The torment that blazed on his face solidified her belief.

He mourned Alex, almost as deeply as she did.

"Anastasia, you don't know what it takes for me to be like this." Like this? In control? Holding back? "You don't know what you're risking."

"I have nothing more to risk, Ivan."

His head tilted back against her hand, a growl rumbling deep in his chest, as if there was a trapped, starving beast there. He *was* resisting because he feared he'd hurt her.

She had to make him believe he wouldn't, had to make him stop holding back. Her other hand slipped around his neck, coaxing his face down to hers. "The only injury I could have sustained was letting you go without being with you one more time."

She lowered her arms to hug all she could of him, a breath she'd been holding for seven long years flowing out of her in tortured relief. Until he stiffened in her embrace as if she'd electrocuted him.

Oh, God. This could mean she'd gotten it all wrong. That he didn't need comfort, at least not from her. That when he'd said he'd give her anything she needed, he hadn't thought it would be him—the one thing he hadn't offered.

Before she could withdraw in mortification, his formidable body surrendered to her hold. He still didn't embrace her, but he gave her license to hug him. So she did. Hug him and hug him. His sighs were the very sound of agonized enjoyment. They reverberated deep in her marrow as he rested his forehead on hers, swaying with her to the erratic cadence of their heartbeats.

Then suddenly he was pushing away. Before letdown burned her to ashes, she was swept up in his arms. Where she'd despaired of ever being again.

Forgetting to breathe as he strode inside the house, she savored the weightlessness, the powerlessness, the soaring he always made her feel when he carried her like this.

His effortless steps paused halfway up the stairs to the upper floor and he looked down at her, his eyes probing hers. "This is what you want?"

Instead of answering him, she nestled her head more securely against his chest. "My bedroom is the last door in the corridor."

That rumble of voracity that had always melted her revved beneath her ear. He hurried through the upper floor that was all her living space, crossing inside her bedroom in seconds. The moment he closed the door, he let her slide down on his hard body and pressed her against it, letting her feel how the tremors shaking her body echoed in his.

Unable to wait another heartbeat, her hands convulsed in his hair, her lips gasping for his. The moment she reached them, she took them in a wrenching kiss, every moist glide and thrust of her tongue confessing how much she'd longed for him. It reminded her how much she'd lost, how much she'd lose again.

But she had him now, and she would hoard all she could of him.

She'd barely started when he tore his lips away. Crying

out, she surged up, desperate for his breath so she could breathe, for his heartbeat so her heart wouldn't stop, needing his taste to fill her up for the desolate future without him.

But he'd only broken the kiss to melt more down her neck, her breasts. His growls of pleasure and need were elemental, set off jolts of hunger in her core.

He wanted her now. She knew he did. With all his indomitable, magnificent being. For now. And she wanted to have every spark of his desire, needed it. Had to have it. If even for one hour.

Too weak still to climb him and wrap herself around him, she could only stand on tiptoe and arch back, offering all of her. Her legs buckled when his erection pressed into her core through their clothes. Moaning, she ground against him, pressing his head harder into her aching breasts. He opened his mouth over her sweatshirt-smothered flesh, nipping one of her nipples.

A cry tore from her as she bucked with pleasure, losing all coherence. "Ivan, please, just *take* me."

With another growl, he picked her up again and carried her where she'd never thought she'd have him—her bed.

His gaze raked every inch of her, igniting her skin wherever it lingered, then he came down over her, his arms a prison of muscle around her. She breathed in the scent of his maleness and protectiveness, fiery and clean and musky. Her mouth watered then her stomach rumbled.

"You're hungry." He pulled back, gaze sharp, tone accusing. He'd constantly worried she didn't have enough food, kept urging her to eat more.

He started to get up and she clutched his hand, the hand that had snatched her from death's jaws, that had taught her what pleasure really was. "Not for food, Ivan."

"Anastasia…" he groaned as he sank back into her arms.

She singed her lips with his heat as she ran them over his cheekbones, his jaw, his neck, loving the feel of the few days' worth of beard he now wore.

At its soft abrasion, she moaned into his skin. "All I want is to feast on you."

And she did, trembling with the enormity of having him in her arms again. Her hands roamed the breadth of his back, reveled in the leashed power of his arms, her lips and tongue delighted in skimming every inch she could reach, every touch and taste everything she'd craved for years. *Years*.

But he broke away from her again, to blaze a possessive trail down her body. He had her writhing in pleasure as he seemed to melt her clothes off. It was only when she found herself naked beneath him in what felt like seconds that self-consciousness assaulted her.

Dr. Balducci had done a masterful job on the scar that traversed her abdomen. It reminded her she'd been taken apart and put back together inside, but she'd gotten used to seeing it, mostly dismissed it. But having Ivan's hands and eyes on it, she felt as if it was the ugliest thing ever, and that it covered her from head to toe.

On a mental level, she knew Ivan would sympathize. But on the sensual one, the male in him, what she knew from ecstatic experience was ferociously carnal and exacting, had to be put off by it.

But as she tried to reach for her comforter to cover herself, Ivan, still fully clothed, captured her wrists. He pinned them beside her head, his knees imprisoning her thighs.

"Don't hide from me, *moya dusha*."

At hearing him call her *my soul*, one of the extravagant endearments he'd used to lavish on her, she sobbed, "I don't want you to see me like this."

Letting go of one of her wrists, his hand went to her chin, making her meet his gaze. "This scar?" His other hand shook as it traced it. "It pains me to see it, as a reminder I could have lost you. But it's also precious because it's proof you survived. And it's beautiful, like every other part of you."

Unable to bear him taking pity on her, she turned her head away as tears of inadequacy slid down her face onto the sheets.

One hand pressed her head persistently, making her look back at him, as his other one took her hand and slid it down his body until it reached the potency tenting his dress pants. Feeling him, so hot and hard and huge, made her whimper.

"That is how beautiful I find it, and you," he whispered.

Arousal overcoming distress, she twisted restlessly beneath him, moaning, "I don't even have words for how beautiful I find *you*. Please, Ivan, don't take it slow. Show me how much you want me, make me grateful I'm still alive."

His gaze filled with storms, but it was absolute care that filled his hands as he settled her back and slid down her body. Realizing what he intended, she was overcome by memories and, weirdly enough, embarrassment.

When she tried to keep her legs closed, he raised his head, his chiseled face flushed, his eyes coaxing. "Open yourself to me, Anastasia. Let *me* feast. Let me heal you."

"I'm healed," she cried out. "Please…"

"Your injuries, yes, but you're far from strong enough to withstand me."

The words *withstand me* unleashed a flood of memories, every sensation of every time he'd ridden her to screaming satisfaction. Though she was dying for him to do so now, to hold nothing back, she knew she wasn't ready for that.

"You can be gentle." She knew he could be, as he had been, heartbreakingly so, that first time he'd taken her. And every time, after their first explosive arousal had been assuaged, when he'd savored her in thorough, tender leisure.

But she saw it in his eyes. He had no intention of taking her that way. He came up to silence her protest before she uttered it, his mouth on her lips as his fingers sought her entrance. She lurched with stimulation as he dipped in, each slow inch a red-hot probe of mind-melting pleasure.

But though she was going to pieces with arousal, after her trauma and after being so long without him, her body felt too tight. Even two of his long, thick fingers felt like too much. He held her eyes as he pumped them fully inside her, drawing the admission that there was no way she'd accommodate him right now.

Rising to singe her in the possessive flames of his gaze, he started sliding down her body again, burned his way in licks and nibbles and ragged words down to her core. Her efforts to pull him up ended when his magnificent head settled between her thighs. Every nerve in her body loosened as his lips and tongue soothed and scorched the intimate flesh she could surrender to no one but him.

He strummed her to one body- and soul-racking climax then another, and another, holding her eyes all through. She was lying stunned, sated, unable to move a muscle when he finally came up to stretch against her, cupping her, crooning to her, completing her bliss.

But she felt every inch of him like cabled steel, coiled on his unspent arousal. Needing to give him relief, she started stroking him, but he captured her hand. Burying kisses in her palm, he tucked her more securely against his massive body before taking her lips.

"Shh, *zvezda moya*." Murmuring another endearment

into her mouth, my star this time, his tongue mated luxuriantly with hers. "I only want to hold you."

She moaned and burrowed deeper into him. "At least let me feel you. I need your flesh on mine."

His caresses stopped, then he rose partially, started shrugging off his clothes. As his body came into view, she realized she'd been right. He *had* become a full-fledged god.

Then she looked down on his promise of endless pleasure lying thick and long and heavy against his chiseled abdomen and nothing mattered but having him inside her.

She tried to wrap her legs around him in silent supplication, but he subdued her with extreme gentleness, wrapped his arms around her instead, letting every inch of his flesh imprint hers.

His lips flowed over her from neck to cheek, his whisper hot and soft against her prickling skin. "Let yourself take what I need to give you, *dorogoya moya*. Let go."

When she finally did, sank into his being and giving, the one thing left in her mind was that he was the only man who had ever made her feel this incredible, this protected and cherished. This man alone had the power to revive her. Or finish her.

Warm, wonderful sensations coasted over Anastasia, making her surface slowly from oblivion. Her eyes cracked open to light peeking between blackout curtains. Blinking, she expected to see herself back in her hospital suite.

In the next second it all came back to her. Everything that had happened since she'd come running home to see Ivan. Ivan, who was still stretched out against her, drenching her in caresses.

But maybe it had all been a dream, and still was. She'd

seen and felt him like this on countless nights. And each time she'd woken up empty and alone.

"I'm here." As if he'd heard her unspoken question, he reassured her of his presence. He smoothed the hair off her cheek, tucking it behind her ear, the heartbreaking tenderness in his caress twisting her heart, spiking desire in her loins.

He'd taken her to bed at sunset. With the sun out again, she'd slept for at least twelve hours. Which might mean that...

He again completed her thought for her. "Your parents came to check on you. They were more than surprised to find me in bed with you." At her embarrassed gasp, something she hadn't seen since he'd come back played on his lips—the tiniest of smiles. "Don't worry, I'd already made us...decent."

It was only then she realized she was in a nightgown, her favorite one, a deep burgundy silk that felt like a second skin. He'd somehow picked it out of all her sleepwear and put her in it while she slept. He was fully dressed again.

"Did they...?"

"They just asked if you were okay. I assured them you were, and your mother insisted I have something to eat."

"Yeah, that's my mom for you. Though she is a scientist, the cure to everything in her opinion is a good meal."

"I ended up accepting tea and a huge slice of delicious homemade apple pie. She served them to me right here."

Her cheeks flamed as she imagined that scenario. With her being a recluse, her parents had never had to deal with any man in her life. Her liaison with Ivan had been a secret, even from Alex. It had been the one thing she hadn't confided in him. And just as she'd thought it time to do so, Ivan had disappeared.

There'd been no one else since. It had been the main reason she'd never moved out of the family home. She'd had no personal life that she'd wanted privacy for.

Suddenly the indulgent gleam in his eyes dimmed, tension replacing it as he got out of bed.

He was going to say goodbye now.

She sat up, her heart suddenly thudding so hard she felt it rattling her whole body.

He looked breathtaking yet haggard. Longing almost stopped her pounding heart as his heavy-lidded gaze raked her, filled with disturbed and disturbing emotions. And she realized.

He didn't know how to say goodbye.

But neither did she. She couldn't say it. She needed him. In whatever way she could have him.

Not knowing how to tell him that, she rose on stiff legs, tried to postpone the inevitable. "You shouldn't have let me sleep all this time. And it doesn't seem you've had any sleep."

His jaw clenched. "Anastasia, we need to talk."

She groped for lightness, even though she was going to pieces. "That sounds ominous."

He clenched his fists, unclenched them. Then he squared his shoulders and stood straighter, as if he was readying himself for a frontal assault. "I tried, Anastasia. Tried to leave you alone, so you can restart your life. But you can't start again. Not yet. And I—I can't leave you."

Her heart did stop this time. Then it stumbled into a gallop of brutal anticipation. Did he mean…?

His next words ended all speculation. "Tell your family you need time to heal, which you do, and come with me." Before elation took hold, he added, "Let me do all I can to heal you."

The plummet from the heights of hope left her unable to breathe for long moments.

When she could finally draw breath, her voice was a rasp. "Is that what this is about? You feel responsible? Sorry for me? Guilty?"

He took an urgent step toward her, his eyes like emerald fire. "I sure as hell feel responsible. For your well-being. And I'm so sorry for what happened, I can barely breathe. And I feel so guilty it erodes my sanity. Guilty that I wasn't good enough or fast enough to prevent it. I want you to come with me so I can take care of you to my obsessive heart's content. But if you're asking if that's all, then no. I would want you with me without any of that. I've never stopped wanting you. I don't think I ever can."

Anastasia gaped up at him, this man she now needed more than life itself. Though he couldn't want her nearly as much, she believed he did want her, as much as he was capable of.

And he was right. She couldn't restart her life yet, couldn't resume her research without Alex, couldn't go back to the same place of work. He'd also been right to try to shield her from the world. It hurt even more being among her family now. And if there was anything she'd ever wanted, the one thing she'd been deprived of, it was being with Ivan.

His eyes seemed to seethe with anxiousness as he waited for her response. But before she gave it to him, she asked, "How long?"

"As long as it takes. As long as you want. Say yes."

Was there really any other answer?

"Yes."

His sharp inhalation said her acceptance took him by surprise. He'd actually expected her to refuse, or at least not to succumb right away.

"Don't you want to know where I'll take you?"

"It doesn't matter if I'm with you. If you want me…"

He gathered her to him, and she felt a tremor in those hands that were powerful enough to crush monsters. "I don't even have words for how much I do."

She fitted into his burning body, felt hers ignite. "Then I'll be with you, for as long as you do."

# Five

A frisson of unease slithered down Anastasia's spine.

With a last look at her phone after she ended her latest call with her parents, who called almost every day, she exhaled.

It had been ten weeks to the day since she'd come with Ivan to Russia. And the ten-week mark didn't have a fond correlation in her mind. Not when it came to Ivan. It had been exactly ten weeks into their first relationship that he'd suddenly ended things. Just days before Alex and Cathy's wedding.

Not that she thought he was about to end it now. This time Ivan seemed bent on being with her, being there for her, for as long as she needed him. His constant dedication to her well-being seemed to be unlimited and unending. She had to continuously try to dial down his indulgence, pull him back from extravagant gestures. To generally convince him she no longer needed any special care.

And though he now let her do things for herself, and
for both of them—cooking dinner had become her enthusiastic responsibility almost nightly—she kept learning
what it meant to be with one of Russia's, and the world's,
premier oligarchs.

Sure, she'd known he was a billionaire, had seen evidence of his wealth and power in so many ways, but the
more she saw, the more it shocked her all over again.

Entering his mansion had been like stumbling into a
level of existence she'd only dreamed of. She made—or
had made—what she'd considered a very good living being
a top researcher for an elite private conglomerate, had lived
her life in her parents' million-dollar house, but this…
This was just mind-boggling. His wealth had multiplied a
hundredfold since she'd been with him in the past. And it
made her…uncomfortable, feeling this unbridgeable gap
between them.

This place alone cost forty million. When she'd said
she'd never thought he would go for such extravagance,
he'd confirmed that. He'd bought this baronial castle with
its own lake, sweeping grounds replete with pine trees and
a staggering forty thousand square feet of living space only
after she'd agreed to come to Russia with him. So she'd
have all the space and facilities to be entertained without
leaving home.

He'd dropped forty million just so she didn't have to
go out!

But she'd realized he'd been right. For weeks she'd been
unable to contemplate being out in public, to see even
strangers on the streets. The idea of meeting any of his
acquaintances and interacting with them made her break
out in cold sweat.

She had, however, insisted he go out alone. He'd refused. He'd locked himself up with her, so that he even

worked across from her in the same room, or in the room he'd made into the nerve center of his cyber tech empire, running one of the major tentacles of Black Castle Enterprises right next to her favorite living room. Apart from the fleeting presence of Fyodor and his team of guards and hired help, Ivan had had no one for company but her.

He assured her he was a loner, with the only company he'd ever had in his life Dr. Balducci and his other partners. Even them he saw only sporadically since they were all so busy with their businesses and now with their families. And he insisted he didn't want anyone else's company but hers anyway.

But even if none of his assurances were to make her feel better, he couldn't enjoy being cooped up in the same place for that long, not even if it was acres wide. But her efforts to get him to go out met with dismal failure. He wouldn't budge from her side.

But for the past couple of weeks, she'd been feeling much better, regaining the desire to actually walk the streets and see people, and yesterday she had actually done it. He'd taken her on a tour of Moscow. She'd been predictable and chosen to start with the famous attractions.

The whole morning yesterday had been spent visiting the *Krasnaya Ploshchad*, or Red Square, followed by the nearby and stunningly beautiful St. Basil's Cathedral, which exemplified Russian architecture. The two landmarks, now starting to get covered in snow, seemed to embody everything she'd ever imagined as Russian. The land she was born in but had never returned to, until now.

Today, it was the Kremlin's turn, where he'd made them jump queues and enter places no tourist was allowed, all through the five palaces, four cathedrals and the enclosing Kremlin Wall and Towers.

"Having a man of your influence for a guide obviously has its perks," she'd told him.

A teasing look had lit up his face as he'd winked at her. "You haven't seen anything yet."

She'd wondered what more there could possibly be as he'd taken them through a heavily guarded wing and into a massive, imposingly ornate office. It had only been when she'd found a man surrounded by half a dozen hulking bodyguards advancing eagerly to greet them that she'd realized what he'd meant, how accurate his words had been.

She *really* didn't remember everything that had happened in the time they'd spent in that man's company. A normal side effect, she was sure, of finding herself face-to-face with the President of the Russian Federation!

The meeting, an impromptu one that could only have been planned at most the day before, lasted for half an hour. During the surreal time, both men had made her the focus of attention and conversation, with the president himself pouring her tea and asking her all kinds of courteous questions.

Then Ivan had said he was taking her to dinner and the president had stood up at once, asking Ivan for an extended one-on-one meeting. Instead of jumping to ask when, Ivan had actually given him an inconclusive answer.

Still stunned from that, and from the whole momentous event, she'd let Ivan sweep her out of the palace complex. Only now, when they'd been in his car for at least ten minutes, did she finally get over her shock enough to speak. She turned to him.

"Seriously? 'I'll see when I can clear a morning for you'? That's what you say when the second-most powerful man on earth asks you for a personal meeting?"

Keeping his eyes on the road as he negotiated Moscow's downtown traffic, he gave that lopsided smile that had been coming easier to him and that twisted everything inside her. "It's the only answer I had to give him."

"You direct your sprawling business empire from home these days, and you have the most efficient system humanly possible in place anyway. You can certainly 'clear a morning' at once for *the President of the Russian Federation* when he asks you to."

At a traffic light he slid her one of those heated glances that brought her blood to an instant boil. "It's not only my business empire I have to take into account while clearing mornings."

*"Seriously?"* Her exclamation was almost a squeak this time. "You might have incurred the wrath of one of history's most powerful and dangerous men on *my* account?"

His lips spread wider at her burst of incredulous anxiety. "I'm too valuable to incur anyone's wrath. I'm also too dangerous that no one, not even him, would act on it even if I do."

Her heart drummed in rising apprehension. "C'mon, Ivan. Even you shouldn't risk putting that to the test, certainly not so you can babysit me. When will you believe I can spend time on my own and bring your obsession with watching me under control? For God's sake, I'm healed, fully, totally. Inside and out. *And* you have me ensconced in this fortress of yours with enough black ops guards to thwart a military invasion."

His gaze lengthened as he seemed to realize that her mortification was real. Then, putting the car in motion again when the light turned green, he pushed the hands-free button on the wheel.

In seconds the call connected and a voice she'd always recognize now emanated from the surround-sound system, answering in that heavily accented English. The president!

"Mr. Konstantinov, so good to hear from you again so soon."

Ivan's eyes briefly landed on her in an intimate caress. "You have Ms. Shepherd to thank for that, Mr. President. She convinced me I could leave her side and come to meet you whenever you wish. You understand that with her recuperating from major surgery, her well-being comes first to me."

"I wouldn't have it any other way. I'll be only too happy to receive you whenever Ms. Shepherdova can spare your vigilant services."

Then with no closing words, both men hung up almost at the same moment.

Ivan turned those incredible emerald eyes to her, that indulgence that always filled them choking her up yet again. "Happy now?"

All tension drained from her body in a rush, making her slump back in the plush leather seat of his Rolls-Royce. "If you call feeling as if I've dodged a bullet happy, then yeah."

The smile froze over his magnificent face. "It really worried you that much?"

"Hello? I had a dozen scenarios scrambling my mind and in every one of them you were targeted for any level of disciplinary action!"

A frown crept over his face. "I wouldn't have arranged that meeting in the first place if I thought it would upset you. I wanted it to be a surprise you'd remember fondly."

"And boy, will I." At his darkening expression, she rushed on. "I *will* remember it in the best way, up until you offhandedly disregarded his request. Then it turned memorable for all the scary reasons."

At his stymied expression, she realized this was a serious enough event she could use to settle the issue he'd been dodging since they'd come here at last.

Turning fully to him, she placed her hand over his arm, found his muscles bunched to the consistency of rock. "Want to know what upsets me? It's that you keep tailoring your every breath to what you think is best for me. That you won't believe me when I tell you what *that* is."

His jaw hardened, yet he made no response as he brought the car to a stop in front of what he'd told her on the way out of the Kremlin was one of Moscow's premier gourmet restaurants.

Before he got out to help her out, leaving the car to one of the guards who followed them everywhere at a discreet distance, he turned to her briefly. In the fleeting moments their eyes met, there was acknowledgment that he understood what she'd meant.

That he hadn't taken her yet.

Over the last ten weeks he'd exposed her to all kinds of intimacy and pleasure, brought her to dizzying heights in every way, except for the way she craved. He hadn't made love to her, hadn't claimed her, fully. By now she wondered if he ever would.

After she'd lost count of the times she'd begged him to take her, she'd stopped counting, and begging. She'd accepted from the start that being with him would be on his terms, that she needed him so completely, she'd take whatever he gave. Because at the time she'd made the decision, and even now, nothing at all from him wasn't an option.

But now that the ominous ten-week milestone was here, his continuing resistance to act on his desire only made her suspect if it even existed. That this wasn't all some kind of debt he'd pledged to himself to pay, to her and to Alex. That would certainly explain his obsession with "healing her."

Yes, she had seen evidence of his desire, felt it, but now

she wondered if it wasn't just the normal reaction of a virile male to an aroused female. Maybe, he thought making love to her that way came with too high a price, that of complicating his exit when he needed to walk away again. Maybe his desire wasn't strong enough for him to pay that price. Every day that passed made her a little readier to accept this explanation.

Feeling his mood had plunged as deeply as hers, she let him lead her into the restaurant in silence. The moment they entered, a tall, thin blond man, the maître d' presumably, came rushing toward them. A smile of eagerness broke through what looked like permanent disdain as he greeted Ivan.

As he led them inside at once, bypassing everyone who crowded the entrance waiting to be seated, every head turned to look at them. It was clear that most, if not all of the diners recognized Ivan, giving her a taste of what it meant to be in the company of a celebrity and under the microscope of public scrutiny.

Before they could be taken to the most exclusive table in the establishment that the maître d' had promised, half a dozen men and women stood up from a table in their path. Ivan stiffened as he saluted them without stopping, but they surrounded them, gushing in excitement over him and looking curiously at her.

Turned out they were waiting for Ivan to consider investing in their start-up. Having his ear in person was like a windfall they were ready to prostrate themselves for.

Realizing Ivan wouldn't give it to them, she turned to him and murmured for his ears only, "Apart from the president, it would be nice to meet live Russians who aren't your reverent employees."

His breath heated her neck as he whispered back,

"You'll find those who wish for my favor are even worse sycophants than those already on my payroll."

But true to his ongoing quest to grant her every wish, he accepted the group's eager invitation to sit at their table.

Taking the plunge, she sat across the table for eight from Ivan, so that she could talk to others for a change. Not that there was much talking at first. It seemed the others were at a loss what to do with Ivan now that they'd gotten his attention. It was clear they'd expected him to turn down their invitation, had probably hoped at most for an invitation to call him directly. Now that he shockingly sat among them, they were as clearly overwhelmed by the godlike brooding entity who dominated the whole restaurant.

They grew more flustered when they ventured to speak, doing it in Russian, only to have Ivan answer in English. They tried to accommodate him, but none of them could hold more than a basic conversation in English. For some reason, Ivan never spoke Russian to her except in endearments though he knew she was fluent. She'd left Russia at only two, but her parents and Alex had continued to teach her. Wanting to put the others at ease, she spoke up in Russian, inviting everyone, starting with Ivan, to follow suit.

After that, to her surprise, being among a group of people, strangers but young and spirited, turned out to be far easier than she expected. It was an even nicer surprise to find herself falling back into the ease of her previously sociable self.

And all the time, she felt Ivan's gaze on her, even as he interacted with everyone, letting them court his favor but generally taking control of the gathering. And though he did it all smoothly, masterfully, every time one of the men had an aside with her, she felt a spike in the heat of his focus on her.

Basking in what she chose to label as jealousy, something she hadn't felt from Ivan before, she turned to the guy on her right. The man she was introduced to as Mikhail Popov was around her age with boyish blond good looks. He had been the funniest throughout dinner, and the easiest to read. His expression mixed blatant admiration of her with extreme awe and maybe a little envy of Ivan. More than a little tipsy now, he'd tapped her forearm to catch her attention. She turned to him and he stared at her blankly as if he'd forgotten what he'd wanted to say already.

Suddenly he blinked, then exclaimed, "Ah, yes. I heard that Mr. Konstantinov bought a mansion fit for a czar. Does it really have nine bedroom suites, two wine cellars and two indoor pools, not to mention thirty acres of gardens and grounds and a twenty-car garage?"

Anastasia smiled at his slurred, list-like question. "I haven't actually counted the suites, or the maximum occupancy of the garage, but that sounds about right."

Mikhail sat back in his chair, looking stupefied. "Now that's putting his money to good use, getting a place large enough to accommodate all of his mistresses at once."

His words fell on her like a kick, hitting her where she'd been shot, cut open and put back together. Not even the bullets or the post-operative wound had hurt that much.

To suppress her reaction, she turned blindly to yet another man who drew her attention on her other side. She didn't really hear what that other man said, didn't know what she said in answer, her stomach churning harder as she felt the intensity of Ivan's gaze flare up. She had no doubt he'd noticed her condition.

Then without preamble, he stood up and threw down his napkin, silencing everyone at the table at once, not to mention almost the whole restaurant.

He beckoned to the maître d', who came running, muttered instructions about settling everyone's bill. He walked around the table to her and her heart thudded at the barely leashed wrath in his predatory approach. For a moment she dreaded being alone with him. Yet to resist would probably cause a bigger scene than the one already unfolding, so she rose silently to her feet.

She wasn't sure if she managed an acceptable goodbye to their stunned and apprehensive companions, but she doubted they even noticed. They were too busy shivering at the malevolent glare Ivan turned on Mikhail. Ivan had noticed the blond man had been the one to upset her, and seemed to be calculating appropriate retribution. The poor drunk man probably had no idea what he'd said wrong, and most likely wouldn't even remember saying it at all when he sobered up.

Grabbing Ivan's arm, she tried to rush him away. She could have sooner moved a concrete pillar. As her nerves screamed in dread that he'd escalate right here and now, it seemed her mortification got to him. He suddenly turned his gaze to her, his eyes probing, solicitous. Taking advantage of his distraction, she tugged at him again and this time he let her steer him toward the entrance, where their coats and car were brought over.

The moment they were in the car, he insisted on knowing what Mikhail had said to upset her so much, but she managed to dodge his questions all the way back to his mansion.

Once inside, she tried to rush up to her suite, the one he didn't share. Whatever intimacies he'd been drowning her in, he'd always ended up leaving her to sleep alone.

As she started climbing the marble stairway to the upper level, he caught her hand.

"If you don't tell me what the man said, I'll have to go back and get it out of him myself."

She turned on him, her heart twisting in alarm, her voice sharpening. "You leave that poor guy alone."

"Not if he said something that disturbed you so much. Your face contorted as if what he said caused you physical pain."

How could he read her so accurately? And not at all at the same time?

It was she who gripped his hand now, needing to abort his aggression. "Promise me you won't go near him. Mikhail would probably drop dead of fright if you walked up to him and gave him one of those terrifying stares of yours."

"Tell me what he said!"

Wincing at his thundering demand, she let go of his hand as if it burned her. "He said nothing, okay? I just felt nauseous all of a sudden. It seems I didn't notice how much I ate while I was talking to so many people."

The muscles in his formidable jaw bunched, worked. "So that's the story you're coming up with to protect him. Now tell me the truth." When she only stared at him defiantly, he exhaled forcibly. "I promise I won't do anything to him if you tell me."

Hating to repeat Mikhail's words, furious with Ivan for trying to force her to, she stood her ground, took a challenging pose. "You'll promise you won't do anything to him regardless. And I don't have to tell you anything I don't want to."

Unable to chart his reaction, this man who expected obedience as his right, a moment passed in charged silence, as their gazes clashed.

Then, finally, she felt the tension gradually leave his tightly coiled body, the vicious fire in his eyes abating, until they were again the pools of cool emerald she now knew hid fathomless, roiling depths.

Finally conceding that she'd won, he sighed. "I won't do anything. And you never have to tell me anything you don't want to. But I'm asking you to please tell me. I can't bear knowing something hurt you, and I don't know what it is, how I can erase it, how I can stop it from hurting you ever again."

Reaching for her hands again, he pulled at her stiff body, brought her flush against him, letting her feel every inch of his hard perfection. Immediately the body he'd serviced and pleasured for ten long weeks wept for his ownership.

But because he hadn't really owned it yet, and with Mikhail's comment giving her fresh reasons why he hadn't, this time she resisted the need to succumb to him. The desire she'd been giving in to, willingly, breathlessly, since that day he'd taken her to her own bed, suddenly felt pathetic. She'd let it blind her to something that had always plagued their relationship, the prior one and this one, that she basically knew nothing about him. That nothing about the way he behaved with her made any sense. That with him, she couldn't form an opinion of the past, chart the present or predict the future.

But ever since he'd pulled her back from the brink of death, she'd accepted not knowing, had even told herself she didn't care to know so that she didn't have to make a decision or take a stand. But it ended now.

But Ivan's burning lips and hands were roaming her flesh, igniting her every inch against her best effort to resist. Before she could attempt to push away, he swallowed her protests, those hard yet lush lips mastering hers, his powerful tongue driving inside her mouth, filling her with the need to surrender again, to beg for him again.

But she couldn't do this again. Not if it meant a return

to the status quo he'd imposed. Of him being so close, yet farther than the stars.

With an act of will she hadn't thought herself capable of, she tore her lips away from his sensual onslaught, pushed out of his embrace. It took him so much by surprise that he let her go so abruptly, making her stagger back.

After lunging forward to steady her, Ivan let her go. He looked down at her as if she'd slapped him.

Though she hated having to do this, after everything he'd done for her, she hardened her resolve. This was as much for him as for her. It was unfair to him if she continued taking advantage of his uncontrollable need to protect and indulge her. Not when it seemed to be at the expense of his own needs and life. He'd put everything on hold to be there for her, as he'd promised he would the moment she'd come out of anesthesia.

By now she knew he'd keep his word forever. As long as he believed she needed him he'd stay with her, be there for her in every way he could think of.

Except the way she really wanted and needed.

His inability to be with her fully, intimately, forced her to face one possibility. That this was all for her, and there was nothing in it for him. And she couldn't do that to either of them.

Swallowing the rising tide of misery, she whispered, "I—I do want to tell you something."

His face lit up with a surge of eager supplication. "You know you can tell me anything."

"Can I?" Not finding the right words to say what stormed in her mind, she gave a nervous laugh. "I do tell you a lot of things, then you do what you unilaterally see fit anyway."

He started to protest, then stopped. There was no denying that he'd been overriding her. All for her own good in his opinion, but he'd done it nonetheless.

"But I am thankful you did it." She held up her hand to stop his usual protest. "And yes, you have to take my thanks. But it just has to stop, Ivan. You can't go on like this."

"I can, if you let me." Then, as if he heard his own words, he backpedaled. "But I promise I will pull back as much and as far as will make you comfortable."

"You're still making this all about me."

"It is all about you."

"No, it isn't, Ivan. There are two of us here. I suffered an ordeal, and you helped me through it. You were the only one I wanted help from. But time passed and my needs have changed and I no longer need that kind of help."

All light in his gaze was extinguished, making the ache she felt perpetually in her right side throb harder.

"Is this what you wanted to say to me? That you no longer want to be here?"

Her insides knotted tighter at the bleakness in his eyes, his voice. "I no longer want what you think is best for me. I want you to start considering yourself again."

"I am very much considering myself."

"No, you're not. And it's enough, Ivan. You've gone way beyond what I dreamed anyone could do for me. Now it's time for you to be with those you really want to be with."

His hands clenched at his sides, his whole body tensing. "What the hell is that supposed to mean?"

"Y-you know what I mean."

Suddenly something scary unfurled in the depths of his gaze. "This is about what Popov said to you, isn't it?" When her gaze wavered, unable to bear the brunt of his incensed one, he rasped, "Hell, Anastasia, just tell me what he said." When she hesitated, his eyes grew beseeching. "It was clearly about me and I have the right to know what it is, if only to tell you my side of it, whatever it is. I already promised you I wouldn't retaliate."

Knowing there was no way she could still hold out now that he'd put it that way, she reluctantly, haltingly told him.

"It was silly to react that way, but it did remind me that this artificial bubble you've created for me has nothing to do with your real life. You've interrupted it to come to my rescue, to stay by my side. But you now have to go back to your…"

She faltered as that terrifying thing in his eyes expanded, like a dragon unfolding its wings and preparing to spew fire.

It was more frightening that he sounded totally calm when he said, "That miserable piece of scum. I'll make him pay for that."

That had her pouncing on him, grabbing his arms in alarm. "No, Ivan, you promised."

His face looked again as demonic as it had when he'd been defending her and Alex, vanquishing their attackers. He gently unhooked her spastic fingers from his flesh, pulled away. "If I'd suspected he'd told you anything like that, I wouldn't have promised to spare him. This changes everything."

"No, Ivan, just let him be. It's not like he was trying to stir up trouble. What he said was the vodka talking. But then it's only expected for a man like you to have—" unable to say the word *mistresses* again, she just shrugged, her shoulders so taut they almost cramped "—you know."

That seemed to pour fuel on his terribly calm, and more terrifying for it, wrath. "A man like me? Do you or Popov or anyone else even think you know what kind of man I am? And it's only expected that I have mistresses? In the plural? At once? Do you think I have them all lurking around, on hold, while I play house with you? Or maybe I put you in bed at night and go make the rounds of my stable of kept women? Or worse, I have a harem all in one place as Popov suggested, to observe my convenience?"

"That isn't what I thought, Ivan, what upset—"

Her words choked off. Though there was much she didn't know about him, there were some things she was sure of. Beyond knowing that he had his own brand of unwavering integrity, he had this aloofness, this fastidiousness about him. What he'd just suggested, what translated Mikhail's comment in jarring detail, couldn't have any basis in fact.

She kept staring at him helplessly. Before she found the words to tell him her conclusion now, to beg his forgiveness for jumping to the wrong one before, Ivan's simmering gaze cooled down until self-reproach took over his expression.

"I'm sorry I overreacted." Though his voice remained as calm as before, it was now devoid of that dangerous viciousness, filling instead with entreaty. As she felt horrible that he was the one apologizing he made it even worse by adding, "I'll give Popov and his partners an in-depth interview to make up for the way I behaved tonight."

"That's great." She breathed in relief, glad for them, though it only made her more chagrined at how she'd behaved, how this had developed. "But I'm the one who overreacted, Ivan—"

His hand rose, interrupting her. "And you had every right to. You have no reason to trust me, Anastasia, with the way I left you in the past. What I do now doesn't erase it, doesn't exonerate me. I just never want you to be upset, never again, and certainly never on my account."

"Trust doesn't even factor into this, and it wasn't why

I was upset. You had a life before you came saving mine, and it would have been only natural if you had—"

"I didn't, Anastasia. I had no mistresses."

"Please, just let this go, Ivan."

"No, Anastasia, I need you to know this. I had no mistresses, in the plural or in the singular, not even one-night-stands." His gaze lowered for a moment before he raised it back to hers, showing her inside him, the endlessness of his dark, tormented loneliness. "I've had no one since you."

# Six

Anastasia felt her heart, the whole world, grind to a halt. What Ivan had just said...

*I've had no one since you.*

The words sank in her mind, each one making no sense individually. Together they made even less sense.

She replayed them again and again, examining them for something she'd missed, or misunderstood. But there was nothing hidden or vague. He'd just said these words as clearly as could be.

*He hadn't had sex with any other woman since her.*

Then everything started to spin in a vortex of questions and confusions, a dozen hows and whys flying about around an epicenter of incredulity.

She felt as if everything inside her had been scattered in disarray, her whole belief system and rationalizations in shambles.

If he'd left her, but had never sought another... If he'd kept an eye on her, but had never come back... If he'd come back only in her extreme need, remained with her, but still wouldn't be with her fully…

What did it all mean?

She stared up at him, lost in his solemn eyes. This was too much, too unbelievable. She had to say something to do it all justice.

Then she opened her mouth and all that came out was a blurted "No way!"

His eyes widened in astonishment. Then the seriousness of his expression melted on the widest smile she'd ever seen on his face, which was exactly what her graceless exclamation deserved. To top it all off, he treated her to another first. He threw his head back and laughed.

It seemed laughing was such an alien activity to him that it brought tears to his gorgeous eyes.

As his fit of mirth eased, he brought up both hands to wipe his face. Then he looked at them, examining the wetness in amazement. That only reinforced her opinion that this had never happened to him before. Or at least he'd thought it could never happen to him again, for surely he'd laughed when he was younger. A time she knew absolutely nothing about.

Her thoughts scattered when she suddenly found him looking down at her as if he'd like to sink his teeth into her and gobble her up whole.

Then he only said, "Yes way."

Her every inch started to burn again at the wickedly sensuous way he'd said that. And though it made her want to launch herself at him, tear at his clothes and beg him nonstop until he took her, she still had a million questions.

He continued to take her, do everything imaginable to her, with his eyes. But since she knew he wouldn't deliver on what those eyes promised, she quelled the pounding between her legs, tilted her head up. "And are you going to explain that?"

Scooping her effortlessly by her buttocks against his great body, he nuzzled her neck. "There's nothing to explain."

He felt so good she had to struggle to resist wrapping herself around him and begging him to take her right there on the stairs. She barely managed to pull herself away enough so she could look up into his eyes. "Oh, yeah? You drop a bomb of this magnitude on me—something that should be totally unbelievable—and you expect me to just take it in stride?"

Another of these frowns that always made her feel the sun had died gripped his face. "You don't believe me?"

"I said it *should* be unbelievable. Just the idea that a man like you would remain…celibate…" The word sounded so weird, so absurd. "For seven years! There has to be a big explanation for that. One you're not volunteering."

He eased her back on her feet, dropping his hands at his sides. "Again with this 'a man like me' thing. So let's have it. What kind of man do you think I am?"

Her cheeks blazed under his chilly gaze. "I don't think there are others like you for you to be a 'kind.' I only have theories from experience, backed up by the few facts you make available to the world. But really, when it comes to sex, any man wouldn't go seven years without it. And a man of your wealth and power, not to mention your looks and your…appetite, it's implausible you would."

"So you don't believe me." This time it was a statement.

"Of course I do." Her protest was vehement. It hadn't crossed her mind to question the truth of his statement. "I just don't understand how you didn't…why you didn't…"

He cut off her stammering, capturing her and raising

her off the ground again and into his power, wrapping her thighs around his hips. "*You* didn't."

His surveillance of her had been that thorough?

But of course it had been. She doubted anything could be kept a secret from Ivan if he decided to uncover it. But it was still hard for her to accept that he'd found out what had gone on behind the closed doors of her life.

Suddenly, she wanted to call him out on it. At least, to challenge him. She'd made it too easy for him so far.

Arching backward, she let her long hair fall over his arms crossed over her back. "How can you be sure of that?"

The heat in his eyes rose, the hardness pressed between her legs becoming that of steel. "I'm sure. I've been watching you."

Another stab of arousal pierced her core, even as a chuckle burst on her lips. "And now I'll hear that song scoring your every move and glance."

The hands squeezed her buttocks harder, sending delicious electricity coursing through her. "What song?"

She locked her ankles more securely around him, her eyes getting heavy under the onslaught of hunger "Y'know, The Police? 'Every Breath You Take'?" She sang the lyrics, somehow keeping in tune despite what he was doing to her. "Stalker much, Ivan?"

The flare of voracity in his eyes made her think that he would give in to desire this time, lower her right there and mount her. And oh, how she wanted him to. But then he let out a ragged breath and started walking up the stairs with her still in his arms.

"It would have been stalking only if I made you realize I was watching you." He paused a beat. "And I was watching Alex, too."

"Neither of us had a clue." Unable to let Alex's memory derail her current concern, she forced a smile. "But you've been watching me since you came back and no longer try to hide it."

"That's different." He grimaced as he shouldered open her bedroom door. "Or maybe it isn't that different." At the foot of her king-size bed, he bent and laid her with extreme gentleness on the turquoise satin quilt, what he'd said he'd picked to reflect her eyes, hovering over her with arms planted on both sides of her head. "If it bothers you, I'll stop."

She had two options. Surge up, clamp him with her arms and legs, bring him on top of her and risk a repeat of most nights since they'd come here, ending with her sated yet more frustrated than ever, and with this conversation aborted. Or resist the compulsion of his lure and her lust, and insist on getting answers. Once and for all.

She rose to her elbows, making him unfold to his full height. She almost swooned back again at the sight of him looming over her, oh so visibly aroused and crackling with hunger.

It was experience saying it would go nowhere that made her sit up. He kneeled in front of her, opening her legs and pressing between them. She knew that position by heart by now. According to him he'd become addicted to her taste. And at the first sign of weakening, he'd have her naked and in the throes of one orgasm after another. Like most nights he'd tire her out with too much pleasure. And then she'd wake up to find herself alone.

Not tonight. She pushed back against him when he tried to prostrate her in front of him. "Can you? Stop? I was just thinking that it has developed into some sort of obsession."

"No, it hasn't." He leaned back, so tall that even on his knees his eyes were level with hers, combed the luxurious ebony silk that had fallen over his forehead back in a self-deprecating move. "Developed, I mean. It has always been one."

"Why? Why did you do it? Why did you watch us all these years?"

Solemnity came into his eyes again, making them even more compelling. "Because I needed to make sure you were okay."

"And when you realized *I* wasn't, as evidenced by the fact that I couldn't move on, why didn't you do something about it? Wasn't that the whole point of watching me?"

His lips twisted on what looked like self-contempt. "I should have done something about it."

She fought the urge to catch those lips that had owned her every inch and pleasured her beyond coherence. "But you didn't. Want to tell me what stopped you?"

He lowered his eyes, escaping her beseeching ones. "Whatever it was, I should have found another way to be with you. It's yet another thing I will never forgive myself for."

Knowing she'd get no answer from him on this point, she tried another tack. "You only came back when our lives were at stake, so it's clear you wouldn't have come for anything less. So why didn't *you* move on?"

With each question he looked as if he would have preferred if she tore off his nails instead. But there was something else with this one. It was as if he'd never actually put the reason into words, even to himself.

Then he finally raised his eyes, and what she saw there almost knocked her flat on her back. "Because as long as you didn't find someone else, I considered that you were still with me."

A tremor started in her deepest recesses, one of searing, incredulous hope. "So if I'd moved on, you would have, too?"

"I very much doubt I would have. I had no way of finding out before I was with you, but I've since discovered that I'm monogamous."

He was monogamous. There'd be only one woman for him. Her.

This was too huge. Too…everything.

Unable to hold back anymore, she surged forward, hugged all she could of him in trembling arms. "You must be part wolf as I always suspected."

He kissed the top of her head, then dragged his lips against her hair, down her forehead, her cheeks. "It's very likely." He pulled back just enough to look into her eyes, and she saw the feral danger simmering in them. "But if you had moved on, I would have come back just to take that other man apart."

Delight swirled inside her at his possessiveness. "Now that's not wolf-like. That's pure dog-in-the-manger."

"I know. That sounds really messed up." His eyes sobered, making her almost cry out in dismay. She'd meant it teasingly. But it was clear he was ready with self-recriminations. Taking her arms off him in utmost care, he stood up. "It *is* messed up. *I* am."

Every nerve firing in alarm at the turn this conversation had suddenly taken, she scrambled up. "Is this what you really believe?"

He squeezed his nape in a punishing grip. "It's a fact."

She swept a hand across his chest, almost afraid he'd push it away. He didn't. Instead, he leaned into her touch as if he couldn't help himself, letting out a tortured groan.

Breath hitching with emotion, she unlocked his viselike hold on his neck and caressed it. "And does this fact have something to do with why you left, why you stayed away?"

"It does." An expression she'd never seen before, a tortured, defeated one, came into his eyes. "I thought you were better off not being anywhere near me."

She reached up and pressed a kiss on his stiffened lips, needing to absorb his distress. "And it didn't occur to you to let me have a say in what I thought was better for me?"

He growled in self-disgust and stepped away from her. "Just look what you did after I left you. You should have hated me, should have gotten over me. You didn't. We both know if I'd given you a choice, you would have wanted to be with me even if it destroyed you."

"You almost did anyway when you not only left me, but left me so suddenly and without an explanation."

His teeth made a grinding sound that made her wince, his eyes blazing like a cornered wolf's. "I wanted it to hurt, so you'd forget me. When I realized I hurt you *too* much for you to ever venture into another relationship, I took solace in the fact that you were at least safe and successful. And I told myself that you might still find someone."

Taking the opportunity to infuse a measure of lightness into the mood, she teased, "The someone you would have come back to take apart."

His eyes squeezed shut. "I already admitted I'm messed up."

She reached up to cup his face. "Well, I'm messed up, too, now, in case this is what's still stopping you."

"You're *nothing* like me, *moya dusha*." His hands covered hers over his face, his eyes full of so much emotions, it was dizzying. "You have no idea what I am."

"I got a pretty good idea since you came back." The shake of his head told her what she'd always suspected, that whatever she'd extrapolated, no matter how extravagant, wasn't even close. She caught his face again, pleading with everything inside her. "Then don't keep me in the dark any longer, Ivan. Don't push me away anymore. Tell me."

His eyes flared with such fierceness it made her gasp. Then he shook his head again, turned on his heel and headed for the balcony. And though it was already freezing out there, he threw the shutters open, as if he was escaping a fire.

Grabbing a thermal shawl off the back of the brocade couch by the balcony, Anastasia wrapped it around her shoulders and stepped out after him.

It was a crisp, clear night, the moon a waxing gibbous. The air was still, making the cold bearable. She watched him as he fisted his hands on the marble balustrade and tipped his head back as if he was gasping for breath.

He looked like a knight of old, silvered by the moon, carved from the night, invincible, incomparable, yet weary from battle. As if to accentuate his reaction to her approach, the wind gusted suddenly. His body stiffened more as she neared him, as if it was cast in bronze, the only animate things about him his satin mane rioting around his leonine head and his clothes rustling around his imposing frame.

"Ivan, please."

He turned as the wind died down and the moonlight deposited glimmers in the emerald of his eyes. Stepping closer, mesmerized by his magnificence, she reached for one of the hands that had saved her, took it to her lips.

His growled protest and attempt to withdraw his hand made her cling to it, cover it in kisses. "Besides everything you've done for me, letting me in, letting me understand, would be the best gift I could ever be given. Give it to me, *please*."

Without warning, she tugged his hand. She hadn't even intended to do that. Surprise made him jerk forward the step that separated them, ending up pressed against her from breast to calf. Her hand released his, went to his head, sifting through the silky locks, bringing it down to hers, pressing her longing against his forehead with lips that shook on a litany of pleas.

His groan sounded as if it tore through all his vitals to rasp on his lips. "I can't, Anastasia. I *can't*."

Holding back tears, she let him go gradually, only so she wouldn't sag to the ground. "As you wish, Ivan. Like you said I have a right not to tell you anything I didn't want to, it goes the same way for you."

Turning on her heel, she walked back into the warm room, felt him following her, closing the balcony door behind him. She heard his breathing leveling out and she knew what would come next. He'd take her back in his arms, start to arouse her, worship her, give her everything he thought she needed, but the one thing she truly did. Himself.

And she couldn't take it anymore.

She *was* healed, was her old self again. Or maybe even a new self. One that couldn't drift in this realm of coddling and contradictory behavior and withheld explanations anymore. One that needed answers. Direction. Solid ground, whatever it was, to stand on.

The moment his hands landed on her shoulders, she whirled away. "I'm sorry I pushed, Ivan. But I don't need you to put me to bed. I can handle that on my own. I can handle giving myself pleasure, too. I've been doing it for years without you, after all. You also seem fine being without me, in the past and now."

His huffed laugh was vicious, bitter, as if he'd never heard anything so ironic.

But it no longer mattered what he felt, that he'd never wanted anyone but her. Not if he didn't act on it. And it was time to make him choose a path.

"I can accept that you can't trust me with your secrets—"

"It has nothing to do with trust, Anastasia." His objection was vehement. "I would trust you with my life and far more."

"Whatever your reasons, I can live with knowing only what you choose to reveal to me. You were right, about what I would have done had you given me a choice in the past. I would have wanted to be with you, no matter the price. Even now, without knowing what is so unspeakable about you or about the reasons you left me that you can't divulge, I still want you, Ivan. I *crave* you."

At his urgent step, she raised a hand to stop him from coming closer, afraid she'd settle for whatever he gave her if he touched her again. "But I can no longer accept this status quo you've imposed on us. I can no longer exist in this limbo." She paused, to brace herself for what she was about to say, to surmount the fear that when she did, it might end everything. Then she said it. "So it's up to you, like everything has ever been. But this time I get to give you a choice, Ivan. Either take me, or let me go."

Ivan's heart felt it might race itself to a standstill.

Anastasia wanted him. She'd been craving him from that first night. But tonight, with everything coming to a head, they'd come to an impasse. And her hunger was killing him.

All he wanted anymore was to snatch her up into his arms and plunder her like she'd been begging him to for the past ten weeks of torture.

But he hadn't taken her because he'd brought her here for her, not for him. Because he didn't want to make it any harder for her to walk away once she was fully healed, if that was what she felt was better for her. He knew he'd only drown her with him, like he had in the past. He'd been assuring that she had a way back, a way out.

Now she was giving him a choice.

*Either take me or let me go.*

He should let her go. She was healed. As much as she could be without the passage of time. There would always be echoes, throughout her life, moments when she choked up, when she was thrown back in time and into the middle of the ordeal. But her PTSD had been controlled, and she was as stable and strong as he'd hoped to get her. He should let her go so she could continue the part of getting better that only returning to her normal life, away from him and the rarefied environment he'd created for her, could achieve.

He *must* let her go. Even if her eyes pleaded with him not to. He had to draw on his reserves of strength, what he'd expended to keep away from her all these years, what had miraculously kept him from plundering her every time she breathed near him in the past weeks.

But he had no more strength. It had been long depleted. He'd been running on fumes, on prayers, on the sheer tendrils of sanity he had left. That was all he had to prevent him from dragging her deeper in with him, into his fathomless abyss of a soul, into the inescapable grasp of his passion.

But she wanted him to.

She had no idea what she was inviting.

But she didn't seem to care.

If he took her now, and then she changed her mind, could he let her go? Could he walk away again?

Did he even know how anymore?

As the debate raged in his tortured mind, her eyes squeezed tight, her whole face crumpling on despondence as she turned away, heading to the en suite bathroom.

He watched her walking away, one slow step after the other, as if she feared she'd shatter if she moved too fast.

He, too, was afraid to move, lest he let out the maelstrom raging inside him. Then he heard the shower running.

The images bombarded him. Of her stepping under the pummeling water, eyes closed and lips open, her silky, golden hair streaming down her back to her perfect buttocks, her healed, lush body gleaming, the water kissing it everywhere...

He wanted to stampede in there, feast on her, wrench pleasure from her depths, make her weep with satisfaction again.

But he knew she'd never succumb to his pleasuring again. She'd let the hunger gnaw her hollow before she did. For she didn't need release, she needed his possession, his dominance. She needed to lose herself in his passion, and sate herself with his invasion.

He felt the last tethers of his control snapping. They lashed about inside him, catapulting him after her.

She wanted him. She got him.

God help them both.

# Seven

Ivan walked into the bathroom and his heart almost burst.

Anastasia was in the large shower stall, her back to him, leaning her forehead on the marble wall, as if the steaming jet beating down on her was almost too much for her to withstand. Without seeing her face, he knew she was weeping.

She hadn't wept in weeks now. She'd even started to talk about Alex without her eyes filling, without choking on the misery and finality of his loss. And he'd managed to take her back to that terrible place of vulnerability, where she felt so anguished and helpless. But he hadn't been able to tell her what he felt would only burden her more. Knowing his past would have been just one more scar for her to sustain.

But that wasn't the only reason. He had to be honest with himself. He feared she'd be horrified, repulsed, if she found out the truth about him.

His slow approach toward her suddenly stopped at a slam of realization. That this could have been the real reason he hadn't confronted her before he'd left her in the past. Maybe he'd dreaded if she'd known, she would feel relieved to be rid of such a monster, would have tried her best to forget him, to replace him.

Dog-in-the-manger, as she'd said.

He was more messed up than he had realized.

But even knowing so, there was nothing he could do about it now. Even if he overcame his own aversion to exposing the ugliness and madness in his past, telling her now would only disturb her more. And this he wouldn't do.

But if he couldn't satisfy her need to know, he could offer her what neither of them had been truly alive without. The all-consuming intimacy that they'd never be able to find with any other. At least he could give that to her for now. While she still wanted him. The man she thought he was.

His steps resumed as he started to unbutton his shirt. By the time he opened the shower, he was still clothed but he couldn't wait any longer to have his hands on her.

It all happened at once. He got drenched, she gasped at feeling his entry and he was wrapped around her, taking her from her slump against the wall back against his thundering body, into the shelter of his no longer containable passion.

She twisted around to face him with a cry, her eyes streaming with both water and tears, glittering with one unspoken question.

He answered it. "I can't let you go."

He tried to obliterate the distance she'd put between them but her trembling hands flattened against his soaked shirt, pain filling her eyes. "I can't have this be the only reason."

A self-deriding and loathing huff escaped him. "The one thing that stopped me from taking you was trying to do what was best for you. For me, holding back has been a hell second only to the years without you, to when I lost Alex and thought I'd lost you, too."

He thought, hoped, his confession would appease her, at least explain his behavior. But what she did next had him so stunned his heart forgot to beat.

Anastasia slapped him with all her strength.

That wasn't saying much, compared to the blows he'd sustained in his life. But from her, it brought him to his knees, figuratively, as he realized just how much he'd hurt her.

She glowered up at him through the jet of water, her enraged eyes the most beautiful and overpowering he'd ever seen them.

"That's for all these years of hell." Then both hands slammed on his chest, wet, sharp lashes of fury. "And that's a reminder to stop making unilateral decisions on my behalf." Next she pummeled him, as if she wanted to storm his being, to break down his barriers. "And that's for driving me mad with your contradictions, with all the things you think you're protecting me from." Then her hands were knotted in his hair, bringing his face down to hers for an openmouthed, desperate kiss, her voice a hot tremolo breaching him to his very core. "And that's for saving me, for being the only one I'll ever crave. The absolute best and worst thing that has ever happened to me."

Before he could try to even think of how to deal with her lightning-fast mood changes, she pushed him away again, hands clawing at his shirt as if it was her worst enemy, tearing at the sodden material, ripping off the buttons he hadn't undone.

"And that's for coming in here still clothed," she panted

as she attacked him, lips and teeth suckling and biting at every inch of flesh she'd exposed. "For making me wait again."

Everything that had ever held him back, every shred of control, every dread, every heartache, snapped, unleashing the longing and hunger that had been accumulating inside him.

Grabbing her hands, he pinned them above her head against the wet wall, while his other hand skimmed her lush curves greedily. But Anastasia wouldn't be held back anymore, squirmed to escape his hold, to continue exposing him to her hunger. He lasted only moments before he stopped her fumbling efforts and shredded the remainder of his clothes,

Shoving them away, he kneeled before her, looked up at her, this woman who embodied everything that mattered. As she sobbed his name over and over, he rubbed his lips, his whole face against her scar, the evidence that she'd survived, that he'd been given a second chance, one he'd almost wasted.

"Anastasia." He reiterated her name like a prayer, soul and body rioting with savage poignancy as he rose and lifted her off her feet.

As she crushed her swollen, hard-tipped breasts against his chest, rubbed her firm belly against his steel erection, he wrenched back at her lips. "No more waiting, *moya dusha*, never again."

He boosted her efforts to clamp her legs around his buttocks, fusing their lips as he flexed his hips until his erection nudged her entrance. He went blind with arousal as her hot, molten core scorched him, her face scrunching with extreme lust as she opened to him fully.

But as he began to ease himself inside her, she bit down hard on his lip. "I can't bear slow or gentle. Give me all you have, all your strength and greed. Devastate me. Finish me."

"Anastasia, *moye serdtse*..."

And she was his heart. He could have more easily withheld his next heartbeat than deny her what she needed. Holding her gaze, he thrust inside her, hard and fierce, invading her with the power they'd both been going mad for, stretching her beyond her limits. Her scream of agonized exultation tore through him as she consumed every inch of him in her clenching hunger.

At last, he thought, groaned, over and over. *At last.*

Incoherent with the pleasure, with the possession, but still needing more, he filled his savage mouth and hands with her flesh, needing to plunder all that she was, leave no fiber of her being unclaimed. Her body yielded to his invasion while he watched greedily as wonder, pleasure and relief splashed across her magnificent face, squeezed out of her in splintered cries.

He'd filled her depths with that first ferocious plunge. He dropped his forehead to hers, overwhelmed, transfigured.

"At last, *moya dusha*..."

Her graceful back was a deep arch, letting him do it all to her. "Yes, Ivan, yes... I missed you, went insane missing you. Give me everything now. Ivan, please, now..."

Obeying her, he withdrew all the way out of her, roaring at the loss before ramming back into her tightness, that sheath of absolute ecstasy and oblivion that he'd craved until he'd become a shell of a man.

She was everything. The perfect fit, the end of his exile. Every glide inside her, the reality of their merging, the unimaginable pleasure of it, sent him straight out of his mind.

Her whimpers were delirious as her slick flesh clamped around his length with a force he was only too familiar with. He had craved it to the point of insanity throughout the years, and far beyond in the past weeks.

But she was tightening even more around him, contracting in forceful waves, her cries sharpening, getting more desperate, and he knew. She was already orgasming. She wanted him that fiercely, was that aroused, it had taken only a couple of thrusts to drive her over the edge. He pushed her hard over it and into an explosive climax, wrung her voluptuous body of every last drop of sensation and satisfaction.

He built the momentum of his thrusts all through her orgasm, until he was jackhammering inside her, until her whole body stiffened around him again, inside and out, absorbing all the ecstasy he rode her to. Her breath came in tortured keens as she hovered once more right at the edge of devastation. Then she exploded again in his arms. Her flesh rippled around him as bursts of completion convulsed through her, wrung him from the deepest point where he buried himself inside her, her screams stifling.

He withstood her storm as she expended every shudder and tear. Then he finished her as she'd always craved him to, impaling her beyond her limits, lodging himself at the gates of her womb and letting his own pleasure scorch through his length, filling her.

Her convulsions spiked at the first splash of his seed, sending him spiraling out of control along with her in the throes of a release that was the most powerful he'd ever experienced, even with her.

Plummeting into a realm where nothing existed beyond being merged with her, he rocked them together as they rode the aftershocks. All he knew was that he was still pouring himself into her, feeling her enveloping him inside and out.

Anastasia. His again.

It had been everything, beyond description. Yet not enough. Nothing had ever been enough with her. He'd always wanted more, always would.

Unable to stand any longer, he sank down to the marble floor, barely aware of the water still raining down on them. Only she had ever made him powerless. Since he'd first seen her, she'd been his undoing. Now he wrapped himself around her, the woman who'd been made to take him whole, to fit within his arms and being.

He realized she'd gone limp in his arms only when she lurched, a gasp seeming to restart her breathing. Her eyes, slumberous and replete and adoring, snared him, ate him up whole, sending fire raging through him again. She was a goddess of temptation and benevolence and fulfillment, one he'd always felt unworthy of. It never ceased to humble him that she, miraculously, wanted no one but him. Gratitude and greed surged inside him, making him crush her against him as he drove all the way inside her again.

Her eyes squeezed shut as she gasped, her core contracting around his fully engorged erection, making him thrust deeper into her, wrenching moans from both of them. Her eyes snapped open, scorched him with the amalgam of pleasure and pain that intensified her one-of-a-kind beauty. She brought his face down to hers, merging their lips, too.

His mind was a total blank as his tongue mated with hers in a languid duel. Though he'd been kissing her almost nonstop through the past weeks, this was different. This was total, complete. Tasting her while holding back, he'd felt like Tantalus, unable to ever quench his thirst until he'd felt he'd shrivel up and expire. Drinking from her lips now that they were sharing their bodies in profound intimacy again was a revival. Even her name described what she was. A resurrection. His resurrection.

Soon the leisurely pleasure caught fire, and she was

writhing in his arms as he pounded himself up inside her until they exploded simultaneously into an even fiercer, more prolonged orgasm.

An eternity later, he relinquished her mouth to gaze down at her. Her head fell back, her face drugged with satisfaction.

Then those lips he'd kissed swollen and deep red moved, and that beloved voice poured out in a heartbreakingly tender melody. "I want you again, Ivan. And again. I want to make up for all the time you wouldn't let me have you."

At her words he hardened again immediately. It was as if their previous two times served only to whet his appetite. As it always had. Whenever he'd taken her in a fury of haste, the explosive satisfaction had only left him wanting more, the kind of pleasure that only slow love-making would bring. And that had been when he'd been ignorant of one paramount fact. That no other woman would do.

Now that he knew every cell in his body was her personal property, no matter if she would have him or not, his desire frightened him with its magnitude.

But she did want him the same way. She wanted him with everything in her. For now. And for as long as he could have her total desire, he would give her his everything.

Adjusting her in his lap, over his erection, he began to move inside her again. He luxuriated in possessing her, in exploring her body and plumbing the depths of her responses as he loved her. He gave her two more screaming, heaving orgasms before he took his own roaring release.

After he'd rinsed and dried them both, he scooped her up and headed toward his bedroom this time, where he intended to keep her for as long as she would stay.

It was only when he was walking the huge corridor

leading to his suite that she stirred in his arms, her question slurring. "Where are you taking me?"

He bent to kiss those swollen lips that could barely articulate words. "To my bed. Where I'll take you properly."

It sometimes seemed impossible.

Well, it always did, actually. That Ivan could give her even more pleasure every time he made love to her. But he did.

Ever since that day six weeks ago when he'd given in and given her himself totally, every time he took her, it was even better, more carnal, yet more profound. He'd been very eloquent and copious with expressing his passion. Far more poetic than this science nerd could ever be. He told her every time he touched her, it was like he tapped into another realm, where neither of them had limits, where the potential for pleasure and unity was infinite.

Anastasia sighed, stretched in bed, every cell buzzing with bliss as she watched Ivan through the open door of his gigantic bedroom, theirs now. He was coming into view then disappearing as he walked to and fro in the attached living room, his deep voice barely audible so as not to disturb her as he no doubt settled a business matter with a subordinate.

She'd never felt like this before, not even with him. Their rapport had been growing with every touch, every glance and word, as if the ordeals they'd endured together had somehow given each a direct link to the other's very essence. Now they were learning to perfect each channel of communication between them, every spark of sensation. The most incredible thing was his becoming that vocal in expressing his feelings, in communicating his thoughts and memories.

Not that he'd ever crossed some lines. He hadn't put a

name to those feelings, or ever went back in time further than when he'd been establishing Black Castle Enterprises with his partners, whom she'd discovered were more than brothers to him. It had been okay with her, as she'd thought it was only a matter of time before he let her in all the way.

But that had proved the only blot in the perfection. That she by now believed he never would.

Suddenly, the bone-deep contentment of waking up in his bed evaporated. Getting up, she put on the turquoise silk robe he'd bought her, another thing that echoed her eyes, which he loved to see.

Walking to the balcony, she opened the blackout curtains, let the cool late November daylight in, looking over the sprawling, snow-covered grounds, trying to shake off the dip in her mood.

She was being too silly, too greedy, needing to reach as deep inside him as he had inside her. But she had to live with the fact that there was far more to him than there was to her. Or anyone else for that matter. What had made him this incomparable man that he was had to have been experiences and tests that she couldn't even imagine. No doubt things he wanted to forget, might even regret. If he couldn't let her in that far, probably thinking she couldn't handle it, it shouldn't bother her. That it did was her own problem, not his. A problem she should deal with, once and for all.

"Did I wake you up?"

She whirled around at Ivan's vocal caress. She'd been engaged in such a struggle with her wayward thoughts that she hadn't heard his approach. He was behind her, then around her, encompassing her in his cherishing power.

She met his heated smile with her own. "I just woke up because you were no longer beside me."

"Now I am, and it's the only place I ever want to be." His breath flayed her lips, hot, virile, filling her lungs and being. "No one should wake up this beautiful. No one should be this beautiful, period."

Starting to tremble with that urgency for him that never abated, she ground herself against his hardness. "Look who's talking."

He pressed her back against the French window, driving one pant-clad powerful thigh between her quivering legs where her robe opened to expose them. "Tell me, Anastasia."

He always urged her to tell him everything she was thinking, everything she wanted. It was as if he needed access to her very soul, to her every whim and need so he could satisfy them. Which he did. Apart from that one huge part of himself he never let her near, he was giving her everything there was to give. While she held nothing back from him.

Now she gave him what he asked for, full capitulation. "I find everything about you painfully, *distressingly*, beautiful." To accentuate her admission, she slipped her arms from around his neck, pushed his open shirt farther apart and covered the perfection of his chest in compulsive kisses. "Every inch of you, every move and word and touch, every callus and scar… It all delights me, drives me out of my mind, even more the more I'm exposed to you, the more I have of you."

His gratification—especially when she mentioned calluses and scars, which must be trophies of that blacked-out time in his past—was so ferocious it burned her. Though it had always disturbed her to formulate theories how he'd acquired them, tracing them with her fingertips and lips, feeling them raking against her skin, had always sent her clear out of her mind with lust. She found them as arousing and beautiful, awe-inspiring as every other part of him.

He ran his fingertips down her arms, slowly, tantalizingly, until they reached her hands, and he untangled them from his shirt. Then giving her such a wicked glance, he turned away from her. She watched him sit down on the couch facing the balcony, amazed all over again how the fever of anticipation and urgency only increased with every sexual encounter. Her heart shook her as he sprawled back, spreading his great body for her to drool over.

Then he beckoned. "Show me, *moya dusha*."

She called on all her self-control not to run to him but rather play the game of slow seduction he seemed to want. She undulated toward him, conscious of the robe slipping off one shoulder, exposing a generous swell of one engorged breast, and the effect that had on him. Black pupils ate up the emerald of his eyes, the rock hardness tenting his pants expanded, and the smoldering smile became purely predatory. Prolonging the moment and reveling in her ability to arouse him always and completely, she took her time to reach him.

But once her knees bumped his, she lost the fight. She collapsed over him under the weight of the seven years of unremitting craving she'd only started expending. Slowing her descent with shaking hands against his unyielding shoulders, she straddled his hips, her robe riding up her thighs. His eyes burned into hers with smug satisfaction until her lips crashed down on his.

He opened his mouth to her urgency, let her show him how much she needed everything he had. And she did. Her hands roamed his Herculean chest, his granite abdomen, until they reached his massive manhood, as she lowered herself to press her drenched core against it.

"I want you, Ivan. You just breathe, *I* just breathe, and I want you. All of you." She reached for his belt buckle, eager to unsheathe the formidable length of him.

At her feverish moans he stopped her uncoordinated

efforts. Sighing in ragged relief, she let him take the lead, luxuriated in his domination, what he'd so maddeningly made her work for.

His hands roved her curves, pushing the robe off her burning body, his every move loaded with the ruthlessness of a starving predator unleashed on a prey long kept out of reach. It didn't matter that he'd spent the night feasting on her. Their fire consumed them only to rage higher.

His pupils flared and subsided, giving his eyes the illusion of flashing emerald. Then he bent to the breasts he was kneading, grazed and suckled her peaked nipples until he had her writhing, her breath fracturing, her arousal soaking his pants. After his devastating homage, he swept her around, spreading her naked on the couch. Opening her thighs wide, he took them over his shoulders as he came down on his knees between them. Before she could mutter a protest, he buried his lips in her flowing readiness. She shrieked at the feel of his tongue and teeth, opening herself fully to give him total access to her intimate flesh, what had always been his.

Then he nipped her bud, and the slam of pleasure told her that one more suckle or graze would finish her. And she didn't want release this way, even if she knew he was addicted to giving it to her. She was addicted to *him*, to merging with him, feeling his potency invade her, fill her every emptiness and loss and need.

"Ivan," she gasped. "I need you inside me."

Growling, he heaved up, caught her plea in his savage mouth, sharing her taste on his tongue. In one fluid motion he rose, lifting her in his arms. But instead of taking her to their bed, he took only a few steps before he stopped abruptly, pressed her with her steaming back against the cool, smooth wall. Capturing her there with his massive body, he locked her feet around his buttocks, thrilling her again with his strength. Then he leaned back, freeing his erection.

As always, the potency she'd worshipped so many times, that had possessed her during so many long, devastating rides to ecstasy, had her mouth watering, her core clenching. The intimidating weight and length of it thudded against her swollen flesh, squeezing another plea from her depths. He glided his incredible heat and hardness through her molten lips, sending a million arrows of pleasure to her womb. But he didn't penetrate her until she cried out.

"*Fill* me."

Only then did he ram inside her. Pleasure burst from every nerve ending at his carnal invasion. She was addicted to this, the first almost unbearable expansion as he stretched her beyond her limits around his length and girth. It was always a shock so acute, so exquisite, her senses flickered.

"Every single time, *moye serdtse*, you feel even better," he growled. "Anastasia…if only I could devour you whole for real." And it felt he tried to, his teeth sinking into her shoulder like a wolf tethering his mate in the throes of a feral copulation. Then he withdrew.

It felt as if he was dragging her life force out with him. Her arms tightened around his back, her hands clawed it, begging his return. He complied with a harder, deeper plunge until he forced her flesh to yield fully to him. Only when he'd breached her to her very core did he quicken his tempo. Every withdrawal was a maddening loss, every plunge excruciating ecstasy. In her heightened state she was aware of every sound and scent and sensation. Her cries that blended with her muttered name on his lips… The carnal sounds of their flesh slapping together… The musky scent of sex and abandon… The glide and burn of his hard flesh inside her. They all combined to rocket her to the point of combustion.

When she couldn't bear it anymore, he gave her what she needed, as he always knew just when, how hard and fast. He hammered between her splayed thighs, his erection pounding inside her with the perfect cadence and force to unleash everything inside her. She shattered in his arms.

Sensations radiated from the pinpoint of insanity where he was buried deepest. Currents of release crashed through her, squeezing her intimate muscles around him, drawing out every jolt of pleasure from her every inch. She felt him everywhere, igniting her every nerve ending, invading her heart.

Knowing he'd inundated her with satisfaction, knowing she now needed his, and his total domination, he roared her name and exploded in his own climax. With one last plunge he filled her to overflowing, sharpening the throes of her release. She felt him pulse the last of his seed into her depths, completion imbuing her as she slumped over his chest...

A rumble beneath her ear jogged her back to consciousness. "Perfection, Anastasia. Every single time. And more."

Feeling boneless, she tried to nod her spinning head in agreement as he carried her and started walking, still buried within her depths. Knowing he'd carry her to bed now, she drifted off again.

Jerking out of her sensual stupor as he laid her down, she twisted around sensuously in the cotton sheets imprinted with his scent and that of their intimacy, compensating her for his loss as he left her body to strip fully.

Coming back to her, he gave her his full weight, which she always begged him for after the storm, his heartbeat a slow thunder against her decelerating one, completing the spell.

She was drifting off when he rose off her, dragging a crisp sheet over her cooling, enervated body. She tried to rouse herself, and he spread soothing kisses over her brow.

"Sleep a while, *moya dorogoya*. I exhausted you and now I must refuel you."

Knowing he'd get them breakfast, she sank back in his indulgence and the echoes of his scent and passion.

Ivan took his time preparing breakfast, to let Anastasia rest. He really shouldn't have taken her twice in a row like that, after a night when he'd done it three times. His insatiable need for her frightened him at times. But at least it only seemed to delight her. She was always hungering for everything he could give her. And he gave her way too much at times.

He now walked back into their bedroom with a tray laden with everything she loved. His lips spread, remembering her accusing him of having a nefarious plot to fatten her up. He'd admitted he would enjoy having more of her to fill his arms, to fondle and squeeze and worship.

Not that he didn't find her perfect no matter her weight. But it was such a relief that after weeks of escalating delight in each other's company, her appetite had returned. She was also back to exercising and had never been more, as she'd said earlier of him, painfully, distressingly beautiful.

Placing the tray down on the bedside table, he luxuriated in watching her sleep off their latest lovemaking. Her lush body was tangled in sheets the color of her hair. Her thick lashes fanned her softly flushed cheeks, her lips swollen with his passion and her wild locks strewn over his pillow.

Suddenly, a white-hot spasm stabbed his gut as images of her bathed in her own blood and Alex's tore into his mind. Seeing her that way now, the image of health and contentment, had emotions raging through him. Every violent emotion, sublime and searing collided inside him, buckling his knees. He sank down on the mattress, a shaking hand reaching out to touch her, to assure himself all over again that this was the reality, that he had her with him, safe and whole and happy.

Her eyes fluttered open, absolute welcome and joy filling them at once. He forced himself to breathe, struggling to banish the brutal images that assailed him regularly back into the deepest dungeon of his memory.

Stretching and yawning delightedly, she sat up, looking like a goddess of voluptuousness, her breasts full and firm, her waist nipped, her thighs long and sleek, her hair gleaming gold around her strong shoulders. His body roared all over again. He tamped it down as viciously. It was enough he'd been all over her the moment he'd found her awake, not even giving her a chance to freshen up or eat. He really had to do something about his perpetual arousal, the need to possess her as many times as she could withstand every single day. He shouldn't unleash seven years' worth of deprivation on her. Even if she was breathlessly willing.

But she was now getting on her hands and knees, slinking toward him like a mischievous cat, rubbing against him very much like one, before turning all human female, pressing her softness into his hardness, turning his arousal to distress.

Pushing him on his back, she lay on top of him, pressing her every hot inch to his. "It's *you* I want to feast on."

He gazed up at her, needing to tell her so much, yet still unable to, the unuttered confessions a constant burning coal in his throat. "I'll be right here after you eat. I'll always be there for you to take your fill of me."

Next moment, her response made him like everything had come crashing down.

Wrapping one lock of the hair he'd grown longer as per her request, her smile inexorable seduction, she asked, "Always? Even when I go back home?"

# Eight

Anastasia could no longer keep the knowledge from herself.

Not that she'd really kept it hidden. It was just she hadn't given her all-encompassing, overwhelming emotions for Ivan a name, not since he'd come back. But it had been a constant in her life, even when she'd thought he'd left her forever.

She loved him. Had always and would always love him.

But though he behaved as if he loved her as passionately, as absolutely, and was profuse with extravagant actions and endearments, he never put his emotions into those words. So neither had she. And in spite of everything he'd done, everything they'd shared, she dreaded that he'd one day suddenly end it again.

And that wasn't another attack of anxiety or paranoia. She had reason to think what she did. It had started that morning two weeks ago, when she'd introduced the subject of going home.

He hadn't answered her, had done it smoothly, heaving up to engulf her in kisses and coddling, feeding her breakfast before making love to her again.

He'd expertly avoided the subject since, diverting the conversation each time she tried to take it there.

By now she knew if she left it up to him, she'd never go home.

Though he'd been struggling not to show it, he'd been on edge, anticipating that his evasive tactics would soon run out, and they'd have a confrontation. She feared that when that happened, this rarefied state they'd been living in would come to an end. And this time, he *would* let her go.

Just minutes ago, she'd reached critical mass. She couldn't go one more hour without finally having this out.

Her footsteps faltered outside his office before she came into his view. He always left the door open, as if perpetually afraid she'd need him and he wouldn't be aware of it at once.

She inhaled one last bolstering breath and walked in.

His eyes flashed that all-out welcome at her sight. He rose at once from his massive mahogany desk with the multiple computer screens at his back. But his eager steps slowed down when he saw her face clearly. She was sure she looked as tense as she felt.

The momentary slowing turned into urgent strides that had him catching her by her shoulders in an anxious grip in seconds. "What is it, *moya dorogoya*? You're not feeling okay?"

Gripping his hands she tried to stem his anxiety, what could soar at the slightest provocation. "I'm fine, really. Don't start worrying. I just...wanted to talk to you."

His face emptied. But in the blankness she could see one important fact. He knew what she was going to talk about. And if he could have done anything to stop her, he would have. But she'd cornered him this time, and he could do nothing to escape the subject. And he hated it.

It made her almost back down. How she hated to force this confrontation, too. But it had to come, sooner or later. And now she knew it would, she could no longer postpone it and live in this progressively debilitating suspense.

Gathering all her strength of will, trembling inside in apprehension at the possible outcome, she said, "I've tried to bring it up before, but you clearly weren't ready to discuss it. I let it go as long as I could, Ivan, I really did. But I can't do it anymore. Even after what happened, the condition I was in when I first came with you, being with you here has been the most magical time of my life. But…"

His hands caught her arms again. "There shouldn't be any *buts*. It is magic, being together. And I never want anything to break the spell."

"I've thought about it long and hard from every angle, and now that I'm healed, inside and out as much as I ever will be, I've changed my mind. I won't sit back and let you pull strings to honor Alex's memory. *I* will do that. I owe it to him, to our parents and to Cathy and the kids. I owe it to myself. Only then can I get closure and change my path."

His jaw muscles bunched, but he finally nodded. "Very well. If you will let me orchestrate this to the best outcome, you can be the one to make the final steps and announcements."

Grabbing his hand, she planted a fervent kiss in his palm. "Thank you…" He started to protest and a finger on his lips silenced him. "Just let me thank you, Ivan, please. I need to give you my thanks far more than you hate receiving it."

He gave another reluctant nod, before his eyes lightened, as if with relief. "If this is why you want to go back…"

She had to stop him. "No, it isn't. I do have a life back in the States, Ivan, a life I want to go back to. But I need you to tell me what going back would mean for us. I know you thrive on solitude, but I don't. I needed it for a while, to regain myself and my stability. But I can't continue being with you in such isolation from the rest of the world."

"Why not? It has been perfect that way."

"It has been more than perfect, but it has also been like a pocket universe, an alternate reality. We can't exist in this bubble forever. You have friends who're as close as family to you, and I do have a family. Two families."

At her last words, something dark and terrible filled his gaze. Something elemental. Bleakness? Revulsion? Even despair?

When families had been mentioned at the beginning of their relationship in the past, he'd only said he was orphan, adopted and abandoned again at an early age. It had been her cue never to mention family to him again, avoiding mention of her own in deference to his sensitivities.

But did it go beyond sensitivity? Did the scars of his childhood go way deeper than what she'd ever estimated? Did he abhor the idea of family, especially one that would invade his life, as hers would, through her?

If this was true, where would this leave them?

Heart pounding with trepidation, she ventured a direct gaze into those grim eyes and broached the subject that had been an unspoken taboo between them. "I realize family isn't something you consider kindly, and rightfully so, but my experience with family is nothing like yours. I—I love my family. I need them."

The sheer pain that came into his eyes made her hate

herself for causing it. His next words, forlorn and agonized, hit her even harder.

"I thought you needed me."

"I do. Oh, God, I do. But needing them, too, wouldn't make me need you any less, wouldn't interfere in our relationship."

His whole face twisted as if unbearable bitterness had just flooded his mouth. "It will. And I can't abide something coming between us."

Dreading his answer, she knew she could no longer dance around the subject, had to ask him pointblank.

"What will you do if—*when*—I go back to my life, the life that includes my family? Will you disappear again?"

This time he said nothing, his silent rejection far harsher than if he'd spoken it. A dozen emotions seethed in his eyes as they fixed on hers. It felt as if he was trying to bend her to his will, to make her relinquish this intention. And she had to face what she'd long avoided facing.

Ivan was incapable of leading a life among others. He was the wolf she'd once jokingly accused him of being. A lone wolf. If she wanted to be his mate, it would be either him or the rest of the world.

But though it would have been a terrible choice, knowing the nature of his scars, she *would* have chosen him over anything. *If* she didn't fear his inexplicable moods, what stemmed from his unknown and not-to-be-known past. If she didn't dread his future abandonment.

But there was so much she didn't know about him, and about the reasons he'd left her in the past. With so many things she couldn't understand about him, so much he hid from her, she couldn't bet her heart, her life and future on him.

It felt as if her heart broke for real, and, her chest was

tightening over its jagged pieces, until she couldn't stop herself from crying out with the pain.

Her desperation released some shackle that had been holding him back and he caught her in a fierce embrace.

"Don't leave, *moya dusha*. Don't leave me."

She sobbed her desolation. "I never want to leave you. But I can't remain here where I have no life outside of you."

"Then I'll make you a life. Anything you want."

"I only ever wanted you. Going back doesn't make this any less true. It's you who's putting an impossible condition on being with you. You don't have to be involved with my family in any way if you don't want, but you can't expect me to just cut them off, too. You don't have to come back *with* me. Just say you will be back *for* me."

Again, his oppressive, horrible silence in the face of her entreaty, where all doubts mushroomed, shrieked for her to cut her losses. To go now, before leaving him became impossible, or even worse, before nothing much of her survived leaving him.

Feeling like she was reaching inside her chest and ripping her shattered heart out, her shaking hands undid his grip on her arms. "I want to go back to the States now, please, Ivan. You are free, as always, to do what's best for yourself."

Ivan had done what Anastasia had asked him.

He'd taken her back to the States. He'd insisted he'd be the one to drive her to her parents' doorstep, even when she'd tried to convince him Fyodor had better do it.

She hadn't wanted him to come with her in the first place. Extending the goodbye for all these hours, and up until these last moments, had been brutal, for both of them.

But he couldn't let her out of his sight before he saw her safe inside her family home. Only his overpowering reluctance now let her walk to their door on her own, rolling the single suitcase she'd packed from the innumerable things he'd bought her.

He sat in the car watching her go, paralyzed, unable to move a muscle or make a sound to stop her.

Knowing he *shouldn't* stop her.

All he could do was cling to her every nuance as she rummaged shakily for her house keys. She hadn't told her parents she was coming home, didn't even ring the bell. She probably didn't want to hurt him with the sight of her family receiving her in tearful welcome, when she thought his hang-ups stemmed from having no family of his own.

Her consideration tore at him all over again, her every move as she fumbled to open the door more slashes to his bleeding psyche. Then without a last look, she stumbled in and closed the door.

The moment she did, Ivan felt his heart being crushed. Literally. What else explained that stab that sank into his heart, making him lurch forward, his head shaking on the steering wheel and his lungs tightening on what felt like broken glass?

Giving in to the agony, he almost wished that it was a real heart attack, and that it wouldn't spare him. Almost. He couldn't wish for his life to end as long as Anastasia existed. As long as she needed him. As he knew she did.

But she needed more than him to complete her healing. She needed to resume her life. He'd tried to put that moment off for as long as he could, plying all his diversion tactics to postpone it. But even before she'd confronted him yesterday he'd already known. If he loved her, he should let her go.

And *how* he loved her.

He'd long admitted to himself that the all-consuming feeling that had blossomed into life from their first meeting and had only intensified as he'd gotten to know her, was love.

No. Far more than love. He now fully knew what his brothers, Antonio, Rafael, Raiden and Numair, even Richard, felt for their soul mates. This absolute admiration and allegiance, this endless desire and devotion. And he wanted with her what they had with them.

Union, children, permanence. Everything.

But that also meant being in extreme proximity with his own family, since they were a close and constant part of her life.

In her efforts to convince him that going back home, reentering her family's life wouldn't impact him or their relationship, she'd as good as pledged he didn't have to see any of them. But he knew this was impossible. How could he make her live in this abnormal state, torn between him and those who'd raised her? How could he force her to split herself in two, part for him and part for them, keeping the two halves separate, with her contentment lost in the middle?

He couldn't. He'd taken her away knowing it was best for her. He shouldn't have pressured her to remain in isolation with him the moment he'd realized it was no longer the case.

And now she was here. Back among the only people in the world he couldn't bear being around. The ones he had to abide if he wanted to be with her again.

Suddenly, the talons that had sunk in his heart retracted, letting him breathe. Because something was becoming clear.

Right now his agony was only over the idea of separation from her. None of his misery in these past hours had been about the aversion that had ruled his life since he was twelve. None of it had anything at all to do with his family.

Even if the dread of being around them wasn't gone, it was *nothing* compared to the unimaginable desolation of being without Anastasia. The idea of putting up with their presence in his life for as long as they lived, of even developing a relationship with them for her sake, wasn't abhorrent anymore. It even bordered on being welcome. As long as it made her whole and serene, as long as it afforded him the miracle of her presence in his life.

He had no idea if she even loved him a fraction of how he loved her. But that, too, didn't matter. Whatever she felt for him now was more than enough.

For a second chance with her, this time for life, he was willing, eager, *happy*, to put up with anything.

He couldn't believe he hadn't figured this out before.

Starting the car, he put it in reverse and backed up into her parents' driveway, in the exact same place he'd parked that first day he'd asked her to go with him.

This time, he would ask her to *be* with him. Forever.

Within ten minutes of being with her parents, Anastasia had expended all the hugs and kisses and the delight of seeing them again. Now an awkward silence descended on them. She really had nothing to say to them.

It wasn't only Alex's loss that gaped between them like a black hole that would forever suck any real brightness out of their relationship. They truly had nothing new to say to each other. They'd been talking regularly while she'd been in Russia, with her keeping them updated about her health while they'd kept her up-to-date with the incidents of their own uneventful lives, and the more bumpy adjustments of Cathy's and the kids'. She knew her mother and father had always itched to learn the details of her situation with Ivan—what she'd adamantly refused to discuss.

Now there was nothing to discuss anymore.

Ivan had succumbed to her desire to return home, had been immovable about delivering her here himself. As he had that time when he'd gotten her and Alex home. It had been almost as horrible as those dark days, sitting onboard his jet with him, knowing that the hours had been counting down to separation from him once again. This time for what looked like a final time.

Suddenly, it all hit her.

This could *actually* be the end.

And there was absolutely no way she could let it be that.

She heaved up to her feet so suddenly she made her parents exclaim in alarm. Excusing herself, she told them she had to do something urgently and would be in touch as soon as she could. Then she ran out of the room with them gaping after her.

She couldn't let Ivan go. She wouldn't. Not this time.

In the past, in Russia, she hadn't fought for him, for them. This time she would. Until her last breath, if need be.

Getting her phone out, she dialed his number as she ran to the door. And the phone rang. Not her phone. A phone on the other side of the door. For a second it didn't make sense.

Then she snatched the door open.

He was there, one hand poised on the doorbell, the other reaching for the phone still ringing in his pocket.

Their gazes collided, a thousand volts of longing and relief arcing across the distance between them.

Then there was none, both hurtling to obliterate it.

She flew into his arms. The home that was hers alone, the man who was her haven, her succor.

Her everything.

Ivan kissed her, devoured her, gulping air through her

lips as if he'd been suffocating without her, as she had without him in that short time they'd been apart. As if he, too, had felt his world coming to an end at the thought of losing her.

With tears flowing down her cheeks, she tore from his crushing embrace, needing to tell him everything she would do for him, for them. She grabbed his hand, dragged him behind her toward his car. Midway, she rethought her plan and doubled back toward the house, and up to her quarters, with Ivan rushing after her with his face an adorable mix of perplexity and compliance.

Closing the door of her bedroom, she tackled him down on her bed and stormed him with kisses, tears and smiles.

Then she realized something. Though he was surrendering to her, kissing her back with the same fervor, with the same shaky need for reconnection, that stiffness had reentered his body. Though he'd been unable to stay away, he was still loath to be there.

Putting this matter to rest once and for all was the one thing that could make her stop kissing him now. Pulling back, she was struck by the magnificent sight he made sprawled there, dwarfing the bed, the whole room, his raven hair strewn around his majestic head.

She opened her mouth to speak, but he spoke first, his voice hushed like a fervent prayer. But it was what he said that made her jackknife up, gape down on him.

"Anastasia, *moye serdtse, ya nye magu zhit' byes tyeba.* I can't live without you, my heart. I won't. Marry me."

His words and their meaning registered at once this time. And so did their total shock. He…he…

*Ivan was proposing.*

And she only knew one thing. She had to find her voice, to blurt out an acceptance.

But something held her back. His agitation. It went beyond worrying about her response. It hit pause on her surging jubilation.

She pulled him up. "There's something wrong here, Ivan. You don't seem happy about asking me this."

"I am, or I will be when you say yes."

Knowing there was more to this than he was letting on, she persisted, eyes roaming his face, feverishly attempting to see inside him. "If there's any element of honor or duty or anything else involved here—"

"All my honor and duty and everything else I am *are* all about you." She started to protest and his lips silenced hers, before he pulled back to pledge, "You're everything to me, Anastasia, everything. I love you. I have always and will always love you. Only ever you."

"Oh, God, Ivan, I love you, too. You're everything to me, too. You have always been and will always be. But—"

"No buts, *moya lyubov*, my love."

"Yes, Ivan, but. These things you never told me are still like a rock on your chest, a constant crushing pain. I *feel* them and they hurt me, too. They're *not* in your past, but very much in your present and I love you too much to let you carry them into your future. I want you with every fiber of my being and I was coming to tell you I'd do anything to be with you. But I won't let you spare me, I won't let you hide your pain and suffering from me anymore."

Ivan knew this was it. She wouldn't be satisfied with any more evasions. She couldn't bear any more uncertainty, wouldn't let him carry the burden alone any longer.

Feeling he'd be tearing out thorns that had been long embedded deep in his flesh, where scar tissue had formed layers that now had to be ripped open to extract them, he stalled.

"Say yes first, Anastasia. Say you'll marry me."

"This isn't about me now, Ivan. This is about you. Let me in all the way, my love, let me heal you like you healed me."

At his butchered groan, she contained him in such tenderness, such magnanimity that he'd never known existed, or that he'd ever be blessed enough to experience.

Kissing his brow, the voice he now lived to hear shook with all of her love and allegiance. "Be with me completely, Ivan. Be mine like I'm yours, past, present and future."

Capitulating once and for all, he surrendered all that he was.

His secrets, his sins, his suffering.

Down to the last mutilating detail.

# Nine

Anastasia thought she'd known the worst kind of devastation when Alex had been murdered.

But there seemed to be more kinds that were just as horrifying. And even more shocking.

Ivan. His past. What had been done to him. What he'd had to endure. What he'd been made to do. What he'd had to do to escape, to rebuild himself, to build his life and power.

If she'd tried to guess for as long as she lived, she would have never imagined anything of this nature or magnitude.

But what was too terrible for her to contemplate was not what had been done to him. But by whom. His parents. The parents he'd loved and idolized. The people she'd known all her life, who'd been as much a part of her being as her own parents, and whom she'd loved and trusted almost as much.

And it explained everything. Everything. About him, who he was, how he'd come to be this way, what he could do. It explained his actions, past and present. Why he'd left her, why he'd stayed away even though he'd needed her and Alex in his life, why he'd tortured himself with depriving himself of them. Because he couldn't bear to be near the people who'd bought their own lives at the price of his.

And it explained his turmoil now. If anything was a testament to his love, it was that he'd come offering his heart, his life. He would endure the torture of living that life close to the family that had betrayed and abandoned him in this unspeakable way, just to be with her.

Now the tears that had seeped out of her soul as she'd listened to him, as she'd tried to process the enormity of his injuries, stopped, as she was hit with another realization. Ivan didn't want vengeance. He'd never wished to punish the people he'd trusted most and who'd sent him to hell.

But *she* did.

She wanted to tear down the whole world to avenge him. Since she couldn't, she'd tear down her own world.

She wiped at her tears angrily, but when she rose from her slump in Ivan's arms and looked down at him, what she saw in his eyes almost caused her heart to burst with outrage. That look of vulnerability, of defeat. She suspected what it signified.

He validated her suspicion. "I've been running away all these years from my dread of this look in your eyes, this revulsion when you realized what I really am, what I've done."

Before she could shout a vehement correction, he rose from the bed where he'd poured out his heart and horrors, turned away as if he could no longer meet her eyes.

"But you were right in persisting to make me tell you the truth. You had a right to know what kind of man I am, where I'm coming from. It would have been unfair to you if I let you marry me without knowing what you'd be really getting. I love you too much I feared it would alienate you, if not at once then later. But it's no excuse—"

She grabbed him, spastic hands sinking in the rock-hard flesh of his arms as she snatched him around to face her. "Stop, Ivan, *stop*. It's all for *you*, for the horrors you've endured, for the childhood you've lost. This is sympathy that my heart and my whole being aren't big enough to hold. But the revulsion you see? It's all for those who've done this to you."

The hesitant hope in his eyes, something she'd never thought to see tainting his indomitable wolf-like gaze, made her want to smash everything in sight.

"I love you, Ivan!" This was almost a scream. "I've loved you since I first laid eyes on you, loved you all through the years when I thought you'd abandoned me, and loved you way more when you came back and snatched me from death's jaws, then dragged me back to life. But now that I know everything, now that I understand what drove you, what you are, I love you far more than ever before. *So* much more than I thought I could withstand. But it kills me to imagine what you've been through. It's driving me crazy to know I'd never be able to do anything about it, that I can't reach back in time and rescue the child you were. I hate it, violently, insanely, that I'm helpless to heal the man you are."

His face crumpled in such agonizing relief it made her burst into tears again. The need to protect him from even one more single moment of pain overwhelmed her, made her charge him, pushing him down again on the bed, raining her agony and reiterating her I-love-yous and I'm-sorrys on him.

His powerful arms trembled around her as if he couldn't

believe she was still really there, and really feeling this way. And her rage spiked again.

She tore away from his kisses, seethed, "I might not be able to do anything about your past, but I can and will do something from now on. This crime your parents committed against you was macabre, unforgivable. And though no punishment could ever be enough, I will do everything in my power to see them punished."

He surged to cup her face, the eyes she adored urgent, anxious. "*Nyet, moya dusha*, no! I never wanted to punish them."

"Because you're far better and stronger than I am. They have to be punished, Ivan. They can't get away with this!"

"It doesn't matter anymore. And you're wrong. You *have* healed me. Just seeing you like this, knowing you still love me and aren't horrified by my past, everything that's ever happened to me has ceased to exist. The one thing that burdened me was my fear of scaring you off if you found out. Of losing you. But now that I know it not only didn't matter to you, but you feel this powerfully about it all, about me, nothing else matters." He kissed her trembling tear-wet lips when she started to protest again. "As for my parents…I never wanted to see them, thought I couldn't be around them. But now that you know, now that I know you'll be mine no matter what, I don't mind having them around."

"*I* mind. Even if you've forgiven and forgotten, I can't risk that you'd feel even a twinge of heartache around them, not for the world. And *I* can't be around them either. If I'm around my parents, around Cathy and the kids, they'll *always* be around." She rose on her knees, grabbed his hands in a convulsive grip when he started to protest. "Marry me, Ivan, today, right now, and let's go back to Russia. Or anywhere in the world you want."

Then her streaking thoughts shrieked to a halt. "God, Ivan, I just realized something even more terrible. The people who sacrificed their own firstborn shouldn't be around Alex's children! They should be exposed to my family for the monsters they are so they'd be cast out of everyone's lives."

"Anastasia, please, just let it go. You can't believe Alex's children are in any danger of them. They've been exemplary parents to my siblings, and doting grandparents."

"They've been my and Alex's second parents!" she wailed. "If you could only see how they loved Alex, how they treated him like a beloved son…after they'd thrown *you* away to certain death or worse. Oh, God!"

He pressed her to his heart again, stroking her back, her hair, crooning words of comfort. After everything he'd endured, *he* was trying to soothe *her*.

"I've always understood what drove them to sacrifice me," he said, his voice now more than calm. Peaceful. "It *was* a deadly situation, and they had to make a terrible choice. I never had any wish to confront or expose them and now more than ever I see absolutely no reason to. I'm the one who caused you and I all the heartache, not them, when I let my hang-ups and fears of my past deprive me of you, deprive us of each other. And I'm never doing that again. I also don't want you to give up anything for me. I want you to have your family and friends and everything that makes your life normal and whole. I only wish to share it with you."

Her still-mushrooming outrage choked her all over again. "There is no going back to normal for me, not after I learned the truth about what happened to you!"

He caught her trembling face in a cherishing grip. "I only told you so you'd have access to every corner of me, so there would be no part of me you didn't see, didn't own. Not so you can wallow in a past I already intended to leave behind. My love for you fills me, heals me, makes me whole in ways I could have never dreamed I'd be. And I want us to never look back, to move only forward." His lips clung to hers, as if he needed the contact to breathe. "All you have to do now is tell me everything you wish for in a wedding and in a home for us and I'll make it happen. Even if you want it today, right now, I'll make it all happen."

"You know I want only you."

"See this?" He made a sweeping gesture at her, them, his smile exquisite. "What you feel? This is reward and cure enough to erase ten times the injuries and injustices I've suffered. But you will be my bride, and we will have a wedding, and you will have your family with you. After their incalculable loss of Alex, we can't let them lose you, too. They deserve to be happy for you."

And for the next hour she argued, cried and bargained, unable to think how she'd let him out of this room, how she'd expose him to his parents, who she knew were coming to dinner.

But he patiently, persistently, adoringly countered her every protest on his behalf.

Then at long last, she realized.

This was part of *his* healing.

This was how he'd truly move on.

"Getting married? Next week?"

Those were the exclamations that met Anastasia's announcement at the dinner table.

She didn't know which stunned her and Ivan's parents more. That they were getting married at all, or that they'd set their wedding date for six days from now, which also happened to be Christmas.

He'd finally convinced her not to elope, to have a wedding where all the people in her life would take part. She'd succumbed only because she knew this was important to him and she wanted to give him whatever he wished for. Once that was decided on, he'd messaged his brothers. Six days from today was the earliest he could round them all up.

She looked at Ivan now, her eyes asking if he'd like to say something, but he only gave a slight nod, giving her full control over the situation.

She swept a glance around the table, her gaze unable to rest on Ivan's parents. She now hated them, and hated how Ivan must be feeling sitting so close to them. It amazed her all over again that he didn't show any emotion that even she could detect, nothing in his eyes and vibe but adoration for her.

To honor his wish to make this as normal and smooth as possible, she forced herself to flash a smile at her parents. "I hope that was you being surprised in a good way."

"God, darling, yes!" Her mother's stunned eyes shone with tears as she reached out to squeeze her hand, before turning to her father. "We're thrilled. Aren't we, dear?"

Her father nodded dazedly. "It's just that we didn't know what was going on. And it's so soon we won't have time to do much."

She waved her father's concern away. "There isn't much to do."

She had to make that perfectly clear upfront. Her parents had always dreamed of giving her as elaborate a wedding as Alex's, but with her seeming to be a bachelorette for life, she'd long thwarted them. If she gave them half a chance, they'd go all out. Ivan, too, would go to lengths she couldn't even conceive of to give her a legendary ceremony if she let him.

"We're going to keep it very simple." Before her parents or Ivan could voice any objections, she added, "I actually didn't want a wedding at all."

*Because of Alex* went unspoken but heard by all.

"When Ivan proposed a few hours ago I suggested we just inform you over dinner and elope." At everyone's gasps, she reached for Ivan's hand. "So you've got Ivan to thank that we'll have a wedding. He insisted that Alex wouldn't have wanted us to get married without one. But even had everything been perfect, I'm not one for frills, as you all know. I just want a gathering where everyone we love would be present."

She had to stop to swallow the bitterness that would now perpetually fill her throat. They'd both have to bear his parents' presence at their wedding, smile and pretend that everything was okay.

"Thank you, Ivan." That was her mother, turning to Ivan, her gaze filled with so much Anastasia couldn't fathom. Though she could guess. This was the man who'd saved her daughter, would now marry her and become a new son, after she'd lost her own. It must be all emotionally tumultuous for her. "I doubt any of us would have been able to change Ana's mind."

Ivan gave such a gracious smile. "It's my pleasure and privilege, Mrs. Shepherd. Quite literally."

"Please, call me Grace." Her mother gave Ivan a wary, wavering smile. "And thank you for giving us the chance to see Ana becoming a bride."

Fixing her with a warm gaze, he covered the hand she had placed on the table. "Every mother and father should be there when a man offers his heart and life to their daughter."

A murmur of appreciation went around the table as another wave of searing love filled Anastasia's heart.

She was on the verge of tears, when Ivan's father, who'd been her beloved Uncle John until a few hours ago, rose to his feet, his face splitting on a delighted smile. "We need to toast the bride and groom!"

Ivan's mother, Aunt Glenda to her, and until so recently almost as close to Anastasia as her own mother, followed her husband, enthusiastically sweeping around the table and filling everyone's glasses with the sparkling white wine her father had selected to go with the seafood.

As she filled Ivan's glass, she squeezed his shoulder, looking down at him in such awe and affection. "You're going to be as good as my son-in-law, too, do you know that?"

Anastasia winced at the sight Ivan made with the woman who'd abandoned him, the skewer in her heart turning as she realized their green eyes were almost the same.

She battled to keep tears at bay as he looked up at his mother. Then he made it almost impossible when his face shockingly gentled as he patted her hand, the same unexpected and agonizing kindness in his voice. "Anyone who loves Anastasia can count on me as the best relative they can have."

Looking delighted, his mother beamed down at him. "And as the one Anastasia loves most you're going to be deluged in new relatives yourself. Good thing you can't have enough family!"

Fiery indignation on his behalf lashed her, flinging the sharp words out of her mouth. "Ivan doesn't have *any* family."

Ivan raised his glass to her, his gaze soothing her. "The only important thing to me is that I'll now have one with you, my love." He looked around the room, his gaze containing nothing but genuine geniality. "And clearly many extensions, too."

She nodded tightly, letting him pull her back from the brink, gratitude engulfing her that he was giving her the opportunity to make it all up to him for the rest of her life.

But as if to further inflame her, his mother touched his shoulder again, her eyes probing, pained. "Are you an orphan?"

There was no use. She couldn't hold back. And she didn't.

"Worse. His parents abandoned him."

His parents had the gall to look horrified.

Then Aunt Glenda whispered, "That's *terrible*. Were you very young? What happened to you?"

Clearly deciding to put an end to this, Ivan rose and turned to his parents with an easy smile Anastasia had no idea how he managed. "As you can see I far more than survived. Now I found the biggest part of my soul and I am the happiest man on earth."

Uncle John, his father, looking as if he'd dodged a bullet, laughed and raised his glass. "And now you do have more family than you'll know what to do with. You have two fathers-in-law and two mothers-in-law and a bunch of in-laws—siblings, nieces and nephews. Before this alarms you, let me assure you it's a bargain. We're full of uses, all ready and eager to do any amount of chores and babysit on demand. And we're only slightly interfering."

Her father rose with a wide smile, raising his own glass. "Ivan doesn't strike me as the kind of son-in-law who'd allow *any* level of interference."

Ivan returned her father's smile. "Not even from a superpower."

Swallowing down her agitation, Anastasia volunteered the explanation. "He's not being metaphorical here. Remind me to tell you about the time when he blithely ignored the Russian premier's demand for a personal meeting because he thought babysitting *me* was more important."

All voices rose around the table, demanding she tell the story immediately. And in telling it, she and Ivan relaxed back into their flawless rapport, and what she never thought could happen did. The night turned into an immensely enjoyable interlude, especially when Cathy and the kids came over.

For long stretches of time during the night that extended into the early hours of morning, Anastasia found herself forgetting everything but that she was with the people she loved most on earth, the people who surrounded the union she was forging with Ivan with delight and caring.

But every now and then, the illusion cracked and she saw the truth. The truth that was uglier than anything from a nightmare. Ivan bolstered her, absorbing her agitation as soon as it surged. But even if he'd dealt so incredibly well with what he'd lived dreading—seeing his parents up-close again—she could not do the same.

After their wedding, she would never expose him to them again if she could at all help it. His parents didn't deserve the happiness and privilege of knowing him as he'd made himself, didn't deserve his unbelievable mercy.

With the countdown to the wedding rushing by, Anastasia found herself sliding into stretches of absolute euphoria.

Being with Ivan now that she was certain of his love was a happiness she hadn't known could exist.

He, too, seemed on a constant high.

Yet, it still came in waves. That tension, like a sick buzz of electricity that zapped her muscles, a white noise that scratched along her nerves. Ivan kept assuring her it wasn't coming from him, that he was fine, that being with her had nullified anything he'd feared he'd feel. He not only didn't feel anything negative around his parents, as strange as it might sound, he actually enjoyed being with them.

And then they'd found there was a bonus that neither of them had considered. His siblings.

Cathy and the others, with all their kids, were all over him, as if they recognized he was kindred. This complicated Anastasia's original plan of moving away as soon as the ceremony was over and seeing their families as little as possible. Ivan deserved to have the pleasure of knowing his siblings and being part of their lives, to bask in their eagerness and admiration, in what she knew would turn to love.

And today of all days, it did feel as if it would be impossible to just walk away from their families.

Debating how to handle or time making this disclosure, she walked into the great room that overlooked the Atlantic and found Ivan looking out to the horizon, in one of the rare times she'd found him alone since they'd come here.

Ivan had invited everyone to stay in his Hamptons estate, where they'd have the wedding. He'd been constantly waving his magic wand to give everyone an experience that would never be equaled, mixing the holiday season celebrations with what he called "wedding overtures."

When she objected that this was all a far cry from the simple couple of hours she'd expected for the wedding ceremony, he just kissed her and demanded she appreciate his "restraint", reminding her what it was like when he was extravagant.

His brothers would be arriving a day before the ceremony, and she couldn't wait to see the rest of that unique brotherhood who'd shared Ivan's tragic origins, and who had not only triumphed over unimaginable hardships, but also, like him, had gone on to conquer the world in their own fields of virtuosity.

Feeling a wave of love crash on her harder than those on the beach below, she slid her arms around him from the back. To her amazement, he was surprised. Ivan had always been primed, feeling the slightest movement from afar, even before it happened. He'd certainly never been oblivious to her approach, seemed to feel it when it was only an intention in her mind. That he'd been now meant he'd been too consumed by something.

Her heart started hammering with worry. But he was turning to her, plucking her up and into a kiss that, as usual, overwhelmed her.

When he finally let her feet touch the ground again, her hands roved over his rock-hard body, still uneasy. "You okay?"

"I am now." He gave her another mind-melting kiss. "There's a lot more to take in than even I thought."

She knew what he meant. His family. "Is that why you were off in another realm? Why you're so tense?"

"I was lost in thought, yes. But I'm tense because I'm not making love to you. That is making me downright dangerous. You do remember I put my libido in a deep freeze for years, and now I'm constantly burning. So this—" he brought her hands to his body, sliding them down his chest to his erection, each inch the consistency of steel "—is because of you."

She pouted. "Whose idea was it to not make love to me?"

He huffed in self-deprecation. "I *do* get stupid ideas. Always concerning you. I thought I could last a week with all the preparations and the family and friends around to distract me. Especially since their presence isn't conducive to our kind of explosive encounters. I also thought the torment of abstinence will serve a purpose, make sure I'd give you a wedding night to remember for the next few lifetimes."

"I'll remember each night with you longer than that."

At her hotly aroused statement, he devoured her again.

He was kissing her within an inch of her sanity when her parents walked in. Groaning, they separated, even as her parents started retreating in embarrassment.

But since she did have to try on dresses, and pick one of the dozen Ivan had provided her, she decided to postpone what she'd sought him for, said she was the one who had to go. Her parents accompanied her.

As they walked out, she again felt her parents' subdued melancholy and lingering unease.

Like her, they hadn't truly gotten over Alex's death. And though she had reassured them she knew what she was doing, marrying a man whose rivals called him Ivan the Terrible, who had enough power to tackle a world leader, it was evident they were still worried. She also suspected that even though she'd expanded on the story he'd provided about her and Alex's accident, they still felt something was off about it and about his role in the whole thing.

But since the truth would only hurt them more, she couldn't allay their suspicions. Not now, not ever.

A couple of hours later, after she'd drowned in fairy-tale gowns and picked the one that made her feel least guilty to wear only months after she'd lost Alex, everyone gathered for another of Ivan's exquisitely catered dinners.

Much later, after the younger generation and their kids went to bed, only she, Ivan and their parents remained.

Ivan took the men to the pool table, and she found herself alone with her mother and his.

As each sat sipping her choice of herbal tea, his mother turned from watching the men and looked back at Anastasia.

"You know, Ana, ever since I first saw Ivan there's been this...overwhelming feeling that comes over me whenever I look at him. And it's not because he's the most powerful and important man I'll ever meet in my life. There's just something about him."

Gritting her teeth, Anastasia said, "Yeah, it's called charisma and influence. He makes everyone feel this way."

Aunt Glenda sat up closer, her eyes so earnest. "It's not that, though I do recognize this about him. There's just this...huge side to him I feel he's hiding."

"Yes, exactly." That was Anastasia's mother, sitting up on her other side, making her feel they were squeezing her in the middle with their curiosity and concern. "It's like there's another person beneath it all. Are you aware of that? Do you know who he really is under this...facade?"

"It's not like I'm worried that he doesn't love you as completely as you love him—" Aunt Glenda stopped, seemed to be getting more distressed the more she tried to explain. "It's just...I wonder about what he's hiding. I know it's crazy, but what I feel..." She looked back at him and fell silent.

So recognition *was* haunting her, despite the transfiguring changes he'd undergone, through ordeals, maturation and intention. And she was disturbed, groping for explanations, something to make her feel secure again in the safe, suburban life she'd built, and paid for with his life.

Aunt Glenda looked back at her, putting down her cup, looking frustrated, even agitated. "God, I wish I could explain it. I wish I knew what I was feeling."

Every word had been falling on Anastasia like a scythe, slashing every fiber of restraint.

The last words severed the final tether, and she snapped.

Heaving up to her feet, she shouted, "What you're feeling is recognition, Aunt Glenda. Recognition of the son you sold to slavers, in return for a way out of Russia and a new life in the States. Slavers who tortured, degraded and exploited him in unimaginable ways!"

Ivan had picked up the feeling that something was going wrong across the room. He'd excused himself from his companions at once and had started rushing there even before he realized what was going on.

But it all happened before he could stop it. Anastasia was on her feet, screaming, everything—*everything*—pouring out of her.

He was running now, feeling both their fathers in his wake, cold sweat starting to bead on his forehead, knowing that whatever he did now, it was too late.

Anastasia sounded as if she was tearing apart her vocal chords. "How dare you sit there pretending you're a normal person? A woman and a mother? A human being even? That you have any kind of feelings? You sold your son! Your firstborn! The genius boy who loved you completely and trusted you implicitly!"

Ivan finally reached Anastasia, put himself between her and the others, taking her by the shoulders, tried to make her look at him, to silence her. "Stop. Anastasia, stop. Come with me, please."

But she only pushed against him, twisting in his hold, around his bulk, seeking to reconnect her wrath with its targets, eyes feverish between both his parents now, shaking so hard it was like she was having a seizure. Her voice had become a butchered wail, again making him realize what she now knew of his past hurt her even more than it had ever hurt him.

"Didn't you ever think of the devastation he felt when he realized you betrayed and bartered him? Didn't you ever feel sorry all these years that you sent your own son to hell, to buy yourselves this easy, petty life? Didn't you ever imagine the kind of horrors he faced, the agony and desperation he endured?" She lurched out of his hold completely, no longer Anastasia, but a rage-filled entity as she shrieked her condemnations. "And after everything you did to him—after he overcame it all and became the best man on earth—he never wanted revenge, only never wanted to see you again. *That's* why he lost seven more years of his life, when he could have been with me. He only found me again through tragedy. And for me, he not only let himself be exposed to you, he did what I thought impossible. He was kind to you. He *forgave* you. When you're *monsters*! Monsters who don't even deserve to live!"

Ivan had dragged her in his arms as she screamed, but had been unable to stop her tirade. He now subdued her efforts to fight him away, pressing her head into his chest, murmuring pleas for her to stop. He had to stem the tide of wrath and misery that was undoing her right before his eyes.

But she'd already expended every last spark of energy, now sagged against him, too drained to even tremble anymore.

It was only after he made sure this paroxysm was over, and he'd carried her to the nearest couch, soothed and revived her as much as he could, that he finally remembered the presence of the others.

Turning his gaze, he found them all frozen in their exact positions. His parents looked as if their hearts had been ripped out, their faces blank in that shocked denial before the injury registered and the collapse occurred.

"K-Konstantin? Kostya?"

His mother sounded as if someone was choking her as she said his name, and the nickname she'd used to call him with.

Giving Anastasia one last kiss, begging her again not to move, to let him handle this, he rose to his feet.

There was no escaping it anymore. Here was the confrontation he'd lived almost three decades dreading.

Coming to stand before his parents, he nodded. "It's me."

Looking as if they thought they were losing their minds, they reached out their hands to him, as if to make sure he was real.

"That's—that's the explanation for wh-what our hearts have been telling us about you…"

"We thought you were lost to us all these years ago…"

His beyond shell-shocked parents talked over each other, then stopped.

Then his father's face crumpled as he staggered back as if under a bone-crushing blow. He would have fallen on the ground if Ivan hadn't caught him and lowered him onto an armchair.

The moment he straightened, his mother was clawing at him, crying, then bawling such ugly, violent sobs he felt as if she was being torn apart inside.

Ivan had dealt with death, with danger and violence of the most extreme magnitudes. But against tears, especially Anastasia's and now his mother's, he was totally powerless.

Looking around, as if seeking help, he found Anastasia staring at him limply. Her parents had sat down, looked as if they'd turned to stone. No help was coming from any of them.

Forcing himself to contain his mother, he led her to sit in the armchair next to his father, who was weeping, too, si-lent tears that were somehow even more distressing to Ivan.

Knowing this had to end, once and for all, he went down on his haunches before them. "My view of this isn't as harsh as Anastasia. She's angry on my behalf, far more than I've ever been on my own. I understood you made a terrible decision, to save Katerina and Fedora and Ivanna and Dimitri, not only yourselves. And maybe you didn't realize what would happen, what they'd do to me. But as I told you before, I survived, and then some. And now I have Anastasia, and I love her and I am happy with her, beyond comprehension. I know it won't be easy, living with this now that the past is exhumed, but—"

His father lurched forward, his hand trembling to Ivan's face, his eyes blood-red. "We believed that you died."

Ivan's jaw clenched. "It was always a possibility to die there."

His father shook his head vigorously. "No, no, we were told you died in a car accident before you even reached the academy you were supposed to join, what we fully believed was a legitimate institution."

Ivan stared at him. Did he mean…?

"We never suspected *anything* of what Ana said. We thought we lost you to a senseless accident like we lost Alex!"

His mother again snatched at anything she could hold of him, ended up grabbing his jacket, his shirt, his hair. "You thought we abandoned you? Sold you? *Bozhe moy…*"

She burst into another jag of demolishing weeping as she pitched forward to kiss his hand and bathe it in her tears.

As he tried to drag his hand away, his heart stuttering in his chest, his father grabbed his other hand.

"It was years before we could get over our grief and guilt for sending you somewhere without us. Just that we weren't there for you, that we thought you died alone, almost drove us both mad. It was only having to care for our other children that forced us to continue to function. If we'd known anything about the true nature of that place, if we even suspected for a second you wouldn't get the best treatment, wouldn't be achieved and happy there, that we wouldn't see you again soon, we would have rather died than send you there."

Ivan stared at the parents he'd once loved with everything in him, whom he'd missed and felt their loss like that of a vital organ.

And he knew one thing.

They were telling the truth.

# Ten

Ivan had felt his whole belief system being rewritten once before. When everything told him that his parents had abandoned him in the worst way possible.

Now everything said they hadn't. Every cell in his body screamed it, had been screaming it since he'd looked into their eyes again.

The knowledge was absolute, incontrovertible.

This time no amount of circumstantial evidence would convince him differently.

And it was like an earthquake was unleashed inside him, sending everything crashing, the pillars he'd built his life around collapsing, pulverizing each other and everything else.

He vaguely realized the pain he was feeling was only the beginning of a process that would reform his memories, his psyche. There was no escaping letting the process take its course, no ameliorating the pangs of this excruciating rebirth.

He could only do one thing.

Kneeling before his parents, his hands shook as he took a hand from each, his heart squeezing as he felt how fragile they'd become. This wasn't only a sign of aging, it was the unremitting effects of loss.

His loss. He knew it.

He let them know he did. "I believe you. And I will never be able to beg your forgiveness enough for believing any differently of you. My only excuse is that it was horrific, not only being in that hellhole, but being without you. I guess at first I needed to believe you sacrificed me so I could let you go, and let hope and life itself go, so I'd escape my prison. Later I needed to believe it so it would harden me, so I could survive."

His parents collapsed over him, deluging him in the agony of their tears, disbelief, relief…and love.

Feeling as helpless as he had when he'd arrived too late to save Alex, unable to rewind the past and erase the damage, he hugged them with all he was.

"Forgive me for suspecting you, for depriving us of all these years we could have been together since my escape."

They both wept and shook and hugged him back until he felt their long-fractured hearts splintering again. He had to stop the vicious circle of pain and regret, had to start them on the path of healing.

Pulling back, he forced a smile on his numb lips. "But I know you'll forgive me, even if I don't deserve to be forgiven. I know because I'm blessed like that. I committed the same crime with Anastasia. I deprived her of seven years when I could have loved and worshipped her, because of my hang-ups and misjudgments. And she not only forgave me, she saved me and promised to love me forever."

He looked back at her, found her sitting up rigidly, her face gripped in a storm of emotions. Dominating all was love. For him. And for his parents. And such relief. But it was the total lack of recrimination, the absolute alliance and understanding that she gave him unconditionally that gave him the ability to forgive himself, so he could give his all to her, to his parents.

Knowing she wouldn't intrude on these moments with his parents without an invitation, he reached out an arm to her, begging her nearness, letting her know there was no breath he wanted to take without her.

She staggered up to her feet and hurtled toward him unsteadily, throwing herself at him. It was like catching life itself when he wrapped her in his arms. She was more than that to him. She was the reason for, and the orchestrator of, his rebirth.

Then she was reaching out to include his parents in their embrace. Her apologies were as pained and profuse as much as their dismissal and their thanks. They insisted it was because she loved Ivan so much that she couldn't bear thinking he'd go unavenged that this all had come to light, and been resolved.

Surrounding them all in his protection and love, Ivan looked at his parents. "I need you to put it all behind us, to only look forward. Anastasia taught me this, too."

His mother burst into another jag of sobs. "I can *never* forget or live with what happened to you."

He pulled her tighter into his embrace, soothing her renewed anguish. "Whatever I went through, it all worked out for the absolute best. And it's not because I became so much stronger or because I'm now wealthy and powerful, it's because of this." He gave the most precious people in his life, the reasons for it, another squeeze, making them all shudder in relief. "Finding Anastasia, loving her, having her love, and reuniting with both of you—these miracles far surpass my ordeals, erases them. I even think it's only fair to have paid that price in advance, for your priceless blessing. So just love me like I love you, and let me make you all happy again."

For an interminable time afterward, Anastasia and Ivan's parents flooded him in every poignant and thankful emotion and he submerged them in the endlessness of his love.

Then, feeling it was the beginning of a new life for real, she knew it was the right time to take it up that final notch.

Rising from the couch where he'd taken them, where she'd been plastered to him with his parents on his other side, she stood before him.

"All this?" She gestured between them and to his parents and around the room to hers. "It only gets better. You have one more miracle coming."

Vulnerability flooded his face once again, as if he was still afraid, would always be unable to believe he could possibly have all this. She had a feeling he understood what she was about to tell him. And could barely bear the enormity of even contemplating it.

Drowning into his emerald eyes, she pulled him up and shared what she'd discovered right before she'd gone searching for him this afternoon. "Yes, *moy lyubov*, you'll have one more person to love and who will love you forever. I'm pregnant."

The extent of Ivan's jubilation at her news continued to stun Anastasia.

Two nights ago when she'd announced her pregnancy, he'd looked as if he was disintegrating under the brunt of too much joy. After promising his parents that they'd continue talking later when he wasn't literally out of his mind with exultation, he'd swept her to his bed.

Not that he'd made love to her. They'd both been too hectic with emotions they'd just needed to be wrapped in each other's arms, to attempt to contain it all and come back down to earth.

He'd made love to her the next morning, though, taking them both to the very edge of their mortality. He'd said he was done waiting for their wedding night, even if it was only one more day away. He claimed that if he'd waited, she wouldn't have had a groom to walk down the aisle to. Not a correctly functioning one, at least. And she'd wholeheartedly approved his strategy.

Now there were less than twenty-four hours to Christmas day, and their wedding.

Dragging themselves from the depths of satiation she and Ivan had just reluctantly left his suite. According to the many messages he'd gotten throughout the night, all his brothers had arrived. According to the many knocks on the door they'd had, everyone gathered downstairs was waiting for them to have an early Christmas since their wedding had confiscated the actual date.

They now descended along one arm of the bifurcated marble stairs, to an incredible sight.

That of everyone they both loved.

And they all did something that made her burst into tears again.

They treated her and Ivan to a standing ovation.

Feeling her knees buckling, she clung harder to Ivan. He swept her up in his arms at once, as if he'd been itching for an excuse to do so, drowned her in a kiss that sent the whole world spinning.

She clung around his neck and kissed him back as deeply to the background music of raucous cheers and hoots. She vaguely discerned the unfamiliar voices among those of her family and friends. Those of his brothers and their wives.

Curiosity and impatience to see those men who'd shared so much with Ivan, who were a major reason he'd survived, had become the incomparable force of nature he was now, overwhelmed her. It would have taken nothing less to make her cut their kiss short.

Looking avidly at the crowd as Ivan resumed descending the stairs with her still high up in his arms, she almost gasped. The collective of his brothers, now on their feet, was staggering. It was as if she was looking at different versions of Ivan.

She was thrilled to see Dr. Balducci—Tonio as Ivan called him and insisted she did, too. Now his terrible misunderstanding with Liliana had been resolved, and she was now his wife, he looked on top of the world. The others she recognized at once from Ivan's descriptions of them. Each was totally unique. Yet they all looked as if they'd been made from the same higher-being material. As they had. They'd all been chosen by The Organization for being prodigies, then they'd been forged in the inferno of ordeals into the best and most powerful versions of themselves.

And those men had in turn picked women who were clearly their perfect match. Each woman stood beside her man, as magnificent as he was in her own way. She only hoped she looked anywhere near as worthy and fitting standing next to Ivan.

Everyone let the newcomers approach Ivan and her first. Ivan put her down on her feet so she could meet them. Not knowing how to welcome those formidable beings who towered over everyone, she started with Antonio Balducci, extending her hand, lips splitting in delight at seeing him again. And he set the rules for this encounter. Her former surgeon and savior pulled her into an affectionate hug, telling her that he'd be her brother-in-law now. His new bride, Liliana, followed suit, expressing her delight that she'd have yet another sister.

The rest of the introductions were as enthusiastic and warmhearted, with her being hugged and kissed and doted on by all, even his brothers' children. There was quite the array of them. Raiden and Scarlett had six alone, adopted and biological. The others had two or three and a couple were working on the next one. Even the newest wife, Liliana, was clearly pregnant. And when Anastasia expressed how incredible it was her and Ivan's baby would be born to find so many brothers and sisters, she was exposed to another round of deluging delight and indulgence.

After they judged Ivan's brothers and their families had gotten enough exclusive time with her and Ivan, the rest converged on them. Or really mostly on Ivan. His sisters and brother and their spouses and children more or less carried him off like they'd been doing the past few days whenever they could, unable to get enough of him. And that when they had no idea who he really was to them.

No one but both their parents knew, or would know of last night's revelations, at least until they all agreed on how to break out the news that Ivan was family in more ways that they thought.

After what she could only describe as the best Christmas lunch in the history of the planet, everyone decided it was time to open presents.

And there were *so* many presents. Everyone had bought presents for everyone else. His brothers and their wives had done their homework to such a meticulous level, no doubt with Ivan's insider's help, they'd gotten every single one of her extended family a unique, incredibly suitable, not to mention lavish gift.

Then came her own present. Something she couldn't have even imagined.

The brotherhood were offering her The Alex Shepherd Research Division, a whole new arm of Black Castle Enterprises that she'd build and helm to Alex's specs and in his memory.

It took hours for her, and for her family, to really wrap their mind around the enormity of this gift.

At one point when she'd barely recovered her wits, she realized one strange thing. Apart from her own gift from the brotherhood—which she was certain had been orchestrated by Ivan—he was the only one who'd gotten no one anything.

Which didn't make sense whatsoever with him being such an extravagant giver.

Which meant one thing. He was keeping his own gifts to everyone for last.

As she wondered what they would be, and when he'd present them, he stood up and invited everyone to dress warmly and follow him into the garden overlooking the ocean.

As everyone rushed after him, it only took stepping outside for everyone to freeze to the spot and gape at the sight before them.

The garden, now covered in snow, had been turned into a Christmas wonderland.

Ivan rushed down the stairs with her dazed beside him, encouraging everyone to follow suit. As soon as everyone descended into the garden, two musical bands, each made of two-dozen musicians and as many singers started playing Christmas carols and songs. The whole place had been turned into an amusement park complete with carousels and rides for both children and adults. And interspersing everything, dozens of *gigantic* Christmas trees towered, magically decorated and lit. Beneath each tree, there were *huge* heaps of gift boxes in the most exquisite wrappings she'd ever seen.

She had no idea when he'd had all his done. Just last night none of that was there. Hell, it wasn't there two hours ago when she'd last caught a glimpse of the garden.

Everyone, even his brothers, seemed to be transported into the fairytale ambiance Ivan had so meticulously created. Shrieks of delight echoed from the children, and laughter from the adults.

Dazed at yet another staggering display of his resources and thoughtfulness, she looked up at him as everyone rushed here and there to sample his wonderland's enchantments.

"Tell me most of these boxes are part of the decorations."

He bent and covered her now-cold lips in his warm ones, singeing her blood and making her forget a world outside him existed as always.

Letting her lips go with one last clinging kiss, he withdrew, teased, "You know I'll do anything you want. You want me to lie, I will."

She shook her head, looking around at the trees. "Even if you got every single person multiple Christmas presents, it still wouldn't explain those…mountains!"

He swept her off her feet again and headed for one of the carousels where all his brothers were taking their children for a ride.

"I did get everyone more than one present. Including everyone who works here and their families, all the event-planning people preparing our wedding tomorrow, the catering team and the music bands and anyone who had a hand in all this."

She jumped up in his arms and drowned him in kisses and love and thanks, on behalf of everyone he'd thought of.

Laughing, he stepped on the revolving carousel's platform and raised her on top of one of the undulating horses. Effortlessly jumping up behind her, he wrapped his arms around her, his hands caressing her were the evidence of their love was growing into a new life.

Putting his lips to her ears so she'd hear him over the lively holiday music and singing and the myriad sounds of joy, he said, "How about you make the rounds telling everyone you've already thanked me on their behalf? Now that I think about it, the number of projected thank yous is making me reconsider giving anyone anything."

She threw her head back on his shoulder, looked up at him, saw the edge of real aversion and anxiety in his light-heartedness and grinned. "No can do."

His body tensed around her as he scowled. "If you won't save me, I'll just courier everyone their stuff."

She burrowed back deeper into his body, savoring his heat and hardness even through their thermal clothing. "No, you won't. I'll make the rounds with you as you give everyone their presents, and you'll take the gratitude you deserve like a champ." Before he could protest, she invoked that carte blanche he kept renewing every single day. "I so want to meet everyone who run this impeccable place, who made all the fabulousness of today come to life, who'll make the undisputable perfection of tomorrow. In short, all those amazing beings who actually live up to your expectations and demands."

His eyes took that intensely adoring cast she'd gotten addicted to and couldn't live without. "Anything that pleases you." Then he mock-shuddered. "Now I must take my anti-thanks medication in preparation."

She hooted with laughter. "I'll have a talk with Tonio and Liliana about developing you a vaccine."

He joined her in laughter, before they both turned to shout and laugh with his brothers and their families. Afterward, they sampled each ride, talked and laughed and played and sang with all their guests, then proceeded to distribute his tons of presents.

And all through, Ivan kept her at his side as if she was as vital to him as his beating heart. As she knew she was. As he was to her. This indescribably incredible, magnanimous man who had unbelievably chosen her to love for the rest of his life.

At the end of the enchanted day, what everyone said qualified as one of the best days of their lives, excitement and happiness were coursing through Anastasia, making her downright giddy.

But to her consternation, after all the bustle had died down, she felt as if a freezing hand was squeezing her heart.

It was that darkness that had lurked in the back of her mind, that hadn't been resolved after yesterday's revelations. That unease that had been coming to her in waves, even among the ocean of rapture of last night and today. It now surged, crested, loomed over her like a tidal wave about to crash.

She'd just entered the bedroom suite with Ivan when it did.

She had no evidence. She just *knew*. Where that dark unease had come from. And what it signified.

The truth.

What was even worse than her worst nightmares.

She had no idea how she continued interacting with Ivan until he entered the bathroom. Then feeling as if she was walking with her own two feet to the slaughter, she headed toward her parents' suite.

The moment she entered and found them both sitting there in silence, looking like automatons, the knowledge solidified.

"I felt it, Dad." Her voice sounded alien in her ears. "When the revelations were being made. Even among the upheaval, I felt it. You know something more about Ivan's past. You more than know. You had a hand in it."

Her father looked at her as if he'd sustained multiple stab wounds and was silently bleeding to death.

"It was you, wasn't it?" she rasped. "You're the one who did this. You're the one who sent Ivan to hell."

Her father rose to his feet as if from under rubble, aging before her eyes, looking as if he'd have a stroke.

"It was me."

The whispered words speared Anastasia in her gut.

Her mother.

Turning away from her father, she looked at the woman who'd given birth to her, whom she'd loved and believed in all her life.

What she saw in her mother's eyes brought her whole world crashing down, crushing her beneath its debris.

"Your father and I...we were marked for liquidation," her mother said, looking as if she'd taken a decision to end her own life. "We were beyond desperate when I learned of The Organization. I approached them for a deal, and my only bargaining chip was Kostya. He was such a prodigy... I knew they'd do anything to get their hands on him. They said if I convinced my friends to let them have him, they would get us all out of Russia and give us new lives in the States. So I made a plan to indirectly convince them that it was a great opportunity, so they would never realize it was I who initiated the bargain, or learn of its true nature or that of those I made it with.

"And there was not a single minute that passed since when I didn't regret it, not one breath that wasn't poisoned by his memory or the taste of my crime. When I thought Kostya died in that accident, I was almost relieved that fate chose to end his torment before it began. Everything I did since was aimed at trying to make it up to Glenda and John, to atone. Not that I thought anything would or could. Then I saw Ivan, and everything inside me screamed, even though it seemed impossible. I only told your father when we found out who Ivan really was."

Her mother lay down on the couch, curled up, shaking, her eyes dry. She must have already expended all her tears.

If desolation and death had a sound, they would sound like her mother did now. "I deprived my friends of their son, and fate only bided its time before finally retaliating in kind."

Then there was silence.

And in the silence, the cacophony of realizations attacked Anastasia.

Her mother had sold Ivan in return for their safety. She believed Alex had died to settle the cosmic score.

Anastasia herself had lived a life of security and freedom at the expense of Ivan's despair and degradation.

The enormity of it all held its breath over her like a vast, black cloud. Then it detonated.

And there was nothing more.

Surfacing from the nothingness was terrifying.

She wanted to remain there where she'd once hidden, where it was dark and silent, where she was sinking in an eternity of pain-free paralysis.

But oblivion was relinquishing her to awareness, expelling her to its mercilessness. She was already feeling, hearing. And once she opened her eyes, she'd see what she couldn't bear seeing. Ivan. Frantically hovering over her, going insane with worry.

From the voices with him she knew he'd brought Antonio, and Isabella, a surgeon, too, and the wife of his partner, Richard Graves. They were both assuring him she was physically perfectly fine, that fainting was not unheard of in the early months of pregnancy, especially after the physical and emotional tests she'd endured in the past months.

She pretended to be still passed out until they left, hoping Ivan would leave, too.

But she soon had to admit that he never would. The man who'd stayed by her bedside for weeks, then remained by her side since, would stay here forever. He wouldn't leave her until he made sure she was fine. When she would never be again.

Giving in, knowing that it was better to get this over with, she opened her eyes.

The look on his face translated the gnawing anxiety in his voice, making her almost close her eyes again. It hurt to see him like this, feel him caring, now that she knew the atrocious truth.

The truth that destroyed everything.

He covered her face in kisses, his tremors transmitting to her heart in shock waves of despair. "*Moya dorogoya, moya dusha*, I'm here. You're okay."

Unable to look at him anymore, she averted her gaze and nodded. "Sorry for the scare. One moment I was upright, the next everything just went dark. I'm fine now."

His fingers, gentle, persistent, caressed her cheek, tried

to turn her eyes back to him. "This is my fault. I taxed you." He bit off a vicious self-imprecation. "I shouldn't have made love to you, let alone repeatedly long and hard. I'm an animal."

The shard of agony embedded in her heart twisted deeper, forcing her to look at him. She couldn't bear him feeling guilty over her, when it was on her account that her mother had consigned him to a horrific fate. She owed him a debt that could never be repaid.

"You didn't tax me, Ivan, and you know it." Before he could take her in his arms again, she rose to a sitting position so he had to pull back. "But everything *is* catching up with me and I do feel tired. I can't see myself doing much for a while. I—I think we should postpone the wedding."

Expecting him to argue, he again floored her by the extent of his consideration, agreeing at once. "Whatever you wish. If the wedding is part of what's putting stress on you, we can always gather everyone right here, exchange vows and send them on their way."

She was desperate to stop his pampering. If she didn't make a stand she'd find herself married to him within the hour.

She shook her head. "I just need a postponement. I hope nobody will be too upset."

His eyes filled with indulgence. "Everyone can cool their heels until you're feeling up to it. Don't worry about anything but feeling stronger, *moya dusha*. The world can stand still or even go away completely until then for all I care."

Feeling it would hurt less if she were the one to go away, forever, she pretended to nod and fall asleep again.

Knowing he wouldn't leave, she turned her face away from his vigilance, unable to stop the silent tears from pouring out of her soul.

\* \* \*

It had been three days since Anastasia had fainted.

After he'd had Antonio and Isabella examine her again, and again, to reassure him she'd bounce back given time, Ivan had gathered everyone the very next morning, Christmas Day, what should have been their wedding day, and announced the postponement of their wedding.

She'd spent half that day in bed, and the other half curled in an armchair, barely saying or doing anything. The next day everyone had gone back to their homes.

Anastasia had asked to go home, too. Her parents' home. Feeling more worried and confused by the second, but wanting to give her whatever she wished for, he'd taken her there. He'd been trying to placate himself that early pregnancy, the revelations, the days among such an overwhelming crowd, had proven too strenuous for her. But every time he went to her, it became clearer, until he could no longer lie to himself.

It now pained her to see him.

But he'd been unable to ask why. He was terrified she'd tell him she was having second thoughts.

It was unimaginable, but the only reason he could think of anymore. That now she realized it was going to be real, and she'd tie herself to him for life, through marriage and through a child, his reality had finally sunk in, and she was horrified about what she'd let herself in for.

But three days in a hell of dread and uncertainty had proved his limit. Though knowing for certain would finish him, he couldn't let her evade him any longer.

He'd just arrived at her parents' home and again they weren't there. The maid had opened the door for him, telling him Anastasia had just gone up to her room.

In a matter of seconds he was knocking on her door. He'd heard her moving inside, and he had a distinctive knock, so she knew it was him. The prolonged silence that answered his knock screamed with her reluctance to let him in, to see him again.

This was it, then.

Whatever it did to him, he couldn't force himself on her. If she didn't want him anymore, if it hurt her that much to see him, he had to leave her alone.

He'd cross that threshold for the last time. When he left, he'd have no more reason to go on living.

At long last, she opened the door, and any lingering hope that he'd been wrong was incinerated under the inescapable proof of her desolation. She looked as finished as he felt.

His heart about to ram out of his rib cage with the need to take her in his arms, to beg her not to recede, not to shut him out of her heart, he met her bloodshot, swollen eyes.

"Why?" At his butchered groan, she said nothing, her breathing becoming strident. He broke down then, begged, "Is there anything I can do to make you love me again?"

She staggered back as if he'd hit her.

Surging forward to abort her stumble, he grabbed her arm, but she jerked it back as if he'd electrified her.

His arms fell limply to his side, crippled by a defeat he hadn't even felt when he'd been young and helpless and at the nonexistent mercy of the monsters who'd imprisoned him.

Breath emptied from his chest, for what felt like the last time. "I guess I was always waiting for this, for you to come to your senses."

Shaking, starting to sob, she fell to the bed. Dropping her head in her trembling hands, she rocked to and fro, moaning as if her soul was bleeding out of her.

He kneeled in front of her before he collapsed, his own

soul escaping him with the tears he'd never shed since he was a child except on her account.

"Don't, Anastasia, don't do this to yourself. Don't feel sorry for me, or feel bad because you gave me hope or made me a promise. I beg you. Don't languish in bed, don't lock yourself from the world to escape your life altogether because I'm in it. I left you once when I thought I'd only bring you danger and anxiety and misery. I'll leave again, because I only want you to be happy and at peace. I just came to tell you this. That I'll always be there for you, and for our child, in any way you let me. But if it hurts you this much to see me, you don't have to see me ever again."

Her weeping escalated with her inability to draw full breaths anymore. Unable to bear her anguish, he exploded up to his feet and stumbled towards the door.

His shaking hand was on the doorknob when Anastasia's words hit him like a bullet between the shoulder blades.

"I'll tell you why. I owe you that. When you know, it will be you who won't ever want to see me again."

Anastasia watched Ivan turning around, hating her very existence even more for the destruction and defeat marring his face and slumping his body. Desecrating his soul. She'd done this to him.

Before she lost all ability to speak, she told him everything. The atrocious, crippling truth.

All through the account she tore out of the depths of her desperation and shame, he remained leaning against the wall as if he'd been riveted there, staring at her as if he couldn't understand a word she said.

By the time she reached the most relevant part, she felt she'd never stop weeping again. "I l-loved my mother until

I learned of the heinous crime she'd committed against you. Now I h-hate her...want her punished. I need you to promise me you will punish her. I need you to punish *me*. I can't live knowing my life has been bought at the expense of yours."

Ivan continued to stare at her. And stare at her.

Then he finally pushed himself away from the wall, came closer with such care, as if she was holding a knife to her own throat and he was afraid she'd slit it if he moved any faster.

His voice was so hushed it was almost inaudible as he rasped, "Do you mean you still love me?"

"God, Ivan, is this the only thing you got out of everything I told you?"

"It's the only thing of any importance."

"No, God, no, you're *not* doing this. You're not brushing this aside. You're not refusing to avenge yourself again."

"You know I never wanted that. I forgave my parents even before I knew they had no hand in what happened to me."

"They're *your* parents. It's up to you to forgive them. But she's *my* mother, and you don't get to forgive her. I don't. Do you hear me? I will never forgive her. I'm leaving this house tomorrow and I'm never coming back."

He was kneeling before her again, his eyes clearing of the ravages of the tears that had made her want to inflict some serious damage on herself, his lips curving into that intimate smile that stirred her insides into mush. "Of course you're leaving this house. You'll be in *our* home, and you're coming back here only for visits."

"No, Ivan, you're *not* smiling!"

His smile only widened. "I actually want to laugh out loud and do a backflip. It's only out of respect for your still raging wrath on my behalf that I'm being so restrained."

He was blithely dismissing this catastrophic discovery that had shattered the very pillars of her existence.

Her crushing misery morphed into exasperation making her hiss, "This is deadly serious, Ivan."

"And I'm as deadly serious when I say I've never been this relieved. I thought I lost you and my world was ending and then you tell me this, and I'm like, 'Really? That's it? That's what she almost gave us both heart attacks over?'"

At her chagrined screech, he took both her hands, pressed kisses on them before pressing them to his heart, his gaze becoming pure persuasion. "I swear on the most precious things in my life—you and our coming child—that I really, *really* couldn't care less what your mother did. I'm not the child who went to The Organization, or the young man who escaped it, or even the man I was until I came back for you months ago. I'm now the new me, the one who loves you, the man you own. And this man has no place in his memory except for every single second since he met you, and every single second in our future together. This man is endlessly grateful that his life path—the horrific parts included—led him to you and made him into the man you love. This man cares about absolutely nothing else, as long as you love him."

His every word was a jolt supercharging her heart with a surplus of love for him that she felt she'd burst with it.

Struggling to contain it all, her hands fisted on his chest, her whole body shaking. "You can't still love me when I and my own have been the curse of your existence!"

He shook his head. "The only times I felt I was cursed was when I thought I'd lose you. And during the past three days when I thought I already had."

Feeling her head would explode with the need to get him angry, she started to protest again, but he surged, sealed her lips with his, letting her taste his life and love, his relief and delight. But it was tasting his smile that made her pull back, her blood seething.

"Ivan, you *can't*. *I* can't let you forgive. You must exact vengeance, carve out pounds of flesh, preferably from me."

He only hauled her into his arms and laid her back on the bed, enveloping her in a full body hug. "I'm taking all hundred and forty pounds of your precious, libido-igniting flesh." His eyes filled with teasing, and a trace of lingering insecurity. "That is, if you love me."

She drummed her feet on the bed in frustration. "If? It's because my whole being is ninety percent made of loving you that I'm losing my mind here."

He threw his head back and laughed, before squeezing her hard. "See this? This is exactly why I'm not only not angry with your mother I'm even glad she did what she did. It didn't only mean saving everyone, it meant saving *you*. Saving you so you'd grow up into this irreplaceable creature, so I can one day find you, and love you for the rest of my life."

Stymied beyond expression or endurance, she started weeping again. "Ivan, oh, God, Ivan, you're too much… and I love you too much, it hurts. It's *excruciating* when I think—"

"Then don't think. Or think only of this. That if I'd known the real price of my family's salvation, and yours, I *would* have paid it willingly then. I would do anything at all for you now. And knowing that, do you think I'll do nothing while you feel this horribly? Do you think I can rest while you break your own heart, and hate your mother to avenge me?"

"But I can't just forget, Ivan. I can't forgive her."

"But I want you to. Your mother did a terrible thing, at terrible times, and she's been punishing herself, eaten by guilt ever since. She has made up in every way possible for my family, and for yours. And she not only lost Alex, she feels it's her fault. That is far more punishment that any mother should have to endure, no matter her crimes. Have mercy, *moya dusha*. Forgive her here…" He pressed his open palm to her heart, making her sob and burrow into his hardness and heat. "Pity her. And most of all, love her again. I need you to. I don't want any anger or disappointment or bitterness to eat at the magnificent light and beauty inside you."

Her tears stopped. There *was* such a thing as being moved beyond tears.

His smile became crooked. "I am being partially self-ish here, since I'm the primary beneficiary of your light and beauty, the one who has the most to gain from it in the form of endless pleasure and fathomless love."

She rose to look down on him, everything inside her capitulating. Loving him beyond endurance, she whispered, "You miracle of a man who loves me beyond my wildest imaginings no matter what. You avenging angel who will avenge anyone but yourself. Will you take me as your wife, Ivan? Will you let me have and hold you, love and cherish you, support and defend you, lose my mind over you and give my very soul to you, so that not even death will us part?"

He held her eyes in utmost solemnity. "I do."

Before she could kiss him, he beat her to it. In seconds he had her arching beneath him, begging for his invasion. But he pulled back, poignancy and teasing a heady mixture in his eyes. "So when will you officially make an honest man out of me?"

And she did something an hour ago she'd thought she'd never do again. She giggled.

He really was a miracle. And a miracle worker.

Raining kisses on every part of him she could reach,

she said, "As soon as you can get your scattered troops to regroup."

As if he'd been coiled and waiting to launch into action, he sprang up, got out his phone, started barking orders for everyone to fall back into formation.

Half an hour later, he looked down at her in triumph. "As per your command, *moya dusha*, tomorrow you become Dr. Anastasia Konstantinov."

Pulling him down over her, loving him fiercely, endlessly, she sighed into his lips. "Tomorrow, and forever."

Before he claimed her, took them both back from the brush with devastation to their exclusive heaven, he pledged, "At least that long."

# Epilogue

"Forgive yourself, Grace."

At his words, Anastasia's mother turned to Ivan with a gasp.

She'd been subdued all through the wedding ceremony, and now during the reception she'd walked into a corner as if she wanted to disappear. Everyone thought her state was recurrent desolation over Alex's loss, and Ivan and Anastasia let everyone believe that. The secret of what she'd done would never get outside the four who knew it.

"I forgive you," he said. "And I do thank you for saving my family, for saving yours. But mostly for saving Anastasia. I would have forgiven you had you cost me all my limbs for this alone." As the woman's eyes filled, he persisted. "And I also want you to believe that Alex's death wasn't punishment for you, or else fate must have seen fit to punish me and everyone who loved him, too, since his death hurt us all irrevocably."

As her tears fell, he reached for her arm, gave it a gentle squeeze. And she crumpled against him, too weak to do anything but accept his absolution, letting him take her in his embrace.

He pressed a kiss to her forehead, this woman who'd once been a second mother to him, the mother of the love of his life, the reason for everything he was and did.

"People in sweeping upheavals and grave dangers make terrible decisions. But whatever your sins against me, just that you've saved Anastasia, so I could find her so many years later, love her, live for her, evens the scales and way more. Anastasia loves you. It's why she was so hurt. But I promise I'll do everything to heal her so she will open up to you again. It's what Alex would have wanted. For us all to be happy, to honor his memory. And in his memory, there will be no more losses and injuries. Never on my account, or on my watch."

A choking sound made him turn around. And there she was, Anastasia, his bride, looking far better than his wildest fantasies. She was his reward from fate, with every blessing the world had to offer in her eyes.

They'd exchanged vows an hour ago, were now husband and wife. One. At last and forever.

He extended a hand to her, and she took it at once, let him reel her in so she faced her mother.

He pressed a cherishing kiss against her flushed cheek, murmured his love and encouragement. Returning the kiss, her eyes filling with that gratitude he'd yet to make her stop feeling, she turned to her mother.

"We'll be all right, Mom. Thanks to Ivan."

The woman reached out a hand, asking Anastasia's permission for intimacy. His palm caressed Anastasia's back, urging her to take her mother's hand. As soon as she did, the woman pulled her into a brief, though fervent hug.

Then, as if she didn't want to push her luck further, with tears running down her face, Grace turned and rushed away.

After watching her mother's departure, Anastasia turned to Ivan, face brightening, eyes igniting.

Before he could scoop her to his heart again, a big hand slapped him hard on the back. *Dammit.*

"So tell me, Wildcard, how do you feel now you're a married man?"

He turned to Antonio, who was grinning at him wickedly, everything right with his world again now that he'd gotten his Liliana to forgive, *and* marry him, too. Something Ivan had had a hand in.

While he'd been with Anastasia in Russia, Antonio had called him in a bleak state, asked him to come take what amounted to his last will and testament, to give to Liliana after he'd left, ostensibly to commit accidental suicide on some frontline. Ivan had rushed to his side, then to Liliana's to make her stop him. Which she had.

Ivan had rushed back to Anastasia the next day. She'd still been sleeping so long in those days he doubted she'd even noticed he'd been away.

But when Antonio's wedding had come just a week later, he'd begged off being his best man. Anastasia hadn't been up to attending weddings at the time, and he couldn't have left her. And he couldn't bear seeing his best friend get the love of his life, when he'd felt he'd eventually lose his.

Did that make him a terrible friend? Yeah. Probably.

Antonio sure would never let him live it down.

Pulling Anastasia into his side lovingly, he crooked an eyebrow at his best friend. "Why don't you tell me first? You're an old married man now, while I'm fresh off the altar."

Antonio looked down at his wife of only two months, going positively goo-goo eyed. "It's simple really. I'm the happiest man in existence."

"Oh, no, you're not!" Ivan growled, actually annoyed at his friend's claim.

"Oh, yes, I am." Antonio all but stuck his tongue out at him.

"It's my wedding, and if I say you're not, you're not!"

The two women looked at each other...then burst out laughing.

As he and Antonio turned to their wives, demanding in mock severity what they found so funny, the rest of the gang, as Anastasia called them, converged on them.

"So what are you ladies busting a stitch over?" That was Isabella, sauntering over with that serpent husband of hers slithering right behind her. Yeah, Ivan still wasn't a fan of Richard Graves, a.k.a. Cobra. Neither was Richard a fan of his. They were both perfectly fine with this.

"Yeah, we want in on the belly laughs," said Scarlett, Raiden's wife.

Anastasia and Liliana turned to the ladies, laughing harder than ever.

"There's just something hilarious about watching these two Olympians bickering," Anastasia spluttered.

Liliana hooted in laughter. "And not any bickering. The twelve-year-old variety. Time stopped for them the day they met, it seems."

"No, it didn't," Ivan growled. "And we don't bicker!"

"You tell them, brother." Antonio squared off beside him, as always joining with him against any others.

"Oh, you bicker. You're experts at it." Eliana, Rafael's wife, gave Antonio an affectionate nudge. "Just admit it."

"It goes beyond expertise. It's a matter of survival for you boys. I don't think you can live without plucking at each other's shiny feathers." That was Jenan, Numair's wife, who'd become the leader of the gang of wives, just like Numair had been and remained their brotherhood's leader. "So what was the subject of the squabble this time?"

Anastasia feigned a shudder. "I'm afraid if we tell you, we'd have a full-scale war among all of you on our hands."

Liliana nodded in mock trepidation. "Yes, we shouldn't say. To preserve the peace within the brotherhood."

It was the men who now spoke up, each demanding in his own inimitable way to know what the Bones/Wildcard duet had been saying behind their backs that they should be punished for.

Anastasia and Liliana finally pretended to break down under duress and divulged the sensitive subject of the debate.

As expected, each man protested, claiming the title of Happiest Man In Existence for himself, each ready to duel for it. Finally the bickering escalated to jabs and shoves, among the raucous laughter of their delighted and adoring wives.

Suddenly, all the men froze. As did Ivan.

It took the women moments to realize that the men weren't playing a collective joke on them, when they all rushed to get out their phones.

Ivan's heart hammered so hard he jumbled his password to open the screen twice. He had the same difficulty in bringing up the latest message.

After reading it, he bit his lip, for fleeting moments wondering if this was some kind of prank, wishing it was. And knowing it couldn't be.

Then he raised his gaze to his brothers, saw confirmation of that in their solemn eyes.

This was no prank. It was really him.

Cypher.

Their Black Castle brotherhood's long-lost brother.

He was texting them on the line that not even their wives had access to. With a message made of only five words.

Expect a visit…soon. Cypher.

Many hours later, the reception was over and the impromptu meeting he'd had with his brothers had revealed no insights into Cypher's message, or any projections about future developments.

Head filled with nebulous worries, Ivan now walked into their bedroom suite with Anastasia in his arms and clinging around his neck.

As he lowered her down on their bed. But as he came down half over her, started kissing her, she stopped him. And he knew why.

He'd previously explained who Cypher was, leaving out as much as he could. Which clearly hadn't satisfied her. She had more questions. Ones he didn't know if he ever could, or should, answer.

"Have any of you texted Cypher back?" she asked.

"If we could have we would. Cypher is the only one in our brotherhood who's my equal in cyber powers. He hid from even me all these years. I have no idea where he's been, what he's been doing. Or even who he is anymore."

"You all looked so…shaken at his message."

"We hadn't expected to hear from him after all these years."

"You said it didn't end well between you. All of you?"

"Yes." He *hated* talking about this, would rather be extracting molars without anesthesia. Before Anastasia could hit him with another question he only had to evade, he stretched her arms above her head. "Now enough of this. Let me make love to my bride."

And for a very long time, he did just that.

After he'd drowned them both in the ecstasy of their unity twice, Anastasia stirred in his arms.

He was savoring the drugged cast in her eyes and his own satisfaction when her question hit him out of left field. Damn. He'd managed to forget everything that existed outside of this room. Until now.

"Does this visit Cypher said to expect worry you?"

He rose above her, smiled reassuringly, and told her his very first, and what he intended to be his very last, barefaced lie.

"Of course not."

\* \* \* \* \*

# MILLS & BOON®

## *Desire*™

**PASSIONATE AND DRAMATIC LOVE STORIES**

---

## A sneak peek at next month's titles...

### In stores from 17th November 2016:

- **The Baby Proposal** – Andrea Laurence *and*
  **The Pregnancy Project** – Kat Cantrell

- **The Texan's One-Night Standoff** – Charlene Sands *and*
  **Maid Under the Mistletoe** – Maureen Child

- **Rich Rancher for Christmas** – Sarah M. Anderson *and*
  **Married to the Maverick Millionaire** – Joss Wood

---

*Just can't wait?*
Buy our books online a month before they hit the shops!
**www.millsandboon.co.uk**

**Also available as eBooks.**

# MILLS & BOON®

## Why shop at millsandboon.co.uk?

Each year, thousands of romance readers find their perfect read at millsandboon.co.uk. That's because we're passionate about bringing you the very best romantic fiction. Here are some of the advantages of shopping at www.millsandboon.co.uk:

* **Get new books first**—you'll be able to buy your favourite books one month before they hit the shops

* **Get exclusive discounts**—you'll also be able to buy our specially created monthly collections, with up to 50% off the RRP

* **Find your favourite authors**—latest news, interviews and new releases for all your favourite authors and series on our website, plus ideas for what to try next

* **Join in**—once you've bought your favourite books, don't forget to register with us to rate, review and join in the discussions

Visit **www.millsandboon.co.uk**
for all this and more today!